DANGEROUS

BOOK FOUR: AGE OF HONOR

TAMARA LEIGH

WWW.TAMARALEIGH.COM

THE WULFRITHS. FIRST. IN BETWEEN. IN THE END.

The late middle ages. England's king seeks to recover the French lands of his ancestor William the Conqueror and claim the continental throne. France's king aspires to seize the remainder of his royal vassal's lands and retain his throne. So begins the Hundred Years' War, the backdrop against which the formidable Wulfriths of the AGE OF CONQUEST and AGE OF FAITH series continue their tale.

A LADY OF DANGEROUS DEPTHS

Though Lady Dangereuse of the Wulfriths may not have loved, she has certainly lost. Widowed young, she is devoted to managing her lands while helping her young son overcome the trauma of losing his sire. But when the injured knight who rejected her betrothal years ago falls into her hands, she turns her efforts to gaining the confession of one who may be more responsible for the violent death of her husband than she. If that means detaining him, so be it. As she seeks the truth of what deprived her son of a father, she is unprepared for suffering inflicted on her people by those intent on keeping her unwilling guest from delivering intelligence to the King of England. And more unprepared when a heart gone cold warms to her husband's hated rival.

A KNIGHT OF UNTOLD REGRETS

Mission compromised, Sir Rhys de Arell finds himself pursued from France to England and into the path of a lady whose misplaced kiss saw her wed to a man he once counted a friend. Though he has put the death of her deceitful husband behind him, she has not—and believes a reckoning is due. Injured and in the power of one who is owed an apology but not a confession, Rhys is unsettled when her son becomes attached to him, and more when attraction for the lady leads to a kiss that feels far from misplaced. With his pursuers wreaking havoc on her lands to recover what could save English lives, can he salvage his mission as well as prevent her son from losing his mother? And if such treacherous depths cannot be navigated, how is he to walk away from the lady a second time?

From USA Today Bestselling author Tamara Leigh, the fourth book in the Age of Honor *series unites the Wulfrith family with the De Arell's of* Baron of Blackwood, *the third book in* The Feud *series. Watch for NOTORIOUS in Autumn 2023.*

For new releases and special promotions, subscribe to Tamara Leigh's mailing list: www.tamaraleigh.com

DANGEROUS: Book Four (Age of Honor) Copyright © 2023 by Tammy Schmanski, P.O. Box 1298 Goodlettsville, TN 37070 tamaraleightenn@ gmail.com

This novel is a work of fiction. Names, characters, places, incidents, and dialogues are either the product of the author's imagination or are used fictitiously. Any resemblance to actual events, locales, organizations, or persons, living or dead, is entirely coincidental and beyond the intent of the author.

Cover Design: Ravven

Ebook ISBN-13: 978-1-942326-62-5

Paperback ISBN-13: 978-1-942326-63-2

"He hath made every thing beautiful in His time."
~ Ecclesiastes 3:11

CHAPTER 1

Le Tournoi d'Honneur
Northern England, 1350

L ady Dangereuse of the family Wulfrith had little care for Rhys de Arell, and yet compared to what her husband felt for the knight, that little could be considered much.

Staring at the disgruntled man she wed four years past, again she wished she had not attended the tournament that was one of several held across the country now the pestilence had finished harvesting a third of England's population—including members of her family.

Aching over those lost long before word could be sent her, silently she amended her assessment that what was known as *The Great Mortality* was finished. There were yet reports of outbreaks in isolated areas which had escaped the merciless scythe when first it crossed the channel from France in late 1348. As should be apparent to all, no corner of England was too distant nor blessed to elude the evil.

1

Still, that being of little concern in the north, Dangereuse's husband had insisted she accompany him to *Le Tournoi d'Honneur*—The Tournament of Honor. When she had asserted she could not leave their young son in the care of his heavily pregnant sister, with resentment Benoit had bent some. Though he coveted time with his wife absent a child between them, he had announced Sebastian would also make the journey.

Now Dangereuse wondered if it would have been better to leave behind their son who once more suffered an ear infection. For the Wulfrith in his blood he was strong, but that did not make him immune to life-threatening illness, and since birth he proved vulnerable to those of the ear with which Benoit reported he himself had been afflicted—and survived without coddling.

Anxious over his recovery, an hour past she had slipped away from the jousting field and returned to their host's donjon to ensure the servant into whose care Benoit had given their son was not negligent. His temperature remained elevated, but not as high, and she had soothed him to sleep by giving him the breast.

Upon returning to the field, she found her husband brooded more deeply than last eve when, amid the tournament's opening day revelry, he was forced to suffer Sir Rhys' presence in the great hall. And greater his displeasure in suspecting his fellow Wulfen-trained knight looked upon Dangereuse lustfully. She had sought to dissuade him of that, but made it worse when she captured the knight's regard and glared.

Having seen and misinterpreted the exchange, Benoit had gripped her arm and accused her of flirting. Maintaining composure as best she could, she had told it was not so, discreetly broken his hold on her, and said she was for bed.

Grudgingly, he had apologized, but since her response was

not meant to manipulate but distance herself and return to their son, she had declined to remain at his side.

Though he was a good husband despite insecurities that sometimes made her feel suffocated and occasionally saw her accused of loving Sebastian more, there were times she nearly disliked him. And *had* disliked him last eve when he joined her in the chamber and, with no regard for their two-year-old, sought to claim his husband's rights over her body. Their son had awakened, and it was an hour before she could settle him and return to the bed where Benoit snored beneath a pillow clamped over his head.

Now this day, for missing the joust that advanced her husband to the next round to continue representing the English side to which he had rejoiced in being assigned— doubtless more so for Sir Rhys representing the hated *French* side—he was vexed she once more put Sebastian's needs ahead of his own.

She *was* more concerned about their ill child than his success in a game of blades. Too, though she would not speak it, she had greater feeling for Sebastian than Benoit despite aspiring to love her husband since they wed. Regardless of the depth of her feelings for him, he should be equally concerned for their son. She knew he loved the boy, but often jealousy over attention lost to Sebastian cast a shadow across fatherly emotions.

Returning Benoit to focus where he scowled at her from the far side of the tent, Dangereuse raised her chin. "Again, I apologize, but our child is sick, and I refuse to make merry as if he is not."

Breath raised his shoulders, then he strode forward, pulled her into his arms, and kissed her hard as done when most anxious about her feelings for him.

She did not like it, but having found the quickest end to his branding of her was to feign passion and do the same to him, she ground her full lips against his thin ones.

As if shocked by her response, he jerked back his head and pressed fingers to his mouth. When he withdrew them, they were tinged by the blood of lips cut on teeth. "Oh, had I the time to tame you, little wolf," he said and gave a long, slow smile.

He liked naming her that, though in wedding him she had traded the surname Wulfrith for Royston and was no little thing for gaining a bit of height on him once she fully matured. And he certainly liked trying to tame her, though he never would. Still, the mostly dutiful wife said, "There will be time later. Now whom next do you face on the field?"

That smile becoming a baring of teeth, he released her. "Rhys de Arell."

Had she not been so concerned about Sebastian, she would have guessed that for how tightly wound he was, especially since Sir Rhys had earned greater renown than he for jousting skills imparted at Wulfen. Though she had known they might meet on the field, she had prayed not, even if Benoit was the one who failed to advance.

Setting a hand on his chest, she pushed a smile onto her lips. "I have every faith in you."

The vulnerability in his eyes reminded her of a boy, then was gone. "Do you?" It was said with accusation.

Knowing his thoughts were of last eve when he believed she flirted with the warrior he would soon face, her palm itched for the sting of whiskered flesh, but maintaining control, she said, "Did I not wed you, Benoit?"

His upper lip hiked. "Would you have if *he* wanted you?"

This being the first time he contested the question she often posed when he needed assurance of her devotion, it was not guilt that made her hesitate, but surprise. "I wished to wed you, and that I did, Benoit."

"With incentive."

It was true, but she had liked him well enough, and he had desired her, unlike—

Of a sudden, he snatched the braid draping her shoulder and dragged on it, drawing her close and pinning her hands between their chests.

"Benoit!" she rebuked, unaccustomed to rough handling beyond proprietary kisses she gave back for instinctively knowing passivity would lead to further trespass. Fortunately for him, he did not also have a braid. *Her* yank would relieve him of hair.

He raised the braid and pressed his lips to the crossings of black stranded with premature silver passed down through the Wulfrith family, though only two of her generation boasted it —her eldest brother and her.

"Incentive or not, to our end days you are mine as I am yours, Dangereuse."

She had heard that many times, but only sweetly spoken. Might there now be threat about it?

He gave a satisfied chuckle, released her, and jutted his chin at the tent flap. "As I must prepare for the contest, tell Ferrand to make haste."

He spoke of his brother who squired for him and might forever for the inability to complete his knighthood training at Wulfen, Ferrand having sought his release three years ago and Dangereuse's sire, the Baron of Wulfen, making no argument of it.

As discussion of Benoit's behavior must wait, she turned, but he stopped her with, "When once more I best Sir Rhys as done at Wulfen, I expect my wife to be in the stands showing love and support, not fawning over our son who is no longer a babe."

Teeth hurting for the effort not to speak what should wait lest it affect his showing in the contest, she inclined her head and resumed her departure.

"A favor from my lady wife!" he thwarted her again.

She swung around and, as he advanced, looked to his neck around which hung the silver ribbon she had tied to his arm this morn. Customarily, such favors were given by a lady to a knight who dedicated his performance to her, whether she was easily attainable for being his wife, moderately attainable for pursuit by others, or painfully unattainable for belonging to another.

"Already you have my favor, Benoit."

"I wish something that better expresses your love and constancy." He drew off the ribbon and thrust it down her bodice. "A sleeve will serve."

Something not frivolously given since it was integral to a woman's gown and greatly missed if not recovered, but it was not possible with this gown. She extended an arm. "I would give it, but these sleeves are not detachable."

He frowned. "Those of the new gown you wore last eve detached. I helped fasten them. Why not this gown?"

"'Tis more costly in time and embellishments, and as you insisted on four new gowns, I determined only two should be so extravagant."

His fairly attractive face reflecting distress, he said, "I did not provide enough funds?"

He had, which strained their finances since he but served his older brother who, as heir, had gained the family lands. Thus, on the day past having noted her husband did not appear surprised by Rhys de Arell's attendance of the tournament, she had wondered if his pride was responsible for new garments sewn for husband and wife.

"Well, Dangereuse?"

"The funds were sufficient, but as Bastian is quick to outgrow his garments, I put coin toward clothing for him."

His cheeks spotted. "That is not what I told you to do."

Increasingly bothered—and angered—by the change in him since he received an invitation to the tournament, she said in the imperious tone he detested, "I did what I thought best, and I am right since I did not need detachable sleeves on all my—"

"Whilst I am being armored, return to our chamber and change."

Her head jerked as if slapped. "What say you?"

"As I intend to wear your sleeve, you must return here within a half hour."

"You would have me risk waking our son—as you did on the night past—though sleep is his greatest comfort?"

His only answer was to step past her, toss back the flap, and call, "Ferrand!"

The young man who had departed the tent upon Dangereuse's arrival entered and said with apology, "My lady."

Near always with apology, she reflected on exchanges with Benoit's brother whom she liked but agreed was a poor fit for Wulfen training, there being too much soft in his spine despite a good facility with weapons.

She gathered breath. "I shall leave you and my husband to it."

"A half hour," Benoit reminded as she moved past. "I need that sleeve."

Prickling in the roots of her hair, she cast behind, "You do not," and stepped out into a day more brightly colored for dozens of gaily-striped tents erected by the participants.

7

In the next instant she was snatched back inside, and her gasp of surprise became a cry of pain when her breasts slammed into a solid chest.

"Benoit!" Ferrand protested.

Ignoring his brother, her husband thrust his face near hers. "I need that sleeve."

Breathe through your anger, she silently—desperately—counseled lest the temper her sire, mother, and beloved step-mother helped her gain control over was loosed.

"Wife!"

Here a breath. Another. And one across which she said coldly, "You will have my sleeve. And quickly."

Strangely, his sudden shift from anger to relief repelled, and again she wished she was not here. Had neither come, perhaps they could have made this a rare lazy day abed, talking and cuddling while Sebastian climbed over them and giggled at things he thought funny and tried new words by poking and pointing at what he wished named.

Benoit set her back, then strode toward the table on which lay pieces of armor that would protect his body when he charged at Sir Rhys. "Armor me, Ferrand, then you shall prepare my destrier."

Dangereuse turned toward the young man and offered a smile she did not feel but he deserved for protesting Benoit's mishandling of her.

He served his brother well, and for that she did not think her husband aware of what she sensed. Ferrand resented Benoit, and she thought it might be jealousy for what his brother gained that he had not—knighthood at Wulfen Castle, a fortress renowned for training up England's finest defenders.

She exited the tent. Rather than hasten to the donjon, once more she breathed through anger, then acknowledged the rashness of her solution to delivering a sleeve without disturbing their son. But would it be better to defy Benoit alto-gether? If she did, might it so incense that his concentration failed and he lost the joust to Sir Rhys?

She looked to the other tents and the knights and atten-dants too occupied to pay her notice, then stepped to the side of the tent. There she drew the meat dagger from her girdle and began cutting away the pale green sleeve that would expose that of her white chemise.

It took longer than it would have had she scissors, but soon enough she freed the casing with its elbow-to-wrist buttons. "As told, quickly," she muttered and started around the tent—only to falter over the feeling of being watched.

The offender was located easily. Not only had the man of shoulder-skimming blond hair presence for his height and muscular build that was accentuated by a well-cut tunic of orange, but unlike others among the tents, there was no move-ment about him—rather, what appeared suspended move-ment, as if the sight of her doing what she had done halted him.

Sir Rhys de Arell, handsome countenance even more agree-able than four years earlier when last Benoit and he jousted, eyes so blue their color was known at fifty feet, hiked his eyebrows.

As the only response for this was either a natural show of embarrassment or unnatural derision, Dangereuse raised the severed sleeve and kissed the precious favor he would see upon Benoit when the two charged each other.

Smile slight, he touched what she had failed to notice. The ornate sleeve of a lady's gown was fastened to his arm—and not destructively cut away but properly detached with its lacings still bowed.

Certain for this Benoit had demanded the same from her, silently she counseled, *Breathe through it.*

Then his smile enlarged, revealing amusement could still make something charmingly crooked of it all these years later, and as she started to give her back to one who had not wanted her as Benoit had reminded, he bowed curtly.

Dangereuse swallowed indignation, snatched her eyes from those dancing over this half-sleeved lady, and entered the tent.

When the two within turned, she said, "As promised, *quickly!*" and flung the sleeve at her husband's feet. "For the ruin of a new gown, consider it an even greater expression of your wife's constancy."

"Dangereuse!" He started toward her.

She sprang outside and, relieved Sir Rhys had departed, headed for the stands where any who noticed her—and there would be many for the Wulfrith silver in her hair—would see she was missing a sleeve. And soon learn of its wasteful sacrifice.

CHAPTER 2

Irony? Rhys de Arell considered as he brought his destrier around to confirm what was glimpsed the moment after his lance struck his opponent's shoulder and the same was dealt him. Whereas he had remained mostly upright, Benoit had gone sideways.

Though the force of Rhys' strike was mostly responsible, it was aided by slippage of the saddle that further unbalanced its rider and caused him to lose the stirrups. Now that leather seat sat askew on the destrier whose reins were caught by an attendant of the lists as another attendant waved Royston's squire toward the prone knight.

As those in the left-hand stands cheered for the *French* side gaining another victory and those on the right expressed discontent over a loss for the English, in memory of the last time the two met over lances when Rhys was the one cast out of the saddle, he murmured, "Irony indeed." Then as expected of the victor, he flipped up his visor, thrust his splintered lance high, and shouted, "House De Arell!"

The same as others attending Tournaments of Honor held across the country in preparation to resume the war with France now survivors of the pestilence were coming out of mourning, all here supported the English. Hence, the victorious cry of those assigned to represent the French at tournament was that of honoring their family name as opposed to the other side's cry of *All hail England!*

As the roars of those supporting the *French* participants drowned out the dissenters, Rhys looked to the stands where members of his immediate family stood applauding him alongside relatives that included his step-cousin, Lianor—she whose sleeve was fixed to his left arm just below the spaulder of blackened, embossed steel protecting his shoulder.

He had not had the heart to refuse her favor, but he should have lest it encourage the attentions of one ten and six to his twenty and four. He felt some attraction for her, but were anything to come of it, that would be years from now when she was fully woman and he, having further served his country and taken responsibility for the castle being raised on his sire's barony, was nearer a mind to wed.

"Nay, my lady!" shouted an attendant near the English stands. "Depart!"

Defiantly, she of silvered black braid and ruined gown raised her skirts and went wide around the man seeking to intercept her. Moments later, as Royston's *devoted* brother raised him to sitting, she dropped to her knees beside them.

Though the presence of a lady on the field did much to calm the joyous—and not so joyous—din, it was not sufficient for the exchange between husband and wife to be heard. But it was seen.

Benoit had recovered enough to express displeasure that had Lady Dangereuse stiffening and drawing back from the face thrust near hers, and further his anger was seen in shoving aside his brother, staggering to his feet, and casting off his helmet.

Aided by Squire Ferrand, the lady rose to a height just above her husband's and set a hand on the arm to which was bound the sleeve whose removal Rhys had witnessed—so fierce that detachment he had concluded Benoit had insisted she provide a favor like that worn by his rival.

I am glad he has not broken your Wulfrith spirit, he had thought when she returned to the tent with the ruined sleeve.

Now whatever she spoke caused her husband's face to darken further.

"'Twas no mishap!" Benoit was heard around the lists.

Having remained astride, Rhys thrust down his lance and dismounted in preparation to face the one who accused him of something foul—the same that once Rhys had accused Benoit.

As spectators' voices ascended again, this time in anticipation of an encounter beyond the joust, the defeated jabbed a finger at the victor striding forward with hand on hilt. "It was De Arell who—"

Daring to draw near Benoit now reaching for his own sword, Lady Dangereuse and Squire Ferrand rendered the rest of his words unheard. Whatever their desperate entreaties, it made him blink and look around as if unaware he had an audience, then he broke free. Declaring he would inspect his saddle, with a hitch in his stride he moved opposite.

His brother hastened after him, but the lady paused to retrieve his helmet. As she bent, she looked to Rhys, and he held her gaze until a flash of what appeared liquid silver drew his regard to the neck of a bodice that appeared low only for her bend causing the tops of her breasts to crest. Then the silver was gone.

Imagined? he wondered, returning to her face as she straightened with her husband's helmet in the same hand with which she had bruised Rhys' eye long ago. Certes, there was naught imagined about her slashing gaze.

Rot it! he silently profaned, certain she believed he had looked upon her with lust.

She swung away, then exhibiting more Wulfrith spirit, set her chin high and followed her husband and brother-in-law toward the gate through which Benoit's destrier was taken.

Though tempted to continue to where he had thought silver poured from her bodice, it was time to conclude the joust so its spectators could withdraw for refreshments ahead of the final contests.

Rhys drew breath that expanded his chest against the breastplate fashioned of the same steel as the spaulders that were attached to it with leather straps, then bowed to both stands. Receiving more praise from those on the *French* side, and some supporting the English side, he returned to his destrier.

A quarter hour later, shed of armor and the stands emptied, he stepped onto the field whose ground was being leveled by men in preparation for the next contest. As he strode to where Benoit had fallen that had yet to be raked, he nodded at those who paused to look his way. Whether they wondered over his return or accepted he, like others, wished to survey the field on which he would soon compete again, they resumed their work.

Shortly, he saw what was not imagined, it now fouled by dirt. It was not liquid silver but the soft of a ribbon, doubtless the same worn by Benoit during earlier jousts and traded for a severed sleeve.

He swept up what the lady had bestowed on her husband, and as he drew it through his fingers, let his mind fully venture back to that other contest between Royston and him.

Bare months before the war with France commenced in 1346, a joust was held outside Wulfen Castle in honor of those to be knighted and soon to cross the channel with their king, including Rhys and Benoit who served as first and second squires to the aging Baron Wulfrith.

The two had been fairly friendly rivals through most of their fourteen years of training from page to squire to knight, their abilities well matched. However, when Rhys began surpassing Benoit, which eventually earned him the title of *first squire,* strain had risen between them. And greater it became days before the joust when it was learned the baron might offer the hand of his eldest daughter to Rhys, heir to the Barony of Blackwood.

Dangereuse's first betrothed having broken their families' arrangement two years earlier, foregoing his inheritance to wed a commoner, she had resisted other betrothals until her eighteenth year. At the joust attended by scores of families whose sons trained at Wulfen, Rhys had looked nearer on her than in all the years since his training began. Not that he had been in her company often. Indeed, their exposure to each other was mostly at a distance, the eldest Wulfrith sister residing at the nearby Stern Castle with her womenfolk. Once he became first squire to the lady's sire, several times he and Benoit had accompanied their lord to his family's home.

Though Rhys had been attracted to her lovely figure and face, mass of raven black hair shot with silver, and self-assurance, knowing he would soon go to war and longing for new experiences absent the fetters of a wife, he had offered less encouragement than she. Not that she offered much, her gaze more assessing than flirtatious, smiles more thoughtful than spontaneous.

Seemingly more genuine attention she had paid Benoit who, hopeful of being considered worthy of a Wulfrith bride though he had neither lands nor title, had taken every opportunity to draw near and engage her in conversation. Had he noticed the baron's disapproval, it had not put him off.

Though Benoit's warrior skills were formidable, they had been more so the day of the joust at Wulfen as if his life depended on besting every participant, which included those to be knighted and those coming up after them. When at last only two remained, Baron Wulfrith's first squire faced his second in the lists—no great surprise since their esteemed positions were earned by excelling in all things warrior.

Rhys having bested Benoit at jousting more often than not, the surprise came during their first run at each other when a glancing blow to his shoulder from which he should have recovered—unlike Benoit nearly knocked over the back of the saddle—sent him sideways. And off.

The worst of it was being dragged with his boot caught in the stirrup. As cries sounded from those watching death fast on the heels of one who might go to his grave before gaining spurs and a Wulfrith dagger, he threw his arms up around his head to shield it from pounding rear hooves. And that was when he saw what he was not meant to see. His saddle's girth strap had not broken. It was loosely notched, which his adopted brother, Eamon, would not have allowed. Here, foul play.

Then his boot had released. As he rolled away, he heard gasps and sighs from those in the stands, then Eamon was beside him, turning him over and demanding to know if anything was broken.

His first thought was to reach his destrier, but despite protecting his head from thundering hooves, it had struck the packed ground when the stirrup loosed its hold on him. Thus, consciousness wavered and his tongue was so thick he could not command Eamon to secure his mount to ensure whoever loosened the strap could not set it aright to cover near murderous duplicity.

By the time he was able to send his brother after his destrier and rise, what seemed minutes had passed, during which Benoit was proclaimed the victor and many pressed around the defeated one.

Unbeknownst to Rhys at that time, his sire also believed foul was in play. Seeing his son recovered, ahead of Eamon he had reached the destrier secured in a paddock beyond the tents. But too late. The strap was notched more loosely than permissible, but not so much the minor blow should have caused an expert rider to lose his seat.

When a dirtied and soon to be bruised Rhys joined his sire and brother, he had told them though he could hardly count the notches while being dragged, the gap between strap and underbelly had been greater.

They had not questioned him, confident he did not seek to cover an inability to remain astride. Hoping to learn who might have tightened the strap, they had questioned the squire who tended the horses ahead of returning them to the stables.

Though Rhys did not want to believe the deception was Benoit's doing, since the second squire had more to gain than any others jealous of Baron Wulfrith's first squire, he was not surprised to learn that when Ferrand delivered the victor's horse to the paddock shortly after the arrival of Rhys' destrier, he had insisted his brother's mount be tended immediately for a limp.

Pressed to reflect on what had transpired, the squire had said after he finished examining the leg and finding no fault in it, he noticed Ferrand was before Rhys' mount fondling its muzzle.

After re-notching the strap? Rhys had wanted to ask. However, clearly the young man had not witnessed that. Rhys was not close with Ferrand for their age and training gap, but he seemed a good lad and devoted to honoring his Wulfen training though more effort was required of him than many. For family, had he dishonored his training and himself?

That being the only sense Rhys could make of what happened, he told he would confront the *victor* alone and found him in his tent.

As Benoit's attempt to conceal dread behind surprise was so exaggerated it reeked, Rhys' suspicion became belief. As for Ferrand who assisted his brother out of his armor, exuding fear and guilt, he had retreated to a corner while Benoit righteously denied wrongdoing.

Then the cheat had gone too far in accusing Rhys of envy and pride, claiming he who believed himself invincible sought to blame his inadequacy on the rightful victor when it would better serve to be a good loser.

Self-control dealt a blow, Rhys' fist had dealt its own blow. Thus, it was a scene of squires punching, grunting, and cursing that Lady Dangereuse happened upon.

If only he had seen her before once more drawing back his arm. If only she had not tried to insert herself between them. Though able to decrease the force behind his fist, it had landed center of her chest and staggered her back into Benoit's arms.

Rhys had been mortified, and not only for harming her. As a young woman, his stepmother had also sought to prevent warriors from injuring each other and was so gravely injured she could not bear children.

Lady Dangereuse having interrupted the confrontation between those soon to be knighted, her lunge and retaliatory fist to Rhys' eye had concluded the matter. Or so he thought.

After he apologized to her and asserted Benoit was

unworthy of Wulfen training, he had shaken his head at Ferrand and exited. And found he, more battered and disarrayed than upon entering, was of great interest to fellow knights in training who lingered among the tents, curiosity roused by sounds of the altercation.

Minutes later he was back, having been intercepted by Baron Wulfrith who was alerted to behavior unbecoming those soon to gain knightly swords and Wulfrith daggers. Grimly, he had commanded Rhys to follow, but however he intended to resolve the discord was never known for what they interrupted—his daughter chest to chest with Benoit, hands on his shoulders, mouth beneath his.

The baron's bellow had made the couple lurch apart, then he ordered his wide-eyed daughter to his side and told Rhys to leave.

The following day, neither squire having attended Baron Wulfrith during the remainder of the celebration, the clamp-jawed Rhys and Benoit the cheat were knighted side by side. Blessedly, before Rhys departed with his family, the baron had granted him a private audience.

Offering no excuse for his behavior and none being asked of him, Rhys had said that, regardless of his disagreement with Benoit, he should not have done as he had and apologized. Baron Wulfrith had considered him, risen and embraced his former first squire, and told he had every faith Sir Rhys of the De Arells would honor God, country, king, and Wulfen. Then he had gripped the younger man's shoulder and with regret both seen and heard, said he would have liked him for a son-in-law.

Before Rhys joined the king's army a month later, word found its way to Blackwood that Lady Dangereuse had wed Benoit Royston and would reside with his family until her husband returned from war.

Fortunately, those recently knighted at Wulfen were assigned to different battalions and rarely encountered one another, and no further opportunities were there following the English victory at Crécy. Benoit had returned home rather than participate in the siege of Calais that gained King Edward the coastal town needed to easily transport supplies and men to France in his bid to reclaim his ancestral lands of William the Conqueror and Eleanor of Aquitaine, which had been taken by the French during the reign of England's King John.

In the nearly four years between that siege and the pestilence's retreat, Rhys and Benoit had no reason to meet again. Had not both attended this Tournament of Honor to which the king issued orders posing as invitations, still there would be distance between them.

A pity Benoit had found no excuse to evade the summons, but doubtless aware Rhys would compete here, for that his wife and son accompanied him. He who should not have gained a Wulfrith bride had done so, and though surely due to the impropriety witnessed by Baron Wulfrith and Rhys, he was elevated in the eyes of many despite gaining no lands nor title in wedding her.

Returning his regard to the ribbon belonging to Dangereuse of silvered hair, Rhys saw his fingers had been as busy as his memories, continuing to rub away dirt. Once more, it was nearly liquid silver as befitting its owner who ought to be valued beyond the ability to make other men envy Benoit. But was she?

With a growl, he dropped the ribbon into the purse on his belt. Regardless of the state of her marriage and what had caused her husband's saddle to slip, it had naught to do with he who honored his Wulfen training in fairly facing opponents, even when defeat appeared imminent.

Having suffered no defeat this day, he had a joust to

prepare for and, should he prevail, one more to secure the win for the *French* side. As for the mêlée in which all would participate on the morrow regardless of their success in the lists, there he and the man with whom once he had good relations would clash again.

CHAPTER 3

At this Tournament of Honor, *France* proved victorious in the lists.

Unlike others who begrudged Sir Rhys his unbroken victories for representing the country with whom England was at war, mostly Dangereuse begrudged his success for how it affected Benoit. He was angry enough over discovering the stitching of the girth's strap failed, certain it was made to appear worn through in retaliation for the belief he did something similar to Rhys de Arell, but now the attention paid his hated rival...

Never had she seen him in so dark a mood. Though at times she was wary of his response to events and other people, rarely his responses to her and their son—until this eve when Sebastian received a sharp rebuke for shrieking as Benoit took him from his mother and passed him to a servant so husband and wife could attend the celebration.

The child being red-eared and his nose dripping, Dangereuse had determined she would stay behind.

Benoit had determined she would not.

For that, there would be a bruise on her arm to attest to his insistence—and her restraint. If not for the servant's presence and other guests exiting their chambers along the corridor, she would not have yielded easily. If at all.

Now here she was in the great hall, distracting her anger by trying to distract Benoit's as voices and brimming cups were raised to the joust's victor.

Once more hearing Rhys de Arell's name shouted, she put a hand on her husband's arm and leaned near. "You are sure you do not know what is keeping your brother?"

He moved his glower to her. "Worry does not become you, Dangereuse. Leave the matter be."

She feared for Ferrand since even if De Arell was responsible for Benoit's unseating, the squire would have to answer for not carefully watching the destrier nor checking the saddle before the contest.

Oh, were we alone, Benoit, she thought. Then wishing they were farther from the hearth for how great the heat in this place stuffed with revelers, she raised her first goblet of wine and sipped.

Benoit took a gulp of his third fill.

Here something else to which she was unaccustomed. Though on occasion he overly imbibed, not as quickly as done this eve. Hence, more food was needed to soak up the excess.

"Still I hunger, Benoit." She hooked an arm through his and tugged him toward a sideboard laden with finger foods. When he did not resist, she breathed out relief.

They filled small plates, and as they picked at their host's offerings, a jouster eliminated ahead of her husband clapped him on the back. "If a girth strap must fail, yours could not have picked a better time, Royston. As I can attest, Sir Rhys' winning blow is fierce." He rubbed a shoulder. "Better had my pride been a bit battered in losing the saddle than being troubled by this injury for weeks to come."

Benoit snapped around to face the man, and in a voice that carried across the din said, "The strap's failure was no accident. It was the work of one determined to win no matter the dishonor of being a cheat!"

As the man's eyes widened and heads turned, Dangereuse gripped Benoit's arm. "My lord husband, it has been a long day and—"

He wrenched free and shook a finger in the other man's face. "Aye, a cheat!"

"Pardon, Lady Dangereuse."

The voice on her other side making her silently demand of the Lord why this man of all present should be near, she looked around.

Wearing a fine tunic of vivid green, Sir Rhys raised his eyebrows. "I would return your—"

"De Arell!" Benoit snarled.

Now she wished her husband had drunk himself into a stupor, even if he must be carried abovestairs in view of all.

"Royston," Sir Rhys said.

As if once more unaware of the attention he drew, Benoit demanded, "Here to gloat over your ill-gotten win?"

Movement at the victorious knight's side drew her regard to his hand that held something silver.

"Eh?" Benoit pressed.

"You are certain 'twas ill gotten?" Sir Rhys said, then shrugged his mouth. "Here I thought it irony."

As Benoit's face darkened further, silently she appealed, *Dear Lord, aid me in getting him away.*

"As someone instructed me years ago when *I* thought

myself cheated of a win," Sir Rhys continued, "rather than blame your inadequacy on another, be a good loser."

Benoit took a threatening step toward him, but before Dangereuse could move between them as once she had done, his eyes lowered and he exclaimed, "'Tis not enough to cheat me of a win, you think to stick me with a blade, De Arell?"

She startled, and seeing the accusation surprised Sir Rhys as well, looked to the hand in which she had glimpsed silver, though not of a blade.

This day's victor gave a curt laugh, then extended his hand to reveal a looped silver ribbon. "If you truly mistake for a blade that dropped on the field when your wife came to your aid—and I but thought to return for it being a fine favor—you must be full up in your cups."

As Benoit seethed over what he had deemed less worthy than a ruined sleeve, Dangereuse fought the temptation to snatch the ribbon out of that large, weapon-hardened hand.

Though her husband invited mockery this day and her anger toward him found grounds for such, Sir Rhys made it worse. If only he had walked away from that of which he was accused. And were the accusation true, more shame on him for using the excuse of the ribbon to insert himself in the exchange.

But of which he has the right, has he not? her inner voice submitted.

Before she could mull that, Benoit seized the ribbon. "Considerate of you to return my wife's token of great love," he bit, then reached for Dangereuse with his other hand.

"Why, Sir Rhys, you spoke true!" a lovely, youthful voice sounded as Dangereuse allowed herself to be drawn away, hands clenched so she not provide the guests more fodder for gossip.

"Your doubt wounds, Lady Lianor," that knight said. "As told, the only favor I accepted this day was yours."

While Dangereuse was steered toward the stairs and the chamber that would shield them from prying eyes and ears, she lost the struggle against looking around. At the end of the aisle that had opened to them, she saw the comely lady's hand was on the knight's arm, her face tilted up.

Ten and six, Dangereuse guessed, *and perhaps in love with the one earlier favored with her detachable sleeve.*

But is he in love with her? the thought crept in and moved her gaze to his face—and eyes that appeared to await hers. Then the aisle closed up and celebrants resumed earlier conversations or engaged in new ones, some of which surely had to do with the spectacle her husband made of them.

Great her relief when Benoit told he needed fresh air and left her at their chamber's door. Hoping the outdoors was truly his destination and it would calm him, she thanked the servant who had eased Sebastian to sleep. Only after pressing coin in the woman's palm did she understand the reason she was regarded with concern. Dangereuse's hands were shaking, though she did not realize how much until she closed the door and raised them before her face.

Lord, out of what muddy place did this one of Wulfrith blood crawl? she silently demanded for having known little fear before and after *The Great Mortality* made refuse of her sire, two sisters-in-law, and thousands upon thousands of others. Now more she shook for fear of what might come of her husband leaving her here than anger over his behavior.

"No more drink, Benoit," she rasped. "Come back and tell we depart at first light. Come back and sleep it away. Come back and let us mend what you are bent on breaking with or without Rhys de Arell's aid." She swallowed. "I ask little of you. Grant me this."

THOUGH RHYS HAD BEEN RILED in overhearing himself accused of cheating—and more outright than in the lists—when he had disengaged from the group that included Lady Lianor Boursier, he had not meant to fuel Benoit's fire. He had thought to jolt sense into the knave by revealing the accused was near and making it appear he approached only to return the ribbon.

Unfortunately, he had not considered Benoit could be half inebriated, nor was he prepared for the accusation Rhys intended to stick his rival with a blade. He should have ignored the jibe, passed the ribbon to Lady Dangereuse, and withdrawn rather than point out what was obvious to all—Benoit Royston was loose of mind.

"Much regret," he murmured.

"Rhys."

And regret at being found.

Having retreated to an alcove to escape the attentions of ladies drawn to the unwed heir of Blackwood and mull his contribution to Lady Dangereuse's distress as she was ushered from the hall, he nodded respectfully at the formidable warrior who halted before him.

"Sire," he said and straightened from the wall against which he had set a shoulder to observe the participants as they began departing the celebration.

The same as most nobles here, that meant returning to fine tents raised outside the walls since there were not enough chambers within the donjon, those available reserved for the most esteemed guests, which included Griffin and Quintin de Arell and, surprisingly, the Roystons. But then, not only was Benoit a relation of the baron who held this demesne, but Dangereuse a Wulfrith.

The sire considered the son, raised a half-eaten apple, and

took a bite. Finally, he said, "I am not wrong in saying you allow Royston to cast a shadow across your triumph."

Rhys grimaced. "Do you never marvel how begrimed one can feel over unfounded accusations? True, one may not be entirely innocent of wrongdoing, but when far from being the culprit..." He shook his head. "You know I will do my utmost at the mêlée on the morrow, but I do not look forward to competing against nor once again bettering Benoit since his losses will be felt by ones other than himself."

"You think he mistreats his wife?"

"I tell myself he would not dare—that she is too strong and willful to suffer abuse—but when I made it clear I heard him pronounce my victory ill-gotten this eve, I sensed fear about her."

Griffin de Arell chewed on that—and another bite of apple. "Mayhap 'twas only worry over an altercation between you and her husband, rather than her well-being."

"I have considered that, but if 'tis otherwise, I do not care to be responsible for her suffering should I defeat Benoit again."

"My son, you cannot allow that possibility to affect how you fight and defend yourself, and not only because you are my heir. Though you shall engage in mock war, you will not be moving on a chessboard of pieces easily set aright. God willing, none will die during the morrow's contest, but there will be injuries, and possibly some so grave those who fall may never again be fit to fight for their king."

"Be assured, sire, I shall use well the training and experience gained since earning my spurs."

"And a Wulfrith dagger." The baron jutted his chin at what hung on Rhys' belt that was a match for the one on Benoit's, then said, "Your mother tires, and as I must speak with Barons Boursier and Verdun about quarrying stone from their lands for the castle that shall be yours, I would have you escort her to our chamber in..." He frowned. "A quarter hour should be enough time for her to finish her conversation with Lady Thomasin."

"It will be done," Rhys said, pleased to aid the woman who, though not of his blood, truly was his mother.

Baron de Arell squeezed his son's shoulder. Then striding opposite, once more he indulged in a bite of apple, his fondness of that fruit causing his lady wife to tease it was what first drew her to him. And ever his response was, *Strange I should recall different—that you were offended I was more intent on finishing my apple than addressing the demands of a lady who dared bring an army to my walls.*

No exaggeration that, nor the depth of love grown out of hostilities that had caused much feuding between the families De Arell, Boursier, and Verdun.

Though Rhys would admit it only to himself, the greatest reason for remaining unwed at twenty and four was the belief marriage without the kind of love had by his sire and second wife would be more burden than joy. Hence, even after gaining experience as a warrior knight, he continued to delay in joining his life with another lest settling for less cause him to miss an opportunity to gain much more.

Thoughts returning to Lady Dangereuse, he feared that was the fate of she whose sire had wished his first squire to wed her. Though good for Rhys who would have resented being pressured to marry at that time despite the bride being desirable, it may have proven bad for Baron Wulfrith's daughter. Even had Rhys been a grudging groom, surely he would have made a better husband than the one the lady gained—though from the kiss witnessed by her sire and himself, clearly she had favored Benoit.

Hopefully, when this tournament was done and the Roystons returned to Rhys' past, the two would regain whatever ground their marriage lost as a result of events here. And remain in his past.

CHAPTER 4

A creak of the door. A slash of light. A stumble over the threshold. A curse loudly voiced.

Dangereuse removed her hand from Sebastian's back where he slept in the crib beside the bed and turned toward the intrusive light that met that of the lantern left on the bedside table lest the brazier's glow did not keep Benoit from bumping into something.

"Quiet," she hissed as he closed the door, fortunately not hard enough to slam it in its frame. Better it remain slightly ajar with corridor light squeezing through than their little boy awaken.

Benoit now seen only by lantern light, he halted at the foot of the bed and narrowed his eyes at the crib. "Bastian...Bastian..." he drawled, making their son's name sound foul. "Always Bastian."

Certain he had more drink in him, she bristled, but since venting her anger would worsen matters, she said low, "I will help you to bed." Then she crossed to his side of the mattress and lowered her feet to the floor.

As she started past him to secure the door, he seized her arm.

Gulping down a cry lest those with chambers nearby heard, she peered into his flushed face. "Release me, Benoit."

Eyes moist, mouth convulsing, he said, "No matter how I try, you do not love me. 'Tis as if I am beneath you."

She attempted to wet her lips, but her mouth was dry.

"And you are not alone in believing that," he slurred as he moved his gaze around the chamber. "Were you not a Wulfrith, no room in this *inn* for me."

"Benoit, you have had too much to drink and need rest. The morrow comes soon."

"The morrow comes soon," he singsonged petulantly. "Aye, when once more I seek to prove my warrior skills are superior to those of the man you believe would have made a better husband."

As his hands tightened on her, threatening another bruise, she groped for calm. "No such thing do I believe," she said and silently assured herself it was true. "Now speak no more of this and come to bed."

"You think to command me?" His voice rose. "Because you are a Wulfrith, you believe it gives you—a woman—the right to tell your husband which way to turn?"

Hearing Sebastian's bedclothes rustle, she entreated, "Pray, let us discuss this later. Our son needs sleep."

"As does your husband!" The force of his words spraying her with spittle, he jerked her nearer. "He whose efforts to make you proud could end in the loss of blood, even death."

She would have sharply reminded him she had already expressed concern over his need for rest had not their boy stirred again. Too, there the sound of footsteps and hushed voices beyond the door, indicating more revelers retired for the night.

After silently beseeching the Lord to swell her patience and grant her wisdom, with deliberate huskiness she said, "Come to bed and let your wife hold you."

"Me?" the bitter word sprang from him.

Though hard to continue the charade, she leaned in. "You, dear Benoit."

His hold eased slightly, and with less volume, he said, "De Arell sullied it."

She frowned. "Of what do you speak?"

He dropped his forehead to hers, heaved a sigh that filled her nostrils and mouth with the scent and taste of strong drink. "I had to burn your pretty ribbon."

"What say you?"

"He put his hands on it as if..." He growled. "...he wishes to put his hands all over you."

Struggling to contain fear, she said, "He may want that, but 'twill only ever be your hands upon me."

He knocked his head back, bared his teeth. "Then you know he wants you! Have you betrayed—?"

"Benoit, not so loud!"

A whimper sounded from the crib. Now the beginning of what could become a wail.

"See what you have done!" She strained to free herself. "Let me go. He needs his mother."

"*I* need you."

"He is ill!"

"Mama!"

She peered over her shoulder, and seeing Sebastian grasped the rail to pull himself to standing, swept her eyes back to her husband. The way he regarded their son causing fear to rake her insides, she entreated, "Benoit."

"Mama!"

Returning to the little boy, she saw he wobbled where he

gripped the rail with one hand and reached with the other, repeatedly opening and closing his fingers.

"Mama! Mama!"

"Silence!" Benoit bellowed.

Knowing some in nearby chambers would hear the commotion even were the door firmly closed, anger overrode fear, but not so much she yielded to the temptation to drive a knee into his groin. She thrust it into his thigh.

Releasing her, he stumbled back. However, no sooner did she make it around the bed and reach to their child than he caught hold of her and flung her behind him.

She fell hard, but immediately regained her feet. And went still when he swept their wailing son out of the crib. "Benoit!" she appealed.

Holding Sebastian at arms' length, he roared, "I said be quiet!"

It made the frightened child cry more shrilly and strain to turn his red face to the mother he trusted to rescue him.

Dangereuse raised a staying hand, cautiously stepped forward. "Give him to me."

"Quiet, boy!" He jerked their son, making his head snap.

Praying someone investigated what went here, no longer caring her family would suffer shame as long as she could get Sebastian away from this jealous, inebriated man, she took another step forward. "I will quiet him. I promise. Just—"

"Quiet!" he barked and shook their son like a pillow in need of fluffing.

Dangereuse screamed and lunged, but Benoit turned his shoulder to her and thrust her against the wall beside the window.

As she staggered around, he shook their son again.

Then the door burst inward, and once more corridor's light flooded in. A blur of movement revealed the one who entered wore green, and she glimpsed other figures beyond the threshold as Benoit barked, "De Arell!"

He was here? Before she could verify it, her husband dropped their son on the bed and pushed past her toward...

Was it truly his hated rival? It mattered not. What mattered was getting Sebastian away from here.

Landing her knees on the mattress as the warriors crashed into each other, hearing grunts and curses amid the pounding of skin, muscle, and bone, she scooped up the shrieking child. It was a struggle to keep hold of him as she half crawled to the other side of the bed that would deliver them near the door and decrease the possibility of being caught between the two who overturned a small table, but finally her legs were over the side.

Trying to press the flailing Sebastian's face to her shoulder to keep from adding to the horror of what he witnessed, she moved toward the door and saw a lady enter and reach to her.

Had Dangereuse any doubt it was Rhys de Arell who came to investigate a domestic quarrel, no longer. Here the noblewoman who married his widowed sire years ago and, unable to bear babes, made her stepson her own and adopted two children of common birth.

As Dangereuse neared Lady Quintin, a shout of pain not of Benoit turned their heads, and Dangereuse saw blood on Sir Rhys and the slashing blade of a Wulfrith dagger in her husband's fist.

Both women screamed, and an elderly man who had watched from the corridor hastened inside.

Benoit turned from his rival who hunched over his injury and above her son's cries shouted, "You dare trespass! Get out!"

At the sight of the bloodied blade angled toward him, the grey-bearded man halted. But Lady Quintin, who surely longed to go to her son, gripped Dangereuse's arm and pulled her toward the door.

"That is my wife!" Benoit thundered.

Then so much happened in what seemed a madly twisting dream that Dangereuse thought she might ever question the truth of it.

Benoit ran at her as Sir Rhys unfolded and lunged.

The elderly man grabbed Benoit's arm and was dropped by a fist.

She landed a foot in the corridor and was wrenched back by her braid.

Lady Quintin lost hold of her, and she tightened her arm around her son.

She slammed back against Benoit, and Sir Rhys shouted, "Accursed knave!"

Then there in her husband's fist was the dagger, and instinctively she clamped a hand over that wrist.

When he jerked that arm to the side and her with it, her feet went out from under her, Sebastian screamed in her ear, and the unbalanced Benoit dropped with them.

Somehow—likely Sir Rhys' arrival as much the cause as her seeking to keep the blade from coming near her child—the husband of Dangereuse and father of Sebastian was impaled by his prized Wulfrith dagger.

What followed was further disjointed, but most clear was the bloodied knight prying her son from her and passing him to Lady Quintin, her struggling as she was drawn away, and her cry of, "Why could you not leave be the ill between you, Rhys de Arell? Why could you not leave that foul ribbon in the dirt? 'Twas only good for the burning!"

Then somehow she was in his arms, and when the fight went out of her, it was a quaking Dangereuse he carried to his parents' chamber. There, Sebastian sobbed and clung to Lady

Quintin as if he might never be coaxed out of the stranger's arms.

Or was it Dangereuse who could not be coaxed out of arms she ought to reject? She whose hands gripped fistfuls of a green tunic? She who found comfort where there should be none?

Her as well, she admitted, but still it was hard to loose her hold on him and settle where he lowered her.

Through a blur, she saw and heard Sir Rhys' mother express concern over the injury done him and him assure her it was nothing that would not heal. Then he was gone and her boy gentled into her arms.

The next time she saw Sir Rhys was late morn the day of the mêlée that went forward as if none were slain on the night past. All those involved in the incident having been commanded to the great hall at the shockingly swift conclusion of the investigation into what had widowed a wife and unfathered a son, Dangereuse was forced to once more leave Sebastian in the care of a servant.

Despite it feeling as if she peered through dark rippling water, straining to see and hear all that went above as she awaited the findings, she had been very aware of Sir Rhys where he stood fifteen feet to her right, and more so for earlier noting his limp in addition to cuts and bruises. As he had changed out of his bloodied garments, she could not be certain where Benoit cut him, but possibly it was serious enough he had to forego participation in the mêlée.

At last, the long-standing sheriff of this shire pronounced Benoit Royston's death an accident. Therefore none were at fault but a man who drank too much and dishonored Wulfen training envied by many.

Still, Dangereuse feared otherwise, that though Benoit was not murdered, he had killers beyond himself—and she was among them.

Weakened by fear for Sebastian who was unusually quiet this morn and resistant to being held though his ear remained inflamed, further diminished by flashes of violent memories and lack of sleep, she had to grip the table's edge to steady herself and keep her eyes from going to those standing to her right—in addition to Sir Rhys, Lady Quintin beside her husband who was less handsome of face than their son, the elderly nobleman whose nose had been broken, and three other guests who had observed the events from the corridor. However, continuing to feel the gaze of one to her left whom earlier she glimpsed slipping into an alcove, she looked there.

Ferrand stepped out of the dim.

Though not surprised by the misery on his face, she did not expect a bruised eye nor his arm in a sling.

Whether the girth strap failed on its own or was Sir Rhys' retribution for believing the same worked on him, Benoit had made his brother suffer.

Aching for him, she thought, *I am going home to Wulfenshire. Home to the Barony of Wulfen. Home to Stern Castle. Home to my womenfolk. What of you, Ferrand? Is there anything for you at your home? Or just as there is no longer anything for me and my son under that roof, is there naught for the squire who no longer serves his brother?*

Deciding if she could find a way to aid him she would, she gave her back to all and returned to Sebastian to await the arrival of kin who had been sent word to come for them.

CHAPTER 5

Castle Lillia upon the Barony of Wulfen
Wulfenshire, England, December 1353

W hat foul night is this?" Dangereuse whispered as she leaned into the window embrasure, allowing sleeting rain carried on autumn's chill end to fleck her face and robe.

Though uncertain how she came by the sense of portentous ill that began after her husband's death, it was borne out often enough she suspected it a gift in answer to prayer she never again be caught wrong-footed as on the night her and her son's world was upended.

She looked around as if to confirm Sebastian slept peacefully in the crib alongside her bed, but of course he did not, having been given the small chamber off the solar. And now that he was nearly six winters aged...

She pressed her lips.

Her eldest brother, the Baron of Wulfen and England's renowned trainer of knights, believed her son would make a far better warrior than a man of God.

"But..." she breathed, then here in *the alone* of a widow whose child no longer sought even the pillow of her breast, looked from the misty inner bailey below to the outer bailey whose fog was set aglow by wall lanterns doing their utmost to part the dark of night and absorb the light of sleet bred by rain and snow.

"Better the Church," she affirmed the peace of a monastery would be a balm to Sebastian who, though too young to make sense of what happened that night, surely carried its horror within.

The older he grew, the greater control he gained over emotions that could make him difficult, and though his outbursts were mostly in the past, at times she sensed they bubbled beneath his skin. Thus, it was imperative she find a replacement for the priest who had left shortly after her arrival at Lillia, in part for his advanced years, in part for the new castellan being female.

"Aye, 'tis the Church for you, my son," she said.

And heard again the response of her eldest brother. *As a warrior is in your boy's veins, Wulfen training will serve him best. Plant him in the Church and still he will be a warrior—a discontented, perhaps dangerous one. Entrust him to me, and I will do all in my power to transform that discontent into good that honors God, country, and family.*

Distantly acknowledging the sleet striking her face had become more fierce, once again she grudgingly considered his argument despite it being more disagreeable now he urged her to begin Sebastian's knighthood training upon attainment of his sixth rather than seventh year.

She shook her head, leaned out the window that should already be fit with panes of horn for the coming winter, and extended her tongue to catch ice on it.

A sweet sting, then the fragile crystals melted into water she pressed to her palate, just as she did rain that fell from a summer sky, cooling rather than chilling.

Wishing for the warm months when she could ride across the lands of Lillia that had been a barony in its own right until its heiress wed Baron Garr Wulfrith two hundred years past, she murmured, "Fearless Lady Annyn Bretanne," and not for the first time thought it fitting she who loved the tale of that ancestor best was now Lady of Lillia—albeit temporarily.

As she drew back from the window, lightning flashed as it had before the rain began freezing. Momentarily blinded, she heard thunder she hoped would not awaken her boy, though he might jump into her bed and allow her to hold him. Since he slept deeply once aversion to being sent to bed yielded to the calm of lying prone, more likely the thunder would rouse her sister-in-law who, over seven months pregnant with a child not of Dangereuse's brother, slept poorly.

Murielle Marshal, wed to Rémy Wulfrith to assuage the king's guilt over her ravishment that could have been prevented, had become Dangereuse's charge when Hector named his sister keeper of Castle Lillia that was to pass to their youngest brother once he was knighted. Thus, she was to prepare Rémy's unwanted wife to become lady of the castle for the day he presided here.

Though Murielle was unhappy with the dizzying turn her life had taken—the man she loved slain, a babe in her belly by way of violence, and wed to the sacrificial Wulfrith who disliked her as she did him—she was respectful, mostly punctual, and made an effort to learn what would be expected of her once Dangereuse passed all the household keys to her. Unfortunately, the young woman had become somewhat less compliant these past weeks, advanced pregnancy causing greater discomfort than earlier bouts of nausea and vomiting.

Of course, Rémy made the transition easier for her by staying away as he should not. Though the two had spoken vows quickly, albeit not soon enough to conceal the babe was conceived outside of wedlock, Dangereuse was fairly certain their marriage had yet to be consummated.

Not only had her brother returned to his training the day after they wed, but in all the months since he had not visited his bride.

A less intense bolt of lightning returning Dangereuse to the present, she renewed her vow to do all she could to ease her brother's marital woes so he and Murielle would at least find satisfaction in being good stewards of the land and their people, then reached to the shutters. Before she could close them, shouts sounded from atop the outer bailey's walls, then more lanterns were being lit.

Had they visitors this late at night? Or was something afoot? Though the lands of Lillia were mostly peaceful and the castle well garrisoned, she leaned toward the approach of ill for this portentous feeling and that twice last month brigands had attacked travelers en route to northern England. There had been no deaths, but horses and valuables were stolen and those who resisted beaten. Hopefully, the combined efforts of Lillia's fighting men and the Sheriff of Wulfenshire— Murielle's uncle—would end the lawlessness.

Hearing more shouts and the rattle of portcullis chains that indicated whoever came was welcome despite the hour, Dangereuse latched the shutters. Then she turned into the solar she had taken for herself when the ailing castellan passed a month after she arrived to relieve him of duties that became more onerous once the steward resigned his post—yet another unwilling to answer to a woman.

"Not a moment too soon," Dangereuse muttered as she crossed the chamber that, with its large table to one side of the hearth, served well she who rose early to conduct as much demesne business as possible. Thus, she did not disturb those sleeping in the hall. Equally important, sooner her work was completed for fewer interruptions, which allowed her to spend more time with Sebastian and his schooling, as well as Murielle who must master household matters before advancing to administration of the demesne as would be necessary during her husband's absences.

Dangereuse encountered none until she descended the stairs. There she was met by Puck, the short, sturdy man-at-arms who had the great hall's night patrol and was assisted by an aged mastiff and wolfhound.

"Sounds we have visitors," he said in a voice so coarse one need not see the scar on his throat to know injury was done it sometime in the past. "What would you have me do, Lady D?" he named her as done since the day of her arrival. Though she had meant to correct him for what sounded a lack of respect, he had leaned near and said, *Bein' a Wulfrith and all, I doubt not ye can be dangerous, but yer name is a wee intimidatin' for those who wish only to serve ye well. More, do ye not think it long?*

Lest laughter offend, she had inclined her head. Thus, most retainers named her *Lady D* and, secretly, she liked it.

Dangereuse looked past him to the castle folk who could not have gained more than an hour's sleep on their pallets and hoped any disturbed by those come into the hall soon returned to their rest. Of course, if the visitors did not enter through the great doors...

She took Puck's arm and drew him toward the kitchen corridor. "I shall send you outside to bring our visitors around to the back. Since the remains of the cooking fires yet cast heat, it will be appreciated in such foul weather."

It was only when they entered the brightly glowing kitchen she realized she sent him out in tunic and chausses alone. "We must get you a mantle!"

"Nay, I did not get big and meaty and survive worse than the opening of my throat by running from danger let alone discomfort, Lady D. Stay here and let Puck the Ruck do yer biddin' quick like."

Puck the Ruck, she mused as he crossed the kitchen, opened the door on the wintry garden, and closed it behind him. Though often he called himself that which brought to mind a great heap, it lightened her mouth nearly as much as the first time he proudly spoke the rhyming name.

While awaiting his return with the visitors, she added logs to one of the dying fires and set out bread, cheese, ale, and cups. Upon catching lowered voices and footsteps in the garden, she snugged her robe's belt and, ensuring the lapels crossed well to conceal her chemise, opened the door.

Ferrand was there in his oilcloth mantle, having had charge of this eve's perimeter patrol that was to intercept any who approached the castle and, once it was determined they should be granted admittance, escort them inside.

"My lady," said the man he had become since his brother's death, those intervening years spent upon the Barony of Wulfen for Hector honoring her request to find a position for a squire without a lord. One was had at Castle Lillia and, after some difficulty her brother attributed to him being dominated by Benoit, he had risen through the ranks. Were he a knight, he would be a contender for the position of captain of the guard when it became available.

"Squire," she titled him as was his due in the presence of men-at-arms who answered to him, though on occasions their meeting was other than business, he was simply *Ferrand*—and *Uncle Ferrand* to Sebastian who had been unenthusiastic about acknowledging their kinship until he realized his uncle was just as uncomfortable being addressed thus.

Her brother-in-law crossed the threshold ahead of others also wearing mantles upon which moisture beaded and drew her aside. Surprisingly, the light here revealed something his face had not reflected since The Tournament of Honor —uncertainty.

"What has happened?" she said, then caught her breath when she saw the men-at-arms who entered behind bore a sizable man of fairly short blond hair who was not only bootless and reduced to under tunic and hose of fine fabric, but soaked through and bloodied. "Dear Lord, was it the brigands? Have they slain this traveler?"

"He is not dead," Ferrand said, "but you ought know—"

"It matters not." As Puck closed the door, she hastened past the men-at-arms and slapped the large table used to assemble platters of viands for meals shared with the castle folk. "Place him here—gently!"

"Hold, my lady!" Ferrand came behind her.

"It can wait, Squire. This man's injuries cannot." She continued to the cupboard where medicinals and bandages were stored for accidents inherent in working a kitchen amid fires, bubbling liquids, popping grease, and keen knives.

She opened the doors, grabbed salve and a ball of bandages, and was sharply pulled around.

"Lady Dangereuse—"

"Loose me, Ferrand! As I am not squeamish, I can tend him until the physician is summoned from...I believe he traveled to the village of Falls Vale."

Further protest opened his mouth.

"Do as our lady commands, Squire," Puck said with warning, though the younger man ranked higher.

Ferrand heaved a sigh. "Very well, see for yourself."

That she did when, after setting salve and bandages alongside the man lowered to the table, she turned toward her a face bristling with many days' growth of whiskers. Her throat closed, and the recoil in her body went down through her feet, fixing her there with a hand on his broad jaw.

Despite a battered face, she knew it. Not that she had never seen it in such a state, each of their significant encounters ending with damage done his handsome visage, including that which saw her clinging to him as he carried her to his parents' chamber. Effortlessly. Gently.

"We can see to his injuries, my lady," Ferrand said.

Slapped back to the present, Dangereuse realized she was transfixed by the man. And in her brother-in-law's voice was something she had not heard in a long time—apology, as whilst he labored for Benoit.

Ignoring it lest her inner trembling slip out, she looked to where he drew near. "Forgive me, Ferrand. I ought to have listened."

His smile was sorrowful. "Else I should have blurted it. Now allow us to tend him."

"Nay, I shall." She returned her regard to the knight who had somehow fallen into her hands. As she drew her fingers from his face, once again she wondered, *What foul night is this?*

Then she told herself there was good in it—that were this the portent of ill earlier felt, it did not adversely affect her nor those dear to her. This was all upon Rhys de Arell whose misfortune could be due to God exercising His right to exact vengeance.

Could be, the voice within reminded that though this man had played a part in her husband's death, she had no real evidence of the extent. Though much she had brooded on it, never had she thought to seek it. But now...

Might she learn the truth about the broken girth strap that pushed Benoit to a dark place and turned him violent—not only toward his brother and wife but their son?

If there is a confession to be had, how do you propose to draw it out? questioned the cautious side of her she ought to heed more than the knotted side.

"My lady?" Ferrand ventured.

"Heat salt water to clean his injuries," she instructed, and after he withdrew reluctantly, looked to Puck. "Put an iron in the fire lest cauterizing is required, then bring vinegar from the cellar."

As he hastened away, she looked back at The Tournament of Honor's victor.

And there that voice again. *If he caused the girth strap's failure as Benoit believed, what will you do, Lady Dangereuse of the* honorable *Wulfrith family to which you belong—first, in between, and in the end?*

Pressing her lips inward, she considered Sir Rhys' torso and arms to which clung the tunic with its water-diluted blood-stains. Only then seeing he quaked, the fire having yet to generate sufficient heat, she ordered one of the men-at-arms to find a blanket, then beckoned to the other who had come out from beneath his mantle. "Aid me in getting him out of these wet garments."

His eyes widened. "I can do that, Lady D. Ye need not—"

"I know a man's body well enough to have made a child with my husband. Now be quick ere this knight is lost to England."

Despite their combined efforts, it was difficult to remove the tunic from one so tall and muscular, but at last Sir Rhys' bruised and cut chest was fully exposed and, more importantly, his sword arm. The latter having suffered no mere flesh wound, it would require stitches to muscle as well as skin, meaning a physician was needed to provide a better chance of him wielding a blade again.

That gave her pause, and she was ashamed by the consideration he might no longer be worthy of swinging a sword. Worthy or not, she would not withhold care. As soon as possible, the physician would do his best for the knight, then she would see about gaining answers to questions over three years aged—even if Sir Rhys' stay at Lillia must be prolonged.

Truly, Dangereuse? That voice again.

Ignoring it, she had the man-at-arms compress the arm with a kitchen towel to prevent further blood loss. When his fellow soldier returned with a blanket and spread it over the knight's lower half, she directed the two to remove the hose beneath that cover. Though she *was* familiar with a man's form, since she must clean the arm and chest wounds and there was no need to scandalize her men, better they treat with the more intimate parts of the body.

You would keep him at Lillia beyond what is necessary? the voice pressed as she reached for one of the towels Ferrand had set on the table with a bowl of steaming water. *Bastian is here, just as he was there the night Sir Rhys came to your aid.* That *the boy cannot know for the rescue of mother and son ending in his sire's death.*

She faltered, then assured her conscience that during this man's recovery there would be opportunities to learn the truth. And she would ensure Sebastian never knew the one who had crashed about the chamber with his sire was at Lillia lest he was snatched back to that night and the ground regained in the years since was lost.

But where am I to hide you? she pondered as she dipped the towel in the bowl of warmed water placed alongside his hip. It was then the men-at-arms' struggle to peel off the hose caused the blanket to slide and bare a hip and upper thigh—on the latter a white scar as long as her hand.

Recalling him bent over the injury Benoit dealt him, wondering if this was that, she traced its path with a finger. It being as flat as it looked, it was no new acquisition. At least three years old.

"My guess as well," Ferrand said low, and she jumped her gaze to where he stood near the end of the table. Since he had not been present that night, she had not known he was aware of the injury Sir Rhys sustained beyond the visible ones. But then, there had been witnesses to what happened in the chamber, and later she learned those events had been more the talk of the tournament than the crowning mêlée whose victory was had by those representing the English side—some suggesting her husband's death was no accident.

That first year, so much gossip circulated about the widowed Wulfrith she had feared she would be unable to keep it from touching Sebastian until some other unfortunate became talk dropped from loose lips into famished ears, but it had mostly quieted. Of course, her brothers had aided, as well as Uncle Owen, none giving more than one warning before taking teeth and bending noses.

Of a sudden, both men-at-arms grunted over their success in removing the hose, then the one triumphantly holding it said, "Some bruising on his legs, Lady D, but no broken flesh, nor does it appear he was so long exposed his toes froze."

Meaning she would not have to tend him below the waist.

"Are you sure you wish to do this?" Ferrand asked, once again with apology.

Finding his eyes on the finger with which she traced the scar, casually she withdrew it lest she appear guilty. "I am sure," she said, then pulled the blanket up over the knight's bared hip and wrung out the towel. As she moved to his head, she eyed his torso to determine where to begin and saw he no longer quaked. With an approving turn of the lips, she looked to his face.

And found half-open eyes upon her.

CHAPTER 6

Was he conscious when I touched his scar? Dangereuse rued.

His lids rose higher. "My squire...traveling companions..." His voice was so rough he sounded three score aged. "Where?"

She looked to Ferrand who said, "We found him beneath a tree. No others, no horse, no weapons. Just as you see him here."

"Brigands?"

He nodded, but added a shrug.

"Where?" Sir Rhys repeated, more gravel about his voice.

"He needs drink," she said.

As Ferrand strode to the table upon which she had set out refreshments, a tug on the braid draping her shoulder brought her chin around.

Gripping the ribboned end, Sir Rhys said, *"You* are drink."

She blinked. Did this man who years ago showed no interest in marrying Baron Wulfrith's eldest daughter truly equate her with something so desirable as to be essential to life? If so, he was delirious or mistook her for another.

He shifted his gaze to the braid, slid his thumb up the crossings. "And lightning in the night."

Neither did that make sense until she considered the dark strands strewn with silver must remind him of the black of the night slashed by lightning. If so, then for acknowledgement of the silvered hair of a fairly young Wulfrith, he did not mistake her for another but suffered a mind addled by the assault.

Gaze returning to hers, he released the braid, dropped his hand to the table, and closed eyes as brilliant as his sire's.

She thought he lost consciousness, but when Ferrand appeared on the other side of the table and said, "You must drink," he nodded.

The squire elevated him and put the cup to his lips. The knight drank slowly, then gave a shake of the head that had Ferrand setting the cup aside and easing him down.

Hopefully, Puck would soon return with vinegar so the cleansed wounds could be sterilized, that better done while Sir Rhys remained awake rather than the pain of it jolt him out of sleep.

"I shall tend your injuries," Dangereuse said.

He rolled his head toward her, picked his gaze over her, then said with demand that pushed offense up her spine, "Where am I?"

She leaned near. "Why, you are a most unexpected guest at Castle Lillia. I cannot say you are welcome, Sir Rhys, but I shall do all in my power to ensure your stay benefits both of us."

The ice appearing amid the bothersome blue of his eyes told he was lucid enough to suspect her choice of words.

When she pulled back and began cleaning cuts that would scar a nearly flawless chest she told herself was not unlike Benoit's—but was, for how perfectly it tapered into abdomen and hips—he hardly flinched. But all changed when Puck returned with the vinegar.

Now to tend his most dire injury, of which she believed him unaware since threat to the sword arm of any fighting man could rouse him such that he must be restrained. Either the arm was numb from loss of sensation, or shock was greater than lucidity.

"Puck, Squire Ferrand, I need your aid," she said and felt the knight's eyes follow her as she moved to the other side of the table.

When she shifted the towel cinched about his injured arm to expose the wound, he demanded, "What do you?"

"Your sword arm took a blade deep. Do you not recall?"

He jabbed his elbows into the table to rise, then shouted as Puck and Ferrand forced him down. When he proved even a seriously injured De Arell was not easily overwhelmed, causing her to order the men-at-arms to pin his legs, still he fought. "Do not take it! Do not!"

Struggling to keep hold of his arm, she put her face near his. "The injury is serious, but the physician shall determine whether it must be removed. God willing, he returns to Lillia early on the morrow."

"I am to believe you?" he growled.

She raised her eyebrows. "You have no choice. Now allow us to clean the wound so your arm is not lost to infection."

"One always has a choice, Lady, even if 'tis utterly sacrificial."

"In that you are right, Sir Rhys."

His eyes moved between her and his bleeding flesh, then grimly he bore her efforts to preserve his arm—until the vinegar. He shouted, slammed his heels into the table, arched his back.

Unable to harden herself against his suffering, she said,

"Forgive me. Now hold, for the worst is past and all that remains is the bandaging." *For now,* she did not add, knowing the burn of vinegar would be naught compared with that to which the physician would subject him.

His exhale buffeted her face. "For now," he said what she had not, then as if relief was had in knowing the arm would not be severed this eve, his muscles eased, head turned opposite, and lids lowered.

Hopeful he had begun a journey so far down inside himself he would remain senseless until conveyed to a place that best concealed his presence, Dangereuse wiped her bloodied hands on a towel and reached for salve.

"Lord, he is strong," Ferrand murmured, releasing his hold on the knight's other arm.

Declining to comment on strength it sounded he admired though surely he suspected the same as she that Benoit's death began with the suspicious failure of the girth strap, she said, "I know you ordered another patrol upon your return, but I must ask you to go out again and search for his traveling companions. If they were injured, finding them now could mean the difference between life and death."

"It is as I planned to do as soon as you had no more need of me."

Fleetingly, she reflected how sad it was it should take separation from his brother by way of death to bring out the best in Ferrand. "Then go, but leave a man to aid Puck in moving Sir Rhys out of the kitchen."

He looked to the knight who continued his journey into senselessness, then instructed one of his men to follow.

When the door closed behind those who flipped up their hoods to protect against the sleet, Dangereuse began salving the arm with more confidence for certainty her unwelcome guest would not rouse again.

She was wrong.

He spoke, seemingly to someone near the door beyond which lay the great hall. Since it was done with a slur indicative of dwindling consciousness, she continued to concentrate on her ministrations.

"Lady D, see who is here," Puck said low.

She looked up. And gasped.

Barefooted and tunic askew, her boy stood before the door that granted him entrance with nary a peep for the oil she had applied to its hinges this morn. And here she stood behind a table on which lay a man, her hand on his muscled chest.

As she snatched it away, Sir Rhys said, "You look much like..." These words she made sense of, though they were just as slurred as the others that now echoed the name of her departed husband. "Aye, like Benoit did when..."

When this knight and her husband began their page's training at Wulfen, she pieced it together amid the struggle to do other than observe this encounter.

"Mama, who is that man?" Sebastian pointed with the hand gripping a toy soldier Hector had gifted him.

Dangereuse was so relieved he did not recognize Sir Rhys from that night—at least at this distance—she broke free of her stupor. "'Tis a knight who has been hurt and I seek to aid. Now Puck the Ruck shall take you to the hall and rouse Amanda who will see you back to bed." She referred to the maid she had employed upon arriving at Lillia, a matronly woman Sebastian seemed to like though the quick to smile and laugh Amanda was more quick to express displeasure over his inappropriate behavior.

Her son shook his head. "First, honey milk."

Whether it was the firmer hand taken with him this past year to prepare him to enter the Church, Amanda's example of how to deal with foul moods and offensive demands, or the desperate need to see him depart the kitchen that fueled her resolve not to yield, she did not know.

"First, sleep, Bastian," she said, then to Puck, "Take him and rouse Amanda."

The man grimaced but moved to do her bidding.

Unsurprised by stubborn on her boy's face, she said in a tone he did not like for its backbone, "Do you disturb any in the hall, I will put away your toy soldiers for a sennight."

His arm jerked, and she knew were it an egg he held rather than a wooden figure, yellow would run through his fingers.

"Aye, a sennight, Sebastian," she spoke his name in full to impress on him she was serious.

He sighed, and when Puck extended a hand, took it and asked, "Ride your back, Puck the Ruck?"

The man grunted. "Up the stairs, providin' ye be quiet and wake none, lad."

"I be creepin' like a mouse," Sebastian mimicked the man's rustic speech, though not cruelly as told by a playful grin. Then as he was urged toward the door, he peered over his shoulder at the man whose silence she hoped indicated he had exhausted the last of his consciousness. "That one is a fierce warrior. Be careful, Mama."

Returned to the night her two-year-old screamed and flailed and saw things he ought not, as if through a glass sooted by fire, she watched as he departed. And wondered if, from across the room, he *had* recognized Sir Rhys, even were he unable to place him. Or was his warning but a reflection of games played with toy soldiers she must get away from him were he to commit to a path other than the one her brother wished for him?

Though she told herself it must be the latter, she had to swallow a whimper.

"Sebastian," Sir Rhys rasped. "I think I knew...that his

name." He turned his face, revealing lids so narrow the blue was barely seen. Then no blue at all.

Momentarily, Dangereuse closed her eyes, then feigning ignorance of the soldier watching her, returned to her ministrations.

CHAPTER 7

Words, those of Rhys weaving in and out of those of others, most prominently a woman's.

Certain they were but echoes of ones already spoken, he resisted making sense of them, preferring to remain beneath the agony that had deprived him of consciousness. Though there was also pain in these depths, it was dull in comparison. Hence, better he stay down here while he healed up there.

Wrong, lad! A De Arell does not dwell in the dark. He razes to the ground those walls and brings light to the ruins. More words from the past, but these were clear, given by Griffin de Arell to his six-year-old son.

Now words from Sir Owen of the Wulfriths who had concluded his page's training—*Do you close eyes and heart when faced with steep challenges, the only way before you will be down. Then you shall have to climb anew, which can be done only if you are given another chance to prove worthy of your training.*

His resistance faltered, making it feel as if a whetstone

were dragged across his aches and providing a foretaste of the sharp pain to come should he abandon the depths.

Then came the words of Sir Owen's older brother, spoken long before the pestilence claimed the Baron of Wulfen—*Regardless of the suffering of a warrior worthy of knighthood, he faces his challenges with hand to God, head up, shoulders back, sword at the ready.*

Sensing the presence of Griffin de Arell and those who partnered with him to form a man and warrior out of a boy, Rhys swam toward the surface. Though each stroke and kick intensified the pain in his sword arm, he bore it—and more easily when the memory of what felt a caress to his thigh offered the balm of distraction.

Seeing again a stunning woman standing over him, her braid in his hand, he sensed he should be able to name her. Then out of his mouth came the words, *You are drink.*

Had he truly said that, suggesting the sight of her quenched thirst better than any brimming cup?

He had caressed the crossings of the black braid stranded with silver and also named her *lightning in the night* like what had slashed the sky as he and his companions rode for shelter before the rain began to freeze.

Consciousness had dipped but was alleviated by the offer of drink and distant recognition of the man who held the cup. Somewhat revived by the ale and the woman announcing she would tend his injuries, he demanded to be told where he was.

She had stiffened, bent near, and said he was an unexpected guest at Castle Lillia, a name not unfamiliar for it being the northernmost fortress upon the Barony of Wulfen. That and what next she spoke—*I cannot say you are welcome, Sir Rhys, but I shall do all in my power to ensure your stay benefits both of us*—jolted. He knew he had not been thinking clearly, but it was worse than that. The second he set eyes on the fairly young lady of silvered dark hair, he should have known her. And Ferrand Royston.

Now he recalled Lady Dangereuse's hands on his chest moving with detached efficiency that should in no way bother, and yet—

Ache tore through Rhys' arm, sweeping aside the memory as if it were a table cleared by an angry drunk, and now pain in teeth he gnashed to keep from voicing his suffering.

Though hopeful he neared full consciousness and this the extent of what he must bear, it was not. The effort to keep from shouting made him quake, while the breaths he forced in and out raked his throat as he peered into the dim cast by a low-burning lantern on the wall to the left.

Were a brazier here, its coals lit to ease the chill, there remained no glow about it. Either such consideration was not afforded him or the coal exhausted. If the latter, likely this dark hour was nearly the last before dawn when surely someone would revive the brazier to heat the air nipping his face.

But there is fire and heat here, he resentfully acknowledged. *From shoulder to fingers much fire. Unless—*

Struck by the possibility that pain was imagined, aware some who lost limbs continued to feel them and the specific ache of the injury well after the severing, he ceased breathing.

Might his arm have been removed atop the table once he lost consciousness? Though Lady Dangereuse told it would be for the physician to decide, perhaps she lied. Or the physician had come and, determining the arm should be removed, taken it.

"Pray not!" Rhys exhorted, his beseeching barely heard for how dry his throat. His next breath making him groan, he moved his left hand beneath the blanket. Acknowledging he now wore a tunic, whereas on the table he had been absent garments and his only covering that of a blanket, he closed a hand over his sword arm.

Rhys de Arell remained whole.

Praise, Lord! he sent heavenward. *And let this not be the extent of Your compassion. Heal my arm so it serves well again, and aid me in being worthy of Your mercy since surely many trials lie ahead ere I rejoin my fellow warriors and—*

"Knave!" he named himself. Upon awakening in the kitchen, he had asked after his squire and the others, but had he received confirmation of their well-being?

"Show them mercy, Lord," he pushed past lips that would crack if he did not gain drink. "Let not such ill as was done me befall them. No matter how unwelcome I am at Lillia, let me be glad I am here for them also being present."

His swallow hurt all the way down. As he chided himself for discomfort insignificant compared to his arm that could be lost by day's end, a door to the right opened.

In response to his head turning toward the light of a torch, a voice said, "I did not expect ye to rouse, Sir Knight. Pardon for neglectin' the fire. And pray, do not tell Lady D."

Lady D, he turned that over as wood met metal as the man set the torch in a wall sconce. Then came footsteps that made the floor groan. "She be disappointed in one who meant only to rest his eyes and went a bit beyond."

More than a bit, Rhys thought as he looked to the squat man and saw it was not a brazier he approached but a small fireplace in what must be an outer wall.

Puck. Was that not what he was called? Fairly certain, he said, "I need drink, Puck."

"Ah, forgive, forgive." The man altered his course, and as he drew alongside the narrow bed, Rhys noticed the small table to the left where a pitcher and cup sat among other items. Puck poured the red of wine, likely heavily watered in consideration of one as much in need of moistening a dry throat as finding ease in alcohol, then eyed Rhys. "Ye need aid sittin' up?"

"I would be glad of assistance."

It was so quickly given, he nearly shouted over the pain, but when diluted wine coursed his tongue and moistened his throat, the ache shafting his arm eased some.

The man returned the cup to the table and lifted the smallest of two pots. "Now some of this, eh?"

"What is it?"

"Medicinal powder Lady D put on yer tongue when ye returned to sleep in the kitchen. And a good one 'tis for relievin' pain so one can rest."

Do I wish to return to sleep? he questioned. He wanted relief, but were it to render him entirely senselessness—

"What I mean is this powder have not the sleepin' ingredient," Puck said as if he saw what Rhys should not have let upon his face. "Only relief here, allowin' sleep to follow of its own will."

Angled on the pillow the man had raised behind his shoulders, Rhys pondered if he lied or passed along Lady Dangereuse's lie. However, as his pained arm could render him unconscious again, he said, "I will take some."

When a pinch was dropped on his tongue, its bitterness made him groan.

"Nasty stuff, but as ye shall find, worth every grain ye choke down. Now I will get the fire goin'." The man crossed to the stone hearth that protected the wood flooring.

Rhys ordered his thoughts, then asked, "Any word of my traveling companions? There were three—a squire, man-at-arms, and woman."

"A woman, ye say?" Puck did not look up. "Regrets. Though Squire Ferrand assembled a party to scout the area where you were found 'neath a tree, they returned empty-handed. Unfortunately, new snowfall covered the tracks."

Then neither was there proof Rhys had slain one of the three pursuers as believed. Likely, the man astride had made it a good distance before succumbing to his injury.

To tinder and kindling taken from a basket near the hearth, Puck added logs. "They are to go out again, but as only now dawn is upon us and snow up to the ankles, it could be an hour or more ere the search is resumed—or longer, since there may be more snow mid-morning."

Almighty, preserve them, Rhys entreated, then recalled the gathering storm and dark of night that allied with men who sought to overtake the four pushing their mounts hard to outrun the weather, next his decision to divide his party—his squire and the man-at-arms going one direction, Rhys and the woman another.

Hopefully, it had been for the best, making up for much gone wrong, including the channel crossing that turned rough two hours into the voyage, so greatly sending their ship off course it docked far north of London. Unfortunately, for now Rhys could only pray none of those accompanying him from France were lifeless beneath the snow.

When he looked to Puck, he saw the man had drawn his dagger and angled it low inside the cavity to strike a stone against the keen edge, creating sparks that, on the third try, lit the tinder. He fanned and blew on the smoldering pile, then confident the resulting flames would ignite kindling that would in turn light the logs, rose and sheathed his dagger. "I be leavin' ye to your rest."

"I have more questions."

"Likely not for me to answer."

"Where am I?"

The man guffawed. "Why, still at Castle Lillia." Then he made a face, "Ah, ye mean where in the donjon, eh?"

"Eh," Rhys answered.

"This windowless place is the bedchamber of the former steward. It be at the back of the accountin' room that do have windows to let in light, though set high for this bein' the ground floor just off the great hall."

Rhys suppressed a groan over pain cramping his right hand, and that reminded him of something he should have asked earlier. "The physician?"

"Unless he returned whilst ye and I chatted, not here, and perhaps not for some time with the weather barely holdin' its icy breath."

God in heaven, Rhys silently appealed, then asked, "What of my warrior's gear—sword, dagger, armor?"

"Doubtless taken by yer attackers."

No surprise, but he would not mourn those precious items whilst there was the possibility of greater mourning for those with whom he traveled. "Would you send word to the castellan I wish to make his acquaintance?"

Puck chuckled. "That ye already done."

Had he? This a gap in his memory?

"Methinks what ye do not know is *he* be a *she*." He let that sink in, then confirmed it. "Aye, Baron Wulfrith's sister is Lillia's castellan."

Though there was nothing humorous about that, a laugh escaped Rhys. Naturally, the woman who tended him in the kitchen was the keeper. "Would you tell Lady Dangereuse I wish to speak with her?"

"As soon as she shows herself."

Guessing her still abed, Rhys said, "When will that be?"

"Seein' as early morn is for working the books, likely she

will not come down for another hour or so—unless her rascal rouses early."

Rhys stumbled over that, then recalled voices swirling about a mind going lax. He had brought to focus a small figure near the door—a child briefly seen when he was little more than a babe and by brutish means his sire tried to end his wailing.

Whether he had resembled Benoit Royston then could not be known, but now his features reflected those of the boy with whom Rhys had begun his page's training a bit later than most sent to Wulfen. Staring at the wide-eyed Sebastian, he had considered—perhaps aloud—if he had known the boy's name before, then looked back at the mother. And saw no more.

"There are times Bastian is up out of bed ahead of the castle folk," Puck said. "Though I be not versed in children, methinks the lady's brother right. Better a warrior made of the boy than a man of God. Hopefully, Baron Wulfrith will not have to force the matter for his sister being bent on her son's vocation." He glanced over his shoulder. "The logs catch! Ere long, 'twill be warm."

"I thank you."

Puck nodded. "As I have duties ere I break my fast and gain my sleep, I must leave. Would you have me refill your cup?" At Rhys' nod, he poured and set the cup near the table's edge. "Have ye hunger, Sir Knight?"

Had he? He ought to, especially as already the powder eased some of the pain, but he shook his head.

When Puck retrieved the torch and started to withdraw, Rhys called, "Would you leave the door open so daylight may enter with the sun's rising?"

"I shall."

"And ensure Lady Dangereuse knows I would meet with her."

The man went from sight, then that far door closed. Absent torchlight, the room beyond glowed with dawning light entering through the high windows.

Just as the medicinal was easing Rhys' pain, the fire had begun to take the chill from the room. Still, neither was sufficient to grant healing sleep. Or so he thought.

He meant only to close his eyes against what smoke resisted going up the chimney constructed in the donjon's outer wall, but he began to drift. Then for the promise of greater relief, he allowed himself to be borne on those gentle waves as he prayed for the well-being of those from whom he had been separated—and attendance by the physician.

CHAPTER 8

No matter how she tried, the entries inked weeks past refused to be reconciled.

Dangereuse jabbed the quill in the stand, set her elbows on the tabletop, and pressed fingers against her brow. "Accursed De Arell! 'Tis your fault." Including how little sleep she had after her return to the solar last eve. And it was not only her churning thoughts nor memories of The Tournament of Honor that disturbed. It was Sebastian whose slumber was punctuated by groans heard through the door between his room and the solar.

After failing to ease him out of the dream by rubbing his back and whispering soothing words, she had carried him to her bed and held him. Thereafter, he was silent but restless.

She could not be certain that violent night had visited him as she believed it had the first year following his sire's death, but surely the sight of Sir Rhys in the kitchen stirred long-buried memories. As Sebastian had warned her to beware of one he called a *fierce warrior* though the man wore no armor nor weapons, was that not proof of recognition?

Only some recognition, she assured herself, then tears stinging her eyes, said low, "Why, Lord? Of all who might come to Lillia, why him?"

A sob nearly escaped. As ever, the wall around her emotions was most easily breached by her son, whether a result of fear for him, worry, or frustration. Lowering her hands, she looked to the bed where the top of Sebastian's head was visible above a fur coverlet.

He continued to sleep, and other than occasional shifting, seemed at peace. Of course, when he found himself in his mother's bed, which months past he declared was the baby's way rather than that of one who would become a knight, that peace would end.

Upon rising, she had meant to quietly return him to his bed. Instead, the mother Hector believed overprotective had kept her boy in sight.

"Your fault, De Arell," she repeated, then pushed aside the journal. Standing, she tugged straight the green wool gown she had donned after completing her ablutions, then considered the nearest shuttered window whose thin upper seam was lit.

The sun having risen and reconciliation of expenditures best done later, she would leave her son to his rest and go belowstairs. Since there were always household matters to tend to, she intended to occupy herself with them, excepting those Murielle was to undertake once she was ready for the day.

And what of your uninvited guest? her conscience submitted.

As she had not been alerted the physician had made it back through the snow, it fell to her to ascertain Sir Rhys' state—or at least check with the one entrusted to see to his needs through the night.

Hoping Puck would give a good report so she could stay

clear of the man who had named her things that sounded of one beguiled—and had further disturbed in taking hold of her braid—Dangereuse moved to the bed.

"My boy," she whispered and touched her lips to his brow above long lashes resting atop cheeks that were less and less the plump of small apples, then made her way to the great hall.

As expected, all evidence the room had served as an immense bedchamber last eve was gone, scores of pallets and blankets stacked out of sight in alcoves over which curtains were drawn. As not expected, one would not know the morn's simple meal of bread, cheese, and small ale had been served, the tables having been cleared and benches straightened.

"Lady D!" Puck called in a thicker than usual voice.

Looking to him where he exited the kitchen corridor, she saw a cheek bulged and in one hand a loaf of bread whose upper edge was torn.

They met halfway, and he swallowed loudly. "Ye are down early, and less the need this morn for Lady Murielle coming belowstairs around dawn for honey milk to calm her belly. When she learned what interrupted your settlin' in for the night, she set to playing lady of the castle."

Dangereuse blinked. "Is that so?"

"Aye, she wished yer burdens to be fewer once ye rose."

"Considerate," Dangereuse said, then added, "I imagine she was curious about the injured knight."

He shrugged. "Seemed content enough with what was told her—which was not much, mind."

Then she did her sister-in-law a disservice in assuming she took greater responsibility than usual so she might learn more about their unwelcome guest? "Did she go to the steward's rooms?"

"Nay, been busy in the hall and kitchen. As for Sir Rhys, when I built up his fire a while back, he was roused, in pain, and agitated 'bout his arm. I told there was hope the physician would return soon."

"How great that hope?" she asked, having not peered outside lest the shutters protest or gust of cold air awaken her son.

He grimaced. "The sky has not resumed lettin' down the white stuff, but it thinks on it."

"Then we must pray the physician makes it safely back soon."

"I do, Lady D, and since still there be no word of the knight's travelin' companions, I pray no harm befell them, especially the lady."

She startled. "Lady?"

"That what he told—he be with a lady, man-at-arms, and squire."

"How did they become separated?"

"I did not ask."

Then she must. Were there any hope of locating the three, even if it proved too late to preserve their lives, her patrol must know exactly what happened.

"Ye go to Sir Rhys now, milady?" At her hesitation, Puck added, "He told he would speak with the castellan and was surprised when I said you were that."

Of course he was. "Then like Lillia's former steward, he believes a woman unfit for the position."

"Said naught of that." He raised the bread in readiness to take another bite. "Ye go to him, Lady D?"

She glanced past him. "Is Lady Murielle in the kitchen?"

"Aye."

"Then though I can deliver Sir Rhys no good tidings, I shall see how he fares and learn what I can of his companions." She started to turn away, then asked, "Has another search patrol gone out?"

"Shortly after dawn."

She managed a smile. "'Twas a long night, Puck. Gain your rest."

"In a bit." He sank his teeth into the bread and strode toward the hearth where usually he bedded down despite the noise of a hall coming to life. Ahead of arranging a pallet to the side and sleeping, he would eat and sit a time before a fire whose battle with the cold seeping into the donjon was aided by rushes spread across the floor and aged tapestries clothing the walls.

That last made Dangereuse wish for summer when the hangings could be taken outside, cleaned, and mended. Though since her arrival progress had been made in restoring the donjon's order and beauty, her first priority had been to better the ranks of Castle Lillia's fighting men who needed younger blood to thin the thick of those growing old, her second priority to increase the household staff.

Before the pestilence claimed a third of England's population, Lillia had been one of several jewels in the barony's crown. However, for numerous deaths here and the evolving illness of its former castellan, the demesne had struggled to recover. Then there was the steward. Though following his departure no evidence was found of misappropriation of funds, he had been less competent than believed. But whoever succeeded him would be capable—as soon as a man versed in numbers willing to answer to a woman was found.

Returning her thoughts to Rhys de Arell, Dangereuse moved toward the corridor past the high table and silently entreated the physician, *For your sake, those of the demesne, and that of my unwelcome guest, be safe and come soon, George Mannly.*

Then she opened the door to the steward's study. Pausing, she considered the room of good size that accommodated a writing desk, counting table, and shelving and cupboards that held journals and books. Not only was this place softly lit by clouded light pressing through the upper windows' panes but firelight pulsed from the room in the back corner.

Though Sir Rhys could be in no state to harm a woman—not that she believed him of such bent—she listened for sounds beyond the hiss and crackle of burning wood and touched the hilt of one of two daggers on her girdle. The one with which she cut her meat could be a deterrent, her sire and eldest brother having trained her in wielding short blades, but this dagger was more formidable for its longer reach and keen edges she herself kept sharpened.

It was not a Wulfrith dagger, but it need not be, she reflected as she crossed to the bedchamber from which enough heat radiated it also warmed the study. She did possess one of her family's daggers awarded those knighted at Wulfen, but since it was that on which Benoit fell during their fateful struggle, she had locked it away and had no intention of passing it to Sebastian.

Shoulders back, she entered the small room and looked to the man abed. Face turned opposite toward the table on which sat drink and what was used to tend his injuries, his bedclothes were cast off. Thus, his only covering was the clean tunic found for him that left his lower legs bared—and clung to torso and thighs.

Fearing he suffered a fever of infection rather than the fire's excessive heat, she hastened forward and, seeing moisture on his face and neck, put a knee to the mattress and leaned in.

She need not feel his brow to confirm he was overheated, but that instinctual seeking had doubled when she became a mother and trebled when Sebastian proved vulnerable to ear infections that finally resolved at four years of age.

When her hand on the knight made him groan and turn his face toward her, she said, "Sir Rhys? 'Tis Lady Dangereuse of the Wulfriths." And caught her breath at the realization that rather than continue binding her name to her husband's, she voiced what she held inside. When she wed Benoit, it had been difficult to accept her bond with him should be stronger than that with her family, but it had become easier when their joining produced Sebastian. However, after what was done their wailing son the night of Benoit's death, once more she considered herself primarily of the family into which she was born.

"Ever a Wulfrith," Sir Rhys murmured, and as she snatched her hand from his brow, saw he peered narrowly at her. "But alas, the honorable Wulfriths are a poor fit for one who..." He moved his eyes down her. "Unless I misinterpreted your tone on the night past, the *welcome* extended your unwanted guest sounded a threat."

Realizing she yet leaned over him, a knee on the mattress, she drew back.

However, as she had come to his uninjured side, with little effort he closed his left hand around her arm. As sensation shot upward and slid into the curve of her neck like trailing fingers, he said, "Do you keep the physician from me to work vengeance you believe my due?" When she hesitated over what sounded more accusation than question, he shifted his grip higher and pressed his thumb against the sensitive bend in her elbow. "Is that what you do, Lady Dangereuse of the *Wulfriths?*"

Feeling as if there was no woolen sleeve between her skin and his, she said as levelly as she could, "Were that a consideration, the Wulfrith of me won out. Thus, I give my word the weather is what keeps the physician away." As his eyes delved hers, she added, "And prevents the search parties from locating your traveling companions—a lady, man-at-arms, and squire, you told Puck."

The hard in his eyes easing, he rasped, "Lord, if they are lost..."

"How were you separated, and do you know the direction they went?"

After some moments, he said, "When I realized we were pursued, it was too late to don plate armor and—"

"They were brigands?" she interrupted, and at his frown added, "We have had trouble with them."

"These were not brigands," he said, then continued, "I had the man-at-arms and my squire continue to Broehne Castle upon Abingdale, hopeful a greater number of pursuers would follow them while the lady and I turned opposite—a miscalculation, three of the five setting after us." A growl escaped. "When briefly we were able to go from sight, I sent the lady west, then showed myself. I injured one of our pursuers and, as I dealt a killing blow to another who dropped over his horse, the third came at my back. My only armor a sleeveless chain mail shirt, I was injured. God willing, the lady and the others arrived safely at Broehne."

Dangereuse longed to ask the identity of the woman who might be dear to him. Of course, as he had not named her his wife, she was not that—yet. "Sir Rhys, loose me and I will do what I can to preserve your arm."

He narrowed his lids. "Ensuring my stay benefits you and your *unwelcome* guest?"

After considering her words of the night past that he was right to believe had threat about them, she said, "Just as I think it my right to know the truth of what happened at the tournament that rendered my husband barely recognizable, led to his death, and so affected my son the sweet of him was lost for a time and can yet go astray, I believe the blame is not all Benoit's nor mine to bear."

"*Yours* to bear? As you know, I was there, so tell how 'tis possible blame falls to you."

Recalling exactly how it was possible, emotion stuffed itself so far up her throat she had to swallow twice to get words past it. "You saw what I did that caused him to stumble—"

"*Drunkenly* stumble! And you but acted to protect your son."

"I acted out of fear unworthy of a Wulfrith. He would not have hurt Sebastian."

He drew her nearer. "You speak of one who shook the child to quiet him after thwarting your attempt to get the boy away —an enraged man who used his blade on me, then having no care for the danger of keeping hold of it, sought to prevent you and your son fleeing."

Dangereuse felt as if slapped, though by her own hand. She did not need him to point out Benoit had been out of control. And more the fool she must sound for admitting he was barely known to her that night.

Once more risking being mauled by guilt over his death that had taken years to trim back until more was allocated to Benoit and much held in reserve for Sir Rhys should it be proven he sabotaged the saddle, she said, "You are right. The blame is more his than mine. What I want to know is how much belongs to Baron Wulfrith's vengeful first squire."

As displeasure yielded to anger, further his eyes lit, but of greater note was something else amid the blue—fever not of the fireplace. She berated herself for confronting him at this time, then said, "I fear the heat come upon you is more from within than without, which could mean infection. Regardless of who—or what—is responsible for the failure of Benoit's girth strap, I would not have the loss of your sword arm be upon my conscience. Hence, allow me to tend you."

"What I need is a physician."

"And yet I am all you have," she clipped.

He stared at her for what felt minutes, then something not quite a smile lightened his mouth and he said, "Who would ever guess you would be all I have? But so it seems."

As if his acknowledgment of her claim imbued it with different meaning, she felt her heart shift as though in search of a bit more room, and as he considered her further, she was swept back to the day her sire suggested Rhys de Arell would make a fine husband and she had felt a thrill—before this man made it clear he was not interested.

"So it seems, Lady Dangereuse of the Wulfriths," he murmured, and his lids started to lower. When he raised them with effort, fever amid the blue was more evident. Then he released her arm and closed his eyes.

Staring into his still face, appalled she had to remind herself to breathe, abruptly she straightened. As she turned the covers over him, she looked to the items on the table that were adequate for cleaning and bandaging injuries but not piecing an arm back together.

For that, more would be needed, including assistance and much prayer.

CHAPTER 9

Blessedly, Sebastian had been in a good mood when he appeared in the hall as Dangereuse arranged for what was needed to save the knight's arm.

Saying naught of awakening in his mother's bed, he had displayed having once more clothed himself, washed his face, and combed his hair—and done it well, he proclaimed, then emphasized his achievement by gripping the pommel of the wooden sword gifted by his uncle, Hector.

She could have disputed his accomplishment for his tunic being inside out, crusty sleep in the corners of his eyes, snarled hair, and breath that told he had not cleaned his teeth. However, she was proud of him, though more he sought to please his warrior uncle than his mother who told a man of God must keep his body clean and presentable, it being second only to the cleanliness and order of one's thoughts and words.

After congratulating him on preparing well for a day that would include lessons he disliked, she had sent him to the kitchen to break his fast and gain a cup of honey milk from his aunt, Murielle, who inventoried the great pantry so cooking necessities could be restocked.

Sebastian had turned that direction then come back around. With a troubled brow, he had told he dreamed of the fierce warrior seen in the kitchen last eve.

Again she had been struck by the question of how he had known Sir Rhys was a warrior, and again the answer that though he had been only two the night of his sire's death, he was more aware than believed. She had hated her smile felt a frown cut from her face and tacked back upside down, but it was all she could manage as her heart pounded—and harder when, in struggling for a way to distract him, he asked where the warrior had gone.

It was Puck who answered. Dangereuse having roused him from beside the hearth so he could aid with Sir Rhys, he had told Sebastian the injured knight was resting to regain strength lost during a battle in which he prevailed.

That she had approved of, but not his next words that sent Sebastian running for the kitchen—that if he of the great line of Wulfriths wished strength to win his own battles with fist and sword, he must grow his body tall and muscles big with good food. The encouragement had served, but later she would set Puck aright.

Now, halting just over the threshold of the steward's bedchamber with the stout man, an aged household knight, a man-at-arms, and the sturdy housekeeper who was as versed in healing as Dangereuse, she met the gaze of the coverless man who sat against the headboard, left hand gripping his bandaged arm, perspiration moistening his face and darkening his blond hair.

Possessing an answer to the question in eyes lit by the torch set in the wall sconce, she said, "Still the physician has not returned, nor have we word of those with whom you traveled. As a longer wait could result in the loss of your sword arm, we come to do what we can to save it."

He looked between them, lingered over the basket the housekeeper held, returned to Dangereuse. "Unless you have medicine to put me down into sleep, strong drink is needed." It was said with the unnatural precision of one who strives to keep his voice from betraying physical and emotional states.

"We have the drink needed," she said.

Holding the skin, Puck strode to the bed. "As it shall take a good quantity, let us get ye up to relieve yourself."

"Done shortly ere you entered," the knight said.

Hoping that effort was more responsible for his perspiration than fever, Dangereuse stepped forward.

And faltered when loudly Puck sniffed the air. "I hoped ye had, that 'twas not all on me for forgettin' to empty the basin earlier."

As Dangereuse halted at the foot of the bed, with less precision Sir Rhys said, "For the sake of the women, pray empty it."

"He shall after you have taken all the drink you can and whilst we wait on it to take effect," she said.

He reached for the skin with his left hand. "As I require no aid in drinking, see it done now."

A man's pride, she thought, though she could not begrudge him since she would be as uncomfortable were she the one abed.

Puck unstoppered the vessel ahead of relinquishing it, and as Sir Rhys put the spout to his lips, Dangereuse moved about the room and instructed the others in what was required of them.

Throughout, she felt watched by the man who believed she broke with Wulfrith honor in threatening him on the night past. And she had, though it was not the same as threatening his life or dire injury as he suspected in submitting she intentionally withheld the physician's care.

When all was prepared except for the ropes he rejected being fixed to the headboard and foot of the bed to keep him still, she moved to his right side, lowered to her knees, and sank back on her heels so her eyes were level with his. "Can you drink more?" She jutted her chin at the skin.

"Though I begin to feel the effects for not being one who overly imbibes, more would help but..." His tongue clicked off a dry palate. "...I do not think I can keep more down and fear my bladder will fail." He muffled what sounded a chuckle, then his mouth went the way of a crooked smile like the one shone upon her the day he witnessed her answer to Benoit's demand for her sleeve.

Though she sought to harden herself against him, when she leaned over him to take the skin and felt a tug on the braid that slid over her shoulder, she failed. Once more, he had hold of it. And just as in the kitchen, there was no rough handling of it like when...

She recalled Benoit dragging on her braid, his behavior further proof of how affected he was by renewal of his acquaintance with Sir Rhys. As if repentant, he had kissed the crossings, but were it true repentance, she had been too riled to accept it. And had no opportunity to do so later.

"More silver than when you were a girl," this knight said so low she might have missed it were the words not seen on his lips. "More than when you were a young woman." His eyebrows gathered. "I am sorry you have no husband to... unravel it."

She lurched upright, freeing her braid. And regretted her reaction. She did not think the others heard what he spoke, but their raised eyebrows and twitching mouths evidenced curiosity.

"Let us be done with this," she said and looked to the housekeeper who stood on her other side behind the small table of supplies.

"Needle and thread only," Sir Rhys growled, still fearing amputation.

Offering no assurance, she instructed the man-at-arms to stabilize his right shoulder as Puck would do the left, then began unwinding the bandage.

Their patient remained aware enough to occasionally look upon her, but when she began probing the wound that did not appear infected, she felt his gaze deeply.

She tried to ignore him, but becoming unsettled, peered into blue eyes that ought not bother as they did.

"I *am* sorry," he rasped.

She shifted her jaw. "Fear not. If any takes your arm, it will not be me."

"That is not why I apologize, Lady of the Wulfriths."

She did not want to believe him, but it was nearly impossible not to.

As for the man who appeared moments later—*that* impossible if not for God's hand in it—his dark mantle sparkled with melting ice that had no hope of surviving the donjon's heat.

Lillia's physician had returned.

———

DANGEREUSE WAS SO relieved she would bear no responsibility for the fate of that sword arm that she shared her relief with Sir Rhys who, eyes closed, had shown no reaction to the surprise of all gathered around. Mouth to his ear, she said, "The physician has come. If any can save your arm, 'tis George Mannly."

When she raised her head, his eyes were open, and it was not relief shining from them but alarm. "Do not remove it!"

Then he had been more at peace in hands that could easily fail him than those of a man of medicine. But then, whereas with the physician he could return to consciousness and find the arm taken, with her he might remain whole—for a time.

"Mannly knows his medicine, Sir Rhys."

"I do," George agreed, stepping alongside Dangereuse after removing his mantle. "If the arm can be saved, you have a better chance with me than most."

Were he comforted, it was not obvious in his scrutiny of the physician, and she wondered if he distrusted the abilities of a man not yet thirty and of good build that could see him mistaken for one who belonged to the class of men who fight —and of the nobility for how crisp his speech.

Dangereuse had also doubted him in the beginning, and greater her prejudice when it became apparent the unwed man was attracted to her. But only good was spoken of he who had served at Lillia for several years and eased the former castellan's pain enough that he was able to continue serving the Baron of Wulfen beyond what was expected.

"How old are you?" Sir Rhys asked, words slurred.

Unhesitatingly the physician said, "Of enough years and experience to extend the lives of many, including that of the man my escort and I happened upon en route to Lillia."

As Dangereuse caught her breath, Sir Rhys struggled to rise, causing her to straighten quickly to avoid being clipped by his head. "My man?" he demanded.

"That is as he who spoke with a heavy French accent told, then asked us to deliver him to Broehne Castle to which his party was bound before being forced to divide due to pursuit by..." He frowned. "What did he call them? *Les signaleurs blancs!*"

Translating that to English, Dangereuse said, "White flaggers?"

"When I questioned the same, he renamed his countrymen *continental swine.*"

She startled. Though Sir Rhys had told his attackers were not brigands, she would not have guessed they were the French with whom her king was impatient to resume his war and with more vigor than done since the passing of the pestilence. At this time, though a tenuous truce was in place that was to have been extended by ambassadors sent across the channel last month, preparations were being made for a spring campaign when the weather was more forgiving and channel crossings less treacherous.

"What of my squire who rode with him?" Sir Rhys asked.

"He said he hoped his sacrifice allowed the young man to reach you at Broehne, unaware you had fallen and were brought here." The physician motioned Dangereuse aside and took her place. "Now let us see if months hence this arm can yet wield a sword. Lie back."

Rhys did not want to. He wanted more answers—and to remain present enough to ensure one who appeared too young to decide the fate of the limb did not make an irreversible mistake. However, the drink worked its accursed wonder, lightening his head while the rest of his body felt as if stones fixed to his feet tugged him to the bottom of the sea—those same straits he and his party had barely crossed for the storm lashing their ship.

Rhys dropped onto the pillow and, after glancing at Lady Dangereuse who had moved to the physician's other side, closed his eyes. It was difficult to remain conscious, especially when the wound was probed, but he ordered words he hoped would gain the answer needed—first to ensure the well-being of the man-at-arms, second for greater confidence in the physician. "Will he recover?"

The answer was in George Mannly's hesitation, but his response was honest. "He took an arrow in the back and was long exposed to the cold. I made him as comfortable as possible and Lady Murielle tends him, but I expect him to pass ere nightfall."

"Lord," Rhys breathed, panged by the loss of one who had aided in the mission given this knight under cover of a lesser mission. Longing to hunt down *les signaleurs blancs*—a derogatory name English warriors called their French counterparts for how readily those of the continent raised a white flag when cornered, only then seeking to suspend hostilities and negotiate, he asked, "You can repair my arm?"

"I believe so. As it requires precision to knit all back together, you must take medicine to ensure you remain still."

Senselessness from which he would awaken only when the potion left his body, but of great importance, as was prayer for the man dying beyond this room and the squire and lady who might also be lost for Rhys being unable to keep them out of the hands of her pursuers.

"Lord, let me not have failed them nor my king," he beseeched and hoped his words too slurred for sense to be made of them.

"Half a dropper on his tongue, my lady," the physician said. "That and no more."

For how dangerous it was, Rhys knew from tale of some put down into sleep never to awaken.

A hand on his jaw tilted his head back, then a thumb pulled down his lip and pushed between his teeth to access his tongue.

Wanting to confirm the dropper was only half full, Rhys tried to open his eyes. Failing that, he started to clamp his jaw to blockade his tongue, but the lady's breath smelling of mint made him clay in the hands of one the Baron of Wulfen's first squire had resisted becoming enamored with so he could immerse himself in the challenges and adventures for which he had trained.

How different would life have been had he pursued her? How different were he the one who kissed her rather than the cheat?

He sputtered as the foul tasting liquid streamed across his tongue. Had she not clapped a hand over his mouth and put her weight behind it, he would have expelled it.

Eyes intent on his that sprang wide, she said, "Pray, swallow."

Staring into those lovely eyes, he tried to see what was behind them, but as that drawbridge was raised, grudgingly he choked down the medicine. And missed the soft of her palm when she removed her hand.

Once more he was tempted by the plaited hair dangling over her shoulder, but she intercepted his fingers, closed hers over his, and said low, "Beware of obsession, Sir Rhys. Never can there be anything for you here."

Because his disinterest had allowed Benoit to pursue and gain her.

Because she believed Rhys' victory at The Tournament of Honor was had by the same trickery that saw the cheat named the victor at Wulfen.

Because he had been unable to walk away when he heard himself named a cheat.

Because that and return of the lady's ribbon could have been what pushed Benoit over an edge that led to abuse of his wife and two-year-old son.

"Beware," she said again and set his hand on his chest.

Though he aspired to a smile of even breadth rather than

that of teasing, he felt one side tug higher and, with little thought, spoke words as low as hers, "Aye, beware of lightning...in the night."

Then recalling what was felt atop the kitchen table—a caress on his thigh where Benoit had scarred him—he left her with the fleeting hope that when consciousness returned she would be at his side. And he would be whole.

CHAPTER 10

S now. And more snow.

Thus, it remained impossible to send word to Hector at Wulfen that aid was needed to better protect the demesne and its people from the threat of those more dangerous than the brigands who occasionally injured their victims but had yet to take lives.

Remembering Sir Rhys' man whose light had flickered out on the day past while Murielle held his hand, seeing again tears coursing the young woman's cheeks as Puck drew the blanket over that lifeless face, Dangereuse was surprised when Ferrand shifted his weight and lightly cleared his throat.

For the concern on his brow, she struggled to find her place in their exchange about the search patrol's return this morn that was as empty-handed as on the day past when she emerged from the steward's study following the physician's best efforts to save Sir Rhys' arm.

Vaguely aware she went sideways in resuming their conversation, she rued an entire day had passed since she put medicine on the knight's tongue. And wondered again if she had done something wrong, and for that he had not awakened.

Recalling what she forced herself to witness while he remained still and unaware of the measures taken to save him, she shuddered, then sent up a prayer George Mannly was right.

An hour past, he had returned to the hall after visiting his patient and assured her the fault was not hers—that as Sir Rhys breathed well, likely his body held him under to sooner recover from the trauma—but what if he was wrong?

"My lady?" Ferrand prompted.

Sitting straighter in the high seat behind the table before which he stood, she reproved herself. Whereas the men of his patrol had gone to the kitchen to warm themselves and fill their bellies, her ruddy-faced brother-in-law waited on her, snow-encrusted mantle dripping in the hall's warmth.

"Forgive me, Ferrand. 'Twas a nearly sleepless night."

He glanced toward that corridor. "Still he does not rouse?"

"Still," she said, then, "So no signs of the squire nor lady?"

"None, though we have searched the demesne as far as we dare with more winter weather upon us."

Before autumn is even done, she silently lamented.

"Just as there is no evidence brigands remain among us, my lady, there is none of the continental swine that attacked Sir Rhys and his party." He shook his head. "Befriended by the snow."

Ironically, at that moment a wedge of glittering white dislodged from the folds of his mantle and dropped to the dais.

"As you melt too slowly, and I keep you from fire and food" —she pointed with the feathered end of her quill—"get thee to the kitchen."

He flexed a smile. "With your approval, I will not send out

further search parties but rely on the regular patrol to keep eyes sharp for any signs of the lady and squire."

She inclined her head. "As it becomes too dangerous for so little chance of finding them alive, best we put our hope in them reaching Broehne Castle and that soon we can make inquiries of Baron Lavonne, as well as send word to the sheriff who must be told what transpired and of the possibility hostile French remain upon Wulfenshire." Due to a mission given Sir Rhys, she guessed from his words that entreated the Lord he not fail their king.

"God willing, soon the sun parts the clouds," Ferrand said, then went the way his men had gone.

Knowing it could not be much longer before Sebastian appeared belowstairs, and hoping he did not react poorly to her once more bringing him to her bed to relieve him of what rose behind his lids, Dangereuse set her mind on numbers that were more cooperative this day.

Despite servants going about their duties and an occasional snort or grumble from Puck sleeping near the hearth, her work was uninterrupted, and in less than an hour Lillia's accounting was in good order.

Only after setting the quill in its stand and stoppering the ink pot did she become aware the hand in her lap was occupied with caressing the ends of her braid, which called to mind—

She shook her head. Though loath to return the journals to the steward's study with Sir Rhys in the bedchamber, since Sebastian had yet to appear, she would quietly slip in and out, which would also allow her to retrieve his wax tablets for his writing lesson.

A pity they could not also avail themselves of the study as they did fairly often for its quiet and privacy, but she must keep Sebastian away from Sir Rhys. Even if the latter remained lost to the world, she would not risk her son stealing into the room in search of a good bounce on the mattress he could not know was occupied by the one he named a fierce warrior.

As she descended the dais with the journals, Murielle came off the stairs with a hand on her belly and took a single step toward the kitchen before catching sight of her sister-in-law. Lowering that motherly hand, quickly she adjusted her course, causing her ash-black braids to swing.

"How fare you this day?" Dangereuse asked as the young woman advanced.

Remy's unwanted wife halted. "Better than on the night past, for which I apologize. I know it was for me to oversee preparations for the evening meal, but death is..." Momentarily she closed her eyes. "How does one become accustomed to seeing life desert a body as if 'tis repulsed by the shell that long and lovingly sheltered it? I do not know I can. It is too hard on the eyes and heart."

Not for the first time, Dangereuse's maternal instincts were roused for the young lady she had not expected to like— though it was not Murielle's fault the solution to King Edward's guilt was to make it difficult for Rémy to oppose wedding her. "I am glad for your struggle," she said.

Offense widened eyes that evidenced Murielle had taken her tears to bed after the man-at-arms passed. "How can you be so—?"

"I am glad because one ought not become accustomed to death." Dangereuse touched her arm. "All witnessed much death during the pestilence, and uglier it was than that of Sir Rhys' man. Hence, it is good loss of life still moves your heart. Be glad of it as I am." She started toward the corridor.

"My lady?"

"Murielle?"

"I am grateful for your kindness and consideration toward

one you did not wish your brother to wed. And bears another man's child."

Dangereuse smiled at she who was a hand and a half shorter than the eldest Wulfrith sister. "Not by your choice," she said, aware the same as others of her family the young woman's pregnancy was due to ravishment by the former Baron of Woodhearst—a man who had died and been replaced by Dangereuse's second brother, Warin. "Thus, no fault of yours."

Lids having fluttered down, Murielle nodded. "I never thought to find myself like this. Had I, perhaps I could have avoided it and Rémy might have wed a woman he loves rather than dislikes."

Ignoring that last, Dangereuse said, "Or wed none at all. 'Twas marriage to you that ensured a landless younger brother would have the keeping of Lillia once his knight's training is complete. Great honor, reward, and security in that."

"He does not see it as such." It was said with certainty rather than the beseeching of one who wishes to be assured otherwise.

Nor would Dangereuse have indulged her since it was better to clearly see the road ahead than advance with reaching hands through a fog and hopeful of happening on good things that would mostly prove bad. "He does not," she agreed. "Hence, if you want more than vows spoken under duress, you and my brother must strive for better."

"A steep mountain to climb," the young lady said, peering up at Dangereuse through long lashes. "As I had a love the same as you and lost him by the blade just as you lost your husband, 'tis difficult to have been there and now—"

"Murielle!" Immediately, Dangereuse regretted the whip of her tongue. After all, since as yet her sister-in-law was a Wulfrith in name only, she did not—and might never—know all the tale of the *love* whose loss she believed her sister-in-law mourned.

"I did not mean to offend, Lady Dangereuse. Truly, for you are as near a friend as I have."

Far different from when the two women were first thrown together, the younger wary of her sister-in-law—and not only for her unwelcome marriage into the Wulfrith family. Murielle knew of the rumors surrounding Benoit's death, some positing he had died by the hand of the wife appropriately named *Dangereuse,* though it was deemed an accident and her innocence supported by witnesses.

"You did not offend, Murielle. 'Tis just I have work to do and lessons to complete with Bastian." She smiled tautly, adjusted her armful, and slipped past.

"Will Squire Rémy come to Lillia for Christmas?" the young woman called.

Dangereuse looked around. "Doubtful, though he may be at Stern for the festivities which, if the weather is good and you can safely make the journey, is where you should be reunited with your husband."

Murielle looked to a belly both knew likely too ripe to risk travel in less than a fortnight. "Not this year," she said and smiled just enough to reveal a small gap between her front teeth. "Mayhap next year."

Dangereuse continued to the corridor and, once out of sight, paused. "Lord, as I know it will take much on both their parts," she sent heavenward, "aid Rémy and Murielle in gaining something better than what I had, or at least as much as what I believed I had before Benoit became barely known to me."

She opened her eyes, and as she resumed her stride, heard from the direction of the steward's rooms the voice of one who should not be there.

CHAPTER II

"You cursed! Two times!" proclaimed Sebastian Royston who even more resembled his sire for hearth fire and tabletop lantern showing well one who had drawn nearer than last eve.

Nay, not last eve. The night before. Or was it further back? Rhys wondered as he peered at the boy who had awakened him by lightly bouncing on the mattress where he stood to the left of this knight who might no longer represent the warrior class as well as once he had. If at all.

For the struggle not to look to his other side lest the arm he felt was only imagined, he had yet to speak, let alone provide the answers demanded of him. *Were* they even a consideration for the whelp girded with a wooden sword whose behavior, like his dusty blond hair and brown eyes, reminded he was the son of a cheat.

"Do not sleep again!" he commanded as Rhys' lids lowered, then bounced more heavily. "Tell me what the words mean!"

The shifting mattress causing ache to course Rhys' right

side from what he prayed was still shoulder to fingertips, he said, "Go back to your mother's skirts, boy!"

"What say you?"

There being gravel about Rhys' voice, and guessing his words imprecise for fatigue, pain, and what remained of the medicine that rendered him unconscious, he repeated himself.

"Skirts? I am no baby!"

"Then cease behaving one and go!"

"You cannot tell me what to do. I am the son of a knight undefeated at jousting. When I am very big, I shall be as great as my father!"

Whether Rhys was more roused by the unfounded claim made for Benoit or the next bounce that landed the boy atop his legs, he did not know. What he knew was annoyance bordering on anger portended ill. Thus, his unwelcome visitor must leave, even if frightened into doing so.

With his left hand, Rhys gripped the boy's arm and pulled him so near the wide-eyed face dug up the memory of a very young Benoit finding himself bettered by his fellow page at wrestling. "You will go and not return. Do you understand?"

Though fear lit Sebastian's eyes, his lower jaw jutted. "I want to know what those words mean—sin...signa...blan..."

It was then Rhys recalled where he was before being wrenched back to this room—riding hard with the lady to escape their pursuers, tormented by chill rain, sending the words, *Accursed signaleurs blancs!* into the air rushing past.

Doubtless having spoken the dream aloud, he had been heard by the son of Lady Dangereuse who surely did not know her boy was here.

"Tell me!" Sebastian said with a whine that Wulfen knights would correct once he began training to join the ranks of England's defenders.

"Tell me! Tell me!" As his rising voice further tested Rhys' resolve to give quarter to the defenseless and those who did not know better, he heard the arrival of someone in the outer room—the door striking the wall and what sounded books dropped to the floor.

There would also be swift footsteps if not for cover provided by the boy's shrill cry, "Ah, nay! Caught!"

And such a halfwit Rhys felt to find he continued to grip Sebastian's arm when Lady Dangereuse came through the doorway.

There was wild about her that in no way resembled a wing-flapping mother goose. Here a silvered she-wolf whose cub had gone dangerously astray—or so she believed. And Rhys made it easy to do so.

"Release my son!" She ran forward, and as he complied, swept the boy into her arms.

"Mama!" Sebastian cried as she slashed Rhys with eyes that would make him bleed were they daggers, then began struggling when she pivoted to carry him from the room. "Let me go so I can make him tell me! I need to know!" He thrust hands against her chest and arched his body, causing her to stumble.

Withstanding the temptation to push onto his elbows lest he find he had only one, Rhys called, "Hardly the makings of a knight, boy! Honor your Wulfrith blood!"

That stilled Sebastian who peered over his mother's shoulder as she moved toward the doorway, then he boasted again, "I am the son of a great knight undefeated at jousting."

Now Lady Dangereuse stilled.

Staring at her lovely figure silhouetted in the doorway, guessing she recalled the contests attended by her husband and this knight, Rhys said, "So you tell, Sebastian Royston," then hoping for solitude in which to discover the truth of his body lest it was all devastation, looked to the ceiling.

Instead of departing, the lady said tautly, "You and Sir Rhys had a disagreement?"

"Aye, and he made me mad."

"How did it begin?"

"What?"

Her sigh returned Rhys' eyes to her. "What led to the disagreement, Sebastian?"

"I do not remember."

She turned back into the room, shifted him to her hip, and nodded at the bed. "You came to jump on the mattress and found the knight here."

"Uh huh."

"And?"

"He was talking in his sleep. And cursing! Not bad curses. But maybe. That is why I woke him—so he would tell me what the words mean."

"How did you awaken him?"

"A little jump."

There was enough light between this room and the study to see she briefly closed her eyes. "Only a little jump?"

He shrugged. "He is stubborn like me, so I bounced harder. I promise I did not mean to fall. I could have broken my sword!"

Slowly, as if patience required it, she said, "You fell on Sir Rhys?"

"His legs, but he is a fierce warrior, so it cannot have hurt."

"You know he is not well."

"What?"

She repeated herself, then added, "As you also know little hurts can feel big hurts when one's body is healing. Thus, you should not have awakened him, nor discomfited him by bouncing on the bed."

"He would not tell me what he said. And he tried to tell me what to do!"

"Which was to leave him to his rest, aye?"

He pursed his mouth, jerked his head.

"Well, that you shall do after apologizing to...our guest."

Rhys was surprised. He had expected he would either be left alone to discover if the arm was truly there, or the lady would remove her son from the steward's rooms and return to rebuke him for laying a hand on her child, to which he knew she must be sensitive after what happened that night.

"Now?" the boy said, voice once more leaning toward a whine.

"Aye, Sebastian." She set him on feet that dragged all the way back to the bed—the right side to which Rhys unthinkingly moved his gaze to follow his advance. And in doing so, glimpsed that to which the covers drawn over that half conformed.

A breath he did not know was trapped in his lungs exited at confirmation he had not imagined feeling in that arm, and another when he curled those fingers into his palm and closed his thumb over them. God willing, whatever the physician had done to keep it attached would also see it restored to its former strength.

"What is wrong?" the boy said, the blur of him halting near Rhys' shoulder, concern in his voice sounding genuine. "Did I hurt you? I did not mean to, Sir Knight."

Rhys blinked away excess moisture and looked to the woman who remained in the doorway, lips compressed. Though pride bade him not answer Sebastian's question that exposed a warrior's emotions, he said, "I am grateful for all the physician and your mother did to save my arm."

It appeared the boy would speak to that, but he shrugged

and said, "I am sorry I woke you and jumped on your bed—though 'tis not really your bed."

"I know."

He looked around. "Can I go, Mama?"

In answer, she extended a hand and he ran to her.

"Sebastian!" Rhys called.

He came around. "Sir Knight?"

"*Les signaleurs blancs.* Those are the words I spoke that sounded a curse as I came up out of my dream. It is French for *white flaggers,* which is what many English warriors call the defenders of France who boast mightily of fighting to the death for honor, faith, and people, then wave the white flag when those against whom they are triumphing begin to triumph over them."

The boy made a sound of disgust. "English do not do that."

"Aye, they do, but not so much it is more predictable than not."

Sebastian looked to his mother. "See, I need to know these things."

There was disapproval in her regard, but before she could respond, he returned his gaze to Rhys. "And see, 'twas an easy thing to tell. You made it hard."

Just as the boy made it hard not to laugh.

Sebastian set his head to the side. "That is a strange curse."

A curse only because Rhys had embellished it with the word *accursed.*

The boy sighed and slipped past his mother who followed him.

Rhys was disappointed. Absent Sebastian, he would have inquired about his man who was not expected to survive, efforts to locate his squire and the lady, and the physician's prognosis for full recovery of his arm. But first she must deal with her son.

Hoping she would return soon, he folded back the cover to survey the thickly bandaged arm that was splinted to better hold the stitches since he was certain the bone was not fractured.

"Lessons in the solar," he heard Lady Dangereuse say, "We shall meet there in an hour."

"Aye, Mother," the boy said with formality as if suddenly too old to call her *Mama*.

"Go on, Bastian, and do not trouble Puck. He needs his sleep."

Then she meant to return immediately? Rhys wondered. Was eager to rebuke him for overstepping?

The boy's footsteps echoed in the hollow of a corridor, ceased, and he called, "My sire was undefeated in jousting. Aye?"

Her hesitation told much.

"'Tis what Uncle Ferrand told!" Sebastian prompted.

"Did he?" Her voice sounded slightly choked. "Certes, your sire was exceptional at arms."

"Because he was Wulfen-trained and a great warrior as my uncle will make me."

"An hour, Sebastian, and be ready to work hard," she said, then the outer door closed.

However, she did not directly return to the bedchamber. She muttered something, then there came the scrape and thump of what he was certain were books she had dropped when she hurtled into the room.

She shifted things, and when it became evident she was in no hurry to return to him, Rhys closed his left hand over his right arm and yielded to the ease found behind lowered lids. He wanted to speak with her, his questions being in greater need of answers than what her son demanded of him, but as there was nothing he could do with whatever she would tell, it could wait.

He did not think he slept, but when next he opened his eyes, she was in the doorway watching him, shoulder against the frame, arms folded over her chest.

The she-wolf being exceedingly lovely, though not as beautiful as he recalled the second Wulfrith sister, it took some moments to ask what should be uppermost in his mind. "The man-at-arms, Lady Dangereuse?"

She straightened. "I am sorry. As expected, he passed quickly."

Lord, receive him, Rhys sent heavenward. "And what of the lady and my squire?"

She smoothed the skirts of a practical gown that was far from the beauty of those worn at The Tournament of Honor, then crossed to his right side.

As Rhys stared up at her and wished the silvered braid draped her shoulder rather than ran her back, she said, "Regrettably, naught has changed, but though the snow is now so unrelenting no more search parties can be sent out, the regular patrols keep watch for them."

"Then their only hope is to have made it to Broehne Castle."

"Mayhap not. Were they able to reach one of Abingdale's outlying villages, they should be safe. Of course, if the weather turned one or the other around, rather than go west, they may have gone south deeper into the Barony of Wulfen, or east toward Woodhearst."

He frowned. "Was not your brother, Sir Warin, recently awarded that barony?"

"He was. Thus, this castle, which was to have been given into his keeping, shall be held by our youngest brother once Rémy completes his knight's training."

"Until then, you are castellan."

"As I have been since Rémy wed last summer, both administering Lillia and imparting skills to his wife beyond overseeing the household," she said, then added, "I speak of Lady Murielle who tended your man-at-arms."

Rhys had not heard the youngest Wulfrith brother had wed, which was unusual for one in training to take a wife. However, rather than question what was of no real consequence, he determined to discuss his arm.

And would have had not the lady said in something of a rush, "I feared you would not awaken, it being a full day since I administered the medication."

That surprised on two fronts—what sounded distress over the well-being of a man she could be said to have threatened when first he arrived, and that a day had passed since his arm was put back together.

Most often, men who failed to rouse within hours of being rendered senseless so dire measures could be taken to save them did not rouse at all. Death followed, whether from incorrect dosing or an injury too grievous to remedy.

"You seem concerned, my lady, hardly expected of she who threatened me when I lay bleeding on her kitchen table—at least, it sounded that way."

Her gaze wavered. "Not only have I no wish to be responsible in any way for the death of another, but if you are to give me what I shall need when my son is old enough to learn the truth of his sire's death, I cannot have you expiring."

He tried not to take offense, but wanting better from this Wulfrith said, "And here I thought it possible I misunderstood what sounded a threat that night—that what you said would benefit us both was, instead, gratitude for me coming to the aid of you and your son." Of course he exaggerated, needing none to tell him his response to Benoit alluding to him being a cheat at the joust and proclaiming it in the great hall had played a part in what happened abovestairs.

Eyes flown wide, she made fists of her hands at her sides. "Gratitude?" she hissed.

Inwardly, he groaned. For this, the psalm—*Let the words of my mouth, and the meditation of my heart, be acceptable in thy sight, O LORD, my strength, and my redeemer.* For this, that which his sire had sought to impress on him—*Think much, regret little.*

The lady shook her head. "The truth about Benoit's death is due me and my son far more than gratitude is owed you."

She would be right had he become vengeful in response to the trickery Benoit worked on him at Wulfen with the aid of his brother who now served here. Though Rhys could not know what exactly caused Benoit to go sideways in the saddle at The Tournament of Honor, he knew he himself had not dishonored his Wulfen training by falsely seizing victory.

He started to respond, but his tongue was nearly fixed to his palate. Looking to the small table to his left, hoping drink was in the cup beside the pitcher, he reached and found it was without heft.

"I shall pour for you," she astonished until he reminded himself of her determination to learn a truth she believed he held close.

She skirted the bed, filled the cup, and reached it to him.

Their hands brushed. Wishing the contact did not disturb him more than the sight and feel of her braid, he carried the cup toward his mouth. However, as he had only a single pillow beneath his head, he lay too low to take drink without spilling. Pressing his left elbow into the mattress and turning that direction to raise himself, a groan escaped as pain streaked his right arm.

"Hold!" she said, and when their hands touched as she

took the cup to return it to the table, further he was disturbed as he ought not be with this lady and in these circumstances.

As he eased down, she said, "We must get the other pillow under your head and shoulders." She looked around, gave a huff of annoyance. "I forgot."

"What?"

She met his gaze, and for the first time he noticed though her eyes were the grey-green of most Wulfriths, hers might be better called green-grey for a greater abundance of silver. "The physician used the second pillow to elevate your arm while he stitched. As it became bloodied, I sent it for laundering."

"Then?" he said, though he knew the answer—providing her distaste was overruled by impatience to gain what she thought he withheld.

"If your thirst is to be satisfied, I shall have to aid in raising you."

"So it seems."

As if considering how best to do it, she moved her eyes over him, then turned and sat at an angle on the mattress beside his left shoulder, leaned near, and slid an arm under his upper back.

With her aid, this time when he pressed his elbow into the mattress, his injured arm was less pained. And now with his head near her shoulder and chin at the top of a breast, she was closer than when she had come between him and Benoit at Wulfen and he inadvertently struck her in the chest...when she retaliated with a fist to his eye...when twice he fingered her braid.

She reached behind and retrieved the cup. "Drink, Sir Rhys."

He could not have said what possessed him beyond attraction to which he did not easily succumb and should not with her, but when she put to his lips a cup that wafted the scent of hippocras—wine flavored by sugar, cinnamon, and other spices—he set a hand over hers as if to steady it and felt a heart already beating fast begin to pound.

Her fingers convulsed. Though she must want to snatch them away, which would see him doused, she said tautly, "Drink, and be quick."

He drank—slowly and deeply, all the way to the bottom.

Though he expected her to withdraw immediately, with grudging she asked, "More?"

He was tempted, but so was his bladder that would soon need emptying. "My thirst is slaked."

She returned the cup to the table, eased her arm out from under him, and stood. As he settled back and was struck by the feeling he had lost something, she poured again and said, "For later," then clasped her hands before her.

Though she waited on something he could not give, and he believed there was one at Castle Lillia who could provide a piece of what led to that night, the time between her return to the room and what he needed to know regarding his future as a warrior pushed his patience to the limit.

But once more she proved unpredictable. "As the warrior of you has yet to address the repair of your arm, either you are very patient, else you fear the worst."

Deciding there was no reason to point out there had been only the narrowest opportunity to guide their exchange beyond asking after his traveling companions, he said, "Not the worst, for it is still attached. Too, you told if any could save the arm it was George Mannly."

"Aye, the Lord works through his hands, allowing him to bless others."

He raised his eyebrows. "How blessed am I?"

"When he finished the repair, he told with proper care and

healing you should be able to wield a sword, possibly as well as before."

"Providing I awakened," Rhys reminded her of the caveat that could have rendered the prognosis valueless.

"As you have."

Making no attempt to hide his relief, though it was only *possible* his skill would be restored in its entirety, he said, "Thanks be to God and your Mannly."

She nodded. "Though he said your body could simply be using deep rest to heal, I know he was worried, and for that often checked on you. Upon my return to the hall, I shall send word you have awakened."

"Good, for I have concerns to discuss with him."

Her brow lined. "You are feeling well, aye? It was only your legs Sebastian fell upon, not your arm?"

"That is so and, as he told, it did this warrior no harm."

If that comforted, it was not apparent for her hands tightening at her waist. "He said it was unintentional."

It was a statement, and yet there was question in it—the need for him to confirm her son had not acted maliciously.

"I believe so. Unfortunately, having recently come up out of sleep and discomfited by him jumping on the bed, I was quite annoyed. Thus, knowing it best he leave, even if he must be frightened into doing so, I reacted as I should not have."

"That is why you had hold of him."

"To pull him near and command him to go."

"Instead he persisted in trying to learn what you would not tell—and that is what I walked in on."

Rhys yielded to a smile so slight that had it any crooked about it, likely it would go unnoticed. "Walked, my lady?"

The she-wolf did not flush. This was more a blush. And there *was* a difference. But then she took a step back and angled her body so light did not fall directly on her visage. "I apologize for my reaction, which was that of a mother fearing for her child."

"I understand." He hoped that sufficed for him having witnessed that she, perhaps more than many mothers, had cause to be overly protective.

Face remaining visible enough to see unease there, she said, "Too, you must know I did not want my son nearer you than he came in the kitchen lest he recognize you from..."

She trailed off, and he wondered if she also thought that though the boy had been very young at the tournament, he seemed to have recognized Rhys in some measure.

Lightly, she cleared her throat. "Other than ear infections, with which Sebastian was afflicted at the tournament, he was a happy and fairly easy child. After that night, he became difficult and disruptive." She blinked, and he guessed were light directly on her face he would see moisture in her eyes. "As he has mostly outgrown that behavior, it would be almost unbearable were he to regress. Thus, to ensure his happiness and good future, he must continue down the path he is upon. And that means—"

"A path that will grow firmer once he begins training at Wulfen," Rhys unintentionally spoke over her.

She stiffened. "The same as my brother, you think my son better suited to the life of a warrior for the Wulfrith of him, but I believe the Church will serve him well as he shall serve it. Therefore, I will not risk further exposing him to you lest memories that yet visit his dreams once more disturb his waking hours."

Hearing threat in her words again, Rhys said, "If you are of a mind to bind this injured warrior or put a lock on his door, I give my word I will not seek out your son. 'Twill be for you to keep him from bouncing on my bed."

She raised her chin. "Be assured, that will not happen

again. Now, ere I alert the physician you wish to speak to him, I would know what happened at the tournament between the time I saw you outside my husband's tent and the joust when Benoit's saddle went sideways."

What she insinuated did not surprise, but it offended. And again, rather than think much so he regret little, he said, "You refer to when Benoit demanded the favor of a sleeve like the one his opponent would be wearing, forcing you to cut away what was not made to be detached."

Her breath caught. "What I refer to are events that led to my husband's death that could have been prevented."

Rhys sighed. "You were present at the joust. You were present during the celebration in the hall. And you were very present in your chamber when your drunken husband aggressed on you and your son. So tell, what more truth do you need of the death he brought on himself as confirmed by the sheriff's investigation?"

She stepped near. "I am aware Benoit bears much responsibility, but just as I played a role in his death, so did you. What I wish to know is the *unseen* part you played."

Rhys' ire rose, and as with her son, it was best she leave. Thus, he did not temper his voice. "Did I do to Benoit's girth strap what he did to mine with the aid of his brother? I did not. Though I regret some of my responses at the tournament the same as those during Wulfen's joust, especially when I struck you unintentionally and you put a fist in my eye, just as you are innocent of your husband's death regardless of the guilt in which it seems you like to splash, I am innocent. And even were I not, still Benoit would be responsible for behavior unbecoming a man, let alone one trained at Wulfen upon whom it is impressed to take responsibility for one's emotions and actions."

Her jaw convulsed so vigorously he half expected to hear the crack of a tooth.

"Now before you leave me to my rest, Lady Dangereuse, I ask that you send word to the king and my family of what delivered me here, and I request it done by way of your brother, the baron."

She turned away so swiftly the silvered braid center of her back arced and lashed her right forearm.

"Lady!" he called. "Do you not think it strange your son, who you would not have recognize me, named me a fierce warrior the night of my arrival and again this day?"

She halted, but did not look around.

"I believe he does recognize me, though he is unaware he first looked upon me that night of the tournament. For that, he knew me for a warrior though no weapons nor armor remained about me. For that, he is intrigued by and esteems this *unwelcome* guest despite my incapacity. Whether or not you can admit it, Sebastian was not so young as to be oblivious to the danger he was in, nor to forget what comfort was had in me answering his cries and his mother's."

He was surprised she remained to hear it all, and more surprised when she said so low he barely heard, "I do not want him to remember." Then she departed.

When the outer door closed, Rhys lowered his lids, though not to sleep since the needs of his body must be answered. Rather, to question how much he would regret what he had said for thinking little.

BACK PRESSED to the corridor wall, chin to her chest, Dangereuse stared at the slippers poking from beneath the hem of her gown. She did not want to agree her son recalled more of that night than was healthy, and that he recognized the warrior who burst into their chamber, but having herself considered it when Sebastian blundered into the kitchen and saw Rhys de Arell on the table, it was no difficult thing.

"Woe's sakes!" she rasped. Though she had hoped some good could come of Benoit's rival falling into her hands—that when Sebastian was old enough to know the reason he was fatherless, the behavior of his sire could in part be explained by him being a victim of foul play—Sir Rhys refused to cooperate.

Instead, he maintained his rival, aided by Ferrand, had worked ill on him at Wulfen, and it was mere coincidence the same happened to Benoit when next the two jousted. Though strangely moved to believe him, for the sake of her son and her trust in Ferrand, it was better the man her sire had wished her to wed was a deceiver.

"Why did You let him come here, Lord?" she whispered, then gripping hard the wax tablets she had only just remembered to pluck from the desk before departing the study, continued to the hall.

CHAPTER 12

The snow having ceased and begun melting on the day past, Dangereuse had finally done what Sir Rhys requested five days earlier. Though she had yet to inform him she had sent word of the attack to Hector, she would do so through the physician when he returned from an outlying village—by late afternoon, Mannly had assured her before departing to set the arm of a boy thrown from a barrel in which he and his friends challenged an icy hill.

Dangereuse had excuses aplenty for not herself delivering word to the one the physician told spent time in the steward's study and tended his own fires. In addition to managing the affairs of Lillia, she oversaw preparations for the Christmas feast to be attended by villagers from across the demesne. As most dwelt within a league of the castle, there could be well over two hundred guests crowding the great hall, though should the weather go foul again, far fewer and most would be those who resided at the castle. That made planning difficult, and then there was concern over waste should more food be prepared than could be consumed.

Returning to Murielle's menu, Dangereuse confirmed it was as flexible as possible to accommodate a moderate *and* sizable number of celebrants, then reached for the inventory of food stores to ensure they could supply what was needed.

"Signaleurs blancs!" Sebastian shouted from where he sat cross-legged atop a table near the dais enjoying his reward for writing his numbers up to ten in Latin. Fortunately, the hour earned to engage his wooden soldiers in mock battle was nearly exhausted. If she had to endure his victorious trumpeting much longer, she might begin snapping at those undeserving of impatience—unlike Sir Rhys who had shoveled those words into her son's head.

"Craven!" he denounced his *French* forces. "So craven!"

Dangereuse looked to him as he backhanded the small white flag fashioned out of a piece of paper and splinter of wood he had tied to the arm of a wooden soldier.

"Fight the good fight or fight not at all!" he rebuked.

Unable to suppress a smile, she was glad he did not know she watched. Her boy would not become a warrior, but these last words gifted by Hector were worthy since they applied to all—in Sebastian's case, the wielding of words rather than swords.

But then he looked to her and grinned, making it feel as if the hard of the ribs caging her heart softened. That he who had suffered darkness found light in which to bask was a gift to this mother who strove to heal the innocent mind and heart bruised the night he lost his sire.

The brightening of his smile further gladdened her—until she realized he looked past her.

"I have been waiting for you!" he called as Dangereuse turned her head. "Waiting and waiting since Mother was afraid I would jump on your bed again, though I promised I would not."

"And so here I am," Sir Rhys said, striding from the direction of the steward's rooms clothed in tunic and woolen hose as well as short boots likely provided by Puck. Feeling his eyes upon her, she stood, as did the wolfhound who had lain alongside her chair.

Aware her son and others watched, including Murielle who sat at hearth with servants hemming new tablecloths for the Christmas celebration, she met the knight's gaze. "Since the physician tells rest is essential for the healing of your arm, I expected you to remain in your chamber, Sir Rhys." *And keep your word you would not come near my son*, she silently added.

Bandaged arm now in a sling, he halted before the dais, causing the wolfhound to deeply sniff the air between it and the newcomer. "Then I heal well and more quickly than anticipated. Much gratitude for your concern, my lady."

She raised her eyebrows. "There is something you require?"

"Sir Knight, come see!" her son entreated.

Shooting her gaze to where he had come up on his knees, Dangereuse said sternly, "Sebastian Royston!"

"He needs to see, Mama!"

"Heed your mother," commanded the man whose interference offended.

"But I want to show—"

"Heed her, Sebastian of the Wulfriths."

And further he offended in reminding her son of his mother's side of him, as if the boy must aspire to the standards of a warrior in preparation to devote his life to fighting. Though her brothers sought to influence her boy likewise, their offenses were less grievous than those of this meddler of no relation. Once she got the knight alone—

"Aye, Sir Rhys," her son acceded and dropped his rear onto his heels.

Dangereuse returned her regard to the man of impressive

build, blond hair striped with darker blond, intense blue eyes, and clean-shaven jaw, doubtless that last courtesy of the one who provided the boots.

"Like it or nay, my lady," Sir Rhys said low, "'tis effective to remind your son he represents England's greatest defenders."

Rebuking herself for leaving emotions upon her face and that even now she could not entirely clear them, she set her palms on the table and rasped, "Not only is it not your place to command or correct my son, but you break the word given that you would not come near him."

Frowning, he ascended the dais across from her and, also ensuring his voice did not travel, said, "I did not tell I would not draw near your son. I told I would not seek him out, and my word holds. It is you I sought for not informing me of the progress made in alerting your brother as to what befell my party on his demesne."

It was hard not to bridle further, especially now he was well above eye level and there was reproof in his gaze. Pushing off her palms, she straightened from the table. "When the weather broke on the day past, I sent word to the Baron of Wulfen, as well as the Baron of Abingdale, informing the latter you seek confirmation of the arrival of the lady and your squire at Broehne Castle."

"I thank you, though surely you could have informed me earlier."

She glanced at the women before the hearth, causing them to resume stitching, except for Murielle. "Since I have been very busy, I planned for the physician to inform you once he returns from tending a villager's injury."

Slowly, he looked toward the steward's corridor, then back at her. "I regret I so frighten that you dare not approach me in your own home, my lady."

"You do not frighten me!"

"Disturb, then?"

She glared.

"As for correcting your son and in the manner I did, it was worthy inducement."

Almost wishing it was not, she said, "Tell what an unwed and—I assume—childless man knows about raising boys into men."

He blinked as if taken aback, then stepped nearer, bringing his upper thighs into contact with the table. "I know enough that easily I gained obedience which eluded you. As for how one unwed and childless succeeded, though you may find it difficult to believe, once this man was a boy."

She nearly gasped over him challenging her ability to control her son, but perhaps more because it *was* difficult to believe he had ever been small and vulnerable.

"And lest you forget, I was trained by my sire, your sire, and your uncle. They made me what I am—a man who aspires to be worthy of God, family, and country. A warrior who..." He paused as if to reconsider his next words, then finished, "...agrees to rules fashioned for the betterment of all and plays by them."

Not only did he refer to being Wulfen-trained, but he alluded to his joust with Benoit. As she struggled for a response that would not further interest those in the hall, unexpectedly he said gently, "The boy is stronger than you believe." But then he had to add, "Thus, likely he will prove more fit to wear sword and spurs than a monk's robe and a crucifix slapping at his belly with each step he takes."

"How dare you tell—" She closed her mouth, but her words were too loud and it was too late.

"Mama?" Sebastian called.

Regretting his concern, she hung a smile from her lips and turned it upon him, but it was the advancing Murielle who captured her son's attention with the playful words, "Goodness, Lady Dangereuse, do you not cease teasing poor Sir Rhys, he will think you a dragon, and all know you are not." She moved her regard to the boy who had not liked her at first but had lost that battle. "You agree with Aunt Murielle, do you not?"

The smile that returned to Dangereuse's son was a tentative thing, but it enlarged when Sir Rhys turned to the young woman and said, "I have your word the castellan of Lillia is a woman, not a fire-breathing dragon, Lady Murielle?"

Sebastian gave a cry of delight, next a giggle.

And Rhys, lowering his gaze from the face of Rémy Wulfrith's wife, made sense of the reason the squire had wed ahead of knighthood. As Lady Dangereuse had said her youngest brother spoke vows last summer, it must be due to an indiscretion that would make this young woman a mother and her husband a father in not much more than a month.

Lady Murielle halted, glanced at her sister-in-law, then dipped awkwardly. "You have my word on that, and I am sorry for the loss of your man-at-arms, Sir Rhys."

"I am grateful you were at his side during his final hours, my lady."

"It was my privilege." She gestured at the hearth. "Would you join me before the fire? As 'tis nearly two hours ere supper, I could order drink and small foods to ease your hunger."

Though the day's tedious passing tempted him to accept, he would have declined if not for Lady Dangereuse's sharp breath. "I would like that."

Her smile was all white teeth—perfect except for a space between the upper front. "Then come."

He did not make it far, but Lillia's castellan was not the one who thwarted him. So recklessly did her son descend the table he should have taken a tumble, so swiftly he approached that were these eyes old, he would be all blur.

Having no doubt the man he deemed a fierce warrior was his destination, Rhys halted and looked to Lady Dangereuse. Her posture and expression confirmed displeasure, but she did not try to prevent the inevitable.

And now the inevitable was before Rhys, chin high to peer up the man he esteemed despite being dispossessed of the trappings of one born to the blade. Then Sebastian put his hand on his wooden sword and declared, "Our Wulfen soldiers have fought and beat the foul French—signaleurs blancs all of them."

Rhys wanted to smile, but this was a serious matter, just as it had been for him at a similar age. "Are you certain the soldiers of Wulfen have triumphed over all their foes, Sebastian? Just because a victory seems complete does not mean it is. Just because you surround your enemies does not mean you are not surrounded by other enemies. Just because you think your side superior—and more so for claiming God as your impenetrable shield—does not make it so." *That* among many things impressed on him during his Wulfen training.

"You do not believe me?" The boy jabbed a finger toward the table transformed into his playground and beneath which a mastiff slept with its great head balanced between its paws. "Pray, come see."

Ignoring the bore of Lady Dangereuse's eyes, Rhys looked to the boy's aunt who had paused ahead. "A short detour, my lady," he said and followed Sebastian to where a great number of wooden figures were down and surrounded by far fewer victors.

The boy clambered onto a bench and atop the table, dropped hard to his knees, and swept a hand over his battle-field. "Though our English are half the number, those who invaded Wulfenshire are dead—every accursed signaleur blanc!"

"Sebastian!" his mother rebuked, though surely it was Rhys she wished to chastise for exposing her son to those words. But did the boy realize it was not mere play that French soldiers of ill purpose were on English lands? If so, might one of so few years have enough wit to work through what happened to Rhys and place those events on this shire? Or had someone made it clear to him? His uncle, Ferrand?

"But that is what they are, Mother." He picked up a figure to which a small white flag was attached and thrust it in her direction. "Bad French who show no mercy when others are on their backs, but when *they* are down..." He swept the figure back and forth, causing the fabric to flutter. "...they wave the flag. When I am a knight, I shall show no mercy as they show us none."

"Sebastian, 'tis time you—"

"Not all French are given to waving the flag, and those who are do not always do so," Rhys spoke over Lady Dangereuse.

Not wanting to further antagonize her, he hesitated to continue, but her son said, "Tell me, Sir Knight. I must know."

Feeling for the fatherless boy, remembering when he had felt the absence of a mother before his sire wed again, Rhys said, "It is true the French with whom I had an encounter on English soil were white flaggers, but it can be wisdom, rather than cowardice, that leads to surrender—regardless of whether the warriors are French or English."

"The English are more wise!"

"Many, but not all."

Sebastian turned thoughtful, then shrugged and surveyed his scene of destruction. "'Twas a fine battle, aye?"

Though no sense could be made of the figures beyond the

fallen being French and the standing English, Rhys said, "I can see how our countrymen won the encounter."

"You can?" the boy exclaimed.

"Aye, the commander was skilled at forming battle lines."

"That is me!" He slapped his chest, once more gripped the wooden hilt. "Sebastian of the Wulfriths!"

Having sensed Lady Dangereuse's approach ahead of hearing her footsteps, Rhys merely inclined his head.

"This seems a good place to end your play, Bastian." His mother halted alongside Rhys. "Take your toys abovestairs, straighten your room, and attend to your ablutions."

"'Tis not yet supper!"

"Do it now."

The boy looked to Rhys, silently appealing for aid, but he received only a look meant to remind him to obey.

"Aye," he begrudged and began dropping the soldiers into a leather pouch.

Finding the lady's gaze awaited his, Rhys was struck by an unbidden question—would she ever regard him with something better than distaste and accusation?

Certes, she wanted to say something other than what she did. "My sister-in-law has made a place for you before the hearth." She nodded toward the chair in which the young lady had sat when he entered the hall. Now she was in another angled near.

As for those who had aided with sewing, they withdrew, arms full of linens that could as easily be coverings for the bed as the table.

"And a servant has been sent for drink and viands," Lady Dangereuse prompted, clearly having tolerated her son's exposure to him long enough.

"Kind of her," Rhys said and strode toward the great fireplace whose hearth was as tall as he and as wide as one and a half of him. For that, it was fueled by sectioned tree trunks and thick branches.

Two strides in, he realized he did not advance alone. As if to ensure he did not stray, she followed.

He slowed. As did she.

He halted. As did she.

He turned. Coolly, she raised her eyebrows.

Though tempted to remind her he had not sought out her son—that the boy came to him and wished him to assess his battlefield—Rhys had no reason to be on the defensive. At least, none of his own doing.

"My lady?" he invited her to do her best in rebuking him.

"Now is not the time, here is not the place," she said and resumed her stride to claim another vacated chair beside Lady Murielle.

As Rhys lowered into the one facing them, a servant appeared and set a tray on the small table between the three. "Apologies, Lady D," she said, "I understood there would be two. I shall go for another cup and more viands."

Her mistress shook her head. "No need. Supper comes soon enough."

Quickly, the girl filled the cups, returned the pitcher to the tray, and dipped. As she retraced her steps, Sebastian started toward the stairs, soldiers under one arm and a hand on his sword hilt as if he expected to encounter brigands on stairs he imagined a dangerous mountain pass.

Once Rhys had imagined the same of forbidden stairs leading to the floor where his leprous grandsire dwelt in seclusion lest he pass his disease to others. More than once in defiance of his sire, the boy had gripped his wooden sword ahead of challenging the mountain pass within Castle Mathe. However, each time his courage had faltered or he was intercepted by his beloved illegitimate sister, Thomasin, who now had sons training at Wulfen.

When he looked back at Sebastian's mother who also watched her son's departure, he gained a glimpse of the young woman she had been before the contest at Wulfen. And wedlock. Though the softening about her was fleeting, it was so striking that when her grave expression returned, he did not think he would ever forget how beautiful she presented those few moments he was permitted to look upon the vulnerable, desperately loving Dangereuse of the Wulfriths.

Something in his chest sticking, he picked up the cup of wine in lieu of a ham pie which could wait until he freed his functioning arm.

As he settled back, Lady Dangereuse retrieved the second cup and a sugar-dusted pastry and passed them to her sister-in-law who could not easily reach the tray for the babe in her belly.

After a sip and a nibble, Lady Murielle said, "I believe my nephew is taken with you, Sir Rhys."

He resisted looking to the boy's mother. "He is a spirited lad."

She snorted, and not quite delicately. "He is, and usually reserved with strangers. Were you armored and banging about in great boots, his interest would be understandable, but..." She shrugged.

Resentment flared, though not toward her—rather, those who had stripped him of his warrior's gear and left him to die. Though his greatest desire was justice for the man-at-arms and any others lost to him, he would risk much to restore two of his possessions—the sword whose forging his sire commissioned to mark his son's attainment of knighthood, and the Wulfrith dagger Lady Dangereuse's sire had presented him. The thought of one unworthy wearing either made sour of his stomach, just as it had the night Benoit used his Wulfrith dagger to prevent Rhys from aiding his terrified wife and son.

"Methinks you have drifted away from us, Sir Rhys, and 'tis not a good place you go," Lady Murielle said.

He smiled as he carried the cup to his mouth. "You read me well."

"Merely observant. Where there were few lines upon your brow, of a sudden twice as many."

"Then I should be more guarded with my expression." Continuing to ignore Lady Dangereuse's suffering over his presence, he returned the cup to the tray and took the small pie.

"Surely not amongst friends," Lady Murielle said, evidencing either she was unaware of her sister-in-law's grievance against him or would not judge him for it.

"You are kind, my lady." After he took a bite of the pie that could be eaten whole were he lacking manners, Lady Murielle gasped and pressed a hand to her abdomen.

"Your babe moves," he said.

"Vigorously." Her fairly breathless words ended on a soft laugh that did not linger, nor her hand on her babe. As for her sidelong glance at Lady Dangereuse, it wafted guilt.

For expressing joy over an obvious indiscretion? Rhys wondered. Though surely Lady Dangereuse's nephew or niece was legitimized by belated marriage...

That thought trailed away, and in its wake came another.

It was assumption Rémy Wulfrith sired the child and for that wed ahead of attaining knighthood. But had he not, why join his life to Lady Murielle? Even were they betrothed before, such betrayal would make it easy to terminate the marital contract.

Expecting disapproval from Lady Dangereuse, Rhys was surprised that though her eyes were on her sister-in-law, no rebuke was evident. Then she said mildly, "The sign of a healthy babe, Murielle. God willing, your little one will be that."

The young woman's smile slight, she looked to her pastry and showed more than a nibble's interest in it.

"I hope the physician's prognosis of your recovery is encouraging, Sir Rhys," the castellan of Lillia said in an attempt to turn the conversation.

"It is, and further I am encouraged that there is no longer discomfort in moving fingers and wrist and only a little in movement of my arm and shoulder."

"Then you may regain full use of the limb."

"That seems very possible."

"If not, your left arm was also trained to weaponry."

"True," he said and recalled how, as a squire, he had questioned why time and effort were wasted on such. Her uncle had raised his eyebrows and said, *Think on it, young De Arell, then you tell me.*

Frustrated over how poorly his left arm wielded a blade compared to the right, he had not needed to think far, mischievously making a lesson of his answer with—*Why be content with one warrior at your disposal when there is another on the other side of you eager to enter your service should the dominant one fall?*

Rhys had seen approval in Sir Owen's eyes, then the warrior had said, *A worthy lesson, Squire. Let it be your sixteenth.* And so it was. Though he had heard the trainer of knights bestow it on others—sometimes with a wink at Rhys—since lessons were personalized at Wulfen, it was numbered differently for other squires.

"I am grateful for my training," Rhys said. "Blessedly, as I keep my spare arm in practice, it *is* prepared to undergo strenuous training to become the dominant should it prove necessary."

"Certes, you are of a warrior's bent, Sir Rhys. But not all are."

In those last words meaning—and warning. After thinking much so he regret little, he told himself to let it pass. However, with this woman it was difficult to heed that lesson and another given by her sire—*Only a fool does what he knows in his bones he ought not.*

Thus, Rhys would surely regret his response. "True, though I wager your son is also of a warrior's bent."

Her eyes widened, but he was not the only recipient of further disapproval. As if Lady Murielle had made a pact with him to aid Sebastian in being trained at Wulfen, she came out from behind her pastry. "I also believe my nephew's gift will be that of defending against men who wield weapons against those dear to him."

Rhys would not have thought Lady Dangereuse could sit straighter. She did. "Then 'tis good his mother, who has the greatest care for him, knows better."

As if to make amends for overstepping, her sister-in-law said, "Despite much restlessness, I did think he performed well this day's scripture lesson."

"Restlessness is normal for a boy not yet six, Murielle."

The young woman blinked. "True, and more restless for missing Charliese, do you not think?"

Deciding to help dig her out of Lady Dangereuse's bad graces, Rhys said, "Charliese?"

Lady Murielle nodded. "His cousin by way of Sir Warin."

That was of interest since had that Wulfrith brother wed again following the passing of his first wife from the pestilence, and had he a child old enough to play with Sebastian, Rhys should have heard of that marriage.

"Not that he would admit he misses Charliese since she is a girl, younger, and picks at him nearly as much as he does her," Lady Murielle said, "but when she visited months past, he could not hide how attached he is to her."

Rhys looked to Lady Dangereuse. "I was unaware Sir Warin wed again."

Her jaw shifted. "He retrieved the girl from France when her mother wished to be rid of her. She now resides at Stern in the care of my grandmother's maid."

Illegitimate then, an act of indiscretion while Warin served King Edward on the continent ahead of the sweep of the pestilence. Though it was behavior unworthy of a Wulfrith, he had done the honorable thing in claiming the child though it announced his sin to all.

Surprisingly more forthcoming, Lady Dangereuse added, "Once Warin settles in as Woodhearst's baron, dividing his time between administering his lands and training knights at Wulfen, his daughter will be raised there with the aid of my grandmother's maid until he weds again."

"I did not know that," Lady Murielle exclaimed. "What will Lady Héloise do without her maid?"

Lady Dangereuse frowned. "Did I not tell? Filomena is being trained to take Esta's place."

"Why, that is wonderful!"

Now well outside the conversation and content to remain there since both women were relaxing into it, Rhys finished off the meat pie.

"But what of Filly's family?" Lady Murielle asked.

"They have moved to the nearby village of Ravvenborough so she may visit them often."

"Glad tidings. After what they endured, I am happy for them."

Rhys took another meat pie and downed it in two bites.

"Have you recent tidings of how the babes of Stern fare?" the younger woman asked with further lightness that confirmed it was best Rhys was relegated to the background. Too, it allowed him to more closely observe the she-wolf with her guard lowered.

His reward—which he ought not regard as such—was a smile that softened her mouth. "Just as the baron and Séverine's babe thrives, so does the newborn daughter of Ondine and Sir Sinjin."

Ondine, Rhys acknowledged the second Wulfrith sister who was so beautiful it was said that despite scarring following her miraculous recovery from the pestilence, she remained comely.

"Do you not think that babe gifted the loveliest name?" Lady Murielle said.

"Indeed. Though 'twas to have been that of Ondine's mother, *Mae,* Sir Sinjin wished his wife honored as well. Thus, the name *Maedine,* which my sire would have approved for being fond of distinctive names."

"Certes, no other shall answer to it," the younger woman said, "just as none answer to yours, a name that fascinates."

As it had Rhys until, during his training at Wulfen, he learned it was first held by Dangereuse de l'Isle Bouchard, the maternal grandmother of King Henry II's wife. Though it was not the woman's birth name but a sobriquet for one who did as she wished with little concern for the opinions of others and the Church, it was said she of dangerous bent had embraced it. Rhys had thought it strange the baron named his daughter that, and after the Tournament of Honor that cast suspicion on her for the death of her husband, some said it was a portent.

As if aware of that, Lady Dangereuse said, "'Tis a name borrowed from Eleanor of Aquitaine's grandmother for its uniqueness and bit of intrigue." It was said with finality.

Shortly, Lady Murielle shifted the conversation to ground more easily tread by asking, "Has Lady Ondine fully recovered from the birthing? She has been in my prayers."

"She is up and about, as I have no doubt you shall be after delivering your babe, Murielle."

As if fearful of that, the young woman lowered her chin, then asked, "What of Fira?"

The third and youngest Wulfrith sister, Rhys reflected, and wondered if the pretty freckled and redheaded girl, who would now be of marriageable age, had retained her petite proportions or gained sudden height as some females did like many males moving toward manhood.

"Does her health hold or has she suffered more—"

That would have held Rhys' attention if not for the arrival of one whose entrance caused the cold beyond the closed doors to gust inside.

CHAPTER 13

R hys looked around, and there was the one he had seen only once since his arrival at Lillia—Benoit's brother who had to have played a role in Rhys' unhorsing during Wulfen's joust. The man he had become paused to stamp snow from his boots while the doors remained wide, evidencing others would follow, then he strode toward the hearth. And faltered when he noticed his lady's unwelcome guest was no longer confined to the steward's study.

Guilt, Rhys read again what he had seen about Lady Murielle when quickly she removed her hand from her abdomen.

Though he expected Ferrand to avert his gaze and ignore his brother's former rival, when he halted before his lady who rose to receive him, he acknowledged him with, "Sir Rhys."

"What have you to report?" Lady Dangereuse asked.

With a tone of apology, he said, "Baron Wulfrith has sent your uncle with four knights and five advanced squires to search out those who attacked Sir Rhys' party."

As she looked to the doorway that would soon fill with visitors whose spurred boots sounded on the steps, Ferrand added, "And he has with him a woman he believes is Sir Rhys' missing lady."

Rhys was out of the chair and moving toward the open doors when Sir Owen Wulfrith entered. Noticeably absent a mantle for how chill the weather, the older knight gave him a nod and called, "I know you were expecting your brother, Dangereuse, but I shall have to serve since he is occupied with pressing matters."

More pressing than hostile French on his lands? Rhys wondered.

Then Sir Owen was before him and clapping a hand on his former pupil's shoulder. "'Tis good to see you and in fine form considering your injury."

"I am glad we meet again, Sir Owen, though I would have preferred other circumstances."

"And I." The man leaned in. "My niece must be discreetly told the full of why I come rather than her brother, which is that sickness is upon Wulfen Castle, and even the baron is afflicted."

"The pestilence?" Rhys rasped.

Doubtless anticipating the question, already Sir Owen shook his head. "No deaths and near certainty all shall recover, including your kin and mine. It is mostly of consequence for being so widespread that though now 'tis the practice to move those of debilitating illness to the old hunting lodge to protect the unaffected, their numbers are too great."

The wisdom of the Wulfriths, Rhys reflected. For measures taken during the pestilence, which were even more extreme than those upon the Barony of Blackwood, Wulfen's people had suffered relatively few casualties. Hundreds had died, while at least three and four times as many were lost on other baronies.

Sir Owen cleared his throat. "Thus, as parts of Wulfen Castle have been designated for the ill, others for the healthy, and none are allowed to enter nor leave ere the sickness resolves, when I and those accompanying me to London on Wulfen business returned—absent my nephew, Warin, with whom our king has other business—we were sent to Stern to wait it out. The following day, it was there Dangereuse's messenger, who had read her missive to Baron Wulfrith from outside the walls, came next to deliver word to me I should bring men here to give aid."

"I shall pray for the ill," Rhys said and knew many would be the beseechings sent heavenward from Lillia.

"As I would not have Squire Rémy's wife worry unnecessarily for her husband nor brother who also trains there, best she remain ignorant during the tender weeks left of her pregnancy," Sir Owen said, then glanced over his shoulder. "Now I believe the lady lost to you is found—among other things." Before Rhys could ponder that last, he added, "Though she is mostly silent about her tale, 'tis surely an ill one."

Rhys saw her. Whatever had befallen the woman draped in a large mantle that had to be Sir Owen's, she entered the hall on her own despite a limp, though a squire was on either side as if to catch her up should her legs fail.

"We shall speak of all in the solar," Sir Owen said, and when he continued toward the hearth, Rhys advanced on the lady who had survived something from which he should have protected her.

It was good she of hair that would be rich brown once its order and health were restored did not see him until he was nearly upon her. When she did, her eyes flew wide and knees buckled.

The squires could have caught her, but Rhys reached her first. He whipped his good arm around her to keep her erect, and though he expected her to reject further support for having kept distance between herself and her escort during their journey from France to England, she did not.

"Praise the Lord," Rhys said when she tipped up her face and he saw abrasions there. "I feared I failed you entirely."

Though exceptionally fine of face and figure, the hard of this woman conspired to render her less appealing the same as it did Lady Dangereuse. He did not know all she had suffered in France, but enough that he pitied one who scorned pity.

Thus, he was unprepared when she turned into him, pinning his slinged arm between their chests, and caught up handfuls of his tunic. "You did all you could," she said so low he had to strain to catch words spoken against his collarbone. "Certes, you came nearer death than I."

There was much in those words, and he wondered again what had befallen her between him sending her toward Broehne Castle and Sir Owen taking custody of her.

Wary of what was beneath the borrowed mantle, and fairly certain it was not her own cloak of good wool that should have warmed her adequately, he withdrew his arm and raised her chin. "What happened after we parted, Lady Vianne?"

Golden eyes more luminous for a rush of tears, she pressed her lips and shook her head.

"I must know, my lady."

Another shake, but she peered past him and choked, "Sir Owen knows enough, and that must suffice for now."

As the great doors closed out the cold, he turned with her and, moving her to his side, saw the trainer of knights had drawn his niece and Squire Ferrand away from the hearth—distancing them from Squire Rémy's wife.

Moments later, Lady Dangereuse nodded and sent her gaze across the hall to those who had entered with her uncle. It would have been a glancing look had she not paused on Rhys where he stood very near the woman who should be in London revealing her intelligence to King Edward.

He nodded at her, then called, "Lady Vianne requires food, drink, and rest."

"I will tend her." This from Lady Murielle who began raising her unbalanced body from the chair.

"Worry not, I shall see to our guest," Lady Dangereuse said, surely in consideration of her sister-in-law's unwieldy state, and possibly lest she learn of the sickness upon Wulfen. As she strolled toward those just inside the hall, she called for her uncle's men to take their ease on the dais where refreshments would be delivered.

When she halted before Rhys and looked to his charge, as if the woman at his side perceived threat there, she regained her height and sidestepped to shed his support.

"You are welcome at Castle Lillia," Lady Dangereuse said.

Sidelong, Rhys saw movement beneath the mantle loaned the lady and a pinch of its lapels as if to ensure what was beneath remained concealed, then the disheveled woman said, "I am Lady Vianne Wardieu."

Rhys had thought she would provide the surname of Artois by which she journeyed from France to England. However, as if she could be herself again in her country, despite pursuit by the French who sought to drag her back to the one who might put her to the sword or worse, she had used her family name.

Lady Dangereuse extended a hand. "Come, and when you are settled with food and drink, I will have a bath delivered to your room."

"No bath!" Lady Vianne exclaimed, then sought to correct her forceful refusal by adding, "As I am fatigued, soap and a basin of water will serve."

Not what one expects of a lady terribly disarrayed and come in from the cold, Dangereuse reflected and, from the little her uncle had told, guessed Lady Vianne hid behind the mantle evidence of what she suffered after parting from Sir Rhys.

Since clearly the woman had no intention of accepting the kindness offered her, Dangereuse lowered her hand and met Rhys' gaze. Seeing concern there, she wondered at his feelings for the lady who had accepted his support and made it something of an embrace. Though she told herself their relationship did not concern her, there was a peculiar pang in her chest.

Elevating her chin, she said, "My uncle would have you meet him in the solar in a half hour, Sir Rhys. 'Tis on the second floor, first door on the left."

He inclined his head.

"Kindly follow, Lady Vianne," she said and moved toward the stairs trailed by the woman who could be Sir Rhys' lover.

CHAPTER 14

The sword of the Baron of Blackwood's heir. And the Wulfrith dagger. The sight of both on a table near the fireplace halted Rhys just inside the solar. No plate armor, but better these, though he might yet recover the pieces forged to fit his height and breadth.

"As mentioned, not only was the missing lady found," Sir Owen said where he stood alongside the hearth cradling a goblet.

Other things, he had said, and Rhys had wanted to question that. Distantly acknowledging the fine furnishings of the sizable room that was Lady Dangereuse's bedchamber, he asked as he advanced, "How is it they are here?"

The older knight gestured at the table whose far end was neatly set with writing instruments and books, while a platter of refreshments perched on the near end. "Soon told," he said. "Pour yourself a drink and take your ease while we await my niece."

That Lady Dangereuse would attend surprised, but since she was both castellan and a Wulfrith, sense was made of it.

Having recently satisfied his hunger enough that he could await supper, he eschewed the viands, filled a goblet half full, and settled in the chair before which lay his leather belt hung with the sheathed weapons stolen by a Frenchman. He touched the sword his sire had commissioned for him, next the dagger, and though tempted to return them to his waist, looked to the trainer of knights and said, "I am more grateful than I can tell."

"'Twas not my doing, Sir Rhys." It was said with finality that indicated explanations would await Lady Dangereuse's arrival.

When she came, she was accompanied by Ferrand Royston.

Rhys would have preferred the squire's absence since still he saw the deceitful youth whose aid given his brother had set in motion what led to Benoit bleeding out on a Wulfrith dagger, but it was not for him to decide who should know what was said here. At least, not yet.

For the surprise in Lady Dangereuse's eyes when they lit on Rhys' weapons, she had not been informed of their recovery.

"Sit," Sir Owen said and crossed to the head of the table.

When his niece had taken the chair opposite Rhys, and Squire Ferrand sat beside her, Rhys asked, "How fares Lady Vianne?"

"She ate little, drank much, and now rests," Lady Dangereuse said.

"I thank you for tending her."

Sir Owen cleared his throat. "During a ride to Lillia, we encountered a village bailiff who was unsuccessful in reaching Sheriff D'Arci upon Abingdale, the man being of an age that one of fewer years must soon replace him. He told days past he had jailed a woman discovered beyond the outskirts of the village beside a dead man and she was holding a bloodied dagger." He gestured at Rhys'. "It was difficult to get it from her, but after he and another man did so, they saw the garments beneath her mantle were those of a lady and her bodice torn. As they dragged her away from the dead man, she cursed what she named a foul Frenchman and kicked him."

Sir Owen looked again to Rhys' weapons. "He wore your sword belt as well as his own. The bailiff told once the lady ceased resisting, she spoke little, even when he jailed her, and most of her words were spent on instructing him to burn the gown and chemise she removed beneath cover of her mantle."

Now Rhys understood. "As it was your mantle she wore when she entered the donjon, I believed hers lost."

"Nay, she belted her own with her girdle, making something of a gown of it, and to provide greater warmth for the ride, I leant her mine."

Rhys frowned. "The bailiff did not provide garments to replace her ruined ones?"

"He told he would secure a simple gown, but she declined. Be assured, as he believed her a lady and feared her violated by an enemy of our country, he was attentive to her despite the necessity of locking her away until he could give her into the sheriff's hands. As she barely ate and huddled in a corner beneath a blanket rather than on the cot, for being unable to get word to Sheriff D'Arci amid foul weather, the bailiff asked that I take custody of her and deliver her to the sheriff. Having examined the Frenchman she appears to have slain and being fairly certain she was the lady with whom you traveled, I agreed."

"How did you confirm the corpse was French?" Rhys asked.

"The coins in his purse, and the badge on his tunic being that of his French lord."

That lord being Rollon de Talliere, Rhys thought and, still conscious of Squire Ferrand whom he did not trust, said, "Though I know there must be an investigation, I vouch for the lady. If she slew the man, she had cause, and much of that is told by the state in which she was found. Now tell why you brought her here rather than deliver her to Sheriff D'Arci."

"Alas, as there is sickness at Wulfen, it has struck those of Castle Soaring, including the sheriff who, like Baron Wulfrith, came to the wall to speak with me."

"Is it the same illness?"

"So it sounds—a grave winter ailment such as that which strikes every four or five years, but more serious at Soaring for the loss of two of the elderly, who are always more vulnerable. Blessedly, Sir Percival and the others taken ill begin to recover."

"Praise the Lord," Lady Dangereuse murmured.

"The sheriff sends his regrets at being unable to hunt down the brigands troubling these lands and now these foreign trespassers, Dangereuse," Sir Owen continued. "After I assured him I and my men would take all in hand until he can resume his duties, we rode for Lillia."

"Much gratitude, Uncle."

He returned to Rhys. "So better I can bring to ground what remains of the French dogs who set upon you and your party, start at the beginning."

Though Rhys believed under these circumstances King Edward would be well with Owen Wulfrith and his niece learning of his mission, not so Ferrand Royston. He looked to one whose eyes were bright with interest. "I must ask you to leave the chamber."

The squire blinked, and Lady Dangereuse said, "He is trusted and—"

"Depart, Squire Ferrand," Sir Owen ordered.

Royston's mouth twitched, but he pushed back his chair and, shortly, closed the door behind him.

Feeling Lady Dangereuse's displeasure, Rhys took a sip of wine and began, "As you are aware, Sir Owen, the kings of

England and France formalized a truce this past July. In November, it was determined it was in the best interest of both countries to extend it over the winter months until April of next year. Thus, our king assembled ambassadors to cross the channel and treat with King Jean's representatives in northern France at Guines. Being among the knights tasked with protecting the ambassadors, I was accompanied by my squire and a man-at-arms our king selected for him being trust-worthy—and French to the bone." Prepared for his former instructor's raised eyebrows, he inclined his head. "Aye, but not the heart. Unlike other protectors of the English ambas-sadors, I was given an additional and greater mission—to retrieve intelligence from a lady who would accompany one of King Jean's advisors to the talks at Guines."

"Lady Vianne," Lady Dangereuse concluded.

He looked to where she sat opposite, confirmed, "Vianne Wardieu."

She narrowed her lids. "A spy?"

"One so well placed, easily she moves about our enemy's court."

She frowned. "I noted a continental accent, but 'tis lacking depth that would allow her to pass as French. Therefore, since I am fair certain she is first of England, how did she gain intelli-gence for our king?"

"I am not privy to details beyond those entrusted to me by Edward, but I know she has lived at the French court for nearly eight years—since before our king took the war to France in 1346—and is fairly trusted by our enemy for being the para-mour of King Jean's advisor, Rollon de Talliere."

Disapproval swept the lady's eyes. It was no rare thing for a nobleman to take a mistress—regardless of whether he was wed—but it was less common for a mistress to be of the nobil-ity. At least, openly so.

"Over a month past, Lady Vianne sent word to Edward she had information of such import it must be delivered directly to one of his representatives during the talks at Guines that she would attend with De Talliere. Too, she told that by then she would have more to impart."

Lady Dangereuse set her head aslant. "And yet you did more than bring that information back. You brought the lady to England, which is surely the reason murderous French are upon Wulfenshire."

"That I did, not only because she was adamant she must deliver the intelligence to the king, but for how desperate she was to return to her country."

Lady Dangereuse glanced at her uncle who nodded for her to continue. "Regardless of those things she did to spy for King Edward, I sympathize with her, but I must question whether she remains our countrywoman or plays both sides—or only one side that is not our own."

"You are not alone in considering that, but greatly I lean toward her being firmly our side."

"I pray it is so, but now another thing to be questioned— might you be more easily convinced of her English loyalties because of your...interest in her?"

He knew what she implied, and though he would question it the same were he on the outside of what transpired since removing Lady Vianne from France, it offended. "You suspect such because when my charge sought comfort for her suffering, I did not push her away."

She raised her eyebrows.

"Here is all you must know regarding my interest in the king's spy—were you my responsibility, Lady Dangereuse Royston, the same consideration and comfort would be shown you."

Her eyes widened, and though no more need be spoken,

when Rhys was struck by the irony of it all, the temptation to voice it trampled the advice to think much. "Even were you *not* my responsibility, the same would be afforded you—and more, of which you have much evidence."

Her gaze flickered and lowered over him. Though just as she could not see beneath the table's edge, she could not see the scar beneath his garments, doubtless she recalled the Wulfrith blade that cut him when he defended her and her son.

Sir Owen gave a grunt of disapproval. "Methinks you two chase each other on what only appears to be a playground. Pray, leave that past where it fell so we may return to Lady Vianne."

As ever, it is as bad as being rebuked by my sire, Rhys thought, but acceded it was deserved when he glimpsed excess moisture in the lady's eyes before she looked away.

Acknowledging there was much unresolved between them, he said, "Forgive me, my lady." Then he returned his regard to the knight. "Immediately after the truce extension was signed late afternoon on the third of December, Lady Vianne met me in secret as arranged. With my squire, King Edward's man-at-arms, and three other warriors who were to accompany us as far as Calais where a ship awaited us, we stole her out of Guines."

He shifted his jaw. "For how closely she was watched, her absence was discovered sooner than expected, and ere long we found ourselves pursued. Though our warriors numbered six to their four, it was best to avoid engagement lest it endanger the lady and draw the attention of other French abundantly present for the talks. Unfortunately, as our pursuers' mounts were swifter, they began overtaking us. With little chance of outrunning them and fearing for Lady Vianne were she captured, I instructed her to feign abduction to preserve her life, but also in the hope of safeguarding King Edward's source of information. She played her part well, attempting to swerve aside and turn back toward her lover's men." Remembrance of her performance nearly curved his mouth. "And forcing me to take control of her reins as she screamed and slapped at her supposed captor."

"Well thought," Lady Dangereuse said.

"The distance was closing, and so we went to the wood and had just enough time to spring a trap to which De Talliere's men succumbed more easily for my dagger at the throat of the lady they were surely ordered to return alive. They cast down their weapons and vowed if I spared their lives, they would discontinue their pursuit and report to their lord we went the opposite direction."

Sir Owen snorted.

Rhys nodded. "I believed it a lie the same as King Edward's man-at-arms who named his former countrymen *les signaleurs blancs* and told better we bleed out their lives than provide them another opportunity to take ours. He vowed were we the ones waving a white flag, they would disregard it just as we should."

Rhys paused to reflect how things might have been different had he heeded that advice. The French man-at-arms would yet live, Lady Vianne would be safely in London, Rhys' sword arm would require no healing, and his squire would be at his side rather than, quite possibly, slain.

"No honor in taking the lives of weaponless men who but do their lord's bidding," Sir Owen said.

"As I adhered to, and for that agreed they would not be slaughtered," Rhys said. "There being too little time to secure them, I ordered them to dismount and for our Calais escort to collect their weapons and horses that we would release once we were distant. But then we heard other riders beyond the wood, and the men we spared for the word given us shouted and ran toward their countrymen. Thus, we let the miscreants' weapons lie, spooked their horses to flight, and spurred away."

"And regretted not putting them to the sword," Lady Dangereuse said.

Is that judgment or merely a question? he wondered. "Not in the beginning, my lady, though during our hours' long flight from pursuers who had grown in number, regret gnawed through me as King Edward's French man cursed me for doing what he said was right only in the eyes of God who was blind for the long nap in which He indulged."

"Clearly not Wulfen-trained," Sir Owen said.

Noting worry lining Lady Dangereuse's brow, Rhys said, "Indeed not, though better I understood his ruthlessness after we reached Calais just ahead of De Talliere's men. As the town is held by the English, we were safe inside its walls, but it being imperative we get the lady to England, at first light the next morn we parted from our escort and boarded our ship."

Momentarily he closed his eyes. "Though aware a French merchant ship also made the crossing, it being within sight much of the time, not until a storm struck past midday and drove it near ours did we recognize several of De Talliere's men on deck, among them his son. The storm worsened, and though it distanced our ships, it forced us and our pursuers far off course. Blessedly, when the sun rose the next day, we docked at the Port of Grimsby on the Humber Estuary."

"Northeast Lincolnshire is a long way from Dover," Sir Owen said.

"Especially with the ship carrying De Talliere's men appearing offshore shortly after we secured horses. We alerted the authorities hostile French were aboard and might try to dock, then took the road leading south, hopeful Lady Vianne's pursuers would be detained, giving us time to see her safely to

London. However, lest those of De Talliere devise a means of thwarting English authorities, we rode long and hard, stopping only when necessary and sleeping in the wood."

Rhys paused, looked to Lady Dangereuse, and saw enough stiff had gone out of her that she leaned toward him—seemingly all interest, accusation and judgment no longer evident.

"It had just gone night when we crossed into Wulfenshire, intent on reaching a village upon Abingdale or Broehne Castle before the storm undid us. When I sensed we were followed and lightning permitted a glimpse of riders coming behind, I knew we were as easily seen. As there was no way to determine whether the five men were of De Talliere, English brigands, or mere travelers, I altered our course, angling nearer Castle Lillia. After the next lightning flash, I told my squire and the king's man we would regroup at Broehne and sent them a different direction with instructions to go wide in the hope if those coming behind pursued us, they would be led astray or divide their numbers."

"When the lady and I turned further east, rain promising snow began to fall, and two of those following us set after my squire and the king's man-at-arms. The other three continued to pursue me and my charge. We pushed onward, but as they were gaining on us for Lady Vianne's horse tiring, when we were able to go from sight, I instructed her to head west until she came to the river she would follow to Broehne, then we parted and I showed myself to draw her pursuers to me."

Rhys shifted tightening shoulders. "Amid lightning, I swung my sword against De Talliere's men, two of whom I recognized as those who broke the vows given me." He paused to reduce the dark images to as few words as possible. "I drew more blood than they did, dealing what I believed a mortal blow to one, but then my sword arm was struck from behind, emptying my hand of its hilt. Ere long, I was put to ground and left to die." He drew breath. "Though I have no liking for Squire Ferrand, I am grateful he did not leave me for dead when he happened on me."

Though he might have had he been alone, he silently added as he sat back. "And so here we are, the king's Frenchman slain, my sword arm nearly lost, Lady Vianne assaulted, and my squire possibly dead."

Lady Dangereuse also eased back. "Hopefully, soon we will hear from Baron Lavonne of Abingdale, and he will have good tidings about your young man."

"In the meantime," her uncle said, "My men and I shall expand Lillia's patrol and the frequency of rounds to uproot any who do not belong on Wulfen." He looked to his niece. "What of the brigands who have been troubling your villagers and travelers?"

"They have gone quiet, if not because of the snow, possibly for encountering and wishing to avoid Lady Vianne's pursuers."

He nodded, stood, and looked to Rhys who also gained his feet. "I shall see you at supper." The lady's sharp breath moved his gaze to her. "You object, Dangereuse?"

She moistened her lips. "Of course Sir Rhys is welcome at table. It just seems better for him to continue his recovery in the peace and quiet of the steward's rooms."

"Then you forget he is a knight—one raised high at Wulfen."

"Hardly forgotten. After all, he trained alongside my husband."

After some moments, Sir Owen trampled the silence with, "Aye, first squire to your father and worthy of that highest achievement."

Was there rebuke in his words? Rhys wondered.

As if so, the lady inclined her head stiffly. "As I shall share

Bastian's room, I yield the solar to you and your knights and squires." Then without another glance at Rhys, she crossed to a door diagonal to the solar's entrance and opened it.

"Mama!" her son's voice rang out. "I told Amanda I am clean enough, but—"

"If she tells you are not, you are not," she said and closed the door.

Though their voices were heard, one stern, the other shot through with a whine, as Rhys had no wish to listen in on their exchange, he returned his attention to Sir Owen. "I am glad you came to Lillia and brought Lady Vianne."

Briefly, the man gripped his former pupil's shoulder. "I am aware my niece holds you partly responsible for the death of her husband, but she also faults herself and Benoit."

As she had told, Rhys reflected. "I did play a part that could have tipped Benoit over an edge I did not realize he stood upon, and even had I—"

Sir Owen raised a silencing hand, glanced at the door to the adjoining room, and said, "I know you, just as I knew Benoit—and well enough that I need no explanation of the part you played. What matters to me and my family is that when a Wulfrith warrior dishonored his training by aggressing on his wife and son, you gave aid, the lack of which could have ended as disastrously for her and the boy as it did Benoit. My niece knows this but struggles to fully accept it for how that night affected her son. However, I believe Dangereuse of her broken years is mostly behind her and—"

"Broken years?" Rhys said.

He winced. "Ill spoken, though 'tis as my mother, Lady Héloïse, refers to what came after Benoit's death—guilt and the fierce need to protect her son, which must soon find its end if the boy is to become a man pleasing to God."

"Your niece believes that best achieved by dedicating him to the Church."

"And her family does not." It was said sharply, then the older knight sighed. "Though 'tis good the boy gains control of his temper and impulses, his sharp intelligence is used to bend others to his will, and that is no fit for the Church. Thus, 'tis our belief—and experience with those like him—that if he is provided stability, consistent discipline, accountability to male adults and peers, and a release of aggression through the ways of the warrior, he can become one who defends what needs defending rather than one against whom others must be defended." He nodded. "When the boy turns six in February, we believe he should begin training at Wulfen despite it being a year earlier than most."

"Then you have little time in which to persuade your niece such training best suits him."

"Certes, little time to do it right."

Rhys narrowed his lids. "You would take the decision out of her hands?"

"I do not think it will come to that, but it shall require greater pressure to bring her around—and perhaps a reminder that as she is widowed and her son fatherless, the Baron of Wulfen has final say in matters regarding his wards."

Which she was as much as his nephew. Since she remained unwed though many a nobleman would wish her hand, she herself benefitted from kinship with England's renowned trainer of knights. And it sounded her son would as well, albeit in a different way for being disposed toward military training.

"I hardly know the boy, but the same as you and Baron Wulfrith," Rhys said, "I see a warrior in his eyes and sense it in his bones."

"Now to make my niece accept that," Sir Owen said and turned away.

"I have two favors to ask," Rhys brought him back around. "The first is that I ride patrol with you."

The man glanced at his former pupil's arm slung across his chest.

"Though I have not neglected practice with my left arm and expect to regain full use of the right, more is needed," Rhys continued. "As there is none more capable of dragging the best out of me, I ask that while we are both at Lillia, you engage me at arms on the training field."

"I am honored to be held in such high regard, Sir Rhys, and I thank you that 'tis not mere flattery as it would be if my brother yet lived."

Rhys nodded. "Certes, Lady Dangereuse's sire was a knight above knights and lord above lords."

"For that greatly missed," Sir Owen said. "Blessedly, he could not have left Wulfen in better hands than my nephew's."

Hector Wulfrith whose Christian name Rhys knew from training up behind him. When he had succeeded his father, formally he became *Baron Wulfrith* or simply *Wulfrith* to all but intimates.

"You will afford me a place in your patrol and aid in strengthening my left arm?" Rhys asked.

"Aye, and since your armor was not recovered, I will secure for you a sleeved mail hauberk."

"Much appreciated." Rhys girded his belt, adjusting it until sword and dagger hilts were correctly positioned to easily sweep blades from their scabbards. "I have missed these, but only now realize how much."

A smile touched Sir Owen's lips. "Once I professed the same of a woman for whom I cared more than I should and she..." He trailed off.

Did he speak of one he had loved? Rhys wondered of this man who, as far as he knew, had never wed though his family would have done for him what they did for Squire Rémy who would be castellan of Lillia, the income of which would support a family.

"Long in my past, and there it shall remain," the man said with finality. "Now I must compose a missive Lady Vianne has requested be sent first thing on the morrow providing the weather holds."

Rhys hesitated to question that, then said, "For what purpose?"

"To inform her family she has come home to England, which I sensed she feared would be unwelcome tidings and now, knowing of her time in France, better understand."

Not only for the dishonor of fallen virtue but that she had consorted with an enemy of England, Rhys thought, then dipped his head. "Until supper, Sir Owen."

CHAPTER 15

Supper on the night past had been more tolerable than expected. As Dangereuse had occupied the chair on one side of her uncle, his former pupil his other side, much of the time Rhys had been out of sight and hearing, though mostly due to Murielle.

Seated on Dangereuse's left, she had talked much about preparations for the Christmas feast and expressed interest in the woman who remained abovestairs attended by the physician and a chambermaid. As what Dangereuse knew of Lady Vianne could not be revealed for it being told in confidence, it was for that woman to answer Murielle's questions. Not that she was likely to do so.

Nor answer my questions, Dangereuse thought and silently rebuked herself for curiosity over her relationship with Sir Rhys.

It does not bother she went into his arms, she told herself. *It does not trouble that twice she looked back at him as she climbed the stairs. What do I care if—?*

"Numbers, numbers!" Sebastian complained.

Annoyed and yet relieved by the distraction, she said firmly, "Sebastian!" correcting her boy who had not been pleased his lessons would be in the hall despite usually preferring it over the solar.

Since Owen and his men had occupied his mother's chamber, likely he hoped to explore their travel packs in the belief they were stuffed with weapons, though surely those had accompanied the warriors on their patrol this morn.

"I hate numbers!" He dug his stylus into the wax tablet and raked it over simple calculations that should have been completed by now.

"Enough, Sebastian!" Grateful the morning meal was well past and only Puck and her maid, Amanda, shared the hall with them—one heartily snoring, the other mending—Dangereuse swept the stylus from his fist.

He thrust his lower jaw forward, revealing a lost baby tooth was being replaced by an adult one. "Hate, hate, hate!" he proclaimed, then flung the tablet off the table—just as light and cold air entered through the great doors.

Before Dangereuse could react, a voice belonging to one who ought to be in the steward's rooms, shouted, "Unworthy of blade and lance, boy! Honor your Wulfrith blood!"

Stretched between the need to correct her son and the longing to admonish the man who interfered with her parenting, she was rendered mute—as was the wide-eyed boy who stared at the man approaching the table.

Despite a sling continuing to support Rhys de Arell's right arm, not only did he wear sword and dagger, but chain mail visible between the edges of his mantle.

Uncle Owen's doing, she thought and wished away concern over the healing of one who now looked even more a warrior.

When his eyes moved from Sebastian to her, she glowered.

His expression changed, but not in any way that would endear him. Showing no remorse for overstepping the line she should not have to draw in the dirt between them, he hiked his eyebrows, then raised an arm from beneath his mantle. And took a bite of an apple that looked very small in his hand, though not all because the fruit was many months off its tree, its skin loose and flesh soft.

Being large and all of him proportioned to that height and breadth, it was hard to believe he had ever been the size of Sebastian who, though small compared to this warrior, was big for his age.

When the knight ascended the dais and halted before the table, she stood and, suppressing the impulse to confront him in front of her son, said, "Is there something you require, Sir Rhys?"

The way he thoughtfully chewed—then swallowed—made her toes curl in her slippers, then there was the thrum of his voice when he said, "As earlier I neglected to break my fast, heartier fare than this."

Hating she had to remind herself he overstepped with her son, she gestured across the hall. "The kitchen is through there."

He inclined his head but remained unmoving.

Striving for patience, she said, "Is there something you require of *me*, Sir Rhys?"

"Not I, my lady." He looked to her boy. "But there is something your son requires."

She drew breath. "I am aware, just as you should be aware 'tis for me to deliver it. Now—"

"What do I require, Sir Knight?" Though challenge was in Sebastian's words, more there was flirtation of the sort enlisted by the young when seeking the counsel of a venerated adult.

"I believe you know the answer," Sir Rhys said, "but with your mother's permission, I will speak it."

Though glad he acknowledged having overstepped, she would not allow him to discipline her child.

However, before she could refuse, Sebastian said, "Mother, I want him to tell me. Say he can."

At her frown, he added, "Please."

His appeal a departure from the more usual attempt to charm her into compliance, she hesitated, then returning to her chair begrudged, "You have my permission, Sir Rhys."

He gave her a nod and said, "The marks of godly men are respect and restraint. To learn both, you require discipline, Sebastian."

He scowled. "I want to wield a sword like you. I do not want to be godly. I do not want to know the Bible or that." He backhanded the stylus his mother had set between them.

As her heart lurched, Sir Rhys glanced at the writing instrument that rolled to the edge over which the wax tablet had gone. "Then alas, a poor warrior you shall make." He raised the apple toward his mouth again.

"What?" Sebastian asked.

The knight frowned, then set the apple on the platter of her son's picked over morning meal, and repeated himself.

"I will not be a poor warrior, Sir Rhys! I will be a good—nay, great—warrior!"

"Only if you are as godly as possible."

"Bible men are godly. I do not want to be one of those!"

"As you ought to know, Sebastian of the line of godly Wulfrith warriors, it is not only for a priest—a man of the Bible—to be godly. It is for all men and women."

Emotions flitted across her son's face, then he wrinkled his nose. "I know that. I go to mass with Mother. I pray."

Being aware of something and understanding it are very different things, Dangereuse reflected. And nearly startled when the voice within said, *As is being aware of a man and under-standing him.*

Silently countering that did not apply to *this* man, she determined it was time he leave. "Sir Rhys, my son has a lesson to finish—"

"I will be a godly knight!" Sebastian declared.

Those bothersome blue eyes considered the boy. "Then you must aspire to show respect and restraint."

Sebastian set his hands on the table and leaned in. "I can do that."

"Show me."

"How?"

"Apologize to your mother for your temper, then complete your lesson."

Sebastian hesitated, then looked to Dangereuse. "I am sorry."

She inclined her head. "Appreciated."

"There, I did it, Sir Knight!"

"Acceptable. Now your lesson."

A mischievous glint in the boy's eyes, he raised his palms and shrugged. "No tablet."

Sir Rhys jutted his chin at a place near his feet. "'Tis here on the dais."

Sebastian thrust out a hand, wiggled his fingers.

"Nay, boy. As I did not throw it, you must retrieve it."

"But you can pick it up easy."

"Since willfully you made a mess, it is for you to rectify."

"But –"

"Were you granted entrance to Wulfen, 'tis as you would be taught there," the knight pressed.

"My uncle will let me into Wulfen!"

Once again, Dangereuse's teeth ached.

Sir Rhys raised his eyebrows. "Had he seen what I did upon

entering here, he might decide otherwise lest you do to a sword what you did to the tablet."

"I would not hurt a sword!" Sebastian clapped a hand to his wooden one.

"Retrieve your tablet, boy."

He groaned, dropped his feet to the floor, and started to go the easy way—beneath the table.

"I know of no worthy warrior who would lazily crawl under a table when his feet serve better than his knees," Sir Rhys rebuked.

Abruptly, Sebastian straightened and walked around the table. When he bent to retrieve the tablet, Dangereuse braved those blue eyes. Though she expected smugness about them, there was none. Rather, there was...

She did not know, but fearing he saw tears in her eyes, she turned her attention to her son.

"Got it!" Triumphantly, he raised the tablet as often done with his sword, then puffed his cheeks with air and released it on words wrapped in disgust, "Now numbers!"

"I disliked them when I was your age," Sir Rhys said.

"You *liked* them?" Sebastian made a face.

"Nay, I said I *dis*liked them. For that, I was fortunate to be aided by my older sister and stepmother."

The latter being Lady Quintin who, at The Tournament of Honor, had cared for Dangereuse after this knight carried her away from Benoit's body.

Struck by those images, once more Dangereuse saw and felt Sir Rhys' arms as she gripped his tunic—and ashamedly recalled the longing to remain curled against his muscular chest and forget she had been another man's wife.

"Lord," she appealed, not realizing she spoke aloud until Sebastian whipped his head around.

"Mama?"

Avoiding Sir Rhys' gaze, she latched onto the first excuse she could think of. "I did not realize how fast the day slips away. So you can be done with your lesson and play, make haste, Bastian."

He looked to Sir Rhys. "Help me?"

She caught her breath, said, "If you need help, I shall—"

"I will aid," the knight said, then followed her son around the table to stand between her chair and the one her boy clambered onto.

"I need the numbers again." He pushed the tablet to his mother, then the stylus he retrieved. "Please."

It being a good excuse to put her head down and compose her face, she wrote two sets to be added and subtracted. Then trying to ignore the warmth of the body between her and her son, she slid the tablet and stylus back.

Sebastian set upon the lesson as if she had placed a berry pie before him. As usual, his fingers aided in adding numbers, and she was pleased by how quickly he arrived at the correct answers though Sir Rhys was the incentive. But as ever, he struggled with subtraction.

When he arrived at the answer to the first of those problems, Sir Rhys said, "Close. Unfortunately, close does not win a battle."

Sebastian stiffened, and she sensed he wanted to throw the tablet again, but he said, "Help me!"

Looking sidelong at the knight, Dangereuse saw his mouth tighten. "I am not yours to command, and as you are nearly six years, you know better."

Her son blew breath up his face. "Pray, Sir Knight, aid me."

"Very well. Read out the problem."

He touched the first number. "There are eleven things," he said, then muttered, "I do not know what they are and why I should care."

"Sebastian," Sir Rhys reproached.

A heavy sigh. "And there are three things I must take away from eleven." He held up his hands and splayed them. "How do I do it?"

"Let us try what my sister did to show the importance of numbers and move me toward learning how to work them in my head rather than on my fingers, not only for having only ten, which can be dangerous if one or both hands are busy wielding a weapon, aye?"

Dangereuse nearly groaned. She should have known he would continue encouraging her son to think like one born to the sword.

Sebastian's expression brightened. "Aye, dangerous. Tell me what your sister did. Please."

"To the right of your problem, draw a castle surrounded by an outer wall."

"Why?"

"Draw it."

Shortly it was done. And quite well.

"Now draw eleven swords in front of the outer wall."

"How many?"

"Eleven," Sir Rhys repeated.

Her son laughed and drew very long swords. "Now?"

"Draw three bows atop the wall."

"Why not swords?"

"Bows," Sir Rhys repeated, and when it was done, leaned forward.

Though his arm merely brushed Dangereuse's shoulder, a shiver of awareness leapt to her ribs and swept down her hip.

"That is good, Sebastian. Now as your castle is Lillia, and those without are the enemy—"

"They besiege my castle?"

"It appears. Now name the three defenders atop the wall."

"One is me!"

"I have no doubt, nor that you stand center."

"I do!"

The knight tapped the left and right bows. "What of the two who aid in defending against the eleven?"

"My uncle, the baron. He is the greatest knight!"

"A good choice. Who stands your other side? Sir Owen?"

"Nay, since I do not have as many men as the enemy, I need a most fierce warrior."

His choice of words making Dangereuse fairly certain of the identity of the third atop the wall, her heart lurched.

"Your great uncle *is* a fierce warrior," Sir Rhys reminded as if he also believed as she did.

"Aye, but he is getting old."

"Thereby more experienced, and that is worth much, Sebastian."

"Nay." Her son grinned and tapped the knight's chest. *"You* are a most fierce warrior."

"As you have never seen me fight, you only guess that for me being of fewer years than Sir—"

"Not guessing! I saw!"

Has my heart stopped beating? Dangereuse wondered and, feeling the disquiet of the man beside her, opened her mouth to tell they would work subtraction on the morrow.

But before she could, Sir Rhys said, "Quite the imagination, but if you insist, I shall be one of those who stands your side on the wall."

"Not imagination." Sebastian crossed his arms over his chest. "I *did* see you! The bad man tried to hurt me and pushed mama away and—"

Dangereuse came up out of the chair so quickly it tipped. Had Sir Rhys not slapped a hand to it the same as she, it would have toppled.

"Mama?"

Hating she once more roused his concern, she removed her hand from atop the knight's and, not daring to look at her son lest he see her mouth trembled, said, "Forgive me, Bastian, I forgot I have demesne matters to attend to. Thus, let us suspend your lesson until the morrow."

"But I like this one," he said as he never did when her lessons were interrupted.

"Until the morrow," she repeated, then further disturbed at glimpsing sympathy in Sir Rhys' eyes, scooped up the journals she had planned to work once her boy earned his play. "Amanda," she called to the woman plying needle and thread before the hearth, "I give Sebastian into your care."

"Aye, Lady D."

Dangereuse descended the dais. And faltered. Having yielded the solar to her uncle and with Sebastian likely to return to his room to collect his toys, she determined the steward's study would serve. Fortunately, that destination was believable considering her armful. More fortunately, it would provide solitude in which to set herself aright since Sir Rhys had returned to the donjon for food.

I but need some time behind a closed door, she told herself as she traversed the corridor with snapping skirts and braid sweeping the small of her back.

No tears, Dangereuse Wulfrith. You absolutely will not cry.

CHAPTER 16

Though the impulse to watch her go from sight was great, Rhys did not. Guilt over the unforeseen that had rolled toward Lady Dangereuse like a wheel suddenly come off its shaft made him close his eyes and wish he had done different.

He had known she was discomfited by his interaction with her son, but the boy's behavior roused in him something that ought not be awakened for them being of no relation. However, the impulse to correct Sebastian's disrespect and help him overcome his frustration had made Rhys resist continuing to the kitchen. Thus, where Lady Dangereuse was concerned, once more he failed to think much so he regret little. For it, the boy had swept them back to the night he should have been too young to clearly recall—but did, recognizing Rhys as the savior and Benoit as the malefactor.

"Sir Knight?"

Seeing distress on the boy's face, Rhys forced a smile. "Aye?"

"I am not to upset my mother—my big uncle says so—but

sometimes 'tis hard to be really good. Was it for you when you were as tall as me?"

Not as difficult as it was for this fatherless boy, the hand of Rhys' sire being as loving as it was firm in guiding his son forward each time he strayed off the godly path. Still, Rhys said, "It was challenging."

Sebastian nodded slowly. "I think mother was most upset I told I saw you when that bad man tried to hurt us."

He was perceptive, and though that was not good for Lady Dangereuse in this circumstance, the ability to isolate sources and causes of unrest would serve him well through life—and others, providing he grew into a godly man.

"You were fierce, even after he cut you," Sebastian said as the woman at the hearth rose to take charge of the boy as instructed.

Rhys caught her eye, shook his head, and after a moment, she returned to her chair.

"It sounds you had a fantastic dream," he ventured, though he would not be surprised if the boy refused to acknowledge it as such. "Is it a new one?"

"I have it sometimes, but it did happen. I see it when I am awake, too."

"Since I arrived at Lillia?"

Sebastian shook his head. "For a long time. That is how I knew you when you were on the table." His brow pinched. "Though I do not think I knew your name."

Nor did he know the one he called a *bad man* was his sire, Rhys thought.

"You were brave like I will be when I am big and have a real sword and dagger!"

Weapons only if Lady Dangereuse lost the battle for her son's future. "'Tis much hard work, and not only on the training field," Rhys said, then nodded at the wax tablet.

Sebastian's grimace was fleeting. "Show me how to take eleven away from three without using my fingers so I can still use my sword."

Rhys smiled. "That I can do as well, though first you must master taking three away from eleven."

"That is what I meant."

"Aye, but be aware 'tis a very different calculation though you arrive at the same number."

As if Sebastian suspected being teased, he narrowed his lids, but then returned to the wax tablet. "Eleven"—he ran a finger beneath the swords—"take away three." He tapped the bows atop the wall.

Rhys drew Lady Dangereuse's chair nearer and lowered into the warmth she had left behind. "Here a story, Sebastian. Lillia Castle is under siege. Having three warriors to defeat eleven attackers, the best weapon to wield against them is the bow."

"Uncle Rémy is very good with a bow!"

Rhys nodded. "Unfortunately, though the three of us are also accomplished, each brought only one arrow and—"

"Only one? That is not smart when there are eleven bad men. We can only shoot three."

Rhys nearly laughed. "Until our squires deliver more arrows."

"They better hurry."

Rhys leaned nearer. "Now look long at your drawing, then close your eyes and see it in your mind."

The boy studied it. "Now what?"

"Imagine our arrows flying and hitting their marks."

Moments later, Sebastian exclaimed, "Three on the ground!"

When he started to open his eyes, Rhys said, "Keep them

closed. Now, you see the enemy yet standing who will come over your wall if you do not stop them?"

"Uh huh."

"Count them so you know exactly how many more arrows are needed to keep Lillia safe."

Sebastian squeezed his eyes tighter, nodded eight times, then sprang his lids wide. "Eight bad men, eight more arrows."

"You are right."

"What?"

Rhys repeated, "You are right. Eight more arrows needed."

"And our squires have brought them, and we have shot them and won." Sebastian clapped his hands, then frowned at the tablet. "That was easy, but what if there were two hundred warriors and we had twenty arrows. I could not see that many in my head."

"With such large numbers, there are better ways. This is a good beginning, and more satisfying for helping you understand the importance of calculating numbers."

"I liked it. May we do more?"

Rhys was tempted, recalling when he had responded the same to Thomasin's teaching, but he had overstepped enough. And he was hungry. "Further lessons must be approved by your mother."

He grimaced. "She does not like talk of swords and bows."

"Mayhap she will if you work the problem for her as we did."

His mouth formed an O. "And I could make other problems and solve them the same, aye?"

That is the point of the exercise, Rhys thought. *Make it meaningful and agreeable and one begins seeking knowledge previously forced on them.* "I think that a good idea." He looked to Amanda, and at his nod, she crossed the hall.

"Well done, Bastian," she said as Rhys descended the dais

and strode toward the kitchen. "Before my eyes, I saw you grow an inch."

"Did I, 'Manda?"

"Perhaps not a whole inch, but nearly. Now should we go abovestairs and bring down your toys?"

"Aye, my blocks and soldiers. I want to build what I drew."

"A fine plan," the woman said as Rhys entered the corridor with a smile that lasted until his thoughts moved to the boy's mother.

If emotions resided in the legs, Lady Dangereuse would have limped all the way from the dais to the steward's rooms. And it was his fault for not withdrawing as she wished after his interference with her discipline. For that she was due an apology, despite it being better she knew the extent of her boy's awareness of what went that night, which he was fairly certain had previously eluded her. And there was another thing he believed her ignorant of—providing his assessment was correct.

Halting before the kitchen door that muffled sounds of preparations for the nooning meal that was the most abundant of the day, those of the morn and evening being lighter meals, he considered turning back.

As Lady Dangereuse had not emerged from the steward's study while her son worked the problem, were she still there he could apologize and she would have privacy in which to rebuke him for this trespass as well as when last he offended and she told it was neither the time nor place to discuss it. Was now the time? The study the place?

Not yet, but were she there a quarter hour hence, they could be done with the matter, and when he returned to the outer bailey, Sir Owen would challenge this left arm to do what it must until the right was fully restored.

"God willing," he said, then opened the door and stepped

into the kitchen whose heat would be stifling in summer but was a balm for chill air entering through every crack pried wide.

Tears though she had told herself there would be none. When first they fell, angrily she had swiped them away, but no longer. They demanded release, and Dangereuse could not hold them back.

None will ever know, she assured herself as she neared the bottom of the well from which her tears were drawn. *None will know how deep this hurt for what my son witnessed and remembered as I prayed he would not.*

Recalling Sebastian naming his sire a bad man, hating Benoit had yielded the role of his son's savior to his rival as if it were of little consequence, a sob escaped.

"Cease!" she rasped, and gripping the edge of the shelf on which she had set the journals, stared at their leather-bound spines and, breathing deep, felt ache in rising shoulders as if their bowing were natural.

Disgusted over weakness in legs she feared would buckle were she to release the shelf, she firmed them. "Better," she whispered. However, when she tried to turn into the room, her body would not cooperate. As she waited for what had gone out of her legs to return, her hands on the shelf cramped, but she held to it lest the shame of making a heap of herself spill more tears.

After a time, she looked around at the armchair whose embrace she wished she had welcomed before being overwhelmed by emotion. It was not far. She had only to—

Her legs wobbled. Tightening the muscles, she drew more

deep breaths, but they made her head lighten and black spots dance before her eyes.

"Nay!" she cried. And heard a rap. Was it inside her head?

"Lady!"

Outside, she determined and moved her gaze to the door. And now Rhys de Arell was inside.

As her knees began folding, he grew larger. As she crumpled, he became larger yet.

Then his arms caught her up. Or did she but remember the night he carried her from the chamber shared with Benoit? Were this only imagined, when she came out from under the shroud she would be sore from hitting the floor. Until then, comfort here, like it or not.

I like it, she thought. *And should not.*

CHAPTER 17

Here they were again, though unlike that night long ago, light fled eyes that evidenced weeping and his hold was less secure. However, despite the sling, he got her into his arms and delivered her to the chair.

As he straightened, she beseeched, "Tell me I did not..."

"You did."

She shuddered. "I do not know what happened."

"As you were standing when I entered, I assume your knees locked. Sustain that too long and the senses reel. And surely one is more susceptible amid grief."

She started to lower her chin, but as if accepting it was too late to conceal tears, tipped up her face. "I suppose it *is* grief for learning my boy knows more of that night than believed possible. And him naming his sire a bad man and you—" Her voice cracked, and she pressed a fist to her mouth.

Though impulse urged him to his haunches to offer comfort, he was certain she did not seek that.

She lowered her hand. "Benoit was not a bad man. For your presence at The Tournament of Honor, he just behaved badly, and when his girth strap failed, the threads holding him together came apart for believing you—"

"Wrongly believing," he said sharply. "No matter how hard you slap me with accusations, I stand firm I had naught to do with his unseating."

Fresh tears glittered in her eyes. "That is nearly the same he said of your accusation it was by foul means *you* lost the saddle."

He breathed deep. "If one of us lied—and I believe it—the offender is not the son of Griffin de Arell. Just as I would not dishonor my sire with treachery, neither my Wulfen training." He paused, told himself to leave it be, once again failed with this woman. "If you are looking for a *bad man* in all this, heed the observations of a two-year-old who understood who presented a threat and who aided. And do you require further proof, you have your own observations."

When anger leapt across her face, once more calling to mind a she-wolf, he sighed. "I erred in thinking this the opportunity to address my interference with your son. I apologize."

As he started to turn aside, she thrust up out of the chair. And stumbled.

Rhys came back around, but not soon enough to keep her upright. Hindered by the sling, he pressed a hand to the small of her back and followed her down. But though he expected her to push him away, she hesitated, then as on that night, gripped his tunic and dropped her forehead to his collarbone.

"My lady?"

"'Tis difficult to accept what you tell. Though great the coincidence of Benoit's girth strap also failing, I suppose it must be so."

He nearly stated the failure of his was no innocent thing, but this time thought enough to regret as little as possible. And as if for reward, she turned amid pooled skirts, sank from her knees onto her rear, and slid her hands down his tunic to his abdomen.

Desire. Though Rhys balked at acknowledging it, that was what moved through him, causing fingers denied raven strands striped with silver to ache. And making him question if he had made a mistake in not pursuing her. But had he been open to marrying ahead of proving himself a warrior in full, that possibility would have slammed closed the moment he saw her in the arms of one whose theft of victory cast out what little remained of his friendship with Benoit.

"I am sorry I thought so ill of you," she said. "That night, he lost control, shaking our son as if that would quiet one pained by another ear infection." She dropped back her head and peered at him through tears. "I am grateful you aided us, and I regret the injury done you."

More desire, he thought as her words, then parting of lips, made his heart thump hard.

And harder when she returned to her knees, looked to his mouth, and said, "I would know."

Feeling every muscle strain to hold himself apart, he considered her down the length of his nose. "What would you know?"

"What might have been, though I may regret that knowledge." She slid her palms up his chest, curled her fingers into his shoulders. "I have only ever ventured a glance behind, but now I venture a glance ahead."

He swallowed. "I did not come for this."

"And I did not think I truly wanted it."

He told himself to pull away, but her breath across his lips intoxicated.

Then she tilted her face higher and said, "I do want it."

"Dange," he murmured.

"Rhys," she whispered.

Their familiar use of names intensifying awareness of the differences between their bodies, he pressed his mouth to hers, and when she sighed into him, groaned into her.

Dangerous desire, he thought and kissed her with greater urgency, then gathered her so near her chest conformed to his.

"Rhys."

Her voice like a breeze running its fingers through spring's softly unfurling leaves did something to him not done by other women whose attentions he sought or who sought his—something so wondrous it defied resistance. And something more when her fingers tightened on his shoulders.

Though his cautious side warned against yielding further to the temptation of Dangereuse of the Wulfriths, the incautious side made him angle his head and deepen the kiss.

When she gasped, he interpreted it as passion and permission to further explore one as awhirl as he, though he knew it wrong to move them in a direction that could compromise their honor. And when suddenly she pressed her mouth very hard against his...

Was this greater passion though it felt almost punishment? If the latter, who was being punished? Him or her? Might it even be the departed Benoit?

Rhys stilled his hands that had begun wandering over her and lifted his head. "What is this, Dangereuse?"

Her lids rose, but not enough to meet his gaze, then she dropped back on her heels.

Wondering if she who invited him to taste and explore her mouth would accuse him of trespass and seduction—and wishing he was entirely innocent—Rhys straightened.

"You stopped the same as he, and yet you are not the same," she whispered.

The only sense he could make of her observation being she compared him to the man she had wed, he said, "I am not the same as Benoit—just as you, who oft puts me in mind of a she-wolf, are unlike any woman I have known."

"She-wolf?" Her eyes shot to his. "You set me alongside Queen Isabella?"

He knew King Edward's mother earned that name for vengeance worked on her husband that saw him removed from England's throne with the aid of her lover who, though he gained the queen's bed, failed to gain her son's throne.

"Since I believe naming her such is an insult to the female wolf who nourishes and protects her young as was not our former queen's priority with her children," he said, "never would I equate you with her."

Her gaze wavered. "Then though I am opposed to my son becoming a warrior, making me appear overly protective, I ought to consider it a compliment to be named a *she-wolf?*"

"As intended, though I concur Sebastian is better suited to the ranks of those who fight."

"Because of his Wulfrith blood."

"And Wulfrith spirit." Though Rhys did wish to speak further about the boy, knowing it best to return to what had just transpired between them before it was swept out of sight, he said, "You told you believe I am not the same as your husband. How?"

She was silent so long he thought she would not answer, but she said, "Our kiss. Though I began to feel you sought to brand me and for that aggressed to discourage you, 'twas not your intent, was it?"

Meaning it had been Benoit's? Rhys started to turn over those stones, but they needed no turning. Little surprise the one who resorted to foul play for acclaim and unexpectedly gained a Wulfrith bride had regarded Dangereuse as a possession, nor that she had disliked being made to feel that.

"You wished to know how it would have been with us," he

said, "and I tell never would I have behaved in a way that made you feel you must use aggression to discourage me." He paused, then deciding it best not to say it should be obvious there would have been passion for passion had they been joined for life, said, "When I wed one with whom I wish to pass the remainder of my years, our vows and the ring I place on her hand will more than suffice to tell all she is mine." Then he added, "As I shall be hers."

She stared as if seeking the truth of that, then began rising.

Rhys reached to her, and though she ignored his offer, only when her legs proved steady did he lower a hand that had earlier explored her curves. And wished to do so again.

Lord, help me, Dangereuse silently appealed. Though she told herself their kisses, caresses, and murmurings were in the past and must be evermore, it was a struggle to find herself beyond who she had become in his arms—and outside the shame of seeking intimacy to answer the glancing question that should have remained that.

Now she knew herself capable of feeling far more than what Benoit had roused and that the intensity was mutual. Rhys had not sought to brand her, that fear making her react aggressively as done with Benoit. His was but a response to shared passion.

Still, it was good she cast her husband's trespasses at him. Otherwise...

"I hope in time you will forgive me for behavior unbecoming a De Arell and a Wulfen-trained knight," he said.

She braved his regard. "If I am forgiven for behavior unbecoming a Wulfrith and a lady, I shall afford you the same."

He inclined his head, but remained unmoving as if there was more to resolve.

Not wishing to address it now with lips sore from wondrous plundering and fingers remembering firm muscles, she clasped her hands before her. "Since I assume you satisfied your hunger and thirst after I departed the hall, I shall leave you to your rest."

"No need. As I have hours of training ahead, I shall return to the outer bailey."

She frowned at the arm supported by a sling. "Training?"

"Aye, to strengthen and better the skill of my left arm while the right heals. Though since my knighting I have continued practicing with the left for such an event, lest more is required of it between now and full healing of the other, your uncle shall work with me."

She knew she should not continue comparing him to Benoit, but the thought squeezed in that when her husband practiced at arms she had only seen him wield weapons with his dominant hand.

Realizing she looked through the one who watched her, she asked, "For that you departed the donjon early?"

"Nay, to accompany Sir Owen and his men on their patrol of the demesne."

As Benoit would not have done, another thought slipped in. "All is well?"

"There are no recent sightings of any who do not belong here, nor disturbances in the villages, but that does not mean the brigands who troubled these lands are not out there, nor those who seek to reclaim Lady Vianne." He glanced at the ceiling. "She continues to isolate in her chamber?"

"Aye, my maid checks on her often to ensure she has all she needs."

"Do not mistake her for a coward, Lady Dangereuse.

Indeed, I think her remarkably courageous. Thus, she will descend soon."

Why this jealousy as though he professes love for her, which is his right regardless of how fervently he kissed and embraced me? Dangereuse questioned, next whether he had enjoyed the same intimacy with that woman.

Raising her chin, she said, "The lady will be welcome at hearth and table when she shows herself."

"I thank you."

She stepped past him, tugged at her bodice and smoothed her skirts. As for her eyes, hopefully they were not as red as when he entered. As for her lips, they were tender, but less than when he pulled back from her aggression. As for her braid...

She recalled fingers thrusting up through the hair at her nape, his kiss intensifying, then her retaliation lest he think to reduce her to a thing owned rather than desired. Though she had not known it then, there was a great difference between a hard kiss and a deep one.

As she neared the door he had left open, he said, "Lady Dangereuse."

She turned, felt her braid sweep her back. "Sir Rhys?"

He halted before her. "Since henceforth it will be more awkward between us for how well we now know what might have been, I am thinking this the time to discuss Sebastian."

She nearly looked away. "Now 'tis known he saw and understood more of that night than believed, what is there to discuss?"

"My apology for overstepping, and again after you gave charge of him to your maid."

She raised her eyebrows.

"Further I aided with his math, and he became more enthusiastic once the numbers were made meaningful."

"Meaningful in the context of a warrior," she said, some accusation there.

"Aye, but I think you must agree that had I pressed upon him the importance of numbers in the life of a priest, lack of enthusiasm would have affected his grasp of the process."

She did not want to agree. Thus, she did not respond.

"Then there is the matter of his hearing."

She blinked. "Hearing?"

"After I arrived at Lillia, you said he suffered an infection of the ear at the tournament and it was not the first time."

"Ere attaining his second year, he was struck half a dozen times in one ear or the other," she said warily.

"And 'tis not uncommon for him to ask for clearly spoken words to be repeated?"

"He does on occasion, and though methinks you suggest it indicates something is wrong, 'tis just the excitable boy of him —that there are so many thoughts running through his head it is hard to attend to all that is spoken or asked of him."

"As a child, I had difficulty listening well when all was astir, but I do not think that is all that affects him, Lady Dangereuse. Often he speaks louder than needed."

"As do many boys." It was said more defensively than intended.

"Too, he watches the lips of those speaking, and more so when something is repeated that he missed or misunderstood. Thus, the ear infections may have caused some hearing loss."

"Hearing loss?" she exclaimed.

"The daughter of our smithy at Castle Mathe had numerous ear infections in infancy. Not until she was nearly eight did a healer determine her poor behavior was due to frustration over understanding others and following instructions. Thus, it was not a deficiency of character nor mind, but a mild hearing loss."

Dangereuse started to reject what he suggested, certain as she and her family were that difficulties with Sebastian since he began walking and talking were a result of the trauma of witnessing his sire's death, but she hesitated. Was it possible tantrums and occasional unresponsiveness were caused by frustration over muffled or missed words and the reaction of others who believed him stubborn or defiant?

She looked to hands clasped at her waist and, fearful of this new understanding, breathed, "Oh." Though her boy might not have been as adversely affected by that night as believed, was it preferable he had a physical defect he could not overcome or that one day, amid the godliness and peace of a monastery, ill memories might be conquered?

"Dangereuse?" A hand closed over her tangled ones. "'Tis better to know the truth of an ill thing than allow it to disguise itself as something else."

Such powerful hands he has, she thought, staring at long fingers curved over the mess of hers, broad knuckles, and the back tapering to a thick wrist.

"Always it is better," he restated.

She looked up and thought it strange his piercing blue eyes should warm rather than chill. How could something that appeared capable of putting a hole in one suffuse her with heat?

"If what I believe about your son's hearing is true, something can be done about it."

"Done? If he is so afflicted, I know of naught that can be done."

"As he understands most of what is spoken, he can learn to compensate beyond what he does instinctively, and others made aware of the loss can adjust accordingly."

Dangereuse longed for the chair into which his arms had delivered her following her collapse—to sink into its embrace, fold over herself, and pray through yet another grim revelation.

Resisting the urge to once more brace weakening knees, she said, "It seems much gratitude is owed you—so much I beseech you not to exert further effort on behalf of my son and me since I do not think I can cancel a greater debt."

"Greater, my lady? For the care provided me here, I live. And my charge, Lady Vianne, is safe for your uncle's foresight and the hospitality of your home." His brow smoothed. "If any is indebted, 'tis I."

Deciding to let that argument lie, she said, "Lest our return to the hall add to speculation by those who may have noted this was my destination and next yours, best we depart separately."

He nodded. "As I have kept your uncle waiting long, with your leave I shall go first."

"Until the dinner hour, then," she said.

"More likely supper, since once more the scent of snow is on the air and as many productive hours as possible should be wrung out of the blue sky ere it goes grey again."

"I shall see you then, Sir Rhys."

He stepped around her, and Dangereuse did not move until the tread of his boots faded, then she let her chin fall.

She prayed for her boy. Prayed it was better he hear less than be deeply disturbed by the horrors of that night that yet intruded on his waking hours and dreams. Prayed for wisdom to determine whether the Church or Wulfen was a better fit. Prayed if she wavered, the Lord would make clear the best course, not only to her but her eldest brother who had the power to impose his will on her, which Sebastian would wholeheartedly support if it meant growing up with a sword in hand.

"Lord," she entreated, then opened her eyes and savored

the steady pace of her heart—until remembrance swept her back to Rhys' arms.

She knew not to linger there, but excused the indulgence by telling herself she could more easily put behind her what had happened here were she to comb through the memories rather than allow them to spring upon her when next she saw him.

A quarter hour later, she nodded.

Loneliness and longing for what her brother and sister had with their spouses was responsible for inviting his kiss.

His shortening of her name to *Dange* and the affection implied was responsible for allowing the kiss to progress.

The discovery that what she, on the cusp of womanhood, overheard years ago might not be true—that a woman's enjoyment of sexual intimacy was exaggerated—was responsible for allowing the kiss to progress even further.

The difference between wondrous warmth and speeding heart felt with Rhys and what she experienced with Benoit who had named her *little wolf* was responsible for permitting the kiss to draw dangerously near sinful relations.

"She-wolf," she murmured. And for Rhys' explanation of that, clasped it to her.

Would the two of them have crossed a dangerous line had passion mistaken for branding not put her in mind of Benoit?

She looked around the study, then forcefully said, "We would not have crossed it. We would have returned to our senses. We would not have sinned so far."

CHAPTER 18

Lady Vianne. Perhaps here the truest reason Rhys de Arell would have returned to his senses had Dangereuse failed. The woman having come below-stairs and acknowledged her hostess with a nod, she had ascended the dais and taken the chair offered her beside her protector.

Throughout the evening's repast, Dangereuse aspired to ignore them, which should have been easy since they were several seats removed and she was unable to hear their exchange above castle dwellers relaxing into conversations between bites and sips. However, occasionally the deep of his voice and soft of the lady's was heard, and sidelong she saw their heads draw near and twice the woman close elegant fingers over the knight's forearm. Once he had done the same to her, though that was when she pushed her goblet toward a servant bearing a pitcher of wine.

It was not the first nor second time Lady Vianne requested a refill, but though he appeared to caution against imbibing further, his staying hand could be more an excuse to touch her.

Chest having tightened throughout the meal, Dangereuse wondered if she should have allowed her son the occasional treat of supper in the hall rather than feed him early to ensure a good night's rest. However, the distraction he provided would have been outweighed by her perseveration over observing him conversing as done earlier in seeking greater evidence of a hearing deficiency—a possibility that enlarged each time she saw what Rhys believed her son's instinctive means of understanding lost or muffled speech.

When finally Uncle Owen announced the meal's end, drinking vessels clattered, chairs and benches scraped, dogs emerged from beneath tables to search out scraps, and servants began clearing away the remains and moving furniture to transform the room into a sleeping hall that accommodated the majority of those residing at Lillia.

Though tempted to relieve Amanda who would sit with Sebastian until her mistress appeared, dutifully Dangereuse joined those gathering near the hearth to pass some of the winter night in companionship ahead of burrowing beneath blankets of which there could not be enough when the weather turned pitiless as once more done this day.

Rhys lingered the same as most, as did Lady Vianne, though Dangereuse had expected her to return to her chamber as the fatigued Murielle had done, especially since the woman appeared in need of support as she crossed to the bench onto which Rhys handed her.

Unsurprisingly, Ferrand joined a gathering on the opposite side of the hearth, continuing to distance himself from Benoit's rival as if fearing a confrontation that would render his words more apologetic than what they had reverted to upon Rhys' arrival at Lillia. Not because her brother-in-law was guilty of wrongdoing as Rhys believed. Surely because he thought the failure of Benoit's girth strap was the knight's retribution for his own having failed at Wulfen, though never had he spoken of the jousts nor his injuries the morn after the death of his brother who had surely thrashed him for not guarding his mount well.

As she started to lower to a bench occupied by one of Wulfen's advanced squires, her uncle said, "Sit beside me, Dangereuse," and gestured to the chair on his right angled toward the long, upholstered bench Rhys and Lady Vianne shared with two knights.

Withholding her gaze from Rhys lest his eyes upon her make her flush for how intimate they were earlier, she did as bid.

As Owen of the Wulfriths, believed as formidable a warrior as her sire, considered those with whom he kept company, including other Wulfen knights and squires standing with their backs to the hearth, she realized how exclusive this group and guessed it intentional.

When he gripped his hands between his knees and firmed his gaze upon Lady Vianne, it was confirmed. "You appear sufficiently recovered, my lady."

Silently, Dangereuse agreed her guest of beautifully brown hair fashioned into braids looked healthier for rest, a thorough bathing, and loan of a gown belonging to the keeper of Lillia. The only thing one might question beyond her marked face was the unsteady stride that presented after her indulgence in wine. Hopefully, she was not wont to overly imbibe since such could be the ruin of women the same as men.

Sitting straighter, the lady widened the space between her shoulder and Rhys'. "I am much improved." She looked to Dangereuse. "I appreciate all you provided, including privacy in which to put myself back together after..." Her eyes slid to the floor, then with what seemed grim resolve, she returned to Owen.

"As well as possible, tell what happened after Sir Rhys sent you on to Broehne Castle," he prompted.

Her lips parted, permitting a glimpse of pretty teeth, but no words followed.

"What may seem insignificant, my lady, could be the difference between overtaking and punishing those who followed you across the channel and the suffering of others."

She looked to Rhys.

"Though difficult to tell, we must know," he said, and when her eyes moved to the others about the hall, he added, "We are distant enough that what is told here remains here, but if you would be more comfortable in the solar—"

"Nay, this serves. I just..." She sighed. "When you sent me ahead of you, I departed with little hope of seeing you again and much shame you were unlikely to withstand those you kept from me." Her eyes moved to Owen. "Though afeared of the ride to an unknown place, especially in foul weather, more I shuddered over what would happen were I unable to reach King Edward and was returned to...him."

Rollon de Talliere, Dangereuse silently named the one Rhys had revealed was among the French king's advisors and the woman's lover.

"I know of whom you speak, Lady Vianne," Owen said.

With what appeared disapproval—and hurt—she shot her eyes to Rhys who had shared some of her tale, but then firmed her jaw and continued, "For days I stayed ahead of my pursuers, narrowly avoiding those who grew in number."

"Grew?" Dangereuse's uncle questioned.

"Aye, 'twas not only those of De Talliere seeking my scent. Five—perhaps more—had joined them, and when they passed near, I recognized their voices as being of the English."

"You are certain?"

"Quite. When I was—" She shook her head. "I get ahead of events, but I shall return to those foul Englishmen. In trying to reach Broehne, which I began to believe a different direction for catching no sight of it nor encountering settled communities, the only homes I happened on were those falling into ruin, which I guessed the leavings of isolated souls taken by the Great Mortality. Though I feared sickness in the dark dirty corners, to gain shelter I traded the certainty of killing cold for painful cold."

She rubbed her palms and fingers as if remembering the chill, looked to those waiting for her to continue, then splayed her hands atop the woolen gown draping her legs. "When a better day than the others dawned, boasting nearly as much blue sky as white, it gave me heart to find my way forward. Less cautious for seeing none of De Talliere's men the day before and thinking they accepted I was lost to them, at midday I was sighted by three riders. Though they were too distant to identify, ere they gave chase I knew it was those who sought to return me to France. Shortly, I was overtaken by one of De Talliere's men with whom I was acquainted, the others known to me only by voices that earlier revealed the English of them."

Her eyes returned to Rhys. "Wearing your sword and dagger, Sir Gustave swept me onto his horse. Then after assuring the English—who were surprisingly well dressed— the coin promised them would soon be paid, he ordered them to take my mount and ride ahead to alert the others of my capture."

"Well-dressed Englishmen?" Dangereuse's uncle said. "Of the nobility?"

She jerked a shoulder. "Certes, just as their garments were not of the common, neither their speech."

He looked to Rhys. "You are unaware of English joining your pursuers?"

"Unknown, Sir Owen. Likely after I was left for dead the French engaged the unsavory to aid in bringing the lady to ground."

Dangereuse's uncle thought on that, nodded. "When I assured the sheriff my men and I would seek to uproot those trespassing on Lillia's lands, he told of a squire whose family was set upon by brigands en route to their home in the North. Though he followed the men in the hope of recovering their valuables, wisely he accepted death lay at the end of playing the hero and but observed them at a stream. He said some who cast off their mantles revealed garments too fine for ruffians and the speech of several far from rustic."

"Then it may be the same who joined De Talliere's men," Lady Vianne breathed, golden eyes wide.

"If so, likely they were engaged after reaching Wulfen-shire," Owen said and motioned her to resume her tale.

The cords in her slender neck were so strained, Dangereuse guessed it was becoming more difficult to tell, and that made her grateful Murielle had retired to her chamber since what had yet to be revealed would surely account for how the lady presented upon her arrival at Lillia—a state not unknown to the young woman, as evidenced by the misbegotten babe she would deliver.

Wondering if it would also be this lady's fate to birth a child sown by violence, Dangereuse sent up a prayer that were it so, the babe half of her body would be cherished enough the other half would become little more than a shadow as she had hope for Murielle for how often the young woman caressed her belly.

Lady Vianne cleared her throat. "I nearly beseeched the English not to leave me alone with Sir Gustave for him being desirous of me, but knowing my chance of escape was greater were he the only one I must thwart, I closed my mouth. As we rode opposite the way they had gone, his hands roamed my body, and oft he looked around as if to ensure what he planned would have no witnesses. I bore it, praying for an opportunity to put him on the ground and the reins in my hands."

She swallowed. "It came when he stopped beneath a great pine whose reach was so wide little snow had accumulated beneath it. When he made to dismount, I braced to flee, but he had wrapped my braid around a hand. Before I could take the reins, he pulled me down beside him."

Momentarily, she closed her eyes. "When I threatened to reveal to his lord he had possessed what did not belong to him, he told no thing I spoke would be believed once De Talliere's hope I was taken against my will was dashed by his and his companions' testimony I ran away each time I could have run to them."

As if becoming aware her shoulders bowed, she pressed them back. "I did not cease struggling, and fool that he was in shedding his weaponry ahead of taking what I would not give, he did not cast Sir Rhys' weapon belt as far as his own. Thus, I got my hand around the dagger and put it between our chests."

Vividly recalling the Wulfrith dagger that accidentally bled out her husband's life, Dangereuse felt her skin pale.

"When I warned I would gut him, he tried to take the dagger from me." Her hand came off her lap and clamped over that of the man beside her. "I had no wish to end another's life, but by my hand Sir Gustave was slain."

Dangereuse did not realize her gaze remained on the lady's fingers atop Rhys' until he turned his up and folded them over hers. Whatever coursed her, which could not be jealousy, it freed her of memories of Benoit's bloodletting.

"I am sorry for what befell you," her uncle said, "and

though the sheriff will need to hear the same and more, this suffices."

She inclined her head. "Know that though what he intended was vile, better had he violated me than I be burdened by memories of his death." Catching Dangereuse's startle, and surely noting the surprise on her face, she said, "I speak from the heart and mind of one whose innocent years are well behind me, Lady."

Silently, Dangereuse agreed that being the lover of the King of France's advisor—possibly only to gain information for King Edward—would harden one to the act nearly perpetrated against her. But could it be deemed a good thing she had been prepared for such? Nay, though familiarity with foul trespasses surely allowed her to keep some of her wits about her beneath that tree, such an education could not be named good regardless of how complicit she was in becoming a spy.

Of course, I consider how it would scar me, Dangereuse reminded herself. *I who could not tolerate Benoit's possessive kisses.*

Her thoughts shifting to Rhys' kiss, she looked to his hand holding the lady's. She did not think they were lovers, but there could be something there that might become something more with time and nurturing.

If only I did not care, she thought, *especially since he did not mean to give me reason, but...*

"I would like to gain my rest." Lady Vianne drew her fingers from beneath Rhys'. "As fatigue weakens my legs, would you loan me your arm in ascending the stairs, Lady Dangereuse?"

"Of course." She crossed to the woman she expected more affected by excess drink, though one could not discount exhaustion magnified by the emotions roused this eve.

Arm in arm, they wove among those beginning to collect their pallets and claim a place as near the hearth as possible to partake of the heat Puck would ensure lasted through the night.

When they reached the first landing, Dangereuse heard the hall's great doors open. There would have been nothing unusual in that ahead of all settling down for the night, but there was urgency about some voices. Thus, if not for Lady Vianne's questionable balance, she would have had the woman continue without her.

Assuring herself her uncle could handle whatever disrupted the night, she assisted her guest in removing her garments down to her borrowed chemise and settled her on the mattress.

Grateful the brazier had been tended by a chambermaid who made the rounds of the upper rooms ahead of retiring for the night, she paused at the door. "I pray your sleep is peaceful."

"I would like that," Lady Vianne's voice defied the blanket drawn up beneath her nose. "It has been so long."

Dangereuse sent up a prayer for her healing, then returned to the hall to find that whatever had unsettled it was resolved for the multitude now on their pallets.

"Uncle," she said as he advanced on her. "I heard—"

"Ill tidings delivered from the Baron of Abingdale."

When he halted before her, she asked. "What has happened?"

At the end of his telling, she looked to the corridor Rhys had traversed before her return belowstairs. And was tempted to go to him, though it was not her place to offer comfort.

"No surprise," she said, throat tight, eyes stinging. "Still..."

He squeezed her shoulder. "'Tis late, and some losses are best faced in solitude ahead of condolences. Be assured, the morrow will be soon enough to offer yours."

She agreed, and when he turned her toward the stairs, kept pace though her feet longed to drag.

The morrow, she told herself, *as is appropriate for a hostess.*

WHAT ELSE COULD GO DREADFULLY—EVEN deathly—wrong? Rhys questioned where he had lowered to his haunches to shift the logs, then remained there to rake over the suffering incurred in delivering Lady Vianne and her intelligence to England.

He had known his squire likely numbered among his losses, but confirmation of it for discovery of the young man's body upon Abingdale—a boot projecting from a snowdrift ahead of further snowfall—gripped him so hard he felt unprepared for the tidings.

Because of hope, he thought with guilt-salted resentment. Though less and less he had expected his squire to be recovered whole, he had harbored more hope than he should have. Rhys de Arell had misled himself, and now great ache acknowledging the young man would never be knighted—that in service to his lord and king, a single spurless boot showed where he breathed his last.

He closed his lids and through them observed flames that ought to warm but could not for this chill anger that the desires of others wielded destructive power over the lives of men and women who answered to them. But his anger was not exclusive to the King of France's advisor, nor England's king who benefitted from the intimacy between De Talliere and the lady spy.

Some of it seeped into the fabric of Lady Vianne whose insistence on personally delivering her intelligence to England's ruler led to all this.

He did not want to feel ill toward one who, long deprived

of family and country and having served her sovereign throughout, held close her latest findings so she might cast off what must have become shackles. However, now among those who sacrificed greatly for her was a worthy young man.

Rhys opened his eyes and watched the flames lap at logs with fiery tongues—charring and slowly consuming the bones of trees as was done those of men and women rendered dispensable—in this case for the war between two countries.

Ever men, whether they stand high or low, want what others possess, he reflected, and could not exclude his family, which had engaged in a feud with the neighboring Boursiers and Verduns for more than a generation—one that found no end until this king of England ordered marriage alliances between the three barons while Rhys was a boy.

Unexpectedly, the third Edward's interference had achieved far greater peace than expected, discovery of the truth behind their feud and love between enemies healing old wounds. A pity the same could not be affected between this island kingdom and the continental one. Instead, the marriage between Edward II of England and Princess Isabella of France, which resulted in the birth of this Edward, provided their son a strong claim to the French throne when the last male of Isabella's line passed. For that, this war. For that, spies flitting about both royal courts. For that, murderous French upon Lillia's lands.

"Lord, let what Lady Vianne imparts to Edward save far more lives than those lost," he rasped. "Let it not have been in vain." He stood and, rubbing the healing arm whose sling he had shed, wished for daylight in which to practice his weaponry so sooner he could aid in ridding this demesne of those his and Lady Vianne's presence delivered here. Though Sir Gustave was dead, the others who served De Talliere would seek to complete their mission as required to ensure a welcome home.

"I shall stop you," he said. "And God help me do I put vengeance ahead of duty." Over and again, that last was his prayer until he slept amid dreams fraught with vengeance first, duty second.

CHAPTER 19

December 25, 1353

Was this the sense of portentous ill she believed gifted her to avoid dangerous situations? Or was it merely anticipation of further setbacks bred by a day given to veering off its path?

The latter, Dangereuse assured herself. As this was the day God's people celebrated Christ's birth, it must be.

Christmas Day had begun well with a beautiful pre-dawn mass that marked the end of Advent and the start of the season of feasting that would stretch into the first week of the new year.

The priest of the village of Falls Vale, who arrived last eve with a good number of parishioners, had conducted the service since Castle Lillia remained in need of a man of God to replace the one lost.

Despite the tight fit of those who poured into the chapel ere dawn, good will had abounded. Now with the sun well risen, she was determined it would continue regardless of what must be done to accommodate those from distant villages arriving in greater numbers than expected due to warming temperatures.

Even if portions of viands must be smaller, the ongoing preparations of which Murielle supervised, all would enjoy the meal provided by their lady, in addition to relief from a fortnight of labors.

As the feast that was to have commenced at noon must be delayed two hours to correct the deficit of food as much as possible and provide extra time for those straggling in, the challenge was to keep the guests occupied—especially the children, their excitement raising a din worthy of Sebastian who was eager to lead his peers in all manner of mischief and sought to do the same with those of greater age, most of whom politely disregarded or subtly scorned him.

Though Benoit would have been offended to see his son given the shoulder, Dangereuse approved. Sebastian was fairly highborn, but were he to rise above others, the privilege and responsibility of directing them must be earned.

In the Church, she silently maintained, though since receiving tidings of the squire's death a sennight past, oft she had turned over not only what her brothers believed the best path for her son but Rhys who, though he tried to distance himself from Sebastian as well as Dangereuse, had become an object of fascination.

Not only did the boy attach himself to his great uncle in order to observe Rhys at practice in the training yard when the weather was tolerable, but with some enthusiasm worked numbers as demonstrated by the knight. Each time he arrived at the correct answer, he credited Rhys with his success—and with learning a warrior's strategy.

There was nothing she could do to shift his attention to

another. He admired his great uncle and, to a lesser degree, Ferrand, but he fixed on Rhys just as ever he did her brothers who were not likely to appear any time soon.

Though word arrived two days past that the sickness at Wulfen Castle had abated and most of the ill fully recovered, their Christmas celebrations would be held inside their walls to ensure what they had overcome did not become the bane of others. Thus, though Warin might travel to Lillia once he concluded his business with King Edward, it could be weeks before Hector or Rémy was seen. Of course, that surely suited Murielle, though she did not voice relief her husband was unlikely to appear ahead of her child's birth.

Dangereuse shifted her thoughts to the festivities she had moved from the packed hall to snow-laden hills surrounding an iced pond a quarter league from Castle Lillia.

It had been challenging to arrange for the transport of refreshments and orderly procession of over a hundred guests to this sparkling place where all could be entertained with games and activities that included traversing hills on sleds, shields, and an old iron door, and the frozen pond with bone skates fixed to boots and poles in the hands of those less certain of their balance. However, with the aid of Ferrand, Puck, and others, Murielle now had the time needed to provide a feast worthy of Christmas Day.

Dangereuse, mounted beside Lady Vianne who often appeared at meals and imbibed less than the first night she ventured belowstairs, lifted her chin from the fur collar of her green mantle and raised a gloved hand to sip spiced wine served to combat the cold which the bright of the sun could not entirely dispel.

She lowered the cup, causing the red sleeve of a gown whose skirt was embroidered with black vines to fall over her wrist, then moved her regard from those gliding and poling across the ice to the hill down which Sebastian sledded with Puck.

"'Tis good the hall shrunk," Lady Vianne said as she considered the reveling villagers and castle folk. "When possible, methinks this ought to be part of celebrating Christ's birth." Her mouth curved. "Such purity."

"Now scarred by sleds, skates, and boots," Dangereuse murmured.

The lady looked around. "Just as our Lord was scarred to provide hope ahead of joy, so is the snow and ice beneath which lies good ground that shall green and bloom come spring."

Her words surprised since Dangereuse would have expected that were the surface of the woman scratched—and not deeply—bitterness would be found beneath. "You sound nearly a poet, Lady Vianne."

She gave a little laugh. "I am not unaccomplished with such but—oh!—were that my vocation. But perhaps now I am home." Beneath the woolen mantle provided by Dangereuse, her shoulders rose with breath. "Too long I have been gone, too many years lost. Though I lived in splendor in France, I would not return there even were I believed merely a fickle lover rather than an English agent."

As this was the first time she opened a door into her past outside the presence of others, Dangereuse said, "Greatly you regret the life you chose?"

The woman blinked. "You think I chose it?"

"I..." Dangereuse smiled apologetically. "Forgive the assumption."

Lady Vianne sighed. "I was not entirely without choice, but as the options were no fit for my emotions nor maturity at the time, I fell into a deeper hole from which Sir Rhys kindly extracted me. Not that he had much choice."

"Are you—?" Nearly speaking what she ought not, Dangereuse was grateful those words could cast no light on her.

"Am I in love with that honorable knight?" the lady proved such gratitude was for naught. "Were I open to such and he could feel the same for me, possible. However, I am not looking to belong to any man ever again, and if Sir Rhys' heart is pointed in any direction, 'tis not mine." She raised her eyebrows. "Tell how *you* would answer that question, my lady."

Dangereuse startled. "I have no cause to answer it."

The woman's golden eyes delved hers, then her mouth curved. "And yet I sense something between you even when separated by the span of a room—as if both hold your breath to calm pounding hearts."

Dangereuse gasped. "I know not how you came by this *sense,* Lady Vianne, but I assure you—"

"My lady!"

It was Ferrand who saved her from defending what she wished defensible. He who patrolled the immediate area with others lest they become complacent over the return of peace to Lillia's lands spurred his horse toward her.

She glanced at Sebastian on the shoulders of Puck who climbed the hill with the sled under an arm, then turned her grey-speckled palfrey to receive her brother-in-law.

He reined in, and the slight smile he gave Lady Vianne that was more than he afforded most women with whom he came into contact, made her wonder if he was taken with her the same as a number of the garrison and her uncle's men.

When he looked to her, she prompted, "Squire Ferrand?"

"Sir Owen has intercepted an unexpected visitor." He jerked his chin over his shoulder. "They come now."

So they did. Numbering three, they included her uncle,

Rhys who had joined the outer patrol to ensure the villagers' safe travel, and her second eldest brother who was the only sibling of fair hair. Indeed, so fair that those who recorded their family's history believed it passed to him by the Saxon lady, Hawisa Wulfrith—the first bride of their line whose surname her Norman husband was required to take when his people conquered England three hundred years gone.

Dangereuse raised a hand and, as Warin neared, confirmed the physician's prediction. The scars of his burns sustained last summer while aiding in freeing Sheriff D'Arci's wife and Murielle from the knave holding them at Romary Castle faded. They would not entirely disappear, but that side of his face had become a closer match for the nearly flawless side.

"I shall return to my patrol," Ferrand said, and she knew he might linger if not for Rhys.

As he turned aside, she smiled a welcome at her brother.

"'Tis good to see you, Sister!" Barely sparing Lady Vianne a glance, Warin guided his horse alongside Dangereuse's, put an arm around her shoulders, and kissed her forehead.

As he drew back, she brushed her lips across his jaw. "I thought it too much to hope you would soon appear at Lillia."

He smiled, movement of those muscles making the scarring a bit more visible amid whiskers. "After I finished my business with the king who shall require much of one elevated to the baronage—and who unsuccessfully pressed me to choose a bride from among his eldest daughter's ladies—I paused at Stern. There I arranged for my daughter's move to Romary where she will reside under the care of Esta who has been released from our grandmother's service to accommodate me."

More to accommodate little Charliese who has become attached to the maid, Dangereuse did not say, nor did she need to look to her uncle to know of his reaction to talk of Esta. Just as during Owen's rare visits to Stern, discomfort and something else that caused speculation among Dangereuse and her sisters was on the air here. Though fairly certain their grandmother knew what afflicted her second eldest son and maid, Lady Héloise held it close.

Love gone awry, her youngest sister, Fira, had named it.

Thwarted love, Ondine had suggested.

Unresolved infatuation, Dangereuse had determined—and was hopeful of it, though not for the disparity of rank between the noble knight and servant. Rather, that since the two walked wide around each other, infatuation was easier to bear than love.

"It was at Stern I learned of the sickness at Wulfen," her brother continued. "Blessedly, 'tis nearly past."

"As we have been told. But why are you here, Warin? Though I am glad of it, I question why you do not pass Christmas with your daughter at Stern—or bring her to Lillia. You know I would welcome her, as would her cousin." She smiled. "Not that Bastian would admit it."

"This I know. Unfortunately, whilst I was at court word came of unrest upon Woodhearst."

She glanced at Rhys who, the same as her uncle, listened to their exchange. "You speak of the brigands who trouble these lands?"

Warin settled his hands atop the saddle's pommel. "They or others who believe it their right to take what does not belong to them cause some trouble, but of greater concern is the keeper of one of Romary's sister castles. Though I reproved him for poor management and warned he would be replaced if he did not put all in order, he tests my lordship. For it, the villagers he oversees have risen against him and a recent clash turned bloody."

Since the pestilence had claimed a shocking number of the population, the fairly stable balance between a lord and those who served him in exchange for protection, land upon which to raise crops, and wages, had become delicately balanced. No longer was it usual for there to be a greater number of laborers to work the land than needed. Quite the opposite. And most were aware of the shift that increased the value of their labor, empowering them as never before.

Ever the barons of Wulfen had provided well for their people, giving as was given them, but even their family had to increase compensation to hold restless tenants to the land despite new laws intended to prevent them from seeking opportunities elsewhere. In contrast, the former Baron of Woodhearst had refused to budge and his castellans followed his direction, but life would improve for those people when Dangereuse's brother settled into his new title and set to fixing what was broken.

"Hence, though my men and I must resume our travel by late afternoon," Warin continued, "we will join you and yours for the feast providing you can accommodate our numbers."

Declining to ask how many would further stretch Lillia's foodstuffs, she said, "Happily all shall be provided for." She squeezed the hand of this brother who had known great sorrow during the pestilence, not only sharing the loss of their father but losing a beloved wife. Though it had seemed he might not recover, since he had forgiven their older brother for unwittingly introducing the pestilence to Stern and claimed the daughter fathered while serving King Edward in France, he had returned to a good semblance of himself. There were yet grieving edges about him, but God willing they would continue to dull so when next he wed it would not be only to gain a male heir.

As she withdrew her hand, his gaze slipped past her. For it lingering on Lady Vianne and causing his brow to line, she thought that just as Ferrand deemed the woman worthy of more than passing interest, so did he.

"Forgive me, Brother, this is Lady Vianne Wardieu." Did he stiffen? "Lady Vianne, my brother, Sir Warin Wulfrith."

Slowly, his eyes traveled her, causing the woman's chin to rise, then he said, "Forgive my long perusal which will not render you recognizable as was Sir Rhys whom I did not expect to encounter here—indeed, feared the same as King Edward that his delay in returning to London meant the Baron of Blackwood had lost his heir."

As Dangereuse struggled to keep her eyes from Rhys, the effort warming her more than the heated wine, she heard the woman gasp.

"My lady?" Warin drawled as done with his sisters when he guessed something they did not wish known, though in this case there was no teasing as if—

"Then King Edward told you of his expectation of Sir Rhys' arrival," the lady stated.

"Aye, and was eager for completion of the knight's mission that was to deliver vital intelligence." He smiled tautly. "I can say with certainty it was only intelligence Edward expected to receive at court, not its procurer."

All here understood what was between his words. Not only had their sovereign confided Rhys was to return from France with information to aid with the war, but had revealed the lady spy's identity.

For that, no warmth about his interest in De Talliere's mistress. Regardless of the aid given England these years, which had surely saved lives, she was terribly fallen for using her body as currency. Though neither did Dangereuse approve, the longer she was exposed to the lady who seemed to have made the best of bad circumstances, the more she accepted her.

"Whether I am welcome or not," Lady Vianne said, "I am glad to finally return to England. And much to that tale, which our king shall know as soon as my escort is healed enough to complete his mission."

"Providing the weather remains kind, soon we shall continue to London," Rhys said and looked to Warin. "As you are in Edward's confidence, ere you depart for Woodhearst I shall—"

"Uncle Warin!" Sebastian's voice carried for how near he had drawn. Followed by Puck, he high-stepped through snow. "Skate with me!"

Dangereuse caught her brother's muffled groan. He enjoyed the activity and had good relations with his nephew, but as he had been riding for hours and surely wished refreshment, she called, "I shall skate with you."

"I want Uncle Warin!"

"Mayhap later. His journey was long."

Her bright-cheeked son halted alongside her mount, on his heels Puck who was huffing and puffing for exerting himself with sledding and keeping up with the energetic boy. "But I want—"

"'Tis me or none," she said with firmness that was more difficult to impose since accepting he suffered some hearing loss.

Moving his gaze to Rhys, he appealed, "What of you, Sir Knight?"

As Dangereuse hesitated over withdrawing her offer and returning him to the donjon, which could cast a shadow over the day should he react badly, Rhys said, "I am of the same mind as your mother. Even were I not, 'tis her decision. Thus, you disrespect her—and yourself—by disregarding her."

His support of Dangereuse did not surprise. What surprised was Sebastian's response to Rhys' words and the look accompanying them. "I am sorry, Mother. Will you skate with me still?"

"I shall." She looked to Lady Vianne. "Will you join us?"

Surprise fluttered the woman's lashes, but her halfway smile appeared genuine. "You are kind, but as I will return to the donjon soon, I shall watch." She skipped her gaze over Warin and settled it on Rhys. "May I impose on you to remain so you may escort me to the castle?"

To ensure Warin did not? Dangereuse wondered as Rhys looked to Owen who nodded his assent, releasing him from the patrol.

As her uncle reined around to return to watching for any who might try to work ill on this holy day, he said, "What of you, Warin?"

His nephew, who likely suspected Lady Vianne's wish to distance herself from him, said, "I shall watch Sebastian for a time, then join my men at Lillia."

Immediately, Owen put heels to his mount who kicked up so much snow the sparkling flakes and chips looked nearly a cloud fallen to ground.

"Hurry!" Sebastian tugged Dangereuse's mantle.

Passing her drink to Warin, she said, "Unless you would like to come up on my saddle, Bastian, lead the way."

"I like snow crunching under my boots," he proclaimed, then asked, "You will come with us, Puck the Ruck?"

"I would, but as ye have your mother, and I told the littlest 'uns I would sled them down the hill, that I shall do."

Though disappointment flashed across the boy's face, he said, "'Tis good to keep your word." Then he began the trek to the pond followed by Dangereuse who silently thanked the Lord for this day. It had lost its footing early on, but having landed on its feet—albeit in an altered direction—it was better for it.

CHAPTER 20

The Lady of Lillia, who might have belonged to Rhys had he been prepared to wed when he was not, made his heart strain as he watched her on the ice with her son.

She who had become severe since the day her father and he found her in Benoit's arms, seemed almost the hopeful, bright-eyed young woman he resisted to remain faithful to plans of taking no wife until he applied what was learned at Wulfen in serving his king. Too, he had viewed it as an opportunity to pursue love rather than settle for the convenient and expedient and spend the remainder of his life viewing it as such.

Had he felt then half what he did now for the eldest Wulfrith daughter, would he have bent toward her rather than away? If so, would it have been enough to distance her from Benoit?

Where would we be now? he nearly questioned aloud as she glided backward on skates fixed to her boots, mantle swishing, red sleeves fluttering, gloved hands gripping those of Sebastian who wore skates rather than traverse the ice on the soles of his boots as did most small children. For that, he required his mother's aid in keeping his balance, but did so admirably, not merely allowing himself to be pulled but seeking to work the runners the same as those older than he.

Of a sudden, his feet went out from under him, and he would have landed hard, even taken his mother down, were she unprepared. She righted Sebastian who had cried out in anticipation of a fall, then more slowly moving backward, said something that made him laugh and nod. Shortly, she stopped and released him.

Hands out to the sides, he teetered on the runners. Though they were narrow, they were considerably wider than ones made from iron plate that were permanently fixed to footwear exclusively for use on ice.

The smile his mother bestowed was lovely and once more put Rhys in mind of the young woman left behind.

When she motioned Sebastian forward, he hesitated, and Rhys saw his eyes dart over the others as if he calculated how much humiliation he might suffer.

Dangereuse spoke something, then he drew his arms slightly in and pushed his right foot forward. Some teetering, now the left foot. And twice more, delivering him to his mother.

This cry was of joy. And more joy when she lifted him, put an arm around his waist, and took one of his hands in hers. As if they were dance partners taking a turn about a grand room, they glided forward and around others, including couples who stood nearer than would normally be appropriate.

Now Dangereuse whirled, causing what secured her thick braid to release—a silver ribbon that sought to draw him back to the night of Benoit's death when he sought to return to her one he should not have.

With her son expressing delight, she skated a short

distance, whirled again, and several times more as her silvered tresses unraveled. At the edge of the pond, she halted, and when her hair settled about her shoulders, only the small side braids were intact.

It was good he remained astride rather than join her on the pond, though not for any bodily deficit, his injury well enough healed he could enjoy the ice without great discomfort. Nay, better he was here since there was nothing for him with Benoit's widow despite her response to his kiss. And he should not wish it though she no longer believed him responsible for her husband losing the saddle.

"The Lady of Lillia is lovely of figure and face," Lady Vianne said as mother and son resumed skating. "And such hair on one of few years! It makes her appear forged of tar and steel."

Rhys looked to the woman whose tone was that of one who believed she saw things one did not wish seen.

She raised her eyebrows. "I am thinking tar for adherence, steel for strength."

Hopeful her low words did not reach the man on his other side, Rhys moved his regard over revelers who had not taken to the ice. They ate and drank, kicked leather balls between the pond and sledding hills, and formed snow missiles hurtled at one another.

As he observed the latter who were mostly older boys and girls, sidelong he caught a flash of light amid trees on the eastern boundary of this idyllic place which, outside of winter, would tempt one to lie back on the grass, whether it was newly sprung, sorrowfully parched, or carpeted in leaves.

He narrowed his gaze, seeking another flash that could as easily be an icicle catching light as the armor of one of the garrison patrol. And not as easily, it could be a trespasser.

Thinking it worthy of investigation, he looked to Warin. "Likely what I glimpsed in yonder trees is of no consequence, but I would confirm it." He jutted his chin at the woman. "Pray, remain with Lady Vianne. I should not be long."

Warin opened his mouth as if to offer to investigate himself, but Rhys shook his head. Then, more aware of his belted sword and dagger, he reined aside.

He had not gone far when an alarmed cry he believed of Sebastian made him turn a hand around his sword hilt and peer across his shoulder.

It was the boy, and on the ice between him and his mother lay something of silver, at one end a glint of red. A dagger, and surely a match for his own.

Dangereuse could only stare at what had clattered to the ice when she returned her son to his feet.

"Mama?" he said warily, and it was then she noted the receding din that evidenced what went here had captured the attention of others.

There being nothing she could do about it, she said, "Where did you get that?"

He bit his lip, gave his head a shake that made his skates wobble.

"Tell me."

"Found it in your chest," he muttered, then pointed at the scabbarded weapon whose keen length had been partially exposed upon hitting the ice. "'Tis a Wulfrith dagger. My papa's, aye?"

Feeling a chill and growing colder yet though moments earlier she had considered removing her mantle, she said, "When did you take it?"

"What?"

Anger leapt over him feigning difficulty in understanding,

but reason tamped it down. As he did not yet know what Rhys had learned about his hearing, she repeated herself and saw this time his eyes were on her lips.

He blew breath up his face. "I got it a long time ago."

She wanted to press for exactly how long, it being years since she looked upon that killing blade before hiding it in the bottom of the chest. However, as a child's sense of the passage of time was very different from an adult's, whatever he might tell would be distantly accurate at best. And what did it matter compared to what was of real consequence—that he had not injured himself?

"Where have you kept it?" she asked.

"In a hole I made in my mattress."

Certain he had cut it with the dagger that could have sliced him, outwardly her inward shudder expressed itself.

Sebastian started to draw nearer but stilled when his teetering reminded him his boots were not in contact with the ice. "This is the first time I wore it, Mama, and only because you said I must leave my wooden sword and I needed to protect you."

"Protect me?" she nearly shrilled.

He nodded less vigorously than usual, doubtless feeling his imbalance. "You say 'tis safer inside the walls than outside."

She did when he wished to take his play beyond the castle and she could not accompany him nor make arrangements for others to do so. "The dagger was under your chausses, aye?"

"I put it in my boot and tied the hilt around my leg real good."

And yet it had worked its way out of the boot as well as the tie.

Trying to calm a heart whose beat was so fierce her head lightened, she retrieved the dagger, pushed the blade fully into its scabbard, and slid the weapon beneath her gown's belt.

He reached. "It was papa's, so it should be mine."

For the blood it last shed, never would it be his, but she could not tell him that now. "This is not for a boy, Sebastian. 'Tis for a man trained in arms."

His upper lip began to hike, but as she prepared for a tantrum, what boiled within cooled and he said, "I am sorry."

Her heart jerked as if a stitch meant to close up a wound was firmly knotted. Still, he must be disciplined for going where he was not allowed and taking and concealing the weapon.

Though often she felt almost desolate upon finding herself in *the alone* with none to ease her burdens, she longed for it so she might tame what prowled within. *Later,* she told herself, then said, "You are right to apologize, and 'tis good you understand you did wrong, but you must answer for this."

As his lower lip began to jut, Puck called, "Lady D!"

She looked around and, once more aware of the din and activity, was grateful it had recovered from curiosity over what went here. First, she set her gaze on Warin who remained beside Lady Vianne, then Rhys who had distanced himself and watched her and Sebastian, lastly the stout man treading snow toward the pond with the sled hooked over a shoulder.

"Aye, Puck?"

He halted alongside her palfrey. "Some of the boys would like Bastian to race them—the smallest hill so they may do so on their own."

Her son gasped. "May I, Mama? I am sorry. Really I am."

More she believed that than had Puck arrived before the first apology. Thus, opposing her silent counsel, she disregarded the need for immediate consequences and justified it for him twice expressing remorse and the longing for time to collect herself. "You may, but know we are not done with the dagger you stole."

"Stole?" he exclaimed, then once more exercising control, said sullenly, "I know."

She held out a hand, and he took it and slowly worked his skates to the snowy bank where she unfastened his runners and hers and passed both sets to the young man responsible for fixing them to footwear. Then Sebastian was hastening toward the smallest hill as quickly as his short legs could manage, Puck lumbering after him.

Patting the neck of her horse, she watched their progress until her thoughts strayed to Rhys. She ventured a look at him and saw he moved toward the bordering trees that, though thinned by shed leaves, were nearly impenetrable where evergreens abounded.

Then he returned to the patrol? Had asked her brother to escort Lady Vianne to the castle though he said he would?

Strange. However, deciding to turn her thoughts elsewhere, she looked to the hill Sebastian and Puck had ascended.

Three village boys and her son had settled on their sleds and awaited a push to send them on their way, which would be more exhilarating with each being solely in command of their little craft.

Puck shouted out the count, and when he reached the number *five,* the boys were given a push that sent them down the slope, all whooping over what must seem great speed though Dangereuse could run alongside them, even in her gown.

As they neared the bottom and the ground leveled, she heard what sounded a sharp wind whistling through leaves and saw dark streaks slice the blue sky.

"Take cover!" Rhys bellowed a moment before she identified the sound and sight of arrows flown from the trees.

Punched by remembrance of the feeling something ill moved this way, she cried, "Bastian!" and as killing shafts began landing, started toward the boys who happily climbed off their sleds. But then realizing she could more quickly reach them on horseback than on foot with the hem of her gown weighted by snow—even ahead of Puck who ran down the hill —she turned back.

With all but the youngest revelers understanding what had been joyous had turned dangerous, panicked cries and shouts sounded and those who need not save their children began running opposite the trees. This Dangereuse saw as she dropped into the saddle and caught up the reins, just as she saw several felled by arrows that would turn the snow red.

As she spurred her mount toward the boys who had gone still, aware there was no longer anything to laugh about, more arrows passed overhead.

"Nay!" she screamed and, looking across her shoulder, saw the majority of those hastening to get off the ice were too late. When this batch of arrows landed, they created cracks, and the skaters' incautious movements further weakened the ice. Then like a rapidly spreading disease, the pieces began breaking away and those on them tilted and shrieked as they slid into the water.

"Lord!" Desperately praying He would be merciful, she looked around in search of her son and saw Lady Vianne's horse rear as if struck by an arrow and her brother snatch her onto his mount before hers went sideways.

Now Ferrand was shouting orders to his men, some of whom rode toward the trees while he and others spurred in the direction of the pond.

She saw arrows narrowly miss Rhys as he sped away from the wooded area that had been his destination.

She saw her son push through the snow toward her with eyes wide and mouth agape.

Worse, coming behind him were riders not of Lillia nor

Wulfen, and all nearer than she and Puck. Then one drove his horse ahead of the others as if to trample her boy.

"Do not!" she screamed.

At the last moment, the man veered to the right, leaned so far to the side it appeared he would lose the saddle, and hooked a mail-clad arm around her son.

As he dropped his captive on the fore of his saddle, Dangereuse screamed with fear, rage, and pleading. And again when he and his accomplices turned opposite.

Though fairly certain of who was behind the attack, there was no comfort in the likelihood her son was taken for these men being unable to get their hands on Lady Vianne. And greater pain for Dangereuse knowing had she been a better mother, immediately returning her son to Lillia for his behavior, a pawn could not have been made of him—that he would not be screaming and struggling, just as she who was no warrior would not recklessly follow those carrying her son away.

"Dangereuse!" Rhys bellowed, and a glance over her shoulder through the scattering snow revealed he and Ferrand also gave chase, swords in hand. "Turn back!"

By his command she should ignore maternal instincts? She could not, though there was little chance of taking back her son and much chance she would also be made a pawn, especially since she was nearer Sebastian's abductor than the warriors riding to her aid.

Now the unexpected. The one who had her son yelped with pain and jerked his encircling arm to the side, Sebastian launched off the speeding horse, and a sharp jerk of her reins kept her mount from pounding the small figure that landed face down in the snow.

As she came around, she saw Rhys also narrowly avoided

trampling him and heard him command Ferrand to aid Sebastian, then he shouted for her to go left.

Too late. The one her son escaped turned back and drove his horse hard against hers, cramming his knee into her thigh. Then an arm ending in a bloodied hand into which a crescent was cut—as of teeth tearing into a piece of meat—wrenched her onto his saddle.

Bucking and slapping, she glimpsed Rhys being surrounded by the man's cohorts, then the flash of swords as he fought off those who greatly outnumbered him, and beyond him Ferrand on his knees beside her son.

Lord, let him live and be whole, she silently cried, then bunched a hand and struck the miscreant's jaw. As she cried out over pain in her fist, past her captor's shoulder she saw Sebastian in her brother-in-law's arms and his frightened face turn toward her, bloodied mouth lax as he looked upon what she would have him spared.

Oh, my brave boy, you used the only weapon available to you and defeated a warrior, she praised from afar. *Mayhap a better warrior you* would *make than a man of God praying within the safety of walls.* An instant later, a retaliatory punch sent pain spiraling through her skull. Then all thought passed from her.

CHAPTER 21

Northern border of Wulfenshire

Cold. Might it be but the cold of winter? Or was it death come for her? Perhaps carrying her away?

Lest she lived and her attempt to look at her surroundings alert her captor she was conscious again, which throughout the ride saw her dealt blows to return her to darkness, she kept her lids closed as well as lips against which a groan of ache landed.

Be still and quiet, she counseled. *Hold close the turning of your mind, whether you remain upon Wulfenshire, somewhere in between, or have met your end and shall soon stand before the Lord to answer for your sins. Be still. Be quiet. Be ready.*

"I am here," someone rasped, his breath across the throb at her temple and jaw urging her to rise above the cold.

"Open your eyes and see."

Drawing courage from Rhys' presence and remembrance of Sebastian in Ferrand's arms, the only visible blood about him that which evidenced his attempt to take a bite out of his abductor, Dangereuse lifted her lids.

It was dim here, which likely would be pitch dark if not for firelight well beyond the shadowed Rhys who lay on his left side facing her, a large rock at his back. Were her wrists not bound behind her, easily she could set a hand on his chest.

Lips pressed lest sound escape and reveal to those indulging in the fire's warmth their captives were no longer senseless, she stared out of eyes more visible to Rhys than were the blue of his.

"The same as you, I was rendered unconscious during the ride," he said low, and now she heard thick about his words as if one or more of those renderings was dealt his mouth. "However, I am fairly certain of where we are. You?"

She started to shake her head, but looked closer at what was beyond the rock at his back, then turned her face up. They were in a cave, the ceiling formed of stone interspersed with earth held in place by nets of roots situated above dry ones whose search for water and nutrients proved to no avail.

Lowering her gaze and realizing they were in the cradle of rocks pushing up through the earthen floor, she found some light in Rhys' eyes and whispered, "'Tis a cave."

"It is, and for its ceiling being riddled with roots, I believe it one known to me that collapsed years ago, sealing off the entrance. Hence, either there was another entrance, else a new one created. Regardless, 'tis an ideal base for brigands and malcontents, allowing them to wait out their pursuers."

"Is it upon Lillia's lands?"

"Aye, the northernmost boundary ere Wulfenshire gives unto Lincolnshire. En route to Blackwood to spend Christmas with my family and attend other occasions during my training, oft I paused at this cave—that is, do I correctly identify it."

"When did you rouse?" she asked.

"An hour gone."

She strained for sound beyond the hiss and crackle of the fire she longed to draw near. "I hear them not. Do they sleep?"

"Most have departed, some to patrol the area, others to take game for supper, but three stayed behind. As they have ceased speaking and moving, they may sleep."

"Then since there may be no better time than now, should we not try to escape?"

He grunted. "Have your arms grown so numb you do not know they are fixed behind your back?"

Well she knew it from the abrasive grip of rope and strain in the unnatural press of her shoulders. "I am aware."

"Of your ankles as well?"

She tried to part the upper from the lower, but could not, which she would have known were that rope fixed around bare skin rather than boots.

"Bound the same as mine," he said. "Even if not, you are weaponless just as once more I find myself, the Wulfrith dagger you took from Sebastian as absent from your person as that with which you cut meat."

As she flew her thoughts over all that had happened so she might prepare for what lay ahead, he continued, "From what I listened in on—and is of no surprise—the French and their English hirelings expect to trade you for Lady Vianne, just as they sought to do with Sebastian after the arrow meant to fell your brother struck that lady's horse."

After thanking the Lord that once more Warin avoided death by way of an arrow, she said, "Trade only me, not you?"

"If possible to make the trade without relinquishing me, they shall since vengeance is wished upon the one who carried away Lady Vianne. For that we live, though unless we work a way out of this or are aided by those searching for us, we may die since your uncle and brother will not endanger that lady's life, even did King Edward not eagerly await her intelligence."

Beginning to quake from fear as well as cold, she said, "Do you truly think there is a way out of this?"

"I know it, and that the greatest challenge is finding it with our captors numbering over a score."

"Over a score?" she hissed. "That many?"

"I am fairly certain of it, the three who remain of Lady Vianne's pursuers having hired brigands—likely the ones troubling your lands."

"Lord."

After some moments, he said, "As warmth will bolster your strength, roll toward me, and I will put myself around you."

She drew a strident breath.

"Even were I vile, naught could result from the press of our bodies in these circumstances. Now come to me."

When she was on her opposite side with her back against his front, further warmth was gained from the drape of the mantle that had been pinned beneath her and the fur collar settling in the curve of her neck.

Though warmer, and more for his breath in her hair, she shivered. And lied in telling herself it had naught to do with his broad chest against her upper back...muscular abdomen against bound hands...firm thighs against the backs of hers... knees against calves...

"Better, Dange?"

She jerked her chin and, thinking she had never liked the shortening of her name as much as when he spoke it, wondered how she could be so aware of him under these circumstances.

"'Twill be easier do we set our minds on finding a way out of this," Rhys said, breath caressing her scalp and turning about her ear.

Meaning he was as disturbed as she by the contact that brought to mind their kiss and hands that explored what they could not now?

"Move your thoughts elsewhere," he said as if she spoke them aloud.

She tried, but it was difficult knowing they were not hers alone. Thus, hoping to divert them, she put her chin across her shoulder. "I thank you for coming for Bastian and me. If not for your sacrifice that gave Ferrand time to get my boy away, he might have been retrieved and here with me."

"For pausing to see what transpired between your son and you rather than act quickly after glimpsing silver in the trees," Rhys said, "I failed to expose those in the wood. Had I done my duty, the hue and cry would have been raised before arrows flew. Thus, you praise me for what is little compared to what would have been had I remained true to my training—our captors rendered impotent, and you and yours safely inside Lillia."

Being a Wulfrith and regularly in the company of warriors, she understood his torment and knew he did not seek a defense, just as she would not for her own regrets—the first of not heeding the sense of portentous ill, the second of not returning Sebastian to the donjon for taking the dagger. Thus, suppressing the longing to defend him, she said, "Then for the silver you saw in the wood, you left Lady Vianne with Warin."

"Aye, providing well for her safety, as cannot be said of your people and you."

"'Twas not all for you to do, Rhys. Not only did our captors evade detection by my uncle's patrol, but Lillia's."

"But there was a chance to make that right. As I wasted it, the patrol were unable to defend against the attackers ere much ill was done that required them to turn their greater efforts to saving those under direct threat, including the skaters who went into the water."

And suffered far more cold than I before Rhys put his body around mine, she reflected, then wondered, *How many drowned? How many took arrows?*

"Cease excusing my arrogance, Dangereuse."

"Arrogance?"

He sighed. "Much I have failed in completing the commission with which the king entrusted me—failure such as I have not known. Thus, for embracing more confidence than caution, I could not prevent you being taken."

She shook her head. "You were outnumbered and had to rely on your left arm to work the sword. Had you been able to use the right—"

"Still we would be here. As told, I allowed myself to be distracted."

Once more stung by her own regret, determining he should know she was as aware of her failure, she said, "And I, who not only ignored a sense of ill upon the air but did not discipline my son by sending him back to Lillia, bear much responsibility for how we find ourselves—even, I would say, more."

Rather than vent his next breath on argument, he said, "As we cannot know all that lies ahead, try to sleep."

She wished she could—until it occurred relief from fear of the unknown was too temporary to outweigh the known of being this near Rhys. *Perhaps the only good remaining to me in this life,* she thought, then said, "I do not wish to sleep."

"Then think on how we are to return you whole to your son."

Worthier thought, she acceded.

However, minutes later their silence was shattered by the return of those seeking to recover their lord's mistress, whether she be traitor or victim.

A THRUST of torchlight sought to blind those who remained unmoving despite having time to separate ahead of the arrival of men whose speech was of the continental French and boots over packed dirt resonated as if fashioned of wood.

"See here, Chevalier Pierre!" said the man gripping the torch whose light put shine on a nearly bald pate, his remaining wisps appearing as eager to abandon his scalp as sailors a swiftly sinking ship. "You worried for naught. As you should know by now, a keen blade is the only means of easily thwarting my knots. Thus, our *guests'* greatest liberty is of drawing near for warmth."

He swept the torch to the side, revealing his roughly whiskered face that likely first looked out upon the world forty years ago. And now a grin that was white but for the dark of a missing incisor.

Also seen was Pierre who, were he shorn of short beard, would look younger than the thirty years he appeared. Though his smile was mostly white, his teeth were so crowded, it would benefit *him* to lose a tooth.

"I would apologize for doubting your knots, Sanche, but more smug you would be," he said. "Thus, you must be content with my sire's gratitude upon our return to France—unlike Gustave who, I believe, no longer has need of such." He moved his gaze to Rhys. "I wager you who killed the first of my men can confirm Gustave's passing to Sanche who, jealous of his missing friend, believes he betrayed my sire for coin." He wrinkled his nose. "'Tis no hardship to imagine Gustave doing things to Lady Vianne absent witnesses, but to entirely disappear?" He clicked his tongue. "Dead, oui?"

Feeling Dangereuse's tension, Rhys stared at the man he

had known was De Talliere's son for having observed him during the negotiations to extend the truce.

Silence not the answer sought, that one heaved a sigh, stepped nearer, and picked his eyes over the bound woman. Then he lowered to his haunches and scrutinized her face. "Since learning the name of the keeper of Castle Lillia and that she is of the Wulfriths, I have been intrigued, Dangereuse of dangerous name and silver of an old woman though you have not the years for such."

When he hooked a tress of her hair and drew it through his fingers, Dangereuse tensed further.

"Though you are not to my taste, my sire would find you desirable—and enjoy wrapping himself in your hair." He flicked his fingers free of it, straightened, then said, "As I believe you also have the answer to Gustave's fate, Lady Dangereuse, speak."

Rhys knowing little about this man other than what he had observed—that he trailed his sire like an unweaned pup its mother, the toes of his boots catching light for being fit with polished steel tips—he determined not to rouse him to great displeasure with his attention on Dangereuse. Thus, he said, "Gustave is dead," then covering for Lady Vianne lest somehow she find herself recovered by Rollon de Talliere, added, "Taken to ground by a Wulfen patrol."

Pierre tossed up his hands. "There now—easy! Why our wee island cousins make the simple hard, I shall never understand. Fortunately for you who gave answer, Rhys de Arell, forgiveness." He eyed Dangereuse. "Alas, not for you."

Guessing what he intended, Rhys shouted, "Nay!" and lurched forward to roll atop her, but already Pierre had drawn back his leg. Before Rhys could entirely shield her, she was rocked by a steel toe in the vicinity of her abdomen.

As she cried out, Rhys strained against the rope binding

217

wrists and ankles, then snapped his head around and bared his teeth. "Knave! Poltroon! I will bleed you!"

Pierre slapped a hand to his chest. "You wound!" Then mockingly sorrowful, he shook his head. "Though not as greatly as you did my sire by stealing his whore who may know things that could greatly injure him were they spilled in your king's ear."

Though Rhys knew his weight atop Dangereuse increased her pain, he continued shielding her lest she was dealt another kick.

Pierre glanced at Sanche, then returned to his haunches and narrowed his eyes at Rhys. "Though my sire is so besotted with Vianne Wardieu he insisted she was taken against her will, I say she arranged her return to England to betray the king's advisor who stands to fall from grace—perhaps as deep as the grave should King Jean learn how incautious he is with his English mistress. Pray, confirm that just as you are no innocent, neither is she who despoils the marriage bed of my sire and beloved stepmother."

Beloved because there was truth to the rumor Pierre had wished to wed the young lady before his sire claimed her for himself? Rhys wondered as he continued pressing upon the hurting Dangereuse.

Pierre clasped his hands between his knees and once more appeared to think much as Rhys should have done rather than attend to Sebastian's attempt to avoid taking responsibility for his behavior. "Confirm it, and rather than deliver you to my sire who shall flay you, not only will I trade Lady Dangereuse for the whore but you."

Even if Rhys believed that, his answer would be no different. "Generous, but no further damage would I have dealt my honor."

"Further?"

"Your sire's belief in Lady Vianne's character is without fault. Like Gustave, I desired her. When she spurned me, I refused to believe her devotion to one who is old enough to have fathered her and, if ever he boasted a warrior's build, long ago traded it for indulgence in food, drink, and repose."

Pierre's mouth hiked into a semblance of a smile. "And yet with little effort you took her from my sire."

Wishing he could speak words of comfort to the woman suffering his weight, Rhys said, "*Much* effort—until the lady realized the futility of escaping me and my men."

De Talliere's son rose to a fairly good height. "No man cares to be thought a fool, and less made to look one. But though your offense tempts me to gut you like a pig bound for the spit —which you quite resemble at the moment—I will not deny my father the satisfaction of making you suffer. Instead, I content myself with this."

Trussed as he was, Rhys could only ensure the next kick was dealt him alone. He thrust off the boots he dug in the dirt, rolled over Dangereuse, landed on his opposite side facing her, and had just a moment to peer into her wide eyes before he was struck in the back of the head by merciless steel tips.

CHAPTER 22

It scraped her raw to take food and drink from the hand of the enemy—especially this hand—but what choice had she for how dry her mouth and empty her belly?

"Another drink?" said the traitorous Englishman whose build and hair had been enough to make her suspect it was he who scooped up Sebastian. What made her certain was his bandaged hand. Another thing she knew was he was not of the laboring class, and not only for fairly fine garments. His speech and mannerisms exposed the layers of privilege.

Sitting back on her bound ankles beside Rhys who had been knocked face down ten minutes past, the hair at the back of his head stained with blood let by De Talliere's kick, Dangereuse swallowed a second bite of bread. It went down with as much discomfort as the first, and she guessed it due to tenderness about her lower chest and abdomen that pained her more than her bruised face.

Drawing breath, she looked from the man who had quieted her during the ride with as little consultation of his conscience as Pierre de Talliere, to the wineskin in his hand opposite the one her son bit. "Aye, another drink," she said, then refusing to be ashamed of bodily needs, added, "and soon I must relieve myself." She nodded at Rhys whom she had been trying to rouse when this man appeared. "Alongside sustenance, he shall require the same."

The brigand hunkering on the other side of the senseless warrior extended the skin. "Since our French friends wish him to live a time, he shall be accommodated."

Anger once more moving toward a boil, she ignored the spout and hissed, "Friends? Why? Because for foul deeds committed by their command, French coin fills your *English* purse?"

He shrugged. "I count a friend whoever aids in the survival of my brother and me."

Brother. She turned over what could be relevant in later bringing him to ground providing he was not as free in claiming kinship to another as gathering friends to him.

"Of course, all changes does a friend betray or is no longer useful," he added.

"You are..." She breathed through another cramp. When it eased, she put her lips around the spout and drank despite further discomfort in swallowing. She drew back. "You are loose with your idea of what constitutes a friend."

"Necessity and a means of passing the time." He raised his eyebrows. "I am thinking you have a good idea of who I am, Lady Dangereuse."

By the light of the lantern set atop a rock, she feigned closer scrutiny of the face and figure that belonged to one near her age of twenty and five. "You are a stranger to me, and though I am aware you are not of the common, I cannot say whether you are noble or of the gentry."

He snorted. "You know I speak not of that."

She did but hoped he would tell something to more quickly

end his trespasses across this demesne. Mimicking his indifference, she shrugged. "You are one of the brigands who occasionally trouble my demesne and people."

His eyes sparked. "*Your* demesne? *Your* people?" he dragged those words through sarcasm. "Lord! Grant a woman a little power and she comes to believe her wooden stool a throne. Then for greater vanity and self-importance, those she is sworn to protect are deprived of their rightful places and possessions." He gave a bitter laugh. "Though born of a Wulfrith, first and ever you shall be a grasping Daughter of Eve."

A woman hater, she silently named one who blamed his losses and sins on the fairer sex who failed to do something he could not himself.

She set her chin higher. "*My* demesne and people, God having entrusted them to England's king, the king entrusting them to Baron Wulfrith, the baron entrusting them to me." As color spread up his neck, she added, "As for being a Daughter of Eve, I am not ashamed of my descent from God's beloved."

"Beloved!"

"Aye, the same as Adam who also disappointed his father," she said as she caught change in Rhys' breathing. "Just as all His creation disappoint—and obviously *you* do in thieving from and betraying your countrymen."

He opened his mouth, but whether he meant to dispute or justify his actions, it was not known for the loosing of anger. He lunged, the thumb and fingers of his bandaged hand splayed as if to choke her into silence.

Her first thought was to bite him as Sebastian had done. However, there was a better defense though, as warned by her eldest brother who instructed her and her sisters, she would be pained as well.

Snapping her upper body slightly right to avoid his hand,

she thrust up off her roped ankles and slammed her forehead against his nose. Pain burst behind her eyes, her body recoiled, what felt rain flecked her face, and his cry echoed.

Stay conscious, she commanded as her rear dropped to her heels and she struggled to keep from continuing backward and landing atop her bound arms. Blessedly, she managed to straighten the bend in her back. As she blinked to restore vision, she heard voices and running feet, the traitor's curse and scrabbling in the dirt as he sought to right himself.

"Dangereuse!"

Swaying atop bent legs, she looked to Rhys who had regained consciousness and distanced himself with another roll—one that had to be as much the cause of the brigand slumped against the rock opposite as contact with her forehead that had blood running from the knave's nose.

Peering into Rhys' face that was surely as abused as hers, she said, "I am well." It was false assurance, as much for ache in her head as screaming abdominal muscles. At least, she hoped that was what screamed, that her fear of internal bleeding was unfounded.

"You are not well," he pronounced ahead of the arrival of those come to aid one of their own.

"William!" cried the first who sprang into the encircling rocks, and as others followed with unsheathed daggers, dropped to his knees. "William!" repeated he who appeared several years younger than the sprawled brigand and whose voice was a close match. "Are you—?"

"I told never to speak my name!" growled William.

"Are you greatly injured?" demanded the one who could be his brother as Dangereuse considered the other three who set themselves around their captives. "What did that foul De Arell—?"

"Enough!" William sprayed saliva-diluted blood, then

223

knocked aside the hand reaching to him and got his legs under him. "I shall deal with him."

Knowing pride was behind words meant to mark Rhys as his sole attacker, doubtless more acceptable than her being responsible for his broken nose, and certain punishment of the knight would be worse than that of a lady reserved for trading, she laughed.

"What do you find amusing, *English?*" asked the captor nearest her—the third Frenchman, as evidenced by his accent.

Ignoring Rhys who spoke her name in a way that commanded her to silence, she said, "It amuses that you French did not better choose your traitorous allies. Though *William* will not own to a Daughter of Eve besting him, draw near and see his blood upon me."

De Talliere's man who appeared a dozen years older than Pierre, and from whose eyes shone what seemed intelligence, looked across his shoulder. "Hold, you who fears being known as *William* though surely half the men in England answer to the name."

The brigand who drew an arm beneath his bloodied nose cast Dangereuse a look of loathing but did not reject the hand the younger man set on his arm.

The Frenchman stepped around Rhys, then after considering the face Dangereuse turned into lantern light, touched his chest and executed a bow. "Aubert Marionne, English lady worthy of her surname. Alas, for devotion due my lord, Rollon De Talliere, I can but make your stay more comfortable until we exchange you for Lady Vianne."

"Your lord's son will not allow it," William spat crimson again.

With a roll of the eyes, Marionne turned to the brigand who now stood beyond the two men closely watching Rhys. "Regardless of whether Pierre agrees, it will be done as you ought know by now, *William* who remains unworthy of the coin paid him, the same as his archers who are less competent than promised."

The brigand wagged a finger between Rhys and Dangereuse. "Because of me and mine, you have them."

"As well you know, they are not what we sought," Marionne said. "Thus, a trade which would not be necessary had your men been capable of flying arrows true enough to put through Lady Vianne's protector rather than her horse."

He spoke of Warin who might have lost his life had that archer been as accurate as the one at Romary whose flaming missile embedded in her brother's chain mail.

"'Tis difficult to account for sudden movement," William said.

"Not so for King Edward's archers who are more responsible for his victories in France than his sword swingers. Thus, were your archers truly at Crécy, they were the dregs of those who did your king proud in defeating our army." Marionne shot up a hand as if to shove the other man's next words down his throat. "Oui, the diversion of sending the skaters into the freezing water permitted us to escape as planned, but the iced pond was no small target." He nodded at Dangereuse. "Even her boy could have landed an arrow there." Abruptly, he gestured for William and the younger man to depart.

When they complied, Marionne turned his eyes upon Rhys, "Regardless of whether Lady Vianne is a betrayer, it is my duty to ensure her return to my lord. For that you are here and, does God will it and those miserable brigands not disappoint further, Lady Dangereuse has naught to fear."

Skull feeling as if in a vise, Rhys considered the man ever seen at Pierre's side as the latter trailed his sire—though there had been no trailing about Aubert Marionne. Despite his assurance Dangereuse had nothing to fear, unspoken was Rhys had much to fear in accord with De Talliere's son who made it clear the trade sought was a lady for a lady so his sire would have the satisfaction of flaying the one who took his mistress.

Marionne sheathed his dagger. "Now let us see you more comfortable to ensure your well-being for what lies ahead."

Hope in that, though not for ease of a body in this cold, hard place. Rather, hope for bettering the possibility of escape. "We would be grateful," Rhys said, "but start by allowing us to relieve ourselves ere further we are fouled and you and yours also suffer."

The man eyed him, then shouted across the cave, "William, go for Sanche!"

The Frenchman who had boasted only a keen blade could easily thwart his knots...

CHAPTER 23

Not a Christmas one would wish their child to hold close, Dangereuse thought as once more she considered all to which Sebastian was subjected before her brave boy gained his release. And of course there were the injuries dealt the other celebrants which, she prayed, were not dire.

Fortunately, though as yet there was no end to it for Rhys and her, some good was had for Aubert Marionne taking control of the captives. Sanche having reworked his ropes and knots to permit small steps and minimal use of hands, separately Rhys and Dangereuse had relieved themselves outside the cave beneath frozen moonlight—and under threat of retribution against the other for resistance. Then closely watched by brigands, they were given roasted rabbit and good wine despite Pierre so loudly objecting his words crossed to this side of the cave.

Afterward, two blankets were provided, one atop which they were rebound by Sanche whose rope contraption allowed them to lie side by side and anything beyond slight movement causing the rope encircling their necks to tighten.

Relieved to once more be alone with Rhys and for the warmth of the second blanket covering them, Dangereuse turned her face to where he lay with his shoulder against hers and considered his profile by the light of a lantern. His eyes were closed, but he did not sleep. As she should be doing, he strained to make sense of their captors' mostly English-accented words in search of vulnerability.

She closed her eyes, tried again, but whatever was spoken remained muddled for the mesh of conversations of those who did, indeed, number over a score from what was seen at the pond and here as well when she and Rhys relieved themselves outside. Thus, she returned her thoughts to Sebastian, causing what felt pressure on her chest to increase.

"Fear not for your son," Rhys said. "He is safe within Lillia's walls, as are most your people—perhaps all."

Finding his bruised face with its split lip turned toward her, touched that he sensed her distress, she said, "I pray so, but..." She shook her head and, feeling the rope at her neck, said in a rush, "The things he saw and endured!"

"And yet he who is not yet six overcame what was of greatest threat to him, Dangereuse."

Certain there was more behind his assurance than what transpired this day, she said defensively, "You think that evidence he would make a better warrior than one dedicated to the Church?"

"As you are aware, ere this day I believed him more fit to wield a sword than the word of God, and what he did to his abductor supports a belief shared by your brothers who know better than I. Thus, do you allow Sebastian to be stronger for what happened at the pond, he shall be—with the right guidance."

Recalling her boy thwarting William with his teeth, momentarily she closed her eyes, then said, "My brothers and you may be right. *May* be..."

After a time, he asked, "Your belly and ribs?"

With her mind, she probed those tender places. "As there is pain only when I move quickly or breathe deeply, I am hopeful no great damage was done my belly and my ribs remain intact unlike those of my sister-in-law whose were broken in a similar manner ere she wed my brother. Now tell me of your injuries."

"None further done my arm, and the ache in my head has mostly ceased."

With little thought, she said, "Clearly, you should reconsider coming to the aid of ladies in distress, especially when greatly outnumbered."

His lips curved, causing her heart to lean toward him, and further when a smile that was no fit for the here and now went crooked. "I cannot cease being a warrior for which I trained any more than you can cease behaving a warrior for which you are *not* trained."

Feeling a tug at her own lips, she said, "Certes, I was well enough trained to know how to break a nose with little injury to myself, though likely my forehead will bruise."

"It *has* bruised, she-wolf."

Dangereuse did not want to thrill over him calling her that again, but there was something about lying here beside him. And something more about this achingly sweet awareness they had only each other as if things had turned out different the day he and Benoit jousted at Wulfen.

The alone, she silently named it, though this solitude was far different from what she was accustomed to. *The alone with him.*

"Do I offend again in naming you *she-wolf?*"

229

She blinked. "Nay, far better I like it than *little wolf,* which is what..." She trailed off, but it being too late to leave unspoken, finished, "...Benoit called me."

He went silent, finally said, "As I doubt we will sleep whilst more of them are awake than not, perhaps we ought to speak of what is behind neither of us, which began with Wulfen's joust."

"I think you are right."

"Your sire wished me to wed you, Dangereuse."

"Aye, and I was agreeable for his high regard of you, your skill and integrity, attractive face and body, and things felt even when you showed little interest in me."

His brow lined. "I was unaware you wished encouragement—indeed, thought you more disposed toward Benoit for the smiles you bestowed on him."

She nearly laughed. "Bestowed for him bestowing them on me as you would not and..." Pride nearly stoppered the rest. "...the possibility flirtations with him would move you to smile upon me."

"The power of competition."

She nipped her lower lip. "Would it have made a difference had you known my interest was in you?"

Without hesitation, he said, "I would have resisted."

"Why?"

Further he turned his face toward her as he could not any other part of his body for the rope about his neck. "I found you desirable for beauty, self-assurance, and spirit, but since soon I departed for war and was determined to make good my training and gain new experiences, I did not wish the fetters of a wife. Too, believing marriage without love could be more burden than joy, rather than forge an alliance ahead of great emotion, I determined to choose my wife in my own time to increase the chance of having that with which my parents are blessed."

"Then even had you not lost the joust to Benoit and afterward happened on us—"

"I was *made* to lose, Dangereuse," he said harshly and started to turn toward her. However, when she gasped over the rope pricking her neck as surely it did his, he eased back. "Forgive me."

Swallowing against coarse fibers more snug than before, she said, "Tell me about being made to lose."

He was silent so long she thought he might not, but finally said, "As you know, my saddle slipped and I went over. Whilst dragged, I saw the girth strap was loosely notched as my squire —my adopted brother, Eamon—was too diligent to allow. As I recovered my senses, my father, also believing foul play at work, hastened to my horse that had been led to a paddock. He and Eamon came too late and found though the strap was looser than it should be, not so much that an accomplished rider would lose his seat. When I joined them, we questioned the squire who tended the horses and learned Ferrand had delivered Benoit's mount to the paddock as well and insisted it be checked for a limp immediately. After an examination yielded no evidence of injury, the squire saw Ferrand was alongside my mount and—"

"What you imply cannot be true. My brother-in-law is a good man—would not be party to such."

"I also wished to believe he would not dishonor his training nor himself, but I saw the great gap between the strap and my mount that was different from how it appeared in the paddock. Certain Benoit was behind it, I determined to confront him and found Ferrand assisting in removing his armor. There was no mistaking that young man's fear and guilt as I charged his brother with cheating and Benoit accused me of envy and pride so great I knew not how to lose well. After I landed the first blow, he was as much upon me as I him. That is what you walked in on and sought to end."

"I remember."

"Regrettably, I could not keep the swing meant for him from dropping you into his arms." There was growl in the breath he expelled. "The fist you dealt my eye was the least I deserved. Had I done you grave injury like that suffered by my stepmother who cannot bear children..."

"But you did not, and you ought know I reacted without thought. Never did I think you meant me harm."

He nodded. "Believing the matter concluded as well as possible, I departed. However, my battered state did not go unnoticed. Your sire having been told of an altercation among those soon to be knighted, he intercepted me."

"And the two of you found Benoit and me embracing."

"Indeed."

She cleared her throat. "I did not go to his tent to be with him. After you were nearly trampled, out of concern for one my sire believed would make me a good husband, I went in search of you and saw you enter there. As I neared, I heard shouts and a struggle. And what followed...followed. After you departed and Ferrand was sent away, Benoit told you accused him of cheating as you were wont to do when bested. Because of my sire's esteem for his first squire, I questioned that aloud—and poorly."

"Poorly?"

"After saying I did not believe he cheated, I added, *Did you?* Tears rose to his eyes, and when he turned away, I beseeched his forgiveness." She sighed. "He said honor forbid him do anything so foul—that had he, he would be unworthy of my love to which he aspired. I knew he would have me to wife were I offered, but his declaration so surprised that when he kissed me I could not move, and when he sought assurance I did not believe him a cheat, I was so guilt-stricken I kissed him back and then..."

"...we entered and your sire sent me away."

"Aye, he was angry and silent so long I almost wished he would strike us. When finally he said his plan for me was ruined, Benoit told though it appeared his greatest prospect was serving as a household knight for his brother, he aspired to more and that were he gifted a Wulfrith bride, he would not disappoint."

"He worked that well." Bitterness edged Rhys' words. "Not only did he steal victory at the joust by enlisting his brother's aid, but gained a Wulfrith bride."

"I remind I have difficulty accepting Ferrand's deceit," she said with some reproach.

He smiled again, but this time there was none of the crooked charm about it. "I note you exclude only your brother-in-law from deceit."

Impulse nearly made her protest, but she said, "Though long ere Benoit's death he proved so possessive that at times I thought him obsessed—as if only he should breathe the same air as I—he was not a bad father and husband."

The lines in Rhys' brow deepened. "That is not the same as being a good father and husband. And even more distant that when one is made to feel suffocated by their helpmate."

"You are right. As for what sounds a charge of Benoit wrongfully gaining a Wulfrith bride, you forget you did not want me."

True, Rhys silently acceded, then the thought slipped in, *But were that day this...*

"I do not forget," he said gruffly.

They returned to silence until he shifted his thoughts to when next they met. "I regret what happened during The

Tournament of Honor festivities following the jousting event. Though angered when I overheard Benoit claim he was cheated of a win, I knew it best to resolve the matter later. Still, I assured myself there was no great harm in alerting him to my presence—that it might even wrench him back to his senses. Thus, I sought to return the ribbon that fell from your bodice when you retrieved his helmet."

Her breath caught. "Then for that you..."

"You thought I looked upon you with lust."

"I did."

"I noted your beauty, Dangereuse—what man would not? —but no more." At her nod, he continued, "Unaware of the depth of his inebriation, I was not prepared for his outright accusation of cheating, nor his charge I meant to stick him with a blade. Realizing his control slipped, I should have turned aside. Had I, he might have recovered after taking you from the hall—and you, suddenly widowed, would not have had to ask why I could not leave be the ill between us."

"And leave to the dirt a ribbon that was only good for the burning," she repeated what she had cried as he carried her from Benoit's body, then added, "For you touching it, he put it to flame."

He jerked. "Lord!"

"Unfounded jealousy, and that was his undoing," she said, then asked, "Was it because of the injury done you that you did not compete in the mêlée the next morn?"

"Nay, it was not so dire. I but determined it best to resolve the night's tragic events as soon as possible to see you and Sebastian away from that place."

Greater light reflecting in eyes to which tears sprang, she said, "I am grateful you aided us."

It was the same professed the day she, wishing to know what could have been between them, had sought his kiss, but though now more inclined to embrace her gratitude, he reminded, "Aid that would have been unnecessary had I not engaged with Benoit."

"Unnecessary for you, but who would have been there for us when next his possessiveness of my time and body moved him to that edge? Nay, had you not intervened, Bastian could have paid the highest price—if not that day, then another." She shifted her hand alongside his and slid her fingers into his palm. "It was coming. Though that night I did not wish to believe it of my husband, ever it was coming. And..."

"What?"

"I am ashamed to admit a part of me wished foul play behind Benoit's death so I would have an excuse for his behavior when I must tell our son of that night. Forgive me."

"Forgiven," he said, then closed his fingers over hers. "We should sleep."

"First, would you answer me one thing?"

"If I am able."

"You wore Lady Lianor's favor at the joust."

"Aye, a detachable sleeve."

"Unlike the one you saw me cut away."

"I recall—and that you were angry."

"Because Benoit insisted on displaying a sleeve the same as you, though I would have to return to the donjon for a gown that accommodated the giving of that favor and it could disturb our son whose greatest relief for his infection was sleep. Thus, I ruined the gown."

"A loving mother protecting her young, Dangereuse."

"And a wife who, increasingly, felt bound." A laugh escaped. "Though not as I am now."

Hearing fear in that last, he said, "I shall do all in my power to free you and return you to your son. Now your question?"

"That night, it was obvious Lady Lianor was taken with

you, and I thought you receptive. As you did not wed, was she not the love you sought?"

Then Dangereuse wished to know who turned from who, though such a relationship theirs had not been. Knowing she made herself vulnerable over what might be more than attraction for him despite her warning after his arrival at Lillia there could be nothing for him with her, he said, "Very much I like Lady Lianor, and there was some attraction, but as told, I wish to have more with the woman I wed—for our sake as well as our children."

Might her exhale be of relief? Might her fingers in his feel greater movement of the blood coursing his veins?

"How long...?" she trailed off.

"Dange?"

"How long will you pursue love?"

"Before I settle for an alliance to gain an heir? As it does not solely depend on my wants and needs, I cannot say." He squeezed her fingers. "Now let us sleep."

Though the lowering of her lids took the light from her eyes, it glistened in her moist lashes long after she yielded to exhaustion.

An hour later, satisfied with what he was able to cull from their captors whose words became intelligible as more and more bedded down, Rhys also slept.

CHAPTER 24

Rhys had pieced together enough of the enemy's workings and plans to prepare Dangereuse for a day that began before dawn. At the first stirrings of their captors, he had roused her and told that just as they were bound in the cave, so they would be in a wagon. Gagged as well, they would be transported over the border into Lincolnshire, then east to the coast. There, a ship that would brave the winter sea waited to deliver those of De Talliere to France, as well as Lady Vianne, Rhys, and the brigands promised work with the king's advisor.

Of Lady Vianne's accompaniment, Rhys had asserted that though Dangereuse's uncle and brother would appear to coop-erate with demands presented by a messenger paid to deliver a missive to Lillia on the morrow, they would not trade the king's spy. Somehow, hopefully without injury to any standing the side of right, they would devise a means of freeing Dangereuse while keeping hold of Lady Vianne.

Lord, Rhys as well, she silently beseeched as the wagon rumbled over slowly ascending ground, occasionally lurching across patches of ice that had her snatching breath through her nose as she and Rhys jostled against each other where they lay beneath coarse blankets.

In the beginning, which felt days past though it was perhaps five hours, it had been difficult to remain conscious for persistent ache in her middle and being moved toward panic over the cloth in her mouth, rope threatening her airway, and blankets obstructing fresh air.

Thus far, the greatest relief had was when William's brother raised the blankets to ensure Sanche's rope contraption was unaffected by the captives' shifting. Blessedly, only once had it been necessary for him to loosen the rope against which Rhys' neck muscles strained for his effort to keep Dangereuse from rolling onto her side.

Wishing she could see in the dark the man for whom she felt much—and more every moment—glad for the comfort of met fingers squeezed often to confirm the other was alert, she jerked when the man driving the wagon exclaimed, "The signal!"

A warning received from other brigands riding out of sight, as Dangereuse knew from when Rhys and she were loaded in the wagon. Marionne had told all what was expected during the journey and precautions to be taken with half the English traitors under his and Sanche's command scouting ahead, the other half commanded by Pierre and William watching their backs.

"There another signal, Rufus! Three horsemen approachin'."

As if the young man did not realize his name was revealed the same as his brother's, he who was past due in providing fresh air said, "I am thinking I should knock these two senseless."

Dangereuse suppressed a whimper, and the driver said in a

voice meant for the captives as well, "Nay, Marionne told only do we encounter more than six, it being difficult for our archers to put down all ere harm is done us."

Meaning an attempt to alert the oncoming riders of the wagon's cargo would not benefit the captives and result in the deaths of innocents.

A hand slapped the blanket between Rhys' head and hers. "Hear that?" Rufus demanded. "At your peril—and theirs."

The force of that slap knocking her head to the side, anger shot through Dangereuse. Though the gag made it impossible to breathe well through that emotion, the squeeze of Rhys' fingers aided. Thus, both remained still during the exchange that identified the riders as a merchant and his sons en route to London to take possession of a shipment of spices, and the two in the wagon as freemen hoping to better their prospects in York.

After the parties went their separate ways, a check of the captives provided a rush of fresh air, and shortly afterward the driver announced another signal and said it was time to go to the wood.

He went hard right, and the uneven ground was nearly unbearable for rocking that made her middle ache more and caused the rope to further abrade her throat, but at last the horses were reined in and blankets tossed back.

Now relief for the removal of gags...unbinding of ropes... bladders in need of emptying...drink for dry mouths and food for hollow bellies.

A half hour later, Dangereuse sat distant from Rhys, though not so far she could not see the sides of his mouth had been chafed by the gag the same as hers and how watchful he was of their captors gathered here. Then there was his nearer observance of Sanche who wore his Wulfrith dagger and sword and Pierre de Talliere who had revealed outside the cave this morn he had claimed Rhys' armor—strutting about in those pieces as if unaware they fit so poorly he looked more a squire than a knight.

A fine gift, De Arell, he had taunted as the two were roped in the wagon. *I anticipate slaying many English wearing this armor when next your king dares invade our country. Alas, though I would have you there to witness it, my sire lacks patience in righting the wrongs done our family.*

Doubtless, he had hoped his taunting would provide an excuse to do Rhys further injury with which Aubert Marionne would not interfere, but none was provided beyond what the captive knight exuded.

Before they were gagged again, Dangereuse had asked how he was able to control himself, and he had merely repeated the promise to do all in his power to return her to Sebastian.

I am his first consideration, she thought as she had then— and was as glad of it for her son's sake as well as Rhys'. Were she not in danger, likely he would risk his life to gain his freedom ahead of an opportunity that tilted more in his favor than their captors'. But for being heavily under watch and his feet remaining bound unlike hers, what hope for either of them before they reached their destination which, as overheard, would be this eve and on that portion of the bay nearest a settlement called Old Leake? Little hope, but once they arrived...

"You should be glad I was assigned watch over you and Sir Rhys rather than my brother," Rufus said, and when she turned her chin across her mantle's fur collar to look at him where he leaned against a tree, saw he was not as tall as first thought. She had known she surpassed his height, but not by a hand's width.

He jerked his head at where his older brother conversed with Pierre and Marionne alongside a stream that remained ice-crusted for an abundance of evergreens that thwarted the sunlight seeking to reach the floor of the wood.

The first thing noted about William was he had cast the left side of his mantle atop a shoulder, revealing Benoit's dagger fastened to his belt. The second thing of note was further evidence of what she had taken from him—fresh blood from his broken nose, to which he pressed a cloth.

"Could he get you alone, I do not know I could aid you, Lady. His anger persists for ruin made of looks he counted among the only riches left to him."

After a glance at the archers keeping watch over her as well, which she found more distasteful for their lascivious stares, she ventured, "That sounds there was a time he had many riches."

"*We* had," he said and shot his gaze to the two men, but as if deciding it mattered not what was spoken, shrugged. "My brother and I are not noble, but neither are we common."

"As guessed."

He nearly smiled. "You can take all from a man or give all to a man, but 'tis rare his roots are not seen in what grows above."

Beneath her mantle continuing to press her arms against her sides to ease her aching middle, she said, "From your brother's denouncement of women, I guess your riches lost because of a woman."

"Aye, our stepmother. After the pestilence took our sire, she proved she should not have been trusted to act in our interest. Within a year, what was a fortune to us though it might seem little to a Wulfrith, was squandered. Thus, just as she stole from us, we take from others—and greater our success since gathering men to our side."

"That is sad."

"Why sad?"

"Surely you and your brother hated your stepmother for

her dishonesty, and yet now you victimize others just the same. And are the hated ones."

"We were given no choice."

She harrumphed. "Do right...do wrong. Those are choices available to all."

"Providing one can accept that the reward for doing right is death!"

"Had you not betrayed your country, 'tis unlikely death would be of concern."

His lips twitched. "Ere we turned traitors, William was doomed, perhaps me as well." He glanced at his brother. "An eye for an eye."

She thought she understood, but seeking confirmation, said, "He killed your stepmother?"

He averted his gaze. "He did not mean to push her as hard as he did. Had she not been full of drink, she would not have lost her balance." His nostrils flared. "Not that the world is an uglier place for her absence."

Greater his callousness would anger did she not sense his words were more William's than his. "As told—sad—as is the least your victims would say of you."

His face tightened, and she thought he would further defend the lives he and his brother had chosen, but Aubert Marionne commanded all to prepare to resume their journey.

Her belly tossed its contents, and too soon she and Rhys were returned to the wagon and given only enough time for him to ask how her injury fared and her to exaggerate her healing before gags were fit.

Too soon, Sanche bound them, while Rhys attended to what could be seen of the weaving of ropes.

Too soon, the blankets covered them, which would be easier to tolerate were they able to speak in smothering darkness.

And too soon, Dangereuse's family would risk their lives to carve a way for her out of this.

Lord, be with them and us, she entreated.

Castle Lillia

AFTER A DAY that had Warin roaring over the cruelty of the enemy and how powerless he felt, might this be God's answer to the faithful prayers of others for his own being more demanding than beseeching?

"The Lord cradles our petitions in His hand," Owen alerted his nephew of his interpretation of the arrival of the man standing before the high table gripping his cap in both hands.

Lowering the second missive delivered to Lillia this day, this one intended for the Wulfriths and signed by Pierre de Talliere, Warin considered those in the hall who should be feasting in celebration of Christ's birth but either recovered from injuries dealt by arrows and freezing water or tended the unfortunate ones.

He returned to the messenger. "No apology needed, John of Lincolnshire. Though you know not the identity of who instructed you to deliver this at dawn on the morrow, we are acquainted with him. For that, far better you brought it this day."

Nervously, the man rolled his soft cap. "Much relieved, milord, for I be a man of my word. If not for offer of work on the morrow and coin needed to feed my family these scarce months, I would have done for yer friend as he paid me to do."

Warin felt ache in hands going to fists. "No friend that," he growled.

Before he could set aright harshness that was not John's

243

due, his uncle strode from behind the table and halted before the man. "Though one should aspire to keep his word, since unknowingly you gave yours to one who intends our family and people harm, count the work offered you as the Lord's intervention."

Relief began prying apart the lines in John's face, but they drew near again. "God's wounds! I might have been an accomplice to ill done the Wulfriths." He gulped. "Had I known—"

"You could not." Owen extended a hand. "The coin you were paid."

The man dug it out of what was surely an otherwise empty purse and dropped it in the large palm. "Knowing 'twas evil not blessin' given me, I will have naught to do with it."

Now Warin's uncle took from his own purse and opened his hand. "No evil this, John. Wulfrith gratitude."

The man stared at the coins. "That is much for what little I done—and not as if I thought to do ye and yours a good turn." He jutted his chin at the missive. "Alls I did was mount me old horse and bring that 'cross the border."

"Which, as told, more greatly aids for being delivered this day," Owen said. "Now accept this, warm yourself before the fire, and be refreshed with food and drink ere you begin your return journey."

"I thank ye." Carefully, he picked each coin out of the weapon-hardened palm as if fearing his touch would offend. After snugging them in his purse, he looked to Warin. "My lord."

"Godspeed your journey and good health to you and your family," Warin said.

John turned and crossed to one of the sideboards on which the day's feast had been spread as supervised by Murielle who, Sebastian having turned from her to Amanda for comfort, smothered her own fear over this day's attack by staying in motion.

But not much longer, Warin thought when he saw her straighten with difficulty from the pallet of a youth who had to be resuscitated for how long he was in the frigid water.

Strain in hands once more alerting Warin to fists that were useless in the absence of a target, for which he and the warriors not needed to aid the injured at the pond had gone in search of, he splayed them. But soon they were fists again for remembrance of efforts to recover Dangereuse and Rhys that were thwarted by the rapid division of their quarry in too many directions and melting snow covering the tracks.

"Accursed traitors," he bit, certain this day's atrocities would not have happened if the French had not been aided by men who proved it was only an accident of birth they were English. Though two had been slain at the pond and several of those who fled sustained injuries, there was little satisfaction in that.

"I shall make preparations for us to depart within the hour," his uncle said. "You agree Lady Vianne must accompany us?"

"Aye, and that between here and the coast we determine how best to use her to retrieve my sister and Sir Rhys."

His uncle started to turn away, paused. "We have the advantage and shall make good use of it."

Will it be enough? Warin wondered, then swept up the missive and once more read words written in a spidery hand.

Greetings, Wulfriths. Here my demand for the return of Lady Vianne Wardieu taken from French soil by Sir Rhys de Arell who claims he was overpowered by lust. As he shall answer to my sire, the trade will be Lady Vianne for Lady Dangereuse alone. Now I make clear the fate of your kin do you not cooperate. Though my father wishes his mistress returned to his bed, which may not change even when proven the whore sought to provide your king intelligence, I believe another mistress can be made for him. That is what shall become of Lady Dangereuse of fine face and figure and silvered hair that is as soft as it looks. Indeed, a better whore she could prove once she learns her place—providing such a woman can be tamed without entirely breaking her.

"Which will not compare to how I shall break you, Pierre de Talliere," Warin bit, then read what remained.

Do you not come east to the bay beyond Old Leake immediately upon receipt of this missive, bringing with you Lady Vianne and no more than a dozen men, my ship will set sail not only with Sir Rhys but Lady Dangereuse. I do not doubt the Wulfriths believe it possible to recover their kin from whatever place my sire deems suitable for his spirited new mistress, but blood that need not be spilled shall be. Do not think long on this. Deliver Lady Vianne, and Lady Dangereuse may return to her son. Refuse me and no good end for your kin. ~ Chevalier Pierre de Talliere.

Warin rolled the missive. It was time to inform the French advisor's mistress she would accompany them to the coast, compose a missive to inform his eldest brother of all that had transpired, then lay plans to save his sister without yielding the king's spy. Though should it prove necessary...

CHAPTER 25

S uch a coward Vianne felt—and certainly behaved for how long she pressed her face into the mattress to muffle misery amid prayers groping their way heavenward for those injured in her name. And greater that misery when hours later a response to Sir Owen's missive to her family was delivered her.

All hope of being restored to the Wardieus lost, it decided that for the sake of siblings ill affected by her embrace of France and relationship with the king's advisor it best she not return home, she had entirely lost control as not done in years.

Fortunately, none would know how terrible the blow dealt her since Sir Warin had ordered the one tasked with returning her to the castle following the attack to ensure she remain in her chamber. As that warrior was needed to aid with the injured, rather than keep watch outside her door, he had locked her in and, like the others, forgotten her.

Now with winter's early night approaching, mantle hugged close for the brazier going cold, she stood before a window fit with opaque panes and strained to catch sounds evidencing Lady Dangereuse and Sir Rhys were recovered from those who sought to return De Talliere's mistress to his bed.

However, her chamber being situated at the rear of the donjon and sound resistant to traveling that distance and bending around corners, her mind went adrift. Though she knew she ought to drag it back, she set imagined feet on the imagined soil of the country she had fled and to which her family prefer she return rather than the sanctuary of home. Next, her imaginings swept her to Paris, the palace and court of King Philip and now his son, Jean, the apartments of his trusted advisor, the chamber where—

"Non!" she gasped and, further reviled her accent was altered for having so long resided in France, swallowed bile. However, it rose again with remembrance of what she had become to De Talliere for refusing to wed him years ago. Then there was the pecking—never-to-be answered—question of what little happiness she might have known had she agreed and birthed a child welcome for its legitimacy.

"I must speak with you, Lady Vianne."

She whirled and stumbled back against the window embrasure. As her head clipped the panes behind and gave a crack of protest, she saw the fair-haired Warin Wulfrith strode toward her.

"Stop!" She tossed up a hand.

Having moved from shadow into light, he complied and lowered his eyes over her. Then that stern face whose short whiskers could not entirely cover burns one side of it was moved by a frown.

Feeling as if fire sprang beneath the hand she unthinkingly pressed to her belly, she dropped it to her side. Then widening her stance to firm her feet, she said as coldly as he had looked upon her since they met, "For entering this lady's chamber without invitation, you must be eager to deliver word of the injured."

His heavily lashed eyes returned to hers. "It appears all will survive, though some shall ever be changed by what was done them."

Because of me, she thought, then asked, "What of your sister and Sir Rhys?"

"Yet imperiled for your lover's..." He trailed off.

For how much Vianne hated Rollon de Talliere being named that, she curled her fingers into her skirts.

Warin Wulfrith cleared his throat. "Our efforts to retrieve them having failed for there being too few resources at the time they were taken, they have become pawns in De Talliere's bid to recover his mistress. As for my trespass, I knocked. Had you answered, I would have remained in the passageway and spoken with you there."

Then I so far descended into the dark years following my arrival in Paris I was made deaf? she wondered.

Does it matter? the other side of her countered.

Knowing the sooner this man unburdened his tongue, the sooner she could be free of one who judged her the same as many who knew not the glass-strewn path traveled by one named *whore* and *harlot,* she folded her hands before her. "For what did you come, Baron?"

He drew a missive from beneath his belt, and as he extended it to her, glanced at the table beside the bed. Fairly certain he searched for the missive she received hours past with its seal intact, she stiffened. It was not there, and though he meant to share the contents of his, she would not share what was inked for her alone.

"You received ill tidings?" he asked as she took the missive.

She stilled. "What makes you think that?"

"You have been weeping."

She blinked and, feeling the sore of red-riddled eyes, said, "I grieve for those injured this day and those taken." Abruptly, she turned to the window and unrolled the parchment. When a glance at the bottom revealed the sender, she steeled herself, then read what threatened to so entirely empty her belly its lining might be lost as well.

Pierre being fairly known to her, she should have been prepared, but it seemed he had gone colder and darker for what she was to his sire that his stepmother was not—and he ought not wish that lady to be.

Keeping her back to the Wulfrith who found her distasteful, and for which she could not entirely fault him, Vianne let the words blur and returned her thoughts to the missive delivered her. Then telling herself to accept what was best for all— perhaps even herself considering how alone she was in this cruel world—she turned back.

"You will meet his demands? Trade me for your sister?"

There was enough hesitation to be certain his answer was not as firm as it sounded. "Nay, King Edward expects you. However, for the appearance of cooperation, you will accompany us."

"Appearance," she murmured. "And your plan?"

"Since we depart immediately to take advantage of the expectation we arrive late on the morrow, there is no time to fully form one, but much will be decided ere we reach the coast."

"Then I shall make ready to leave."

He inclined his head. "You do not seem afeared."

Playing the part it seemed ever she was writing for herself, she raised her chin. "Ought I not trust your word I am for London rather than Paris?"

After a slight hesitation, he said, "I aspire to bring all out of this alive and whole, Lady Vianne," and departed without locking her in.

Disturbingly, a half hour later it was he who aided in her mount of a fine palfrey that promised to be of good speed.

Which will not be enough, she thought as, bounded by thirty riders in defiance of Pierre's allowance for a dozen—and among them archers—she rode from Lillia as the chill of night descended.

"Much more I shall require from you," she whispered to the horse she bent over to be nearer its heat and keep the air from hitting her full in the face. "You must also take direction well. *My* direction."

Coast of Lincolnshire

FOR THE CHILL sweeping across the sea separating England from France, it could have been a miserable night for Rhys and Dangereuse as it must have been for their captors who lacked the shelter of a cave along this portion of the coast, but since the two remained in the wagon beneath blankets, they had that warmth and what they passed to each other lying side by side.

That and removal of their gags should have been conducive to sleep, but though Dangereuse had fallen into an uneasy rest —possibly for the injury Rhys feared did not heal as well as told—the warrior of him had resisted. Thus, from conversations in the night, with the sun's light now pouring from unclouded skies that made the ship offshore glow, he knew word of Pierre de Talliere's terms would reach Lillia soon.

For the certainty it would be many hours before Owen and Warin Wulfrith appeared as instructed, there was no urgency about their captors, albeit much enthusiasm when one man patrolling the rocky, sparsely-treed rise overlooking this portion of the coast announced the ship had lowered two small boats.

"I fear they come for you, Rhys." Dangereuse looked to where he sat beside her, their backs against the wagon's bench and ropes loosed sufficiently to allow them to quench their thirst and break their fast.

"They do," he said and wondered how her brother and uncle would rescue her without making the trade. Were any capable of ensuring her return to Sebastian, it was the Wulfriths, but all could go awry. If it did and she survived, she could find herself in France the same as he.

"Is there naught we can do to keep you off the ship?" She nodded at the vessel that appeared to have fair sailing weather ahead.

"Nothing at this time."

"But they will have to unbind you to get you aboard."

"Aye, and just as we are permitted only enough freedom to relieve ourselves with some dignity, threat to one or the other will cut the legs out from under an escape attempt."

She pressed her teeth into her lower lip, then gave a shake of the head that caused sunlight to seek a mirror in her silver strands. "It would be dangerous for me to resist lest harm is done you, but since they believe they are close to what they seek and need me to gain it, I do not believe anything terrible would befall me were you to escape."

"Were your kin here or soon expected, likely not, but the ire of William whose men far outnumber the French merely simmers for you breaking his nose. Thus, were I to run without you and fail, he might punish me by doing you ill."

"But I am needed—"

"Dangereuse, I do not think he would harm you in a way

your suffering would be visible to your menfolk. But harm of the lustful sort, perhaps even to reward his men..."

Her breath caught.

"Forgive me for suggesting what should be unthinkable, but that is the character of these men. Thus, I will not attempt to gain my freedom whilst it is possible to extract an unconscionably high price from you."

"And yet you would have me..." She averted her gaze.

Did he just wish he knew what she left unspoken? He nearly pulled back from asking, then said, "What would I have you do, Dange?"

"Dange," she whispered, then lifted her eyes to his. "You would have *me* pay a high price for my freedom." As the muscle center of his chest convulsed, she continued, "Without considering your fate, you would have me turn my back on you."

He filled his lungs with air that would be painfully cold on a ship under sail. "As we both know, your first consideration is your son as it ought to be. Sebastian needs a mother whole of mind and body, not one who will have to piece herself back together should she suffer what is the worst offense committed against women."

Her eyes moistened.

Feeling the strain of controlling himself each time there had been an opportunity to overwhelm his captors, he said, "Once I no longer war over how my actions affect you, greater the likelihood of escaping those who think to deliver me to De Talliere."

She blinked. "I had not considered that."

"I tell you only so you accept I know what is best."

With a nod, she started to turn her body toward his, but whimpered and bent forward.

He gripped her wrist. "Your belly?"

"Aye."

Rhys slammed his gaze to Pierre who sat before a fire with Aubert Marionne and several archers. No longer wearing the armor with which he had taunted Rhys, having tossed it in the wagon, he reached gloved hands to flames that were reflected in the steel of his boots.

Lord, what I would do to that miscreant given the opportunity, he thought, *and worse if what Dangereuse suffers is more than tender bruising.*

With a shuddering sigh, she eased back against the wagon's forward panel. "Until all is healed, I but need to be thoughtful of movement."

"What you need is a physician." No sooner said than he was struck by how she could be treated sooner. "Blackwood is nearer than Lillia, Dangereuse."

She looked across her shoulder. "Is it?"

"Still a good distance, but that is where you must go since my family's physician is exceptionally skilled in healing."

"Nay, 'tis not so bad I would delay being reunited with Bastian to ease his fear."

It was good she sounded of the belief whatever came she would be going home, but to increase that chance she needed skillful care. "Your boy is stronger than you think. An extra day or two—"

She shook her head, that movement loosing a tress from her fur collar and the stiff breeze making it stream behind her like a lady's ribbon fixed to the sleeve of a charging knight. "Though you may find it difficult to believe, my son feels the hurts of others, especially those dear to him. Months past, he had a fit of temper as he had not in some time when he overheard my sister, Ondine, voice fear over what afflicts Fira."

Dangereuse spoke of the Falling Sickness she had discussed with Murielle in the hall. Though it was not yet certain the youngest Wulfrith's mother had passed it to her, it seemed the boy understood enough to know it could be devastating.

"Still, I believe Sebastian can weather your absence a while longer," he said, "and more easily for word of your recovery being sent to Lillia."

Feeling her scrutiny all the way through, he thought were they not watched he would bend his head and, no matter the rope's cinch, kiss her—perhaps as a promise of what to expect if both escaped, perhaps in remembrance of what could have been if they did not.

Then he nearly laughed. Already their captors knew of the power held over them for the care each had for the other, having wielded it to ensure they remain manageable. Why deny themselves a kiss?

Before he could make good on the answer, William shouted, "Give report, Thomas!"

Rhys looked to where he stood several hundred feet from the wagon, face tilted up as he waited for one over the rise to appear. As he had only once before initiated the contact when a quarter hour passed without the man assuring him none of the patrol saw nor heard anything amiss, when he received no answer, with greater urgency William called another by name.

But then Thomas appeared. "I had to make water! Be assured, all is quiet."

When dismissively the leader of the brigands pivoted to watch those working the oars draw near, Pierre rose and, rubbing warmed hands, turned to his captives. "The time is nigh, Rhys de Arell!" he called, then waved forward Sanche who had paused in conversing with Rufus.

"Pray, not yet," Dangereuse rasped as the rope master and several brigands advanced over ground that was as much rock as sand.

"You will stay here and quietly await your kin," Rhys said.

"Now I want your word that when they free you, you will tell of your injury and have them take you to Castle Mathe upon Blackwood."

Further her eyes moistened.

"Your word, Dangereuse!" At her continued hesitation, he said, "I do not believe I flatter myself in saying there *is* something for me with you though once you warned there was not."

"I did not think there was then," she whispered, "but now... Aye, much, but not if you go from me and never return."

Unable to assure her they would meet again, he said, "Then for me, go first to Blackwood."

Stiffly, she nodded.

Though he was tempted to challenge the laxity of the rope about his neck and kiss her, Sanche and the others, accompanied by Marionne, neared.

"You are drink, Dangereuse," he repeated what he had named her when his injury was being tended and he excused the slip by telling himself his mind had but tipped on its side. "And lightning in the night."

"Rhys," she pleaded as the brigands surrounded the wagon with blades drawn and Sanche sprang into it and swept back the blanket covering them.

The Frenchman's facility with winding, twisting, looping, and knotting rope was fascinating. Though increasingly Rhys made sense of intricacy that rivaled a spider's web, he remained uncertain of how to escape, albeit mostly for being unable to observe how the rope was woven behind his back.

"Though you seek to unravel my secrets, English knight, they remain mine," Sanche drawled once the two were no longer bound to each other and he coiled the rope entirely removed from Rhys and mostly Dangereuse whose lower legs remained bound. Then he gripped the wagon rail and jumped back to the sand.

"Your ride awaits, Sir Rhys," Marionne said where he stood on the side near Dangereuse, then jutted his chin at the boats, one having come ashore, the other rocking behind. "As I believe you will behave in consideration of the lady, I trust it is unnecessary to bind you." When Sanche made an exclamation of dissent, he snapped, "You can play with your ropes again once you have him aboard!"

Rhys did not have to look to Dangereuse to know her thoughts returned to his escape, but even were she not in danger, there was no chance of success since all were intent upon him and armed—of greatest detriment those who could fly an arrow, whether to incapacitate or slay.

"I require no bindings," Rhys agreed.

"Then follow Sanche."

Landing booted feet in the sand and feeling the ache of oft-jolted muscles, Rhys looked over his shoulder. And sent up thanks that though Dangereuse's legs remained bound, she was otherwise freed. After beseeching the Lord to prevent the brigands from further harming her, he said, "Aubert Marionne."

"Oui, Sir Rhys?"

"I trust I need not inform you the lady is ill from the beating dealt by your charge."

The man narrowed his eyes, glanced at De Talliere's son who once more sat his haunches before the fire, then said, "Does it give you some small pleasure to make *Chevalier* Pierre sound a stripling?"

"As you must know, it is no exaggeration despite him being far too old in body to have a keeper," Rhys said. "Regardless, for injury done the lady's innards, it is best she is moved as little as possible—that is, unless you think it will be benefit you to offer her family an unconscious hostage for a healthy one."

Tight lipped, Marionne considered Dangereuse's pallid face, jerked his chin. "Cause our men no trouble, and she shall remain undisturbed."

"I would have your word on that."

Amusement lit the older man's eyes. "The word of a..." He frowned. "What is it you smug English call my wise countrymen who know when to stay and fight and when to vanquish pride and retreat?" He shot up a finger. "Ah, *les signaleurs blancs* when *continental swine* is not enough to express contempt for the French whose mother country most of the English nobility share."

"Your word, Marionne."

"Given. Now..." He swept a hand toward the boats. "I will join you aboard ship by late afternoon, and if the Wulfriths behave, your companion will be Lady Vianne with whom you would have us believe you are more captivated than Lady Dangereuse." He glanced at the latter. "Though my lord's mistress is beautiful, I am observant, and what I witnessed when our men surrounded you after William captured this lady makes me question the truth of your desire for Lady Vianne. Of course, perhaps your affections are easily changed." He chuckled. "Ah, that was a long way around seeing you away, English knight. Go!"

Rhys looked to Dangereuse. After saying to her what he could with his eyes, he drew his mantle close. Then flanked by two brigands who, he silently vowed, would fare better to count themselves his countrymen than not, followed Sanche.

CHAPTER 26

Dangereuse had become accustomed to this persistent sense of ill since Christmas Day, but with Rhys' departure, more it was felt and she could not move her eyes from him—even now he was in the boat accompanied by Sanche and one of the brigands.

Blessedly, though she had feared he would be bound despite Marionne's directive, which could see his life forfeited if a wave or cruel current capsized the boat, he remained unfettered on the center bench facing the ship.

"Just as I suspect Sir Rhys has no great feeling for the errant Lady Vianne, I think you have much feeling for him," Marionne said.

She wanted to ignore him, but recalling what he said before Rhys' departure, looked around. "What is it you witnessed when Sir Rhys was taken by your hirelings?"

He smiled. "I thought you would ask, proving me right about what you feel for him and getting closer to what he feels for you that caused the fight to go out of a Wulfen-trained knight."

259

She glowered. "You talk in circles! Is that the French way?"

She so enjoyed the disruption of his smile that when she nearly bent over a cramp, more she regretted concern softening his expression than the pain—petty though it was.

"Oui, you are unwell, Lady. Most unfortunate Pierre has a temper."

She breathed through the ache, which was nearly as difficult as breathing through anger, then looked to the boat and saw it struggled to make progress.

Lord, she entreated as the second boat came ashore, *command that strong current to prevail over the oarsmen. Send Rhys back to me.*

"My lady?"

Recalling Rhys' assessment of Pierre and what this man told of that one, she said, "A temper? Is that truly your excuse for one of such age he ought to have long ago mastered how to behave a man rather than a child when the answer he seeks is not immediately given?" She might have laughed scornfully if not that it would further her pain. "Still, I thank you for the revelation my son of not even six years is more mature than believed."

Offense was back, but though she expected he would not answer her query, he said, "What I witnessed when William took you after losing hold of your son was a fierce knight likely to escape for his ability to cut through men of lesser skill. But rather than withdraw to come at us later aided by those occupied with saving the others, he joined you in captivity."

She returned her regard to Rhys—and wished he would look around. Though he had spoken words that professed his heart was engaged with hers, was it more engaged than believed? Had he joined in her suffering not because his attempt to retrieve her landed him in the hands of her captors, but for accepting he could not save her there and risking his life to protect her during her captivity—even make a way for her to escape?

"You see?" Marionne said. "Because of you, what Pierre believes of Lady Vianne is likely proven—that she arranged her return to England in exchange for intelligence. Unfortunately, were our king to learn of the breach of security made possible by his advisor's relationship with her, much would go wrong for the obsessed Rollon de Talliere, which could then go wrong for Pierre."

Dangereuse narrowed her lids. "It seems a lot of trouble and danger to try to correct De Talliere's error by returning Lady Vianne to him." She paused to consider how best to word what must be maintained since she did not know what would become of the lady. "If De Talliere's mistress left of her own accord, which I do not believe for having conversed with her and seen her distress at being brought to England, and if she possesses information whose exposure is detrimental to your country, why not render that information obsolete?"

"Two things. It is not known for certain what intelligence she stole, and if she had access to what is of greatest import, it will be almost impossible to alter it without raising suspicions that could harm my lord for his involvement in constructing and championing those plans."

"But if Pierre is correct about Lady Vianne's return to England, how do you know her intelligence has not already been delivered to my king by way of a messenger? In that event, surely it is better to expend effort on altering the plans whose revelation you fear."

"I am more of that mind, but on this I yield to Pierre who holds the lady can be persuaded to reveal what she knows and has told others." He paused as if to let her peel back the word *persuaded* that was but a disguise worn by the word *tortured*.

"*If* she betrayed," Dangereuse persisted.

"Which may never be truly known. However, if she can prove her innocence, not only will she be happy to return to my lord, but he will be most pleased to have her in his bed again. Either way, gratitude will be due his son for retrieving her."

"And you."

He wrinkled his nose. "I do not seek gratitude. I but wish to serve my lord well in being an exceptional companion to his heir."

"Do you not mean *keeper?*"

He leaned forward. "Even the most formidable warrior requires guidance."

"Especially those more formidable for being quick-tempered than with their skill at arms," Dangereuse said, recalling the steel-tipped kick, which the only real warrior present could not prevent, though Rhys saved her from further injury at the sacrifice of his own bound body.

This time the offense Marionne took was so fleeting he had either expected such a response or was benumbed by what he believed the enemy's prejudice. But then of a sudden he reached to her.

She recoiled, but he merely flipped the blankets up to cover her breasts. "The hours between now and the arrival of Lady Vianne will be long, especially do you grow cold lacking Sir Rhys' warmth," he said. "Naught I can do about the injury to your innards, but some comfort in this."

"I would thank you were your consideration not self-serving. Certes, my family will not trade Lady Vianne for a corpse."

He sighed. "Does that prove your fate, I believe it will not be this day, Lady of the Wulfriths. But it is true all shall go better if your menfolk are given no reason to behave poorly."

"No reason? I need no mirror to know my face testifies to rough treatment at the least."

"It does, so let us hope that is greater incentive for your kin to quickly resolve the matter—a somewhat bruised lady for one who maintains she prefers France to England."

Had Dangereuse intended to prolong the conversation, it would have been interrupted by the patrol who appeared on the ridge and called, "All is still! All is quiet!"

William acknowledged the report, strode toward the fire over which Pierre yet presided, and cast Dangereuse a look of loathing before she swept her gaze to the boat that was less small than expected. It seemed the Lord would not answer her prayer that Rhys return to her, but no easy thing would it be for the oarsmen to get him aboard ship where Sanche would refit his ropes.

Digging her chin into the fur collar as she stared at Rhys who was known to her only by the fair of his hair, silently she entreated, *Lord, do something ere the doing becomes more impossible.*

TIMING WAS NOT ALL, Warin thought, but at this moment nearly so.

The patrol's report once more received by those on the shore, and all but one of the brigands who contributed put down by an arrow, he looked from the most recent man quietly dropped out of the saddle to the youngest Wulfrith brother—Rémy who accepted it was killing arrows he must land rather than incapacitating ones lest the cries of the injured alert those below that the Wulfriths were here earlier than expected.

"Do you never miss?" Warin asked low and admiringly.

That made the grim-faced Rémy smile a little. "Far less than once I did." It was said so smoothly Warin longed to praise him for speech that could not better match the depth and strength of a voice whose youthful cracks and sudden pitches were behind him. Unfortunately, the stammering was not entirely resolved, proving its absence was not due to burial but merely rest sometimes long enough to say it slept, other times of such short duration it could barely be said to nap.

Having once more stretched beside Warin in the brittle grass growing between bushes misshapen and ravaged by salt air, Rémy drew another arrow from his quiver. "Tell me when to take down the last knave." He nodded at the brigand patrolling the area on foot above the shore who had the added responsibility of reporting what others of his patrol saw and heard.

"Put him to ground as soon as he ventures this way well out of sight of those below," Warin said and hoped men on the ship would not see him drop. Though at this distance no sense could be made of their shouts, they did not need to be understood to give warning danger was very near.

"Ten more feet this way," Rémy muttered as he rose to his knees and nocked the arrow. "Aye, traitor, then a well-earned rest for you."

Not for the first time since Rémy's arrival at Lillia shortly before Warin and Owen's departure, Warin praised the Lord that Hector had determined their brother of good health should dwell at Lillia during the final weeks of his wife's pregnancy. Doubtless, he hoped a bond would form between the two and be strengthened by the birth of the child he was to accept and raise as his own.

Though it was not for Rémy's reluctance to spend time with Lady Murielle he had insisted on aiding in securing Dangereuse's freedom, he was surely glad for the respite. Had not Owen insisted he greet his wife and assure her of his prompt return, possibly the rift between them would have far less chance of being bridged.

Continuing to move stealthily, Rémy rose to his full height

and assumed the proper stance. "Sighted," he rasped, "and..." He went so still that if not for bright in the eye fixed on his target, one might believe him carved of stone. Then the string flew a beautifully-fletched arrow that performed perfectly its duty by silently dropping their former countryman.

Though certain all the patrol were down, since there was always room for some error, Warin rose cautiously. After peering behind in the direction of those awaiting orders and giving a nod, he gripped his brother's shoulder. "Well done. God willing, soon we recover our sister."

"Not much hope for Sir Rhys," Rémy said.

So told Squire Ferrand who had proven his worth though his Wulfen training ended well ahead of knighthood. Shortly before Warin accompanied Rémy to eliminate the patrol, Ferrand and another had scouted the area. The former had drawn so near the shore he was able to describe the encampment in detail—three campfires separated by hundreds of feet and around which half the enemy sat or stood, gatherings of brigands conversing distant from the fires, tethered horses their riders would not mount again since there was no means of getting them aboard, and location of the wagon both Dangereuse and Sir Rhys occupied before the knight was taken to the boat.

Recalling Sir Rhys' sacrifice of freedom in trying to take back Dangereuse at the pond, Warin said, "If no hope for that valiant knight now, much hope when the Wulfriths aid Baron de Arell in retrieving his son."

Rémy lowered the bow. "Should that transpire, I would a-a..." Momentarily, he closed his eyes.

Ever Warin was tempted to speak the word it seemed his brother's foot caught upon, but as learned long ago, it could so offend that Rémy's speech was further impeded.

"I would accompany you, Warin."

As this was not the time to remind him more training was needed before spurs were fit and, with aggressive intent, he entered a country at war with their own, Warin said, "We look first to doing what must be done *this* day." Then he motioned his brother to follow and the two stretched their legs long to return to their uncle and men.

As they neared, Warin saw Owen mounted alongside Lady Vianne conversed with Squire Ferrand on his other side. Before he could confirm what was being imparted was greater detail about the encampment, sudden movement about Lady Vianne returned his regard to her. There had been lean in her body before, but now she sat stiffly erect, and he saw the swift withdrawal of her hand through the part in her mantle.

Was her guilt—as of one fearing being caught doing something wrong—imagined?

"'Tis time?" Owen asked.

As Warin looked to the older man, he felt thicken the air of anticipation exclusive to warriors about to engage in battle. Thus, he told himself whatever the lady exuded was of no import.

Are you certain of that? his long departed sire spoke to him across the years, and he saw again the newly made squire of him exulting over a contest of quarterstaffs that could have ended in the defeat of an opponent of greater build and experience had Warin confirmed the rules of forfeit were observed after putting an advanced squire on the ground. Instead, he was unprepared when one who observed the rules of forfeit came at him again.

Do you turn your back on what you but deem dangerous no longer, what appears triumph may be treacherous loss in disguise, his sire reproved, then added, *That shall stand as lesson number fourteen, Warin Wulfrith.*

"Warin," his uncle returned him to the present, "what is vulnerable now may not be minutes hence."

And Dangereuse is at stake, he thought as he looked from Owen to the others. "We stick to the plan, but be alert for alterations," he said. "Watch for hand signals and listen well."

After he received their nods, Ferrand and a man-at-arms drew alongside Lady Vianne to protect her flanks while exposing her to the enemy who were likelier to make mistakes if she appeared within their grasp. Though Warin felt the pull of the woman's gaze, he turned his mount toward the sea that, despite the sun caressing its waves and troughs, blew cold air across his face and shifted his mantle.

Beneath the water where the large vessel awaited its passengers with sails lowered, a powerful stir in the depths was evidenced by rocking that made it appear the ship's masts were lances wildly jousting with the sky. And still a long-reaching current thwarted the boat carrying Rhys de Arell distant from the shore.

Lord, let that be Your hand in this ahead of Your hand in what we aspire to now, Warin silently prayed, then drew his Wulfrith dagger. Catching light on it, he sent three flashes southeast.

A moment later, two flashes were given by the scout who remained out of sight of the enemy.

"God be with us," Warin said. "Ride!"

CHAPTER 27

S trange she was more prepared for the unforeseen than her captors. But despite the unlikelihood the Wulfriths could be here already, if any could accomplish that feat, it was the men of her family.

And you, Lord, she silently added, and again at the realization none on the ship had seen what was out of sight of those on the shore so they might sound a warning. Now the horsemen flooding over the rise broke across the enemy ranks, and among them was Warin and Rémy.

The lawless who had put too much faith in the reports of those on patrol—men surely forever relieved of their duty—began scattering. As Pierre, Marionne, and four brigands ran toward the second boat, others made for their horses.

When Dangereuse shot her gaze to Rhys and saw he had come around on the bench, shouts began traveling ship to shore. It was then she realized she wasted the opportunity to aid in her release.

Left on her own minutes earlier, she had drawn in her legs beneath the blankets and, with unbound hands, explored the rope pressing her calves and ankles together. Though she had found the knot, it had been a blind attempt to free the cinched end lest any look her way.

Now with war cries and shouts abounding, she thrust the covers down and bent forward and to the side. Gasping over the ache at her center, she picked at the knot binding her booted ankles.

Hardly had she pried free one of the turnings than Warin shouted her name. She snapped up her head. Not only was his way to her blocked by those who had gained their mounts and brought swords to hand, but brigand archers had taken cover behind boulders on both sides of this stretch of shoreline and begun flying arrows. And with William of damaged face coming for her, there was nothing she could do beyond use her arms to resist him.

And teeth, she thought of how Sebastian had freed himself. *I broke your nose. Give me a chance, and you will have a bite far worse than a crescent of cut flesh to remember me by.*

"Treacherous Wulfrith!" he barked and bounded into the wagon.

Named thus because he and his allies had been bettered— and, regardless of her fate, worse would be dealt them. However, they were not entirely without hope, the degree of *worse* in their hands.

Hoping to keep William from taking hold of her, she slammed her palms to the planks at her back, drew her knees to her chest, and thrust her boots at the juncture between his thighs.

He jumped aside. Though he avoided that humiliation, he took the hit in his upper thigh and went down hard on one knee, but before she could strike again, he yanked her upright.

"Betrayer!" she hissed and, eye to eye with William of no country, once more drew her head back to further damage his nose. But he dropped to his haunches and, as momentum carried her forward, slammed a hand to her back to bend her over his shoulder.

So viciously pain tore through her abdomen that what followed was seen through a haze, and what was heard muddled words from which she pieced together just enough to know what he vowed to do to her would be more painful than what she had inflicted on him.

Moments later, they were out of the wagon. She heard shouts, curses, and the clash of arms, saw below her sand kicked up by boots that traveled no straight line in avoiding the frenzied movements of others.

Only when sea-soaked sand was beneath those boots did the haze begin to clear. Still she hurt, especially when jostled by the hard landing of a heel, but enough sense returned that she began striking at his back with fists and assaulted his front with knees slammed into his ribs.

It did not stop him and probably would not even could she fold over further and sink her teeth into his back, but there was satisfaction in knowing his only way to retaliate was to curse her and squeeze the outside of her thigh so hard she cried out. Then he was splashing through foaming surf and the voices of Pierre and Marionne urged him onward.

Thinking to make sense of the din across the shore, she turned her head as far right as she could and saw all upside down. What first captured her regard were riders on the ridge, notable for how motionless they were as if they watched a performance. However, the role they played was greater than that, as evidenced by the woman who sat between Ferrand and another warrior. Lady Vianne was here.

Certain her presence was for show alone, Dangereuse considered what the three observed. It looked a mêlée, and though those of Wulfen prevailed over the enemy with Warin and Rémy leading the way and wielding their weapons astride, none were near enough to save her for William's archers continuing to loose missiles. And were arrows also flown from the boat?

Shortly, with her hair dragging through sea water up to her captor's hips, William thrust her off his shoulder. With a cry, she landed face up in the bottom of the boat and saw two archers at the fore releasing arrows from the cover of shields held by fellow brigands hunkering behind and to the side of them.

Fortunately, the missiles these men shot ashore would lack accuracy for the boat's movement—and even less for greater movement caused by William heaving himself over the side. Ten here, including the oarsmen sitting center of the boat and Pierre and Marionne at the rear, the latter having come partially out from behind their shields as if expecting the arrows to cease targeting them now she was here.

William was more secure in that belief, planting his feet on either side of her and straightening. "Be quick, Rufus!" he shouted.

Could his brother make it past the warriors of Wulfen? Dangereuse wondered, but though she longed to sit up and watch the progress made against men of ill intent, she lay there awash in pain—until Pierre commanded William to seat her to give more weight to the threat she would be put through if Warin's archers continued firing on the boat.

Thrust onto a bench, she pressed her lips to keep from voicing her ache and surveyed those fighting ashore, the sight of which was unobstructed for the boat being aslant in the water.

As arrows no longer flew this direction, she knew for her sake the Wulfrith bowmen were ordered to cease firing.

Instead, they aided the others in adding to the seven brigands already put to ground.

"Methinks we shall prevail over Wulfrith trickery, Aubert," Pierre said, then exclaimed, "And that of De Arell."

Dangereuse snapped her head around and, seeing he peered over his shoulder, followed his gaze.

The other boat had ceased its advance, the oarsmen staggered upright as if they had been knocked off their bench, a brigand had his sword at Rhys' neck, and Sanche girded with weapons that did not belong to him uncoiled a rope. Rhys' escape thwarted, he would be bound ahead of reaching the ship.

Dangereuse shot her gaze to Pierre de Talliere. "Wulfrith *trickery?*"

He hiked his upper lip. "Your kin were instructed to appear hours from now."

Before she could respond, William snarled, "And would have had you heeded my warning about your choice of messenger."

She glanced at William whose his eyes remained on the shore, concern for his brother touching until she reminded herself of what they were and what they had done. *And are doing,* she silently added when she saw Rufus' blade drop a squire to the sand.

That move allowed William's brother to break free of those closing in on him and draw nearer the boat. For his deliberate weaving to avoid the arrows, it appeared he would make it, but then Rémy bellowed, reined his mount to the side, and released an arrow.

Near the surf, Rufus stumbled to a halt, and as his brother howled with more anguish than anger, looked down at the blood spreading through his tunic's weave where the arrow had entered one side of him.

"Rufus!" William cried.

The young man looked up. Tears brightening eyes soon to close evermore, he called, "Oh, Will! A hole in me! I will not make...old bones." Then his knees buckled and he dropped onto his face.

"God!" William shook a fist heavenward. "I renounce You! You are *nothing* to me!" Then he turned on Dangereuse, gripped her by the front of her mantle, and yanked her off the bench. "As one of yours slew my brother, you shall pay the price—"

"Non!" Marionne clamped a hand over William's arm. "We need her to—"

"Stop her!" a voice Dangereuse recognized as Warin's shouted above the others.

As the two men looked shoreward, she peered past William and saw the only other woman present had broken from her guard who sought to overtake her. Bending low over her mount's neck, she commanded the horse down the slope.

"See now, the whore comes to us!" Pierre exclaimed.

"If this is not more Wulfrith trickery," Marionne said, "perhaps she did not betray your—"

"Oui, she did," De Talliere's son said as the lady sharply turned her horse aside to avoid Wulfrith warriors coming at her. "But whatever this is, we are nearer to getting what we came for. Meaning do you wish to serve our lord, William, you will set aside plans for revenge. For now."

The red-eyed leader of the brigands drew breath that shook his body. "Understood, providing you understand no matter what you say or do, I shall avenge my brother in whatever ways possible once you have Lady Vianne."

"I am well with that—and gutting you should impatience deny me my sire's deepest gratitude." Pierre looked past William who transferred his hold on Dangereuse to her arm, then ordered the archers to ensure Lady Vianne was not over-taken. And sweetened that by promising a gold coin for each pursuer eliminated.

With greater enthusiasm than when it was believed Dangereuse's presence protected them, the men rose above their shields and loosed arrows at those attempting to thwart the lady who, proving her riding skills were exceptional, had less need of aid than others of her sex. And where these archers were concerned, no need at all for their inability to compensate for the shifting boat.

A moment later, Dangereuse's heart was so far up her throat she thought she would choke. Ferrand, who was nearest the lady, fell out of the saddle, a glimpse of the arrow's landing so inconclusive she could not know where it struck.

"Gold well earned!" Pierre announced as the anguish that could not reach Dangereuse's lips came off Warin's. No scream his, but the shout of a warrior straining to keep hold of his humanity as the animal prowling beneath his skin clawed to come free.

WARIN TREMBLED, something to which he was not given since leaving childhood behind—excepting when he was denied being at his wife's side to ease her suffering as she succumbed to the pestilence.

The trembling was not for the injuries done Lillia's people on Christmas Day, not for those dealt him and his men this day, neither for the inability to quickly remove his sister from danger. They contributed, but what decided his body to behave as it did was the possible death of Squire Ferrand for the treachery of Vianne Wardieu and acknowledgment she was responsible for all.

Moments later, he brought his horse around and saw she had reached the surf and heard her shout, "Make the trade, Pierre. I must return to my love."

"Traitorous harlot!" he bit.

"Warin!" Owen called as the last of five brigands who had come between them and the boat reined around to ride at them again. "I have this! Stop her!"

Under different circumstances, he would not have left his uncle to finish the man, this brigand proving twice as ferocious and slippery as the best of the others who would not fight again. However, these circumstances were exceptionally personal.

"God be with you, Uncle!" he answered, then knowing the remaining enemy archers would think him a fine target once he was distant enough they need not fear their arrows striking one of their own, he maneuvered his horse to forge a crooked path to the shoreline.

Still, he felt the breath of an arrow slice past his ear and saw it streak into the water far left of Lady Vianne who urged her borrowed horse into the surf as if she thought to ride it to the boat. Though the vessel had not further distanced itself, there was too much water between it and the lady whose only hope of reaching it was if the Frenchmen risked rowing nearer —or she was adept at swimming a horse and the animal cooperative despite its rider being nearly unknown and the water far from calm and summer-warmed.

"Lady!" he shouted, and she looked from those on the boat who were easily seen for Warin ordering his bowmen to cease firing on them, though the brigands at the fore remained partially shielded.

Eyes he preferred to name dull rather than lovely met Warin's and widened above flushed cheeks, then she turned back and called, "Make the trade!"

Would the French risk coming ashore? Warin questioned and, nearing the woman he would drag onto his horse—hopefully without an enemy archer putting him through—looked around to ensure his uncle prevailed.

Once more, Owen proved advancing age had not blunted his sword skill. With a cry, his opponent landed on the sand, rolled, and ended face down. Then the Wulfen-trained knight spurred to aid Rémy and their men who, with all the horsed enemy now on the ground, turned their efforts on putting down what remained of the archers shooting from behind boulders.

"Sir Warin!"

The Frenchman's voice come across the water returned his attention to the boat, and he saw a brigand stood behind Dangereuse with a dagger at her throat that, for the sizable ruby in its hilt, looked one of those awarded men knighted at Wulfen Castle.

As Warin was meant to do, he reined in short of Lady Vianne.

"There a good Wulfrith!" Pierre de Talliere taunted where he stood beside the blade-wielding brigand, then called, "Come, Lady Vianne!"

She remained unmoving, the breeze causing lustrous brown hair to wave out behind her, mantle to flap, and her billowing gown to expose a hosed calf up to her knee.

"For your sake and that of Lady Dangereuse, come!" De Talliere's son ordered.

Still she did not obey, but neither did she turn aside, and now the older Frenchman spoke something to the younger that made him lean toward the brigand's leader. Whatever words were imparted caused the man to show his teeth, but then he lowered the dagger to his side.

"This is the way of it!" Pierre de Talliere called as Warin

glanced at the second boat carrying Sir Rhys, which had ceased its advance on the ship as if to observe the happenings here. "Do naught, and I give my word I shall unbind your sister's feet and return her to you whole upon the horse Lady Vianne shall swim to us."

That such an arrangement was possible caused laughter to ascend Warin's throat, but the man's next words held scorn in check.

"Agree now, else we force ourselves to be content with leaving you with two gutted women."

As the tide continued swirling about the legs of the horse ahead, Lady Vianne glanced back at Warin who, making no attempt to mask anger and distaste, noted her cheeks had gone pale.

Now it was Warin glancing behind. Though his men had finished off what remained of the brigands on the shore and were moving toward him, he had no choice but to comply lest Dangereuse was put through with the dagger and Lady Vianne pierced by an arrow flown from the boat.

"Keep your word, De Talliere," he shouted, "else my archers shall loose every last arrow, and some of those shafts *will* defy your shields."

"My word is sound!" the man said, quite possibly with a lie lurking behind each word, then he looked to his sire's lover. "Now, Lady Vianne!"

Her shoulders rose as if with steadying breath, then she leaned over the horse's neck, spoke words of which Warin could make no sense, and gave the animal her heels.

Shockingly, as if its rider were implicitly trusted, the horse did as commanded, walking into chill water that rose up its legs and soon skimmed its belly and lapped at the lady's boots.

Was it possible she knew how to swim a horse? If so, surely she had no experience with such in a winter sea. Yet there seemed no vestige of the hesitation she had shown when commanded to the boat, not even when the water moved up her calves, knees, and eddied around her waist as the sea floor fell away and the horse began swimming.

All that was certain was the lady was bitterly cold as revealed by shaking. And more she shook with each surge that drew her and her mount nearer the boat.

"Almighty!" Owen rasped as he halted his horse alongside Warin's.

"Who would have believed?" Rémy exclaimed as he reined in on his brother's other side.

Gaze fixed on the sight, Warin asked of both, "Injuries?"

After assuring him those sustained would heal and the more serious ones dealt their men did not appear life threatening—not even that suffered by Ferrand Royston—their uncle said, "Hidden depths to this Lady Vianne. One might even name her formidable."

"I name her treacherous, Uncle! Not only is she responsible for the ill come upon our family, people, and Sir Rhys"—Warin jutted his chin at the more distant boat—"but 'twas all for naught. Had she pertinent intelligence to pass to our king, it shall return to France with her."

"I believe she was sincere in wishing to deliver it," Owen said, then added, "at least at the time she agreed to do so."

As Warin's anger gathered strength, he heard his men draw rein. Dragging his gaze from the horse that would soon reach the boat and its rider who shook so hard she had entirely folded forward and wrapped her arms around the animal's neck, he peered over his shoulder.

The Wulfrith warriors were halved, though only for the absence of the injured and those tending them farther up the shore, among them a healer from the settlement of Old Leake he had sent for ahead of confronting the miscreants. "Positions, archers!" he called.

As men of the bow began flanking him, Rémy joined those who would enforce the threat that should the word given by the Frenchman turn false, not all on the boat would escape the wrath of Warin Wulfrith whose nature was not vengeful. And yet felt it in that moment.

Sweeping his regard over sand disarrayed by the life and death struggle played out across it, he commanded himself to think clearly, beseeched the Lord for aid, then once more looked to the horse nearing the boat. "Return my sister whole," he growled low, "else far more than the sharpening of my blade will be required to tame this roiling."

CHAPTER 28

The sight was like none Dangereuse had witnessed. Thus, it was a good match for events like none experienced before the night Rhys reentered her life. Though she knew exceptionally good riders could swim horses across deep water, it would have been difficult to believe a woman lacking great strength could do so, and never would she have thought it of a rider whose mount was nearly unknown to her.

However, Lady Vianne was making the crossing, and were she to slide into the sea, likely it would be due to numbing cold, which Dangereuse could not imagine for how chilled she was by the mere movement of air and spray. Not that the discomfort compared to what she felt at her center.

"The French think to make pretty of this," William of dead brother and broken nose said low, "but not I."

His words meant for her alone, she started to look around, but the point of a dagger pricked her back just beneath the ribs.

"Nay, not I." His threat in her ear was more responsible for her next shudder than the breeze growing toward a wind.

Heavenly Father, she prayed, *for how angered and devastated he is by his brother's death at the hands of my brother, he no longer cares whether he lives. Ere he relinquishes me, he will make a lie of the word Pierre gave by sliding in the same blade that spilled Benoit's life.*

Though she longed to shout a warning to Warin, which would alert the French of their ally's intent to act in a way contrary to their wishes and cause arrows to fly, she had little doubt William would slay her immediately. Thus, using what time she had to think a way out of seemingly impossible circumstances, she merely whimpered.

And heard his grunt of satisfaction over the belief she accepted the inevitable.

And felt his hand on her tighten as if in triumph—then ease for being confident of vengeance.

And saw the attention of the others was upon Lady Vianne.

But how to use that vulnerability when, for legs remaining bound, she needed this man's support to stay upright?

Beneath cover of her damp skirt, she strained to angle her heels out in the hope of opening space between them—and nearly cried with disbelief when she succeeded. Her earlier effort to loosen Sanche's intricate knot had yielded results, but though it was not enough to free her feet, were she able to enlarge the gap a bit more, the cinched leather might loosen sufficiently, allowing her to draw one foot out of its boot, then the other.

Aid me! she sent heavenward and, straining again, turned her mind down one path then another, time and again correcting its course to form a plan with some possibility of success.

It was starting to come together when William dug fingers into her arm. "What do you?"

She eased her leg muscles, drew breath all the sharper for an excuse that was far from false, and peered over her shoulder. "I fear my insides bleed. The pain makes it hard not to bend to it."

His eyes widened, and in them she saw reflected the smile on his lips. "A pity I am without pity, Lady." He jerked his head toward where Rufus' insides bled out, whether from a corpse or a body lingering over the last of life.

She hesitated in speaking what would not be well received, but being genuine for the anguish she would feel were she to lose a sibling as well as witness that passing, she said, "You will not believe me, but I am sorry for your loss."

The hard etched in his brow and around his eyes began to soften, but a blink restored it and more deeply she felt the dagger's point. "I do not believe it. You Wulfriths are—"

Whatever he meant to speak was interrupted by shouts from behind.

As William turned her toward the ship, Pierre snarled, "Accursed De Arell!"

Blessed De Arell, she silently disagreed. Though when last she looked to Rhys it was clear Sanche would bind him ahead of reaching the ship, that had not happened, and she guessed it due to his captors becoming spectators over Lady Vianne's feat. Rhys had taken advantage of that to attempt another escape.

As sailors leaning over the ship rails called encouragement to oarsmen in the water who struggled against waves of greater size and strength than those here, Rhys clashed with Sanche—fortunately without needing to watch his back for having ejected those who worked the oars. And that was of greater import since not only must he watch his front as

Sanche slashed with a long-bladed dagger and the brigand with a sword, but for his only weapon being the rope meant to bind him.

"Naught we can do for them. Attend to Lady Vianne!" Marionne sought to return the attention of those here to the one for whom they crossed the channel.

Dangereuse glanced at the woman. Seeing she was fifteen feet out and yet clung to the horse that appeared to be floundering, she returned her regard to Rhys. Neither did William concern himself over the lady's bid to reach the boat. The same as she he meant to impale, he awaited the outcome of that captive's bid for freedom.

Avoiding the reach of a blade, Rhys drew back his arm and whipped the rope again. A cry exited the brigand whose head snapped back when it caught him in the face and dropped him. However, the recipient of the next whip made no sound.

Sanche stumbled, released his weapon, and reached to his throat around which the rope had turned. Before he could free himself, Rhys lunged right and slammed his booted feet against the rail, causing the boat to heave that direction. Then he was over the side and, his end of the rope in hand, yanked Sanche into the frigid water with him. As the boat capsized, the brigand who struggled to his feet was cast out as well.

Dangereuse gasped, and Marionne and Pierre looked around at the mess made of the attempt to deliver Rhys to Rollon de Talliere.

"Your knight favors forfeiting his life sooner rather than later," Pierre drawled as she watched for the knight to surface. "Though it is possible those on the ship will fish out the others, I doubt he would accept a rope thrown to him were he to come up." When only the heads of Sanche and the brigand appeared, he chuckled.

But then Rhys so forcefully broke the water his shoulders and upper chest were momentarily seen.

"Still, soon food for the beasts of the deep," Pierre pronounced.

As William would have me be, she thought and saw the oarsmen struggled harder to reach the ship ahead of succumbing to the cold, which seemed unlikely—though greater their chance than Rhys making it to the more distant shore. And what of Sanche and the brigand who appeared indecisive, neither moving toward ship nor shore but turning frantically where they had surfaced and, seemingly with intention, going under several times?

"Get hold of her!" Pierre shouted.

William turned Dangereuse to the side where the brigands had come out from behind the shields to pull Lady Vianne from the horse.

"Prepare to put Lady Dangereuse over, William," Marionne ordered.

As the leader of the decimated brigands moved her nearer the side, he said in her ear, "My brother was most beloved." Then more deeply she felt the dagger's tip.

As soon as Lady Vianne was retrieved and before attempting to get this Wulfrith inexperienced in swimming a horse onto the beast, he would push in the blade.

Dangereuse looked across her right shoulder. Unlike the two continuing to bob near the capsized boat, Rhys swam this direction. Though he made exceptional progress, he was too distant to help her, and perhaps not even himself once the merciless cold invaded his muscles.

Next, she looked to her kin on the shore and accepted neither could they assist her. Unless the Lord aided in a barely half-formed plan, likely her son would never again run into these arms. Still, some satisfaction in a death different from the one William intended, especially if it thwarted these men, but that was possible only if she acted before Lady Vianne was in their hands.

Loose the arrows ere they can raise their shields, she silently appealed to Warin and Rémy as she slid her hand through the part in her mantle. Then risking the blade slicing through her garments in search of flesh, she pivoted her bound legs toward William. As he lurched back, she closed her hand over the first bit of Benoit's dagger she laid eyes on—not only the cross guard but upper blade as told by pain in her palm. Though instinct demanded she release it, she wrenched the dagger from William and let the force required to do so carry her backward.

With shouts abounding and wonder at what she had managed, she went over the side and struck water so cold she feared losing consciousness. As it closed over her, she tightened her grip on the dagger and told herself she must act quickly to make good what remained of her plan, which was to shed water-weighted garments and free her legs.

Before she had to come up for air, she was out of the mantle and gown, though only for her upper body being freed of the rope this morn that permitted her to release her lacings to ease her pained center.

Now clad only in her chemise and beyond the reach of the cursing William but dangerously near the horse whose legs churned as the men sought to retrieve Lady Vianne, she went under again.

Increasingly numbed by frigid water she had recently acknowledged as being of a cold she could not imagine, as best she could she distanced herself from the horse, bent forward, and set the blade against the rope. As she sawed through it, she prayed and prayed again.

When she had to replenish her air ahead of cutting through

the last tough fibers, she saw one of the brigands had hands on Lady Vianne.

Having hoped she could not be taken for a barrage of arrows flown from the shore, and it clear Warin had not ordered their flight for fear one would find his sister, Dangereuse wanted to scream. And might have had not the violently shaking lady opened her eyes upon her and spoke what looked, "Forgive me." Then she was lifted over the side and out of sight.

Loose your legs! Dangereuse silently commanded and filled her lungs and submerged again.

At last, the rope fell away, but she was so cold and stiff it took nearly all she had left to return to the surface.

And for what? she questioned as she saw the riderless horse making for the shore, the boat with Lady Vianne moving toward the ship, and delayed arrows streaking the sky in their bid to find a gap in shields once more raised. *Aye, for what do I bother?*

CHAPTER 29

The effort to put him through would have been laughable were there a scrap of humor about something as deadly as this.

From what Rhys could see as he thrust through the water, body so chilled he hardly felt ache in his healing arm, thrice from under cover of shields spiked with shafts those on the boat had sent an arrow toward him. But so erratic was the archer's aim that no missiles entered the water near Rhys.

It seemed the miscreants would have to be content with carrying away the lady it had been his responsibility to deliver to the king. Of course, if he succumbed to the cold before reaching Dangereuse—and her kin could reach the two of them—they would be pleased to settle for his death by drowning.

Show yourself again! he silently demanded of the woman he fully accepted could be to him what his mother was to his sire. Though certain he was nearer her than were her uncle and Warin who had begun swimming their horses when she went in the water, for the depth and breadth of the sea before the shore, he could not determine exactly where last she was. And even if he could, by now a current could have carried her away.

Lord, sustain my strength and lead me to her, he prayed as he thrust his left arm into choppy waves and put twist in his body to do the same with the right, both so cold he would have questioned whether they did as commanded were he lacking sight.

Thinking it strange numbing water could as easily incapacitate as a keen blade, next repelled at the realization his mind turned over things irrelevant to saving Dangereuse as though he were abed sinking into rest, he returned his attention to propelling himself forward.

With her kin shouting her name as they also closed in on where they believed she had gone down, over and again he silently demanded, *Where, Dange?*

Then a shrill gasp. Though he knew it might be but a different note played by the brisk breeze, he paused. And nearly slipped under for a body increasingly resistant to his commands.

Shaking so hard he had to grind his teeth to keep from biting his tongue, he jerked around as the Wulfrith warriors shouted, "To your left! Twenty feet!" So she was, tipped up face barely visible.

Though Rhys forced his arms and legs to do what they told they could not, as if he and all the world moved at a crawl, his progress was excruciatingly slow.

He was nearly within reach when he saw her lips move between sharp coughs and heard her mutter, "For Bastian... Rhys...Murielle...Fira..."

"Dange!" He reached, but as his fingers brushed her, she slipped under.

"Nay!" He thrust forward, and feeling hair glide through

fingers that refused to grasp hold of it, sucked air down a throat salted by sea spray and followed her under.

As if God ordained it was time to end the worst of the ordeal, he did not have to go far to find the solid of her. He hooked an arm around her upper back, moved it lower, drew her into his chest, and kicked to the surface.

They broke a rolling wave, and as they slid into its trough and her head dropped back, shouts of relief sounded. Soon Warin and Owen would be here.

Spreading legs and kicking knees high, keeping his lungs as full as possible to compensate for being unable to use his arms to remain afloat, he said, "I am here, Dange!"

Life in her, as evidenced by fluttering lids, then convulsions as she coughed up water.

Feeling as if his mind was shutting down, all he could do as his lower body struggled to keep them afloat was press a hand to the back of her head, move her chin to his shoulder to aid in clearing her lungs, and beseech God to quickly deliver her kin so she have tens of thousands more days.

With or without me, the thought slipped in.

"I have her, Rhys!" Warin sounded distant, though it could not be for the grunt and whinny of the horse stirring the water and Dangereuse being pried from his arms. But it was so, he saw when he raised his lids and recognized his fellow knight despite him looking a smudge against the sky. "You can let her go now."

As he loosed his hold and Warin began the awkward task of getting her on his horse, she murmured something then gave a small cry.

"De Talliere kicked her...in the belly," Rhys said past chattering teeth. "I fear 'tis not...mere bruising."

Though Warin said naught, the fire of his anger scorched

the air as more gently he moved her onto his saddle and into his arms. "Now you." He jutted his chin opposite.

Slowly, Rhys looked around, and only then realized Sir Owen gripped the back of his tunic, elevating his shoulders above the water. Had these Wulfriths not arrived when they did, when next Dangereuse and he were seen it would be as bodies washed ashore.

"Regrettably, unless you can greatly aid, I cannot get you astride," the older man said. "I took a blade deeper than thought."

"What say you?" Warin demanded.

"I will survive," his uncle said. "Now Rhys, I am going to loop this rope beneath your arms and pull you behind. You have only to stay face up."

Only, Rhys mulled and wished *only* were as easy as it sounded.

Clinging to consciousness to keep his head above water, he stared at the sky as the horses returned to the shore more burdened than when they departed. Then finally sand was under him, he was placed beside a fire in sight of the unconscious lady who claimed his heart, and covered in blankets.

Despite a mind urging him to sleep, he resisted, knowing it best he sufficiently recover from shock before going adrift. More importantly, he needed assurance of Dangereuse's wellbeing and the others tended by a healer from Old Leake. Too, there was the ship to see away.

He had been told the oarsmen he knocked over the side had safely reached it and that Sanche and the brigand he dumped into the water had succumbed to a rogue wave. Of course, easier that for work Rhys did underwater to ensure neither man thwarted him—fastening one end of the rope to the boat, knotting its middle section around Sanche's ankles, then the last of it around the brigand. As for those on the second boat, they had scaled the ladder, excepting two who had to be hauled up, one being Lady Vianne. Since the dead would have been cast into the sea, doubtless both lived—unless one was French and his countryman insisted on returning him to France for burial.

If I failed you, Lady Vianne, as Sir Warin does not believe for you seeking to depart England and proclaiming love for De Talliere, forgive me, he silently sent to the ship whose inflated sails had gone from sight an hour past. *Regardless, I have failed my king who might have persuaded you to tell what you decided to hold close.*

Had she held close anything of import, he reminded himself of what he had considered when she insisted on delivering the intelligence, it possible what she was to impart would prove more an excuse for her to return to England than of benefit to Edward.

"Sleep while you can, Rhys," Warin said, having finished consulting with the healer and crossed to this side of the fire. "We depart soon, and as the journey to Blackwood will be completed as quickly as possible, I would have you ride in the wagon with my sister to ensure she is jolted as little as possible." His smile was taut. "For what you endured to save her, 'twill be better for you as well."

Though the pride of a warrior must often be held in check, even were Rhys fully recovered, he would take the wagon over a horse to be the one to protect Dangereuse.

He flexed his jaw that ached from grinding his teeth to keep them from chewing up his tongue, then asked, "What does the healer say of her injuries?"

Warin lowered to his haunches. "Since her passing in and out of consciousness may be due to the cold gone to her bones and near drowning, he cannot ascertain whether she suffers deep bruising or her insides bleed. Thus, she must be tended by a competent physician as soon as possible."

"Blackwood's," Rhys said.

Warin nodded. "I have sent a man ahead to alert your family of our arrival and ensure the physician is present."

"Good. How fares Sir Owen? Squire Ferrand?"

"It appears their lives are not in jeopardy. Though my uncle insists he is well enough to ride now his injury is sewn and bandaged, the squire will travel in the wagon with you."

Rhys looked to Dangereuse and wished her face turned toward him.

"Do I read right my sister's feelings for you are reciprocated?"

He shot his gaze back to Warin.

A corner of the man's mouth rose, making more visible the burns on one side of his face which several days' growth of beard concealed fairly well. "As I carried her to the fire, she spoke something. When I asked her to repeat it, she said she must live for Sebastian. That was expected, but not the name next she spoke—yours."

Recalling those she listed as he struggled toward her after she surfaced, now Rhys understood what was behind them.

"She opened her eyes and asked if you lived," Warin continued. "I told her you did and thought her returned to rest, but she said that had she not her son, she would rue the wasted years between her and the man our sire had known was her match." He raised his eyebrows. "You feel the same?"

Rhys hesitated, but guessing Warin was not truly in need of confirmation and intending to do all in his power to make this fellow Wulfen-trained knight his brother-in-law, he said, "I do not think worse could befall me than were I to lose her ere our life together is begun."

Warin squeezed Rhys' shoulder. "Then with much prayer

for the journey and days ahead, soon to Blackwood." He straightened and considered the sea. "A storm is stirring. Hence, at least a rough day and night ahead of *les signaleurs blancs*—and Lady Vianne who has proven as treacherous as she is notorious."

Rhys understood his anger, and more if what Warin believed of the lady was true. But he also knew this Wulfrith brother possessed soft behind the hard of a warrior's heart— that only when grave offenses were dealt the defenseless and those dear to him was he moved to keen dislike and stiff judgment. Or worse.

Certes, Vianne Wardieu had slammed into the hard side of his heart, and there she would remain without opportunity to redeem herself even were redemption possible.

Inwardly, he groaned over answering to Edward for failing to deliver the lady, then sympathetically over certainty Warin would have to explain how she slipped—rather, *swam a horse* —through his fingers.

The king would not be pleased with either, but as she was last under Warin's protection and he was a Wulfrith from whom more was expected than most, the newly made Baron of Woodhearst would bear the brunt of royal displeasure. And likely Warin knew it, furthering his dislike of the lady.

"Nay, Rémy!" he growled, moving Rhys' regard to the one striding forward. "I will not answer again for my decision, of which you know our brother would approve."

Stubborn all about the young man's broad jaw, he halted. Though the few words they exchanged were spoken low, enough was heard to understand he was vexed at not being allowed to swim a horse to rescue their sister. In this instance, anger proved a fine friend to his speech that was without the slightest falter.

"Rather than waste time objecting to what is done, spend time doing," Warin said and started past him.

"Is that a lesson?" Rémy demanded.

Warin looked around. "As it sounds a good one, aye. Put it to memory and number it as you will." Then he left his brother to calm himself with deep breaths and Rhys to sleep ahead of the wagon's incessant lurch.

———

"ONCE A TRAITOR, ever a traitor, as is more true of the English than others. Hence, in good conscience I could not further infect my country with those formed of your dirt."

Gripping the rail with hands whose feeling and movement she had feared would never be restored, continuing to shake though she wore the dry garments of a sailor and over them a rough blanket, Vianne ignored the man who had commanded her out from under the sheltering canopy to witness his depravity.

"You are an exception, Vianne Wardieu, though only in consideration of my sire," he pressed for a response. "Even if he refuses to believe the lie of you or accepts it and cannot bear to put you asunder, the liberty granted his whore is at an end."

The breeze that had become a wind now buffeting her face and whipping her hair out behind her, she continued to stare into the sea churning against the hull of the ship that forced its way across the channel in defiance of the rising storm—staring and remembering those sucked under. Was it minutes ago? A quarter hour? A half?

"I am sure he will make pretty your prison for his *visits*," he continued, emphasis on the last word making her wish wine coated the tongue pressed hard to her palate. "But it will suffocate, and I am well with that."

Of course he was, just as he was well with casting off the ship the leader of the brigands who took an arrow to the shoulder after Vianne's retrieval. Just as he was well with doing the same to the remaining brigands who defended the boat as best they could. For failing to hold Sir Rhys and Lady Dangereuse who were more likely dead than alive though drawn from the frigid water by two who also swam their horses, those Englishmen had been sent screaming down... down...into the sea.

"Down, down," she whispered.

And startled when Rollon's son said, "Down and dead, all because of you."

Not all, she sought to assure herself. Her plan to return home to her family and England, made possible by dangling greater intelligence than any heretofore provided, had been the beginning of all that went wrong. And more wrong for the innocents along her path. However, there was one as responsible as she—the man she would be tempted to send down... down had she the strength to put him over the rail.

Despite Pierre's hatred of her and the need to protect his family from what she might divulge, for that alone he would not have himself chanced pursuing her across the channel. At most, he would have followed her to the coast and returned home empty-handed. Instead, for his obsession with another lady whose betrothal Rollon snatched for himself and in expectation of gaining his sire's elusive praise, Pierre had sought to expose the traitor of Vianne.

No proof I betrayed, she told herself. *Conjecture only.*

Still, she did not think Pierre exaggerated her fate. Even if she escaped a prison cell or death, it could be years—if ever—before Rollon's trust was restored sufficiently to once more allow her access to his conversations and papers.

Worse than hard imprisonment or death? she questioned,

feeling those fleshy, grasping hands on her that no amount of soap and abrasive cloth could entirely remove.

Envisioning the bars of her gilded cage whose door only he could exit, she breathed, "Worse," and finally grasped what led men and women to go beyond dulling the sharp of their suffering with much drink—to entirely destroy the bodies into which God lovingly poured them.

She gave her head a shake, and lest her Heavenly Father paid her any attention, silently assured, *I will cling to You even do You not cling to me. I will watch for the door You open even do You never open it. I will treasure the strength You grant even do You not grant enough so I not suffocate.*

Pierre harrumphed. "Oui, you who merely play at abduction are at fault for all," he tried again to gain a response—and with his hand as well.

She considered his grip on her arm, then looked up and first focused on the darkening clouds beyond him. Though for an hour or more they had blocked the sun, now their bellies looked ready to birth rain.

When Pierre's fingers dug in, she moved her regard to a face sickly pale for him being stricken with *mal de mer* that twice had him spewing.

Determined to outrun hopelessness and desperation that sought to tempt her to commit a sinful, life shattering thing, she said, "If you contemplate murdering me as you did them" —she jerked her chin at the water below—"greater your satisfaction do I die now by your hand than go down with the ship the same as you."

He glanced at the sky, then feigning fearlessness, shrugged. "Truth in that, but as I believe we shall safely reach France and I will be satiated with exposing my sire's whore, I cannot accommodate you."

That she did not ask of him. Or did she? Might she not merely taunt?

I cling to You, Lord, she silently affirmed. *I watch for the door You open. I treasure the strength You grant.*

Straightening her spine, she snatched her arm free. "As I betrayed none dear to me and count your charges but diseased jealousy for me being loved by your sire, the fault for the ill done others and loss of three of Rollon's men is yours, not mine. You may convince him otherwise, but my love for him is so great I can weather his lack of good sense. And were I moved to overcome it by means I prefer not to resort to, sooner we shall be reconciled."

His face paled further. "What means?"

Now she was the one who jumped her shoulders in a false show of fearlessness. "As once I overheard my sire advise his heir—*When possible, reveal not how well armed you are until in the best position to make the most of your weapons.*"

He was angry, perhaps enough to take what satisfaction was assured him by casting her in the sea, but the sudden pitching of the deck belatedly heralded by the sailors had them slamming hands to the rail to hold against a violent wave. And a moment later he was bent over the rail again.

Vianne endured his retching until the vessel settled enough for her to work her hands down the rail and feet across the wet deck to her shelter. The tent-like structure tucked into a corner opposite another erected for Pierre and Marionne was not much, but its canvas was strong and oiled to deflect rain, and iron loops in the deck were fit with ropes ending in hooks that allowed her to secure herself against being ejected.

Once that was done and thunder and lightning announced that what remained of the day and night ahead would be long, certain she would never again be truly warm, she hugged the blanket to her. And whimpered when the damp deck she sat upon was wet by rain water sweeping beneath the canvas as the ship listed again.

Of course, what she had suffered and yet suffered hardly compared to what might be the tragedy of Sir Rhys, Lady Dangereuse, and Squire Ferrand.

She closed her eyes. "Heavenly Father, I thought I did right in forcing the trade and believed it well planned, but more than it making a greater mess of my life, further I made a mess of the lives of my countrymen. For the life it is believed I chose, I was reviled before, even by my own family, and now...I am hated."

Recalling how handsome, fair-haired Sir Warin had looked at her when first they met, next when he came to her chamber, then this day, she shuddered.

Guessing he was one of the two who swam a horse to save those gone into the sea, again she beseeched the Lord for mercy on the lady and knight, for their sakes as well as Warin Wulfrith who would be more haunted by their deaths were it his efforts that failed them.

Though he would hate her more, that mattered only as far as she allowed it to burden her conscience since there was little chance their paths would cross again—unless she had given him a reason so powerful to avenge his losses it mattered not he would have to get past England's lethal enemies to see it done.

Unlikely, but possible, she thought, then laughed bitterly. What was fear of Warin Wulfrith compared to fear, revulsion, and the shame of returning to Rollon?

"Naught," she said and pulled the blanket over her head as rain beat louder on the canvas and more water surged beneath it, wetting all with which it came into contact. "You are of no danger to me, Sir Warin of the Wulfriths. None."

CHAPTER 30

Castle Mathe
Barony of Blackwood

They had traveled day into night into day with as few stops as possible, though it seemed their arrival at Castle Mathe was less urgent for Dangereuse's brief awakenings, during which she was lucid enough to acknowledge Rhys held her and praise the Lord when assured he and the others would recover.

She had not inquired whether she would survive, the nearest she came to that being the first time she noticed Ferrand was in the wagon. The squire who had taken a bolt through the shoulder had met her gaze as was rare with Rhys and told all prayed for her. After a failed smile, she had asked if she was truly that ill, then without awaiting an answer, turned her face up to Rhys who had made a mattress of himself to take the brunt of jolts. Where she lay on her side curled atop him, she had said softly, *For you.*

For me? he had asked.

Her next smile met with some success. *For you I bother...and me.* Then she had tucked her head and returned to what he prayed was healing sleep.

Now with the sun overhead and their party accompanied by an escort of Blackwood men-at-arms sent to watch for their arrival, Rhys did not have to rise up and peer around the wagon's driver to know Castle Mathe was in sight. Though he longed to look around at what would ever be his home even once he occupied the sister castle nearing its completion, he would not risk disturbing Dangereuse's rest. And need not, for as if the great fortress were memorized words, without closing his eyes, clearly he saw its walls, towers, and donjon framed against a dark frozen wood in winter that would become a black bountiful wood in summer.

I am home, he thought, then spoke into the silvered tangles atop Dangereuse's head, "God willing, you will regard Mathe the same on the most distant day possible I succeed my sire."

"You love my brother's widow," Ferrand surprised for those words spoken low.

Rhys turned his face to the younger man who lay against the wagon's opposite wall, and when Ferrand did not avoid his gaze, said, "Upon my arrival at Lillia, I regarded her as Benoit's widow, but now I see her as Dangereuse who deserves more. That is who I love and to whom I hope to give more. Does it offend?"

Ferrand shook his head. "It does not. It...gladdens."

Now greater surprise—were he to be believed.

"In this I speak true as I have not in other matters," the squire said. "But I shall."

Rhys' chest tightened over anticipation of finally gaining a confession though he required no confirmation of Benoit and Ferrand's wrongdoing. If not for the sound of horses approaching from the castle, he might have pressed for it now, but he said, "I would hear all this eve."

Turning his face aside, Ferrand spoke one word—"Soon."

Those riding from Castle Mathe were here, Griffin de Arell shouting a greeting to the Wulfriths as he rode past. Then he brought his horse around and alongside the wagon.

As he matched his mount's pace to the roll of the wheels, the bright blue eyes of father and son met, and Rhys knew the crooked of their smiles would match if there was not worry about his own and relief about the Baron of Blackwood's.

Then his sire said, "I have been assured though you appear beaten and dragged behind a horse, your injuries will heal. Thus, our concern should be all for Lady Dangereuse." He considered her where she lay atop Rhys beneath the blankets, no laboring about her breathing as during the first hours after departing the coast. "Our physician awaits her."

"I am more grateful—and hopeful—than I can express, sire."

Griffin's smile altered. "Mayhap difficult to express, but not beyond what I can understand, my son."

Much in his words, foremost that from what he knew of the events of these past days and saw in these brief minutes, he understood there was more to this woman being in Rhys' arms than that he safeguarded her.

"Of course, with much thanks to your mother," his sire added.

My mother, he acknowledged Lady Quintin whose body had not borne him but heart had and ever would, just as his bore hers.

The baron jutted his chin at the castle. "She is impatient to receive you and your lady."

My lady, Rhys also named Dangereuse who must survive were he to be blessed with a love like his parents'.

"She would have ridden out if not that your sister, eager to lighten your mother's burdens, fell—which would not have happened had she a hand to steady herself, but she was carrying that little dog as she is not to do upon the stairs." Knowing what would be demanded of him, Griffin de Arell raised a hand. "Just a few steps and only a sprain."

He spoke of the nearly thirteen-year-old Justina whom his mother had taken into their home when the infant of club foot was abandoned. No De Arell blood, but none needed to be a daughter and sister, just as none was needed for Eamon to be a son and brother, the latter's mother having served at Mathe and passed when he was young. As for the little dog descended from the beloved companion of Rhys' grandsire, Justina had given it the same name though she doubled it to *Diot-Diot.*

"Doubtless, by the time you gain the hall," his sire said, "Justina's ankle will be bound up and she will be ready to flutter about you and your lady."

Rhys considered Dangereuse's face that was restful but yet too pale, then looked back at his father. "The same as you with mother, I have fought too hard for Dangereuse to lose her. Pray, help me keep hold of her."

"Whatever power God grants me, I shall wield it, Rhys."

Which he need not be told, just as he need not have asked that of him. Mostly it was a means of further impressing on his sire the waste of time and effort in continuing to put forth prospective wives—even were Dangereuse lost to him.

"Be at ease," Griffin de Arell said. "Soon our physician shall tend her, and to distract you from the waiting, quite the story you will tell me and your brother who will likely arrive within the hour."

The adopted Eamon who preferred the forging of arms to the wielding of swords. Thus, he had served as Wulfen's armorer several years after earning his spurs there. Though he had returned home to Blackwood to serve as a household knight, he was most content overseeing construction of Mathe's sister castles and their iron workings, the first of the fortresses to be given into Rhys' keeping within two years, the second to Eamon within six—providing the work force depleted by the pestilence was not tempted away with the promise of higher wages.

"Quite the story, indeed," Rhys agreed. "God willing, I will not need to be distracted long."

With his horse maintaining the wagon's pace, his sire leaned down and gripped his son's shoulder in the touchingly familiar show of love and support. "Well come home, Rhys."

Fairly certain new lines in that face were pressed there by worry for his heir, Rhys sent up a prayer he himself grew old before the title of baron passed to him.

As his father straightened, the purse on his belt came to notice for a bulge likely due to a partially-eaten apple. Though few things came between the man and his favorite fruit—even one past its season of crispness—tidings of his son's arrival had seen it set aside.

Truly, I am home, he thought, and once more hoped in time it would become Dangereuse's home.

LADY QUINTIN, who had departed a quarter hour past to ascend to the third floor apartment where once Rhys' grandsire resided for suffering leprosy, appeared to have added lines to her face the same as her husband. However, they did her loveliness no disservice, and neither did more liberal silver amid dark hair.

Rhys having paused in relating his tale to his sire and brother, which Warin and Rémy alone expanded on for their uncle requiring the physician's services, eased back from the solar's large table and raised his eyebrows.

As his mother halted alongside her husband, she smiled at her son—blessedly, not sorrowfully. "When I entered, Lady Dangereuse was taking spoonfuls of broth from Justina who has set a vigil over her," she said, then added, "in the company of Diot-Diot."

That nearly coaxed a smile from Rhys.

"Though our exchange was brief for her fatigue, she seemed comfortable and asked after you, Sir Rhys." Now she looked to the Wulfriths. "Once assured of his well-being, your sister beseeched me to pass to her kin that word be sent to her son assuring him she is well and he is to remain at Lillia."

"That has been done," Warin said, "and we agree it is best Sebastian not see her until—"

"What does the physician say of her recovery?" Rhys spoke over her brother and knew he ought to regret his impatience.

Greater understanding than rebuke in his mother's eyes, she said, "Though certain there is more to her ache than tenderness and bruising, he assures me he is honestly hopeful."

"Internal bleeding," Warin growled.

She inclined her head and set her hand in the large one Griffin de Arell raised to her.

Rhys clamped his own hands over the chair arms, causing the wolfhound sitting between Eamon and him to run its tongue over one. Grateful for the devotion of Turo, the descendant of another beloved dog, he set that hand on the animal's neck and asked, "What is the remedy?"

"For how alert and coherent she is when she awakens," his mother said, "fever being slight and color and breathing almost normal, and no blood expelled the one time she retched, he believes her greatest chance for complete healing is to remain as still as possible, which is more easily achieved with medication to ease her pain and aid with sleeping."

"But if her innards are b-bleeding…" Rémy trailed off, jaw jerked as if to release a lock slammed on it.

Compassion all about the lady, she said, "The physician tells that were her symptoms dire, he would risk opening her to see if anything can be sewn. However, as she presents now —and providing it does not change for the worse—more likely the bleeding will resolve on its own than were he to put her to the knife, letting more blood and exposing her to infection."

"Then naught to be done but wait," Warin said with accusation, though not against any at Castle Mathe, Rhys was certain despite his failed mission. Had he to guess its recipient, it would be Lady Vianne now well out of reach of this Wulfrith.

"Aye, wait and be with her," his mother said. "The physician tells she may have visitors the same as the others tended abovestairs."

"After we are done here," Rhys' father said as though sensing his son and the Wulfriths would break from their discussion, then he handed his wife toward the chair she had vacated earlier. As she lowered, the ruby of the weapon fixed to her belt flashed, that and the intricate hilt and cross-guard proclaiming it a Wulfrith dagger. Though she was no warrior, for her warrior's heart her brother had given her what their sire had earned.

"Now complete the tale of your escape from the boat, Rhys," Griffin de Arell said.

Having related how he had thought much so he regret little as his boat struggled toward the ship—and done so until glimpsing the flash of a blade at Dangereuse's back—he said, "I feared for her in the hands of the brigands' leader and was certain my fear justified when William's brother dropped on the beach and it was apparent the blade threatening her was done out of sight of the others who could not make the trade with only a corpse."

He looked around at those waiting on him, ending with Eamon of rugged countenance and good build, the latter a better fit for a head that had been disproportionately large when he was a boy.

This man of common birth, who became a cherished companion long before the death of his mother made him a brother, nodded for him to continue, and as if Turo were in accord, the dog gulped where he had set his chin on the chair's arm.

"I knew I could not reach Dangereuse before he put the blade in her," Rhys said, "which seemed likeliest once Lady Vianne came alongside the boat, but I hoped my escape attempt would move the attention of the French to what William planned."

"It was a sight when first you sent the oarsmen overboard," Warin said, "then capsizing the boat and taking Sanche with you into the water as well as the brigand. For how long it took you to surface, we began to think you drowned."

As had he. "Much work needed to be done underwater to ensure those two did not overtake me—and increase the chance of reclaiming my sword and dagger from Sanche."

Light leapt in the baron's eyes. "Tell."

"I am no master of knots but adept enough to bind an unsuspecting man such that his only way to survive a wave-tossed sea is if aid is quickly given. That is what I did, using the single rope to first bind Sanche's arms, then the brigand's. Lastly, I came up beneath the overturned boat and fixed the rope's end to a bench."

"Ah," Eamon expressed understanding of that to which the Wulfriths were privy and had made provision for what might come of it.

"Believing the second boat would not reach the knaves before the sea claimed them and my chance of surviving the frigid water would decrease if I negotiated it weighted by my weapon belt, what I did was with the expectation the boat would wash ashore with those two fixed to it."

"Thereby regaining sword and dagger," his sire said.

"Aye, and ere we departed, Sir Warin alerted those of Old Leake of a great reward for the one who delivers my weapons to Mathe."

"That may come to pass ere day's end," Eamon said with a bit of the common yet stitched into his tongue, though some believed it should have been corrected when he was given the name *De Arell.* The baron and his lady had let it be, as unashamed as was their second son that his speech evidenced he was more closely tied to the life-giving earth.

"Possibly," Rhys agreed and, over the next quarter hour, finished the tale aided by the Wulfriths who provided further insight. Then, though his body urged him to bed, he determined he would not succumb until he had seen Dangereuse.

CHAPTER 31

Sir Owen slept deeply and Squire Ferrand fitfully, while the other warriors in the immense room that had once been his grandsire's entire world either dozed or rested as the physician moved among them.

As for Dangereuse, her body having been cleaned by Rhys' sister who also set her hair aright as much as possible for being unable to wash the sea out of it, her sleep was shallow and occasionally interspersed with murmurings. But at last, sense was made of her words when she whispered, "Lost to the sea... as meant to be."

"Did you hear that, Brother?" Justina rasped. "Quite clear, and a rhyme! Know you what she speaks of?"

He believed so, having seen her take from William what he believed Benoit's dagger before she went into the water. And there was no doubt she used it to cut the rope from her legs, thereby increasing her chance of survival.

"Methinks she refers to the Wulfrith dagger with which she cut her bindings," he said.

"So fine a weapon lost," his sister bemoaned. "A pity."

He wanted to tell her it was no such thing for what Benoit had made of it and that were Dangereuse awake and of a mind to confide in one unknown to her, she would confirm it, but it was not for him to do.

A great yawn sounded from Turo who surely expected more from his master's son than merely being allowed to accompany him to this place transformed into a sick room.

Rhys, thinking he should have had Eamon take the wolfhound with him when he and those who earlier gathered in the solar returned belowstairs, said low, "Quiet, Turo."

Eyes doleful, the dog shifted them to the mattress where Diot-Diot enjoyed the privilege of being of small size, then sighed his head down.

"Rhys."

He looked around. Finding Dangereuse peered at him through half-open eyes, he smiled. "Aye, she-wolf?"

The corners of her mouth dimpled, and she breathed, "She-wolf."

"She-wolf?" Justina exclaimed. "You make that sound a compliment, Rhys. Tell me you name her that for her silvered hair."

As Dangereuse moved her regard to his sister who sat the mattress' edge and stroked the little dog, Rhys said, "It is a compliment. Though it fits well the silvered black, better it fits for this lady of the Wulfriths donning no sword nor spurs yet being formidable to all who work ill on her loved ones."

"Well, then, I shall not be offended for her!"

"You have been most kind, Lady..." Dangereuse trailed off. "Forgive me, your name escapes."

"Justina de Arell, daughter of Griffin and Quintin, sister of Rhys and Eamon." As if to emphasize her delight in belonging to this family, she gave a nod that caused light to glide over unbound golden tresses.

"I thank you, Lady Justina." Dangereuse looked back at Rhys and opened her eyes wider as though to closely examine a face evidencing more abuse than hers. "You are well? Truly?"

"All will heal," he said, then ventured what remained uncertain by adding, "as shall you."

Her eyebrows gathered, but as if deciding against challenging that, she said, "I dreamt of the sea. Though I long for more sleep, I am glad to awaken from that dark and cold."

"Now only memories that cannot harm you, Dange."

Her lids fluttered. "Was it wrong of me what I did?"

He leaned in. "Was what wrong?"

She swallowed dryly.

"Hold, the lady needs drink," Justina said and rose. With hard-won grace for her wrong-turned foot and the injury recently done it, she skirted the cot and retrieved the cup from the table that side. "Raise her, and I will put it to her lips."

When Rhys eased Dangereuse up with his left arm under her shoulders, the right set in a sling by the physician to mend whatever healing was undone, something like a laugh parted her lips. "Does it not feel we have been here before?"

Encouraged by her teasing, he said, "Indeed, though this time *you* are at your host's mercy, this time *I* the one threatening to prolong your stay do you not speak true."

"That the incentive? Tell the truth and you will...let me go?"

It felt good to chuckle, though there was some guilt knowing it could prove inappropriate should her injury be fatal. "You are right. Thus, speak true so I may prolong your stay—indefinitely."

"'Tis no time for flirting, Rhys!" Justina's pitched voice

caused Turo and Diot-Diot to raise their heads. "The lady thirsts."

He drew back his head, providing space to put the cup to Dangereuse's lips.

But before it settled there, the lady firmed her gaze upon his and said, "My truth is what I hope the same as yours —love."

Justina gasped, causing drops of watered wine to jump over the rim and dot the blanket covering Dangereuse. "'Tis your truth as well, Brother? You shall wed this Wulfrith lady?"

He looked to his sister, shifted his right arm to free his hand from the sling, and reached.

Smiling broadly, she passed the cup to him.

He put it to Dangereuse's lips and shortly returned the cup to Justina. "Now *that* thirst is satisfied," he said, "I shall give answer with a kiss." He did so and, despite her fatigue, she gave back some.

"Still I would hear it spoken," Justina said. "As you wish, do you not, my lady?"

"Words by which to sleep and heal," was the answer given as he lowered her to the pillow.

"Very well, my truth is also love," he said. "For that, I would take you to wife and ever praise the Lord He rewarded my patience by giving me the one I knew I must find."

Across Justina's sigh, Dangereuse said, "You found me— and I you." Then she murmured, "God willing, not too late."

Aching that she questioned her mortality, he prayed the physician knew better what went in her body than she.

Justina scooped up Diot-Diot. "I will leave you," she said, and he was grateful she listened to the inner voice advising her to do so.

When she lurched slightly, he said, "Just as you should not

put undue weight on that ankle, you should not add to its burden by carrying your dog."

She looked around. "I turned my bad one, which already I adjust for. I but needs to adjust a bit more." She flashed a smile and continued forward.

Rhys returned to Dangereuse. Though knowing it best she sleep, struck by the possibility she might not awaken again, he sought something with which to keep her with him a while longer—easily found for the peculiar words she had spoken after telling she dreamt of the sea.

"Dange, you asked if you had done something wrong."

Her lids rose, confusion cleared. "After cutting away the rope, I did as, perhaps, I should not have. Though I could have kept hold of the dagger—at least for a time—I let it sink. I knew how valuable that which should pass to Bastian, but..." She sighed. "'Tis superstition, but never did I want him to even touch that which slew his sire. And when I discovered he had it..." Another sigh. "Memories are powerful, the bad ones dangerously so, but I suppose it was not for me to deny him the opportunity to decide whether he should have a Wulfrith dagger on his belt when he is older."

That last unexpected, Rhys closed a hand over hers that was bandaged for a sliced palm likely received in reclaiming Benoit's dagger. "You rethink your son's future, that rather than enter the Church he receive training at arms."

She blinked. "Do I?"

"It sounds that. And like your brothers, I maintain he is more suited to it."

"But his hearing..."

Thinking she grasped for argument, he said, "His loss is not so great it cannot be compensated for, and who better to aid than England's greatest trainers of knights?" Then hearing Justina ask something on the opposite side of the room and her little dog growl, he looked to where she stood beside Ferrand's cot and saw her shift Diot-Diot to her other arm. Though the dog had been comfortable with Dangereuse, he did not like being near Benoit's brother.

Rhys returned his attention to Dangereuse. "If Sebastian is allowed to go the way of that which comes naturally, the Wulfrith dagger on his belt will be one earned for him being worthy of it."

Her nod was slight. "I fear my brothers and you know better."

"Do not fear. As you are aware, the road of warriors is no straight, flat thing. But though beset with many turns, steep ascensions, and sharp drops, I believe your son—whom I would call mine—shall excel."

"Your son..." Her mouth curved. "Would I could see that." As he was raked again by what sounded questioning of her survival, she said, "If only sleep would leave me be so I might stay longer with you..." Her lids lowered.

He bent and kissed them. "Sleep, Dange. I will be here when you awaken."

And he was throughout the rest of the day and beyond for his mother having a cot placed alongside hers. Each time she roused, often less lucid than lucid, he aided in tending her, told her he loved her, and encouraged her to return to healing sleep.

Then on the third day, an hour after learning his sword and dagger had been delivered to Mathe by a youth of Old Leake, all changed.

———

THE PHYSICIAN STRAIGHTENED. Solemn expression portending neither good nor bad, he looked to those gathered around, then settled on his patient. "Your feeling of well-being is founded, Lady Dangereuse. Were I a wagering man, I would risk coin on the Lord blessing you such that you shall be back at Lillia within a sennight. Nevertheless, still you require much rest and cautious movement ere resuming your duties."

She who had come fully awake an hour past said, "I thank you," and moved her gratitude to her kin, next the De Arells, then Rhys. "And you for staying my side."

He had not thought her aware of his constant presence. That she was made him feel one with her as if already vows were spoken.

As soon as the banns are read three successive Sundays, he assured himself there was no other barrier to wedding providing she was in agreement the same as her brothers and uncle. Though he preferred beginning their lives here, since she took seriously her charge of Lillia, he would reside with her until construction of Mathe's sister castle was complete. By then, Rémy would have his knighthood and be prepared to administer Lillia alongside his wife.

"Rhys?" she said.

"As there was nowhere else I longed to be, 'twas no hardship, Dange."

Her eyes were so telling he wished they were alone.

"Well, then," his mother said, "you will be wanting a hot bath, Lady Dangereuse."

Her future daughter-in-law looked to the physician. At his nod, she said, "Very much."

"Then I shall have a tub and water delivered to the chamber you shall share with my daughter during the remainder of your stay."

"I will see to it," Justina said, continuing to regard the lady as her patient though Rhys' presence had meant more of her time was spent aiding the physician in attending the dwindling number of injured warriors.

All but three had been released, among them Owen who was frustrated for infection setting in, and Ferrand to whom Justina was increasingly drawn though the squire appeared to offer no encouragement—as he ought not for reasons beyond the difference in their ages.

"I entrust the task to you," Lady Quintin said, and Rhys noted as his sister made for the doorway with Diot-Diot, she looked back at Ferrand.

Lord, best I sire sons than daughters, he thought. Even had the squire not worked ill on him, still he would not like the attention of a young woman dear to him landing on a possible suitor. And God help that suitor should he respond in a way contrary to the wishes of this De Arell.

"Justina!" their mother called as she reached the threshold.

She came around, and he guessed the color in her cheeks was of guilt as if caught doing wrong. Were it that, it disappeared when she was told to order a bath sent to Rhys' chamber as well.

"I shall!" she called and went from sight.

"I see no reason she should return abovestairs now there are only two under your care," Griffin de Arell told the physician.

"Your daughter was very helpful, my lord, but..." Though the man did not glance all the way around, the half turn was enough to indicate he also believed Justina paid Squire Ferrand too much attention.

"She leaves behind the girl of her," Lady Quintin said just loud enough for those gathered here. "As is to be expected and accepted, but not this day and not in present company."

She also knew of Ferrand's involvement in Rhys' unseating, and that more than it resulting in his loss of the joust it could have meant his death.

Rhys looked to Dangereuse. The question on her brow told

she did not fully understand what she had yet to accept. Thus, she should be present for Ferrand's confession.

Fairly certain were he to look to the opposite side of the room, the squire's face would be turned to the wall, he told himself, *Not much longer.*

CHAPTER 32

Confession. Though it could have been had three days sooner since Ferrand remained in the physician's care only for it being reported he had begun confiding the tale to Sir Owen, for that and providing his sister-in-law further time to heal, it was best served now.

Dangereuse was comfortably seated beside Rhys when the Wulfriths' uncle entered the solar ahead of the squire. Though it was thought the confessor might postpone the telling when forewarned who else would be present, had he been of that mind, he either persuaded himself otherwise or his former trainer had.

Gesturing to the vacant chairs at the opposite end of the table, Griffin de Arell said, "Sit, Sir Owen, Squire Ferrand."

The latter having paused over the threshold behind the older man whose face had the glisten of one who should be abed, he finished moving his eyes over his audience before resuming his stride.

As he drew out the end chair, he glanced at Sir Owen to his left and Dangereuse to his right, then as if in consideration of his healing shoulder, cautiously lowered. "I am ready as I should have been long ago, Sir Rhys. Is it the beginning through to the end you wish, or would you put questions to me?"

Rhys tried not to pity him, but he did for sensing Ferrand did not seek such. Then there was Dangereuse's palm resting on his thigh, her squeeze entreating him to keep anger sheathed as requested when he revealed what would be told this day. "The beginning through to the end, Squire, and we shall see what questions arise."

Ferrand glanced at Eamon on Rhys' other side, then the Baron of Blackwood at the head of the table, next Lady Quintin, Rémy, Warin, and Owen. "Though I revisit my regrets often, I am grateful Sir Owen aided in making order of what so shamed I knew myself undeserving of Wulfen training."

The fabric of Rhys' tunic that Dangereuse scraped up in her fingers evidenced what little hope remained of Ferrand's innocence was lost. She need hear no more, but knowing she would not depart, he set his hand over hers.

"I am sorry, Lady Dangereuse. Had I sooner accepted my brother was unworthy of you—"

"Squire Ferrand," Owen urged him to correct his course.

He returned to Rhys. "As Benoit and you moved through your page's training, then began your squire's, you were near equals and, I believe, friends."

He believed right.

"But as the competition between you pushed both to excel beyond all others, it became fierce. When you began landing on your feet more often than my brother, he said there was cheating about you. I did not see it, but I so admired him, I accepted he knew best and came to resent you as he did—and more when it was whispered Baron Wulfrith might offer his daughter's betrothal to you. Since Benoit was not our sire's heir, he bemoaned being unable to compete for the hand of one he believed as taken with him as he with her."

As Rhys felt objection in Dangereuse's stiffening, Ferrand said to her, "But you were not, were you?"

Her smile was sorrowful. "I liked Benoit and thought him charming for the good regard shown me, but I was not taken with him."

After some moments, he continued, "Longing for a chance with you that did not depend on title nor lands, he thought that were he the victor of the joust, your sire would consider him for a son-in-law, especially since Sir Rhys appeared uninterested in marriage. I encouraged him until he asked the ignoble of me." Ferrand's gaze shifted to Rhys. "When I protested—and I vow I did—he told there were times when what was trained into us must be set aside to defend against others doing as he believed you did. Then he assured me he had proof your acclaim was gained for being more accomplished with deception than at arms."

Refusing to defend against a lie, Rhys stared.

"Still I balked over the wrong of it and fear my actions would deprive me of my place at Wulfen, which had been hard won for being a third son. I even asked Benoit if desire for the unobtainable made him mislead me." Briefly, he closed his eyes. "Having never before seen him shed tears, I agreed."

He went silent, then addressed Eamon. "That day, for how closely you tended your brother's mount, I thought I would be unable to draw near to loosen the girth strap. There was relief in having a sound excuse to fail Benoit, but then one of the horses groomed by a page roused, and to prevent the boy's trampling, you ran to aid him."

Eamon looked to Rhys, next their father. "As all know, 'twas quickly resolved, but not soon enough." He returned to

Ferrand. "No glimpse did I catch of you whose fingers proved exceedingly nimble for how little time you had."

The squire considered his hands. "They surprised me as well, especially for how afeared I was of being caught."

Eamon's nostrils flared, in his youth a sign fists would follow. However, having mostly matured into a man of calm and thoughtful disposition, he remained seated, hands down though likely they were bunched beneath the table. "Again, I apologize, Brother," he said. "As still I failed you for not rechecking the strap ere you took to the saddle, the only peace I gain this day is confirmation I was conscientious in securing it when I prepared your horse."

"Never did I fault you," Rhys said, "but if you insist on forgiveness, the price is you cease apologizing and put this behind you."

As I must do, he thought, then asked Ferrand, "What of your re-notching of the strap after I was nearly trampled?"

He paled as if recalling the scene in the lists which could have made a murderer of him. "I thought I would retch when you were dragged, and afterward was as angry with myself as Benoit for betrayal of my conscience and honor."

"Still you sought to make it look an accident resulting from my brother's negligence."

"It was what Benoit told I must do, and since I believed knighthood yet within reach, I had to set the strap aright. 'Twas difficult, but for the distraction of your fall, easier than loosening it."

"Thus, your brother stole the win from mine," Eamon said.

Ferrand turned to Sir Owen. "You and others trained me to overcome my weaknesses, but that day I was all weakness. Hence, though I tried to get back to where I was before, the guilt was..." He shook his head. "I could not remain at Wulfen, and I think you knew my time was past."

Receiving a nod, he said, "I returned home to continue my squire's training with my eldest brother's retainers, and when Benoit finished serving the king in France and was welcomed home by the wife he had gained, he vowed to see my training through to knighthood." He looked to Dangereuse. "Just as he did not keep his word to your sire he would become more than a household knight for our brother, he eschewed the word given me."

"And your resentment grew until finally you had to do something with it," Rhys advanced.

"Nay, I did naught with my resentment. However, what became loathing over those four years when he treated you like a possession, Lady Dangereuse, and Sebastian an interloper..."

"Le Tournoi d'Honneur," she said.

"Aye, planned ere I knew who was to attend. When I learned Sir Rhys would be there, I nearly pulled back, but then it occurred it was his due to witness being done to Benoit what had been done him."

Conscious of his hand tensing atop Dangereuse's, Rhys eased it. "You had to know suspicion would land on me."

"Aye, but I thought not enough to substantiate Benoit's claim you were responsible, certain as I was my plan would come together perfectly for having access to his destrier and equipment and time in which to make it appear an accident beyond dispute."

"What did you do, Ferrand?" Dangereuse asked.

"Loosened the stitching of the girth strap both sides and raggedly clipped most of the right to make it appear the thread had worn through. And 'twas done in advance of Benoit's joust with the opponent he needed to best ahead of Sir Rhys since he would not accept his unseating as mere coincidence did it happen with his greatest rival. But though he took a solid hit whose force should have snapped the remaining threads, they held." He shook his head. "After he bested that knight, I was unable to be alone with his mount long enough to fix the strap, and so I could only pray the stitching held through Sir Rhys' contest."

"When it did not, your brother believed me as depraved as he," Rhys said. "That *I* stole a win."

"I meant to correct him. That night when he returned belowstairs after escorting Lady Dangereuse to their chamber, I followed him outside to the stable and his horse's stall. Steeling myself for what was to come, I watched as once more he examined the strap, then revealed my presence by declaring his humiliation and loss were well earned."

Ferrand drew breath. "His hand was on his dagger's hilt when he came around. I thought he would gut me, but he stared as if he did not recognize the brother who made possible his marriage to a Wulfrith. Determined to tell I more than cele-brated his loss—that I was the cause of it—I stepped nearer, but before I could speak, he set upon me with fists."

"When I saw your bruises at the inquest the next day, I knew he had done it," Dangereuse said, "but I thought it was for you not keeping watch over his mount."

"He beat me into unconsciousness. Thus, methinks he died certain Sir Rhys had avenged himself on him." He swallowed loudly. "I did not wish him dead, and yet I hoped the light gone from his eyes would eventually see light returned to yours, my lady. Could I make that day again, I would find a way to contain my loathing, but I am glad what came of my sin is the better life of which his obsession deprived you."

"I know," she said softly, "just as I know you have been burdened and remain so though all is told."

His gaze wavered. "He set it in motion, but I kept it in motion, and for that he is dead."

She raised her left arm from under the table and placed a

hand over his. "You played a part, but Benoit is dead for stealing the joust's win in the hope of gaining me for a wife."

A tear slid down his cheek. "One day, might you forgive me for causing you to endure much and depriving my nephew of his sire?"

She looked to Rhys, and he saw in her eyes a spark of defiance that sought to impress on him she had more right to determine the benevolence shown Ferrand. Even if Rhys was not—and never was—able to forgive, she would go the way of her heart.

And should, he silently acceded, then inclined his head.

She returned to the squire. "I forgive one who was no boy but far from a man when he did his brother's bidding, one who was a pained youth near a man when he yielded to vengeance."

His eyes widened, then he dropped his chin and said, "When I part from you and Sebastian, I shall be freer knowing the end I make of this is as good as possible."

"An end to Benoit's machinations," she reminded. "For you being ever kind and considerate and having served Lillia well, I believe this is a beginning—and a good one. If you think it best to leave us, do so, but know my wish is for you to continue aiding me." When she looked to her kin opposite, Rhys followed her gaze.

Though approval was on her uncle's face, Warin's expression was questionable. For Rhys having trained with him, he knew that brother was sympathetic to the weaknesses of others and capable of forgiving great trespass, but likely the same as Rhys he questioned Ferrand's ability to protect those of Lillia for having allowed Lady Vianne to thwart his watch over her.

As for Rémy of pressed lips, no approval there.

When Dangereuse turned back to Ferrand, he raised his chin and said, "I thank you for your kindness, but I will not give answer now since I no longer possess the excuse of being a boy or youth should I realize I decided wrong."

"I understand." She released his hand.

"If there are no further questions, you may leave, Squire Ferrand," said the Baron of Blackwood.

Silence, and then Ferrand set his hands to the chair arms and pressed upright. "I thank you for hearing me," he said and departed.

Surprisingly, it was Rémy's words that cut through the quiet—and as if with a keenly straight blade rather than jagged one. "I can see how the desire to please and serve one esteemed could entice a man to set aside what he knows he should cling to, but I am uncomfortable with him continuing to serve at Lillia, Dangereuse, especially for his position and little oversight beyond your own."

Though during her confinement in Justina's chamber these past days she and Rhys had spoken of their future during his visits, little of what was decided had been passed to others. As for the squire's fate, that had not been discussed, though Rhys had given it thought ahead of the confession.

"You are also concerned with Ferrand remaining at Lillia, Rhys?" Dangereuse asked.

"Not overly much, though that is because I know what methinks Rémy does not, though I believe Warin and your uncle greatly suspect my intentions."

A smile gentling her mouth, she looked to the Lord and Lady of Blackwood. "Your parents as well?"

"Beyond suspicion," he said, having confirmed what they believed of his relationship with her.

"Then you will w-wed my sister?" Rémy said.

"Providing your eldest brother does not object, I will make her my wife. With me at her side, would you still be wary of

Squire Ferrand serving at Lillia until you assume your lordship and we remove to Mathe's sister castle?"

Rémy pondered that. "Though I am to show grace for genuine repentance, I have yet to be satisfied with how one determines a repenter's sincerity."

"Then allow me to determine it," Dangereuse said. "I am grateful for your concern and aware our hearts can betray us, but I believe if my brother-in-law remains at Lillia while I administer the demesne, it will be good for all, especially the one Benoit cruelly used."

"As you will," Rémy acceded. "Now tell how you think Bastian will react to gaining a father."

She smiled. "Since he admires Rhys, I believe he will adjust ere long."

"I have a s-suggestion. When finally you concede he will make a better warrior than a man of the Church, do so after he presses for it again lest he fear you acquiesce only to make more room for Sir Rhys in your affections."

Rhys had also considered that, but it surprised one still growing into manhood did so.

"I thank you for wise counsel," Dangereuse said.

Rémy stood, and he and his brother and uncle withdrew.

After Griffin and Quintin de Arell gave their blessings for the marriage and assured their future daughter-in-law they were eager to gain Sebastian for a grandchild, Rhys escorted Dangereuse toward the chamber shared with Justina—and hoped to find his sister absent so he could be alone with the woman he expected to be his betrothed a very short time and wife to his end days.

"Let us go elsewhere," Dangereuse said at the sound of Justina humming behind the closed door.

Unfortunately, even less appropriate than the two of them being alone in his sister's chamber was them being alone in his, though certainly it would not be the first time they had such privacy.

"Perhaps Quintin's Bower?" she suggested. "I am curious about it."

He nearly laughed at the name Justina had given the room that long ago served as a prison for the sister of Griffin's enemy who came looking for the brother she believed held captive at Castle Mathe. When Rhys' sire could not produce a man he did not hold, and she refused to believe him innocent, teasingly he had taunted the fiery Quintin Boursier. And found her sire's Wulfrith dagger drawn on him in the midst of his retainers.

Of course, he had been angered. Of course he had overpowered her. However, it was a fine chamber in which he confined her. Had she behaved, she would have remained there until he cooled enough to decide what to do with her. She had not behaved, awakening the household by pounding on the door and casting at it whatever came to hand.

Though she had expected Griffin to return her to her brother's men who awaited her beyond the fortress, he had removed her from the donjon, escorted her to the inner bailey's wall, and locked her in the room now known as *Quintin's Bower*.

"Obviously, Justina told you the tale given her by our mother," he said.

"And most intriguing that." She tilted her head. "Is it true your sire and mother avail themselves of the room on occasion?"

"It is, though as far as I know, only when a guest of high rank passes the night and they yield the solar."

"You will take me there?"

"I will, though I warn it is a room of little account."

"I must see it—and be alone with you there."

Also inappropriate, but he released her arm and said, "As

the weather remains cold, retrieve your mantle while I gain mine."

THE ROOM on the third floor of the inner wall's southern tower did appear to be of little account, but despite its size, simple furnishings, and narrow window whose view was mainly of the snow-clothed wood flanking Castle Mathe, it moved Dangereuse.

"I feel love here," she said.

Rhys paused in lighting the brazier's coals with the torch that had illuminated the corridor and stairs they traversed. "Is that what keeps brushing against me?" he said, then gifted her that crooked smile.

Standing behind an upholstered chair, arms folded atop its back, she gave him a smile of her own. "Mayhap I merely seek a good fit for Justina's blushing beliefs about this room, but..." Once more she surveyed it, pausing on the window, small table, bed, trunk, chairs, and brazier. "Nay, I do not." She frowned. "Do we trespass in coming here?"

Without hesitation, he said, "Had my mother wished to keep sacred this room where I am fair certain she and my sire began moving toward love, she would not have revealed to Justina anything that gave her cause to name it *Quintin's Bower*." He returned to the coals, said across his shoulder, "Ere you are scandalized by imaginings of what might have been told my sister, know my bold mother is fond of tales of romance. Whatever Justina knows of this place has all to do with the heart."

"It never occurred I should be scandalized," she said and, at his chuckle, came around the chair, halted at his back, and slid her arms around him.

"Fire here, Dange." His voice was so deep she shivered.

"Hmm," she murmured, setting her cheek against his back. "Not to be stoked, but soon with my broken years fully behind me."

She heard him set the poker in its stand, then he turned and raised her chin. "At Lillia, your uncle mentioned those broken years."

She began to tense, then eased. "I suppose it natural my grandmother shared with her son what she named those years following my return to Stern."

He slid a thumb across her lower lip. "As I do not believe she knowingly spoke that in your hearing, how came you by it?"

"I happened on an exchange with my oldest brother who was frustrated for how protective I was of Bastian. Now when I become aware of speaking or behaving outside the strength and honor of a Wulfrith, I recall the name given those years following Benoit's death. I hated it, yet was grateful it alerted me to the need to mend those places so I not fail my son as his sire failed him. Of course, knowing one must mend is different from placing the stitches well and securely knotting them."

Rhys nodded. "When Ferrand expressed regret for the loss of Sebastian's sire, you seemed ill at ease."

"I was for longing to remind him Benoit regarded our son as more an obstacle than a gift and that his mishandling of our boy the night you came to our aid portended further ill for their relationship—and evidenced Sebastian fared better being loved and guided by the men of my family."

"You remained silent lest speaking that increase guilt over his role in your union."

"Aye, and I believe the price Ferrand has paid is sufficient to cover his sins."

"I believe you are right."

Being fairly tall, she had only to go to her toes to set her mouth on his, but before she could, he tightened his arms about her and lowered his head.

It was a gentle kiss and soon more. An enthusiastic kiss, then much more. A hungry kiss, then both drew back.

Peering at her out of a face framed by blond hair scattered every direction just as his hands had scattered hers, Rhys said, "Another thing about which you are right."

"What might that be?"

"Love is here."

She laughed. "And 'tis catching," she said, then fingered the healing places on his face. "It feels we traveled a long way to find love. Do you think it felt the same for your parents?"

"I do, and as that made it more precious to them, so it is for us." Gently he touched *her* healing places, then settled his hand on her jaw.

Dangereuse turned her mouth into it and kissed his palm. "I like the alone here with you."

He raised his eyebrows. *"The alone?"*

"It fits, does it not?"

Another crooked smile—and a longing to kiss it. But they were not to soar. Not yet. "Can we talk a while?" She nodded at the chairs.

His smile went further aslant. "For that I lit the brazier," he said, then led her to a chair. But rather than hand her into it, he lowered and pulled her onto his lap.

"Rhys! I like this, but 'tis hardly conducive to talk."

He hooked hair out of her eyes. "A challenge, but as I am certain you shall be mine soon, I am confident patience shall prevail." He drew her nearer, and she settled against his chest. "Now lady soon of the De Arell's, of what should we speak?"

"Of us," she said, then hopeful the Lord would bless them

with sons and daughters, added, "and the children we shall make."

"Fire here," he warned again.

"A challenge," she also named the patience required of both.

And—my!—how she loved that smile.

EPILOGUE

Stern Castle
February, 1354

Fire here, Dangereuse mused as Rhys closed the door of their nuptial chamber on the priest and those who delivered to the wife made of her this day the husband made of him—her kin that included her eldest brother who had fully recovered from the winter sickness and Rhys' that included members of the families whose intermarrying with the De Arells had ended their feuding.

Though the groom's linen undertunic was of thicker cloth than the bride's embroidered chemise that permitted glimpses of her figure, it fit his form so well it required little imagination to know his shoulders, arms, and torso. And none to know his muscular lower legs and feet for them being bare.

He turned to where she sat against the plump pillows. It no longer necessary to keep tucked beneath her arms the bedclothes that lent modesty while their well-wishers were

within, she let them slip to her waist. This her invitation to be
loved in body as she was in heart.

How joyous to be loved in both, the thought slipped in, nearly
granting entrance to the man who did not belong here.

Where Rhys remained unmoving, he said, "You are beautiful, Wife."

Savoring *the alone* with him and wishing him near, she
said, "And yet you, husband of fine face and form, do not seem
as eager as expected, especially since..." That she did not finish
for it sounding a complaint for the month and a half delay in
their wedding. It was not, it being right to give the families of
Murielle and the Wulfriths time to lament what could not be
changed.

"Dangereuse?" Concern edged his voice, and she knew he
guessed another was here who had no place in the front row of
this night nor any row near the one reserved for the newly
wedded De Arells.

As he moved toward the bed softly awash in the light of
candles set around the chamber, she put those sorrows behind
her and said, "To ensure our patience is well rewarded, I would
be in *the alone* with you here."

Understanding in his eyes, he halted alongside the
mattress whose turned back covers invited him in. "Let us
make it worth the wait," he said, then began baring the rest
of him.

When his tunic dropped, all she could say was, "Rhys de
Arell."

"Dangereuse de Arell," he answered, then joined her on the
bed, pushed fingers into her loosed hair, and kissed her so
deeply that all their other kisses seemed almost those of
youths beginning to explore intimacy. Then there was their
responses to what came after...

Later she would ponder how and when she was divested of

her chemise, her clearest recall of their feverish lovemaking being when the bare of her met the bare of him. Though that was just the beginning, as it was more than any beginning she had known, they had not been entirely alone for the one moment she let in the Lord to question why He so blessed them.

The night was marvelously long, and though there were only bits of dozing here and there, when the candles lost their flames and dawn's light stroked the shutters, she longed to remain conscious of the man whose side she hugged and lower limbs she hooked a leg over. But then Rhys tensed.

When it did not resolve, she rose on an elbow and peered into his deeply shadowed face.

"What is it, dear Dange?" he rumbled.

"That is what I ask of you who, I fear, allows troubles to enter here as I did earlier."

"Forgive me. Though I would continue savoring *the alone* with you, my thoughts drift ahead of sleep, and where they drift so trouble that rest remains out of reach."

"I am guessing 'tis the same hovering about me. Tell, and perhaps we can close the door a while longer."

"Though I remain concerned for Rémy, more immediately Warin."

As did she since there seemed naught could be done for her youngest brother beyond continuing to support him through what had delayed their wedding.

"Though the king has absolved me of his French man-at-arm's death and failing to deliver Lady Vianne's intelligence," he continued, "I fear Warin will pay dearly for taking the lady from Lillia though it was only to appear amenable to the trade."

Much that concerned her family. Hopefully, the summoning received by her brother three days ago and ahead of Rhys' arrival at Stern to speak vows would not see Warin stripped of his barony. As Hector had advanced, it could be in regard to that which their uncle sent the king a fortnight past.

Warin having invited Owen to continue recovering at Romary Castle upon Woodhearst, it was there he discovered something slipped into his saddlebag between Lillia and the coast where a ship had awaited those expected to return Lady Vianne to France.

The folded paper that sustained slight water damage when he swam his horse into the sea was bound with twine, and beneath its many crossings a ragged piece of parchment likely cut from one requested of Dangereuse at Lillia. Though what was written on the paper was unseen, clearly inked on the sturdy parchment were the words—*For the eyes of King Edward alone,* and following them two letters that told the sender was Vianne Wardieu.

Though Dangereuse's uncle might have been tempted—perhaps even prompted by Warin—to trespass, which could be easily done for the absence of a wax seal whose ruin would have attested to the breach, Lady Vianne's directive was honored. Hence, whatever Edward beheld upon receipt of the paper was as open to speculation as the reason Warin was in London.

"Likely, Edward believes your brother and uncle's priority should have been to escort Lady Vianne to him when I was captured alongside you," Rhys said.

Dangereuse settled her cheek on his chest that had become her favorite pillow. "As you had little opportunity to discuss this with Hector, you should know he believes your report of the events alongside Warin's and Owen's was well enough received by Edward that if punishment is dealt my brother, his lordship of Woodhearst is unlikely to be affected." Then recalling her brother-in-law who was persuaded to resume his post at Lillia, she added, "And forget not Ferrand owned to losing control of Lady Vianne."

He nodded, but emphasized, "*Unlikely* to be affected. As it was for me to safeguard the lady, the greater responsibility is mine."

"Warin disagrees, and does not regret what it took to free me. As for Lady Vianne..." She recalled her exchanges with the woman, saw again those eyes fixed on her where she had gone into the sea and lips forming words of apology, next what Rhys had confided—his suspicion the lady was given to using drink to dull the sharp edges of life as Dangereuse had also suspected.

"What of her?" he asked.

She raised her head—and wished she could better see his face. "Though for some reason Warin is loath to scatter grace her way, I believe she did what she thought best."

"Then you maintain her decision to return to France could have been more an attempt to aid you than a wish to reunite with Rollon de Talliere."

"You have suggested the same. However, since my uncle discovered that paper in his saddlebag, which could be the intelligence she insisted on personally placing in the king's hands, even more I believe her ride on the shore was done for me."

"I hardly know her, Dangereuse, but I lean that way as well."

"I pray it is so, though it bodes ill if she is not believed by those into whose hands she gave herself," she said, then ushered the lady out of the nuptial chamber, leaned up, and proved she could find his mouth in the dark.

"Might you tempt me again?" he asked when she lifted her head.

"Do we remain awake much longer, I shall." When he

chuckled, she shifted down, sliding her hand from his shoulder to ribs, hip, and thigh. And there her fingers settled on the scar that would ever bear witness to the night he came to her and her son's defense.

Our son, she silently corrected, once more moved by gratitude for Sebastian's reaction to learning Rhys would wed his mother. Blessedly, mostly it had been dismay. More blessedly, it was short-lived. She knew he esteemed her betrothed, but greater her recognition of his shrewd mind when, during Rhys' visit to Lillia at January's end, Sebastian cornered him after learning he was to train at Wulfen to further strengthen his healed arm.

He had reasoned that as Rhys was to be his father, his son ought to accompany him. Rhys had reported it was hard not to smile knowing the direction of their exchange and that he had told Sebastian it was not possible since only boys in training were allowed within those walls.

Sebastian had feigned thinking hard, then asked if it was true the duty of a father was to ensure his son could defend against bad people. Rhys had said it was, providing the son was suited to bear arms, and that another of a sire's duties was to protect his daughters. The boy had spread his feet, folded his arms over his chest, and declared he could more easily protect a little sister if he knew how to use a real sword.

Rhys had agreed, and Sebastian insisted that once he was his sire, he must convince his wife their son was suited to bearing arms and should begin training at Wulfen immediately. Rhys' answer was that as soon as his son proved he possessed patience befitting his age, he would speak with Dangereuse.

Sebastian had shouted with joy and slammed so hard into Rhys' legs to hug them that his wooden sword slipped from his belt and hit the floor.

Thus, it was decided that come spring both father and son would travel to Wulfen and while the former strengthened his arm, the latter would begin his warrior's journey.

"I think Bastian grows to love you, Rhys."

When he murmured what might be agreement, she knew that deep sound warmed the back of a smile, then he said, "He did claim our wedding as an early birthday gift."

"Did he?" she exclaimed.

"As he accompanied me to the chapel."

Dangereuse would have thought her heart too full to love more until it had time to stretch further, but despite remembrance of the day past, that it did. "I am glad he regarded it as a joyous occasion. After yesterday's upset, I feared his mood would strain our wedding day."

"For being in awe of the power of a king, he understands the reason Warin could not attend the wedding, Dangereuse, but as is expected of one his age, he cannot grasp why Rémy stayed away."

"Especially since the aunt lost to him was that in name only for Rémy marrying Murielle and directly returning to his training," she said. "No affection as he is accustomed to seeing between husband and wife. Indeed, no relationship at all."

She recalled her brother lurching from the birthing room days after their return from Blackwood and slamming back against the corridor wall, next her gently prying away the fist pressed to his mouth, then his words, *Dear God, I chose wrong.*

"He is confused by his uncle's mourning," she said. "Even if 'tis not of love lost, Rémy mourns for Murielle—and the babe."

"It appears healthy," Rhys said, having briefly held the child Esta passed to him. "But from what you told of the birthing, he may well have reason to mourn it as well."

"And reason for guilt, he believes." She breathed deep. "The years will tell, and we shall continue praying they tell well."

Longing to return to lightness for what remained of their nuptial night, she said, "We keep letting in troubles when this is our time to enjoy the alone of each other."

"So we do, and here the end of it." An instant later, he elicited a cry of delight when, with the suddenness of a warrior besting an opponent, he rolled her beneath him. "Dangereuse of her blessed years, I would be one with you again."

Blessed, she turned over the word. *No longer broken. Blessed.*

"And perhaps sooner we shall give our son the little sister he wishes to protect," he added.

Raising her head to press her mouth to his, she said, "I would like that."

The kiss was as sweet as it was passionate, and when it was interrupted, the culprit was welcome for it being his gruffly spoken, "You are drink."

Then her softly spoken, "Allow this silvered lady to aid in quenching your thirst—and mine."

Afterward, thinking she could be tempted to spend the remainder of her life here in the arms of the man who found his rest ahead of her, consciously Dangereuse let another step into the light of their love.

Though the years between the joust at Wulfen in 1346 and her joining with Rhys in 1354 had been wearing and lonely, at last the old Baron of Wulfen's wish to wed her to this man was realized. A long wait, and yet necessary since it seemed beautifully binding one's life to another depended as much on finding one of exceptional fit as the timing of that find. God's timing.

"It is done, Father," she whispered. "As you knew was good and right, he and I have become one."

Dear Reader,

If you enjoyed the fourth tale in the 14th-century Age of Honor series, I would appreciate a review of DANGEROUS at your online retailer. A few sentences is lovely. A few more, lovelier.

Watch for NOTORIOUS, the next book in the series, releasing Autumn 2023.

Blessings ~ Tamara

AUTHOR'S NOTE

Dear Readers,

I hope you enjoyed DANGEROUS and the introduction of Lady Vianne Wardieu whose surname may sound familiar. This future heroine is a descendant of Lizanne Balmaine and Ranulf Wardieu of LADY AT ARMS, my first medieval romance published by Bantam/Doubleday/Dell in 1994.

The tale of this lady destined for the heart of Sir Warin Wulfrith will be told in NOTORIOUS, the fifth book in the Age of Honor series that releases Autumn 2023. If you'd like a peek at what I have in store for these two before they reach their *Happily Ever After,* an excerpt is included in ebook and paper-back formats.

As always, thank you for joining me on this blessed pen and paper journey. ~ Tamara

Notorious: Book Five Excerpt

CHAPTER TWO

Paris, France
April 26, 1354

There was advantage in being among the last to perform, it allowing more time in which to perfect words entirely composed in her mind and practice her delivery. But there were also disadvantages. The first was fatigue to which she was more vulnerable for advancing pregnancy that was knotted with fear and worry. The second was nervous anticipation that, dashed each time another performer was summoned ahead of her, was further heightened.

When finally Vianne departed the chamber now empty of all but a handful, she was so tightly wound she questioned everything as her red skirt skimmed the floor of the path to the dais.

How did she appear to the hundreds thronging the hall,

some eager for another performance, others grudgingly pausing in the midst of conversations to show polite interest as required?

Were her chin and shoulders level, footsteps gracefully unhurried, abdominal muscles sufficiently engaged so none suspected she was with child?

Was her composition well enough fixed in her memory that its only fault would be its dark subject matter on an occasion that called for light?

When she took her place before the king whose great chair was positioned ten feet back from the dais, could she truly present this work, or would she fold, instead reciting one more pleasing to him—and Rollon?

The impatient one at the back of my tongue, she silently commanded as she neared the steps of what had been transformed into a stage and pinched up her skirt so her feet did not catch on the hem. Still, she nearly stumbled when Rollon appeared and cupped her elbow.

As he stabilized her ascent, he said low, "Do me proud, my love."

In that moment accepting she must had she any chance of regaining trust and freedom that could keep this child safe, she graced him with what was to appear a loving smile.

When she set foot on the dais, he released her, and she continued forward. Center of the stage, she turned to face King Jean and his boot-licking subjects. Once the murmuring ceased and most eyes were upon her, she smiled as if no greater happiness could be had, flared her skirts like crimson wings, and curtsied so deeply to those unworthy of bended knee she wanted to laugh scornfully. To ensure she did not, she remained bent longer than necessary to compose her face, then whipped up her head as she straightened. And felt the pins fixing her hair at her nape fail.

As if the uncoiling of the braid down her back was part of an act, the faces of many in the audience lit, and she heard scattered applause. None from the women, of course. And neither from King Jean, though appreciation was in his eyes and curve of his mouth. It was the same with his sixteen-year-old son, Charles, who sat beside him. Though the young man now married four years to his cousin continued to look down upon Rollon's mistress, it was obvious to her and others he would like a taste of what the royal advisor enjoyed.

"Entertain us, Lady Vianne Wardieu!" the king commanded.

She dipped her chin, and when she raised her eyes, saw Rollon move behind and to the left of Jean, and just beyond him were Aubert Marionne and Pierre.

Though she had decided to behave, the latter's eyes boring into hers flashed her with memories of the English brigands whose reward for betraying their country was being cast into the sea by Pierre. She remembered their flailing as they were sent over the rails...their screams...

"We wait!" King Jean snapped as if she delayed minutes rather than moments.

Catching the impatient sweep of his hand as she met his gaze, she opened her mouth, but realizing it was her newest composition advancing across her tongue, pressed her lips. Not daring to look to Rollon lest his expression make it more difficult to recall what she had written two days past, she searched backward.

"Mayhap the *lady* overly imbibed this eve, my lord king," Charles said loud enough his voice carried, causing those too imprudent to wait on Jean's reaction to chuckle. Then with that sickly smile he surely thought charming, the Dauphin leaned forward as if to search out further evidence of her inebriation. "As all know, it would not be the first time."

344

Feeling her heart claw at her breastbone and face aspire to the color of her gown, Vianne looked to the tight-lipped king, and knowing greater humiliation would be had with the next sweep of his hand, expelled her breath on the words, "For your birthday, King Jean, that which I call *The Chasm Between Us.*"

His eyes narrowed as surely she would see Rollon's did were she to look his way. Though the title was no auspicious beginning to something he expected to honor him, it *was* honest.

Vianne was not known for dramatic flair during a recitation, but this eve was different. Finding courage in the sweep of her own arm and splaying of a hand, she began, "What terrible sea is this? No warm embrace, no gentle kiss." She touched her lips, leaned forward to peer at the floor before the dais. "Down...down..."

Upon straightening and seeing she yet held the attention of those more given to conversation, she continued, "Whence does it rise, whence does it fall? No soft passage, foul siren's call." Now she turned her ear out as if to attend to that call and leaned forward again. "Down...down..."

Continuing to peer into the depths of her memories and seeing again the men swallowed by the sea, her next words were pitched higher than intended. "Why does it churn, its waves break?" Raising her eyes, she landed them on the glowering Pierre and bemoaned, "No compassion, no pity's sake. Down...down..."

When the hike of his lip showed teeth, she straightened. "Where does it flow, north or south?" She looked up, down. "No tide goes in, no tide goes out." She looked side to side, then once more straight at Pierre. "Down...down..."

If not for movement from the king who followed her gaze by peering around his chair, she would have remained fixed on the miscreant. To return Jean's attention to her, she clapped her hands and demanded, "Who braves its winds, who trims these sails?" Putting back her head as if to look upon those flapping, fraying sheets, she recalled Pierre retching over the side, his belly unable to withstand the lurch of the ship though his gut weathered well the casting of men into the sea. "No weak-kneed lord, none at the rails. Down...down..."

She returned her regard to the entirety of her audience. "When will it ease, when will it still? No land in sight, no more to kill." She closed her eyes, shook her head. "Down...down..."

Then she raised hands as if beseeching God for aid and looked directly at random men and women at the rear of the gathering as she readied to deliver the final lines. "How does one—?"

The words that that followed jammed in her throat as a recipient of her accusatory gaze stared at her out of a face that should be hardly familiar for how brief their acquaintance, that his light beard had gone thick, blond hair grew long, and warrior garments had been exchanged for the lavish dress of a French courtier.

Vianne had thought never to see him again—had prayed the English knight she foiled with what she believed good cause would not risk entering the lion's den of France to wreak vengeance on her. But Warin Wulfrith was here and, doubtless, was the one at the Norman table whose gaze she had felt and back she had seen before he was prepared to reveal his presence.

"Forgive me," she mouthed, not to him but Lady Dangereuse and Sir Rhys—the most recent tragedy for which she was responsible, both surely having died after she swam her horse into the sea to reach Pierre's boat so she could be traded for Sir Warin's sister. As she had drawn near, that lady had wrenched free of a brigand and jumped into the chill water.

There was nothing Vianne could do to aid her, so cold herself she was only half conscious when dragged off the horse. However, she had met the floundering lady's gaze and beseeched forgiveness before being dropped into the boat. As Lady Dangereuse was distant from Sir Rhys who desperately swam to her and more distant from the shore where her brother and his men had slain most of the brigands, the two had to have succumbed to the cold. And now Sir Warin was here to—

"If this painful silence is for show, Lady Vianne," King Jean drawled with exaggerated boredom, "we have no patience for it."

She lowered her arms to her sides. Having scant time to pen her part, she smiled apologetically. "Forgive me. The illness it was feared would claim me continues to addle my thoughts. Do you give me a few moments—"

His hand slashed the air. "You work words well, but on the occasion of our birthday, I expected something better—pretty and uplifting, not ugly and dreary. You are done!"

Deferentially, she bowed her head, then as she turned toward the steps, looked to Rollon so she might know the depth of his anger. But she barely caught his eye before his king's crooked finger had him bending near.

Though tempted to go abovestairs to avoid those to whom she provided more fodder to look down upon the English, fairly certain the long night Rollon promised would be longer yet, she imagined shoving a stick down her spine and crossed to a side table.

As brothers who juggled all manner of items, including eggs, were ushered to the dais, she poured a cup of weak wine. And resisted trying to catch sight of Warin Wulfrith who, unless willing to risk death, could be of no danger to her in the midst of hundreds of French enemies.

He but wished to strike fear in one he could not know was already fearful, surely believing what she professed on that shore—that she wished to return to Rollon, a lie not for his benefit but Pierre and Aubert Marionne into whose hands she meant to give herself despite Sir Warin's attempt to thwart her.

"Exceptional, Lady Vianne!" called one who approached from her left. Though she recognized his accented voice, she startled as if it belonged to Sir Warin whose own Norman-French accent was heavily diluted by the English of him as hers had been before being sent to marry into French nobility.

She swung around and saw here the man of middle years who had been seated at the Norman table—and had unwittingly supplied her bits of information over the years. Relieved he came alone, she wished she could recall his name. Unfortunately, some edges of a mind she believed sharp had become dull these past months, likely due to stress as much as pregnancy.

When he halted before her, she returned his smile. "It is good to see you again."

His lids narrowed. "I glimpse recognition, but though well I recall your name, I believe you have forgotten mine."

She bounced her chin in the direction of the stage where the jugglers raked in expressions of awe and admiration not shown her. "Since my name was announced and even spoken by the king, you have the advantage."

"Had I forgotten it, but I did not. You are memorable, my lady, not only for beauty but compositions of which, alas, *The Chasm Between Us* is only the second I have heard." He set an elegant hand on his midriff, bowed slightly. "Chevalier Joffrey Masse."

She inclined her heard. "Pardon me for forgetting. As told

the king, due to my recent illness, I do not think as straight as usual."

"And yet your gift to him, even incomplete, was exceptional."

"And ugly and dreary," she reminded.

With a playful sneer, he shrugged. "Only those of narrow mind find beauty in the joyous alone."

Doubtless, that the intentional prick of a spur to the flank of the royal House of Valois. Just as the Duke of Normandy who took England's crown three hundred years past had chafed beneath the rule of a King of France, still William the Conqueror's people aspired to autonomy that became rarer with each passing century. It did not sit well with them to be tightly ruled, and less so with the eldest sons of French kings now titled *Duke of Normandy,* meaning at this time grown men and well-seasoned warriors were accountable to the arrogant sixteen-year-old Charles.

"I thank you for the encouragement, Chevalier," she said and, finding some solace in his company, did not immediately distance herself but took another sip, then said, "Blessedly, the jugglers are talented, clearing the sight and sound of me from King Jean's eyes and ears."

The man drew nearer, just shy of making her uncomfortable enough to flit away. "Oui, Jean is less likely to perseverate on not being praised as if a God," he said, "and Charles will fall asleep this eve with his blanket hugged close and a smile on his lips."

She looked sidelong at him. "Careful, you sound almost as English as I."

A corner of his mouth convulsed. "And here I feared I sounded more English than the special friend of the king's advisor."

She was no stranger to allusions and comments about this

English lady's relationship with Rollon, and once before this man had acknowledged that notoriety, but since there was no useful information to cull from him in her current circumstances, there was no reason to continue the conversation.

However, before she could politely disengage, as if he realized he overstepped, he changed the subject. "The Dauphin's wife, Joanna, admires your compositions."

That she had not known, the duchess rarely looking her way while at court. Was what Masse spoke true? Or this a diversion to hold her here? No sooner questioned than she was struck by something she should have considered sooner. Warin Wulfrith had been seated at the end of the Norman table opposite this man, but that did not mean there was no connection between them. What if—?

"The Duchess tells an inquiry into your French ancestry yielded tidings that your mother, who was among the ladies accompanying Princes Isabella to England to wed the second King Edward, was of the family De Morville."

Vianne knew where this was heading, as it did with many who became acquainted with the French side of her—that her ability to paint words into verse had been passed to her by the twelfth-century Elias de Morville whose works were treasured in France as well as England.

"I have no doubt my best writings are due to blood in my veins that sing the songs of my ancestor, Sir Elias," she said and dipped her head. "Now as King Jean requires of his birthday gifts, I should move among his guests."

Giving him no moment to catch her back, she set her cup on the table and made for a group of young ladies who did not like her for being told they ought not, but were more tolerable than the women who warned them away. But as she neared, seeing they were also the destination of Prince Charles, she veered away. Obviously, he tired of sitting his sire's side and sought to use his royal position to gain the attention and admiration of women likely to spurn him were he not France's future king.

"My lady." A hand touched her arm, and she turned so quickly her skirts swept tall boots belonging not to Warin Wulfrith but Ingerger le Grand, lord of Amboise as well as Chevreuse upon which Rollon's manor house was situated.

"My lord!" she exclaimed.

The man with whom she had become fairly acquainted over the years for his appearance at court and more recently her extended stay at the manor, was attractive of face, but less so of figure. Despite his surname, he was slight of height and build. And drawn to her as Rollon scorned each time he was obligated to entertain the lord who permitted him to take game from the woods of Chevreuse.

"You look vibrant this eve, Lady Vianne." He bowed.

She dipped her head. "I thank you, Lord Le Grande."

"And your composition... Though the king deemed it dreary, I thought it hauntingly lovely."

He sounded genuine, but this was also flirtation of which she could make good use were she prying for intelligence. Since now was not the time, she wanted none of it. "You are most kind, my lord. How fares your wife?"

Though annoyance flashed in his eyes, sorrow quickly cast a shadow over it. "Her lingering illness tests my faith and that of our children."

Unthinkingly, she set a hand on his sleeve. "I am sorry. I know you love her well." She did not know that, though from the little learned of his marriage, he was at least fond of the woman.

Regardless, her words served. With a smile of gratitude, he caught up her hand and kissed her fingers. "Hauntingly lovely. Good eve, my lady." He loosed her and turned away.

When he disappeared among the many, the further alteration of her course proved a blessing. She had not expected the doors of the inner courtyard to be open since April nights were cold, but the press of bodies in the overheated hall must have seen them set wide.

She looked around to be certain none followed with eyes nor feet, including Warin Wulfrith who should be conspicuous among the gathering for his stature and blond hair. Since he was nowhere to be seen, she guessed he had departed after showing himself to her, as was wise with Pierre and Marionne beginning to move among the guests. Though the former was unlikely to recognize the warrior who had led the attack against brigands in the pay of the French, despite the way Sir Warin presented this eve and Pierre and his keeper being offshore in the boat carrying Lady Dangereuse toward a waiting ship, the sharp-eyed Marionne might recognize him.

Assured only Chevalier Joffrey had any interest in this lady who had displeased King Jean, Vianne stepped through the nearest doorway onto beautifully-set stone that formed a walkway all around a rectangular, lantern-lit garden.

There were several couples holding hands and walking among vegetation that would be lush before long and one couple who appeared almost of one body for how close their embrace against a tree, but none were near enough to trouble her nor her them. Whereas they sought privacy in which to enjoy each other's company, she sought it to pretend at freedom ahead of steeling herself for Rollon's displeasure she must suffer as calmly as possible to protect one other than herself.

Flinching over remembrance of his hand on her belly, she gave her head a shake, then strode left and, shortly, set her forearms atop a short wall that cornered this section of the walkway. For the lanterns and that she remained fairly near the great hall's light escaping into the dark, she was visible, but as this had become a retreat for couples, likely she would be left to herself for a time.

Leaning into her arms, she fixed her gaze far right of the couple against the tree, affording them privacy for however much time they could steal from whoever would deny them—right or wrong.

"Freedom and safety," she whispered her own longing, then fatigue in every pulse of her body, thought it near tragic that eight years in France—only a third of her life—could wear her so thin she would hesitate to question any who said she was nearer an old woman than a young one. Though she ate, dressed, and lived well, she might as well be laboring in the fields for how worn she was.

In the next instant, she gave a snort of disgust at the presumption her life was as hard as those of common women, many of whom suffered as much or more for being controlled by a man they did not want—and having no soft landing upon the comforts nobility imparted.

If they can persevere despite abundant sorrows that make them feel far older than their years, so can I, she told herself. *And somehow I will.*

Footsteps. And only one set. As they moved toward her, it felt as if her heart snagged on a peg she passed by. Not because her solitude was interrupted. Because something she could not see, smell, nor touch revealed the identity of the man who, the last time they were entirely alone, had shocked her with his sudden appearance.

Unfastening her tongue from her palate, she turned her head toward him.

Had Warin Wulfrith not allowed his beard to thicken, hiding burn scars on one side of his lower face, still he would be as handsome as he presented now—even with eyes harder than hard and darker than dark upon her.

As she forced herself to continue leaning against the wall, he halted a stride from her and said in English, "An interesting performance."

She wanted to swallow, but lest the effort make more evident the lump in her throat, said past it, "Well come to Paris, Sir Warin—rather, *Chevalier* Warin do you wish to continue passing as one who belongs inside the walls of Palais de la Cité."

He looked to those wandering the courtyard as he must have done before approaching her, then in French and an accent far thicker than she knew him to possess, said, "This day, it is Chevalier Warin d'Argent, *Lady*."

On the surface, titled with respect, but barely scratch that surface and there scorn with which she was accustomed when acknowledged by many a Frenchwoman of the court. Determined to remain numb to it, leaving one forearm on the wall, Vianne angled her body toward him and asked, "D'Argent?"

"From whom the Wulfriths descended following the conquering of England by Duke William. Still they hold the Barony of Valeur in Normandy."

Boldly, she scrutinized his garments. "I see, and you make yourself one of them so you..." She returned her gaze to his and, hoping he would not seek vengeance in the presence of witnesses who could be roused by a scream, continued, "...may exact payment for what you have lost despite what King Edward gained." At least, what she hoped he gained from the intelligence she left in England. Unfortunately, for her isolation at the manor, Rollon's month-long absence, and having engaged in no meaningful conversations since her return to the palace, she had no way of knowing if the English thwarted French trickery a fortnight past.

Braving Sir Warin's narrowing eyes, she pressed fingers into the palm of the hand tempted to her belly and prepared to ask for confirmation she had served her country well. Instead, words she had scant time to think through passed her lips. "I never intended your sister harm, nor Sir Rhys and the people of Lillia. Truly, I am sorry—" She broke off.

He had not moved, but a distant look in his eyes told his attention was no longer on her. And when she searched past his shoulder, there the reason—an enemy at his back armed with weapons as was not allowed King Jean's guests.

Silently, she rebuked herself. Despite observation and stealth skills honed to keep her alive all these years, she had known the guard posted outside the apartment was also set to watch over her in the hall. And just as she had caught no sight of Sir Warin before entering here, neither he who also followed her into the courtyard. And would report to Rollon what appeared a tryst.

Write the part! she demanded as the guard advanced, then scribbled it out behind her eyes and spoke it into words, beginning with ones of regret. "Apologies, Sir Warin," she hissed.

All of him tense, the hand missing a sword hilt a mere fist at his side, with threat, he said low, "For what, *Lady?*"

Her answer was a lunge and a slap, which he did not try to prevent though a well-trained warrior—even one garbed as a nobleman of excessive leisure—could easily evade or retaliate against.

And you thought those eyes could not be harder nor darker upon you, she rued as they stared into hers despite the slight turn dealt his head.

There being more to her act that must be played out to protect her unborn child, she spat, "Foul Norman!" then swept around him. Hearing the muffled voices of the couples rise as they reacted to their trampled bliss, Vianne made quick of her steps, causing the guard to falter as she neared.

"A lady alone does not a conquest make!" she called behind, then said to Rollon's man whose uncertainty was almost laughable for how great a brute he was, "Insult only, though I am certain your lord would think punishment due him—providing it does not disrupt our king's celebration."

Then heart intent on bruising her breastbone, tears wetting her eyes, she was past him. As she entered the hall, she caught the sounds of a struggle, curses, and flesh-covered bone on bone.

Determined to escape the celebrants and huddle into silence, as discreetly as possible she traversed the hall toward the corridor that accessed the wing where the apartment lay— praying every step of the way the guard heeded her only so far as her accusation and desire for retribution against Sir Warin convinced Rollon of her innocent venture into the courtyard.

Having seen the second eldest Wulfrith brother fight the brigands on the shore, she assured herself the ferocity of his swinging blade would also be felt in the swing of his fist. Then, though he would hate her more, he would abandon vengeance and depart the palace, Paris, and France.

That is as likely as Rollon embracing this child when it delivers in four and a half months or sooner, she rebuked. *Oh, you fool!*

Dear Reader,

I hope you enjoyed this excerpt of NOTORIOUS, *the fifth book in the* Age of Honor *series. Watch for its release Autumn 2023.*

PRONUNCIATION GUIDE

Achard: AA-shahrd
Ada: AA-duh
Adelaide: AA-duh-layd
Annus mirabilis: AAN-oos Mee-RAH-buh-lihs
Amaury: AW-moh-ree
Artois: AH-twah
Aubert: OH-behr
Audrey: OW-dree
Barra: BAHR-uh
Benoit: BIHN-wah
Briant: BREE-ahn
Caen: KAHN
Calais: KAA-lay
Chanson: SHAHN-sahn
Charliese: SHAH-lees
Chevalier devenu noir: sheh-VAAL-yay DUH-vaan-yoo
noo-WAHR
Colbern: COHL-buhrn
Crécy: KREE-see

Creuseur: KROO-zuur
Dange: DAHN-zhuh
Dangereuse: DAHN-zhuh-ruuz
Darden: DAHR-dihn
D'Arci: DAHR-see
D'Argent: DAHR-zhahnt
Daschiel: DAA-shee-uhl
Dunn: DUHN
Elias: uh-LIY-uhs
Emil: EH-mihl
Ermine: UHR-meen
Esta: EH-stuh
Filomena: FIHL-uh-meen-uh
Fira: FIY-ruh
FitzSimon: FIHT-sih-muhn
Fléau de l'Anglais: FLAY-oo duh LAHN-glay
Ferrand: FEH-rahn
Gisa: GEE-suh
Godfroi: GAWD-frwah
Guarin: GAA-rahn
Guines: GEEN ´
Gustave: GOO-stahv
Gyrth: GUHRTH
Gytha: JIY-thuh
Ufford: UH-fuhrd
Hector: HEHK-tuhr
Héloise: AY-loh-weez
Ida: IY-duh
Ingvar: EENG-vah
Jankin: JAYN-kihn
Jean: ZHAHN
Kenilfairn: KEHN-uhl-faarn
Lavonne: LUH-vahn

Leofwine: LEEF-wiyn
Les Neuf Preux: lay-NUUF-pruu
Lianor: LEE-uh-nohr
Lillefarne: LIHL-uh-fahrn
Lisbette: LIHS-beht
L'Isle Bouchard: LEEL-boo-shahr
Lothaire: LOH-taar
Louis: LOO-wee
Mace: MAYS
Maedine: MAY-deen
Maël: MAY-luh
Marionne: MAA-ree-oh
Mathe: MAA-tay
Mercia: MUHR-see-uh
Moreville: mohr-VEEL
Murielle: Myuur-ee-uhl
Odo: OH-doh
Olivier: oh-LIH-vee-ay
Ondine: AWN-deen
Oriflamme: OH-ree-flaam
Owen: OH-wihn
Paulette: PAH-leht
Percival: PUHR-sih-vuhl
Philippa: FIHL-ih-puh
Plantagenet: plaan-TAA-juh-neht
Ravvenborough: RAY-vuhn-buh-ruh
Reginald: REH-jihn-uhld
Rémy: RAY-mee
Romary: ROHM-ree
Robine: rah-BEEN
Roche: ROHSH
Roslyn: RAHS-lihn
Rufus: ROO-fuhs

Sanche: SAHNSH
Sévère: SAY-vehr
Séverine: SAY-vuh-reen
Signaleurs blancs: SEEN-yuh-luu blahn
Sinjin: SIHN-jihn
Soames: SOHMZ
Stace: STAYS
Stern: STUHRN
Sweyn: SVIHN
Tostig: TAH-stihg
Tournoi d'Honneur: tohrn-WAH DAH-nuur
Vianne: VEE-aan
Villeneuve-le-Hardi: VEE-luh-nuuv LAHR-dee
Wardieu: WAHR-doh
Warin: WAH-rihn
Wulfen: WUUL-fehn
Wulfrith: WUUL-frihth
Yates: YAYTS

PRONUNCIATION KEY

VOWELS
aa: arrow, castle
ay: chain, lady
ah: fought, sod
aw: flaw, paw
eh: bet, leg
ee: king, league
ih: hilt, missive
iy: knight, write
oh: coat, noble
oi: boy, coin
oo: fool, rule

ow: cow, brown
uh: sun, up
uu: book, hood
y: yearn, yield

CONSONANTS
b: bailey, club
ch: charge, trencher
d: dagger, hard
f: first, staff
g: gauntlet, stag
h: heart, hilt
j: jest, siege
k: coffer, pike
l: lance, vassal
m: moat, pommel
n: noble, postern
ng: ring, song
p: pike, lip
r: rain, far
s: spur, pass
sh: chivalry, shield
t: tame, moat
th: thistle, death
t~h: that, feather
v: vassal, missive
w: water, wife
wh: where, whisper
z: zip, haze
zh: treasure, vision

GLOSSARY

BLIAUT: medieval gown
BRAIES/BREECHES: men's underwear with fastening cord
BUSTLE: often made of foxtails, worn under skirt to exaggerate buttocks
CASTELLAN: commander of a castle
CHAUSSES/LEGGINGS: men's close-fitting leg coverings usually of wool
CHEMISE/SHIFT: a woman's loose-fitting undergarment or nightdress
COIF: hood-shaped cap made of cloth or chain mail
CORSET: close-fitting undergarment for shaping a woman's figure (and some men)
COTE: mid-thigh fitted jacket; buttoned up front with close-fitting buttoned sleeves
COTEHARDIE: lavish cote; usually thigh-length for men and full-length for women (buttoned or laced)
DAGGES: fabric edges cut into points
DEMESNE: home and adjoining lands held by a lord

DOUBLET: padded mid-thigh jacket; buttoned up front with close-fitting buttoned sleeves

DONJON: tower at center of a castle serving as a lord's living area

FEALTY: tenant or vassal's sworn loyalty to a lord

FORTNIGHT: two weeks

GARDEROBE: enclosed toilet

GIRDLE: belt worn upon which purses or weaponry might be attached

KNAVE: dishonest or unprincipled man

LEAGUE: equivalent to approximately three miles

LIEGE: superior or lord

MAIL: garments of armor made of linked metal rings

MISCREANT: badly behaving person

MISSIVE: letter

MORROW: tomorrow; the next day

NOBLE: one of high birth

NORMAN: people whose origins lay in Normandy on the continent

PARCHMENT: treated animal skin used for writing

PELL: used for combat training, a vertical post set in the ground against which a sword was beat

PIKE: long wooden shaft with a sharp steel or iron head

POLTROON: utter coward

POMMEL: counterbalance weight at the end of a sword hilt or a knob located at the fore of a saddle

PORTCULLIS: metal or wood gate lowered to block a passage

POSTERN GATE: rear door in a wall, often concealed to allow occupants to arrive and depart inconspicuously

QUINTAIN: post used for lance training to which a dummy and sandbag are attached; the latter swings around and hits the unsuccessful tilter

SALLY PORT: small hidden entrance and exit in a fortification

SENNIGHT: one week
SHIFT/CHEMISE: a woman's loose-fitting undergarment or nightdress
SURCOAT: loose robe worn over armor
TAPETS: decorative pieces of cloth dangling from sleeves and hoods
TRENCHER: large piece of stale bread used as a bowl for food
TUNIC/OVERTUNIC: linen shirt
UNDERTUNIC: shirt worn under tunic; considered underwear
VASSAL: one who holds land from a lord and owes fealty
WIMPLE: cloth headdress worn by married women and nuns, covering head, neck, and sides of face

ALSO BY TAMARA LEIGH
EBOOK, PAPERBACK, AUDIOBOOK

INSPIRATIONAL HISTORICAL ROMANCE

AGE OF CONQUEST: The Wulfriths
AN 11th CENTURY MEDIEVAL ROMANCE SERIES

MERCILESS: Book One Amazon

FEARLESS: Book Two Amazon

NAMELESS: Book Three Amazon

HEARTLESS: Book Four Amazon

RECKLESS: Book Five Amazon

BOUNDLESS: Book Six Amazon

LAWLESS: Book Seven Amazon

DAUNTLESS: Book Eight Amazon

AGE OF FAITH: The Wulfriths
A 12th CENTURY MEDIEVAL ROMANCE SERIES

THE UNVEILING: Book One Amazon

THE YIELDING: Book Two Amazon

THE REDEEMING: Book Three Amazon

THE KINDLING: Book Four Amazon

THE LONGING: Book Five Amazon

THE VEXING: Book Six Amazon

THE AWAKENING: Book Seven Amazon

THE RAVELING: Book Eight Amazon

AGE OF HONOR: The Wulfriths

A 14th CENTURY MEDIEVAL ROMANCE SERIES

VALOROUS: Book One Amazon

BEAUTEOUS: Book Two Amazon

SCANDALOUS: Book Three Amazon

DANGEROUS: Book Four Amazon

NOTORIOUS: Book Five (Autumn 2023)

THE FEUD

A MEDIEVAL ROMANCE SERIES

BARON OF GODSMERE: Book One Amazon

BARON OF EMBERLY: Book Two Amazon

BARON OF BLACKWOOD: Book Three Amazon

LADY

A MEDIEVAL ROMANCE SERIES

LADY AT ARMS: Book One Amazon

LADY OF EVE: Book Two Amazon

BEYOND TIME

A MEDIEVAL TIME TRAVEL ROMANCE SERIES

DREAMSPELL: Book One Amazon

LADY EVER AFTER: Book Two Amazon

STAND-ALONE MEDIEVAL ROMANCE NOVELS

LADY OF FIRE Amazon

LADY OF CONQUEST Amazon

LADY UNDAUNTED Amazon

LADY BETRAYED Amazon

INSPIRATIONAL CONTEMPORARY ROMANCE

HEAD OVER HEELS

STAND-ALONE ROMANCE NOVELS

STEALING ADDA Amazon

PERFECTING KATE Amazon

SPLITTING HARRIET Amazon

FAKING GRACE Amazon

SOUTHERN DISCOMFORT

A CONTEMPORARY ROMANCE SERIES

LEAVING CAROLINA: Book One Amazon

NOWHERE CAROLINA: Book Two Amazon

RESTLESS IN CAROLINA: Book Three Amazon

OUT-OF-PRINT GENERAL MARKET TITLES

WARRIOR BRIDE 1994 Bantam Books (Lady At Arms rewrite)

VIRGIN BRIDE 1994 Bantam Books (Lady Of Eve rewrite)

PAGAN BRIDE 1995 Bantam Books (Lady Of Fire rewrite)

SAXON BRIDE 1995 Bantam Books (Lady Of Conquest rewrite)

MISBEGOTTEN 1996 HarperCollins (Lady Undaunted rewrite)

UNFORGOTTEN 1997 HarperCollins (Lady Ever After rewrite)

BLACKHEART 2001 Dorchester (Lady Betrayed rewrite)

www.tamaraleigh.com

ABOUT THE AUTHOR

Tamara Leigh signed a 4-book contract with Bantam Books in 1993, her debut medieval romance was nominated for a RITA award, and successive books with Bantam, HarperCollins, and Dorchester earned awards and became national bestsellers. In 2006, the first of Tamara's inspirational contemporary romances was published, followed by six more with Mult-nomah and RandomHouse. Perfecting Kate was optioned for a movie, Splitting Harriet won an ACFW Book of the Year award, and Faking Grace was nominated for a RITA award.

In 2012, Tamara returned to the historical romance genre with the release of Dreamspell and the bestselling Age of Faith and The Feud series. Among her #1 bestsellers are her general market romances rewritten as clean and inspirational reads, including Lady at Arms and Lady of Conquest. In 2018, she released Merciless, the first book in the Age of Conquest series, followed by seven more unveiling the origins of the Wulfrith family. And now—DANGEROUS, the fourth book in the new Age of Honor series chronicling the 14th century Wulfriths.

Tamara lives near Nashville with her husband, a German Shepherd who has never met a squeaky toy she can't destroy, and a feisty Morkie who keeps her company during long writing stints. Then there's Boog...

Connect with Tamara at: www.tamaraleigh.com, Facebook, Twitter and tamaraleightenn@gmail.com.

For new releases and special promotions, subscribe to Tamara Leigh's mailing list: www.tamaraleigh.com

Made in the USA
Las Vegas, NV
29 May 2023

72690386R00222